THE FIVE SONS OF LE FABER

Books By Ernest Raymond

Novels

We, the Accused
The Marsh
For Them that Trespass
A Song of the Tide
The Last to Rest
Was there Love Once?
The Corporal of the Guard
Tell England
A Family that Was
The Jesting Army
Mary Leith
Newtimber Lane
The Miracle of Brean
Child of Norman's End
Rossenal
Damascus Gate
Wanderlight
Daphne Bruno I
Daphne Bruno II
Morris in the Dance
The Old Tree Blossomed
Don John's Mountain Home

Trilogy

Once in England
comprising definitive editions of
   A Family that Was
   The Jesting Army
   Mary Leith

Biography

In the Steps of St. Francis

Essays, etc.

Through Literature to Life
The Shout of the King
with Patrick Raymond:
Back to Humanity

Plays

The Berg
The Multabello Road

THE FIVE SONS
OF LE FABER

BY
ERNEST RAYMOND

JOHN GIFFORD LIMITED
125 CHARING CROSS ROAD, LONDON W.C.2

First Published 1946

Reprinted 1968 by Cedric Chivers Ltd., Portway, Bath,
at the request of
The London & Home Counties Branch of The Library Association
ECM - ANTON HAIN K.G.
Printed in Germany

FOR
MAURICE AND SIGRID
NEWFIELD

CONTENTS

PART I

CHAPTER ONE

In the memories of all five sons of Augustus le Faber the little triangular green with the elms shadowing it, and the old mansions and the almshouses on its southern side, lay like the playground of their childhood and the centre of the world. It was the axle round which the whole world spun, and just as an axle is usually motionless, however fast the wheel turns, so the little green seemed quiet and still, though there was a rattle and clangour of traffic all about it, an iron ringing of hooves and wheels, in the Hammersmith and Shepherds Bush Roads, and in King Street, Queen Street and the Broadway. It lay in their memories (till some of their memories ceased) with a kindly light upon it, because of the games they had played there, and the dreams each had dreamed there, in the placid afternoons of childhood. But if the grass and the elms and the almshouses were clearly recalled, a half-light of forgetfulness was advancing over the corners of the scene, because they were thinking of it as it was a long time ago. After thirty and forty years it was a place both vivid and vague, like a scene that comes unsolicited into mind when your thoughts are wandering, or one that is suddenly remembered, for no clear reason at all, on the frontier of sleep.

The green is still there to-day, but the old mansions have gone, and some of the great elms, and there is a large Girls' School on the site of one of the most famous of the mansions and of the almshouses of Iles's Charity. The gas lamps have gone, and the paths that used to cut the green diagonally, and the rails that bordered it, running from white post to white post, and serving the le Faber boys in the office of a tight rope. They would walk along those rails at no little danger to themselves, and Justin, the eldest, the great Justin, the lordly Justin, would always achieve one step more than his smaller and less talented brothers. Men took the rails away forty years later to turn them into weapons of war, and they felled and removed the white posts because they served no purpose standing alone, and then it was that the people swarmed on to the grass and made dust of much of it, and the dust invaded and slowly buried the old diagonal paths. To-day there. is no longer a green carpet under the trees but an un-even earth-floor of greys and fawns, sparsely overlaid with some torn rugs of grass.

But if some of the green has changed, much of it remains just as it used to be. It is curious, and even eerie, that it should have kept so much of its pattern, so much of its old quiet air, considering the heavy events that have marched across the world. A war which pitted the surrounding streets with craters and ruins has not touched the houses on the green. It is as if the green, with the houses facing it, had always stood aside from the movement of history. Always it has had something of the stillness of a village though the iron roar of London could be heard all around it. Always it has been a green sidewater where it was safe for children to play. The small red nineteenth-century houses still stand on its northern side, and so does the red synagogue with the tables of the Law above its porch. And at its eastern end the congregation of grey-stone Catholic buildings, a very camp and settlement of Rome, still stands around the apex of the green triangle. There they are, still in active occupa-tion: the church of the Most Holy Trinity with its tall spire, the almshouses of St. Joseph beside a tranquil garden, the College of St. Mark on the other side of the road, and the grey barrack which used to be a school for pauper children— and, as such, an object of interest and pity to the le Faber boys, who were a gentleman's sons.

However differently they grew, as men, and however their ways diverged, one habit showed itself in all the five brothers: a need to come wandering back sometimes to the old green and to live again, for a little while, in the past. And the other day, driven by this urge of memory, Robin le Faber wandered along the north side of the green, alone. He walked slowly that he might fetch the people out of the past and set them in their places on the green. But when he came to a side-road, called Pemberthy Road, he turned into it and walked more slowly than ever, because now he was looking at the house where he and his brothers had lived. Fifty years and three wars, the advance of concrete and steel in mam-moth formations, speed of travel, migration of people, decay and decline of Western London—none of these matters seemed to have touched that little house. It looked no different, no older, no shabbier. It was still a clean and comfortable little house of red brick with white stone facings, the seventh in a small row of exactly similar houses. The bay window of the dining-room was on the right of the front door, and the window of the best bedroom above, and there was a window over the door; and that was the whole façade. Whoever lived in it now kept it painted and polished and trim. They loved it. You could see this from the spotless lace curtains and the plant in the window, from the gleaming brass on the front door, and from the cropped exactitude of the privet hedge and the glistening surface of the tiled path that led to the threshold.

It was fascinating, and especially to a dreamer like Robin le Faber, to stand here and muse on the old days in that house; to recollect incidents in that little dining-room and in the drawing-room behind and on the narrow stairs and, most of all, in the tiny bedroom at the back which he shared with Justin; to think that, though they were only children then, the future was astir within those small, confining walls; to tell himself that behind that clean front door all those things had begun which must grow and burgeon and enlarge till the fruit fell; both those that were good and pleasant in the memory and those that were unhallowed and dark.

§

This green in the centre of the world was, as you will have guessed, Brook Green. And fifty years ago, when its grass was a good green carpet and the white posts and rails were still around it, on a warm April Sunday, the whole le Faber family, father, mother, and five sons, turned out of Pemberthy Road and walked in a straggling column along the pavement on the north side of the green. It was half-past two in the afternoon, and with such a sun in the sky it was impossible to stay indoors, so the le Fabers had decided to take a walk by the river. The air was as warm as milk; all the trees were sprouting into green buds, except the limes which were breaking pink; and above the feathery tops of the trees a procession of white clouds moved across an infinite transparency of blue. The boys walked quickly in this animating air, and Justin, as usual, led the rest. Robin, the youngest but one, would dawdle and dream a moment, and then run to catch up with the others. Augustus le Faber could not go as fast as his sons, and Beatrice, their mother, kept him company at his side.

Augustus was a tall, fat man of forty-five, with moustaches that curled over pendent cheeks and a paunch which extended so far in front of him that it seemed in advance of his feet as he walked. He wore a grey Norfolk jacket and knickerbockers, and a cap of the same grey tweed. His large, swelling calves were sheathed in thick ribbed stockings which turned over beneath the buckle of the knickerbockers. These light, sporting tweeds suited neither the rotundity of his stomach nor the soberness of Sunday, but they had been put on very deliberately and were now being displayed with a purpose. They were a challenge, a flag. They were a challenge to Brook Green. They were a challenge to all parsons and all old women and all church-ridden people everywhere. They were a challenge to the queen on her throne.

For Augustus le Faber, like many another man of full habit and thick neck, was eager and hot in argument, and ever since the impact of Charles Darwin and *The Origin of Species* upon the nineteenth century he had acquired with the enthusiasm and pride of a discoverer all the arguments against God and the Bible and the churches, and to all who would listen, or, better still, would contend with him, he would expound the unanswerable case, his invective getting hotter and hotter as he did so, and his face and neck redder. His hostility to the clergy was in proportion to the height of their churchmanship, so that nothing could affront him more than the sight of a High Anglican in a cassock (a "Puseyite", as he called him) unless it was a Roman priest in a cassock and cape—or two such priests. And of these last there were plenty to affront him in the vicinity of Brook Green. Perhaps that was why he was happy to live there. A man will hurry towards the thing that incenses him, because there is a pleasure in wrath. One is well alive when one is hot in heart and head. And perhaps that was why Augustus was guiding his family to-day towards the Catholic settlements at the head of the green. It was Sunday, and there should be gross things in action about the doors of the church. It would enlighten the priests, who sought to dominate Sunday, to see the father of a family in knickerbockers and a cap.

Beatrice was dressed in her best, not because it was Sunday, for there would have been loud argument and instruction at 7 Pemberthy Road if she had suggested taking the children to church, but because she had no desire to be different from other women and liked to show her best clothes to the neighbourhood. She wore a dark blue dress with a high neck and balloon sleeves so wide that she must have measured four feet across the shoulders. The waist of the dress was as narrow as the sleeves were wide, and its long skirt, fitting tight over the hips, spread outwards like a slender bell. On one hand was a muff, and with the other she constantly lifted the skirt behind. On her head was a toque with a bird-of-paradise plume. Walking at the side of her portly husband in this tight-fitting dress and plumed toque, she seemed a tall, thin woman, but actually she was not as tall as Augustus whose height was six foot one and an inch.

Ahead of this couple went the boys: Justin, Gerard, Hector, Robin, and Arthur Bossuet—or "Bozzy", the baby of the family; Justin nine, Gerard eight, Hector six, Robin five, and Bozzy three. Justin, leading, turned his head at times, as if impatient at this slowness of the old and the young. He only was in an Eton suit and a school cap. And like his mother he was in this Sunday suit, not out of reverence for the day, for which he had no reverence, but because he wanted to display his best to the world. This was his first term at Colet Court Preparatory School in the Hammersmith Road, and he had learned in these cloisters that all gentlemen's sons wore their Eton suits on Sundays. So he had insisted to-day, with a loud, mounting anger, on wearing his new ceremonial Eton suit, and Beatrice, who was frightened of him, had surrendered.

No one would have supposed that Justin was only nine. Tall and wide-shouldered, with a large face to which an abundance of dark waving hair and a pair of keen, intelligent brown eyes gave a strange maturity, he looked to be eleven or twelve. Justin was always the tallest, the handsomest, and the most striking of the le Faber sons. Gerard, very nearly though not quite as fine a young colt as Justin, wore a blue sailor suit with long trousers; Hector, who was heavy and fat like his father, wore the same; Robin, being only five, was in a white sailor suit and brown stockings drawn tight above his knees; and Arthur Bossuet, who in his mother's view was delicate and must be kept well wrapped up, wore his highwayman's coat of bottle-green broadcloth, with a muffler swaddling his neck, lest winter should assail him with its last spiteful stabs.

And so, in anything but uniform garments, this little regiment of the le Fabers marched towards the hostilities which Augustus had in mind for the Catholic camp.

When they had marched a little way Gerard began to gaze across the green at a large grey mansion half concealed by its high garden wall and its fine old trees. For him this old house with its romantic name, "The Grange", had a fascination above that of any other house in the precincts of the green. Until a year or two ago the Grange had been the home of the most famous actor of his day, Mr. Henry Irving, and many a time Gerard's father and mother had seen the famous man pottering about the garden which he loved or coming through the gates, in his wide hat and dandefied dress, to the carriage that awaited him. Justin also declared that he had frequently seen the man, but Gerard was not sure that he believed this, because Justin, after all, was only a year older than he, and everyone knew that he was a "cocky ass" who must always know everything and have gone one better than anyone else.

Keeping his eyes on the large, flat-breasted house, Gerard dropped back to his father's side.

"Do you think Mr. Irving will ever come back to live here?" he asked, turning grave eyes up to Augustus.

"No. He's sold the house. He'll never come back any more. Not till he's dead, at any rate. He may come haunting it then." And Augustus laughed at his own joke. He always laughed heartily at his own jokes. Sometimes, at better jokes than this, he laughed till his belly shook. "My Joshua, I shouldn't like to be in a house haunted by Henry Irving! I should expect him to come staggering along the passages, clutching his throat and crying, 'The rope! The rope! Cut the rope.' And then I should expect bells to start ringing all over the house."

"Bells? What bells?" asked Gerard, his eyes thirsting for a tale of ghosts.

"The sleigh bells of the Polish Jew," his father enunciated in a slow, melodramatic hiss.

"What Polish Jew? Oh, tell us," pleaded Gerard.

"The Polish Jew whom the Burgomaster murdered."

"Oh, tell us all about it. Tell us. Go on. Tell us."

And even Justin turned back at this mention of murder.

"What happened? What happened?" demanded Gerard, skipping with impatience at his father's side. "Who was the Burgomaster?"

"His name was Mathias, as far as I remember; and the Polish Jew came to his house on a sleigh with all its bells ringing; and Mathias murdered him for his money and threw his body into the lime kiln. And the sleigh bells rang in his guilty ears for the rest of his life. Good gracious, it must be twenty years since I saw Henry Irving in *The Bells*. 'Into the lime kiln, Jew'." As well as he could, Augustus imitated the hiss of Mr. Irving, as he delivered this tremendous line. "And now go on. Don't all hustle on top of me. The tale is ended."

"'Into the lime kiln, Jew,'" repeated Justin, relishing the line. "Was he hung?"

"Who?"

"Mathias."

"Was he hung? No. As far as I remember, he dreamed he was being hanged, and died of the strain. And no one ever knew that he was anything but the most excellent of men."

"I expect there are heaps of people who have done murder, and no one knows anything about it," said Justin cheerfully. And he repeated again the succulent line: "'Into the lime kiln, Jew.'" Savouring it, a slow smile at his lips, he strolled back to his place at the head of the straggling family.

"Shall we see Henry Irving act before he dies?" asked Gerard, turning his head to study again that mansion behind the trees.

"Oh, I hope so. He won't die for a long time yet."

"How long?"

"I don't know. Twenty years, perhaps. He looked a tough old bit of bacon when I saw him last."

Gerard was comforted. "How soon can I go to the theatre? When I'm ten?"

"When you're ten, perhaps."

"Did you ever speak to him?"

"No, I did not. The only times I ever saw him he seemed lost in a dream. Rather like our Robin. Standing about or sauntering along without any clear idea of where he was or what he was doing. His body was in Brook Green, but his mind—Look at that! There's a scandal for you. There's a nice thing to see at the end of the nineteenth century."

Augustus had come upon the enemy. His nostrils dilated above his long moustache. His heavy-jowled face reddened a little, his lips pressed themselves into a firm, straight line, and a fine glaze of disgust added a lustre to his eyes. The triangular green had tapered to its point, and across the road was the church of the Most Holy Trinity. Opposite it was St. Joseph's school for pauper children, and at this very minute (just as Augustus had hoped) some of the children were being shepherded across the road, with a young priest in cassock and cape at their head, and a couple of nuns, in voluminous black robes, sailing behind them. Augustus's eyes followed the young priest, and his head nodded many times. It nodded to express his understanding and his disgust.

"Look at him. Look at the scoundrel. Look at him with that rope round his waist when it ought to be round his neck. I ask you! And that at the end of the nineteenth century!"

The pauper children were hurrying after the priest like lambs after an Eastern shepherd. And behind them, silently, went the black-shrouded nuns like two trained and faithful dogs.

"The massacre of the innocents," pronounced Augustus. "What a crime! Poor little helpless mites driven like sheep into a church to have their minds maimed for ever. To be taught a lot of stuff that Science has completely discredited. To be told that they must believe without question all he says, and that it'd be a sin to turn their intelligences on it and wonder how much of it is rank superstition. To be told that it's wicked to think for themselves. There they go, poor little things, into the mutilating chamber. There they go to have their minds put into fetters from which they'll never shake themselves free. And there are still people who'll say it's God's work instead of the devil's. My God, if I had my way, I'd have all such agents of the devil suppressed. Civilization'll never progress as long as they're allowed to bind up and constrict and cripple the soul of Man."

An old priest, with pink cheeks and a froth of white hair around his temples, the Rector perhaps, had come to the steps of the church and was standing there, both hands thrust between cassock and cincture, while he smiled and smiled upon these dear children of God approaching their Father's house.

"And look at that old villain." Augustus nodded and nodded in understanding and despair. "Look at him. Delighted at getting them in and being able to do his devil's work upon them."

Beatrice protested that "devil's work" was "a little strong", and Augustus was pleased that she had done so. It was exactly what he wanted. Such facile and unthinking opposition justified an outburst of some violence.

"Of *course* it's the devil's work. To bind up and atrophy their powers of free thought *must* be the devil's work, and in an intelligent society it wouldn't be permitted. Anyone is entitled to tell others what he believes, but not to tell them that they must believe it too, under pain of death and damnation—not to tell them that anyone who dares to doubt it will perish everlastingly. That's what they say, 'perish everlastingly.' Damn their infernal insolence. I don't suggest that he *knows* he's an agent of the devil. Why should he? He's only a half-educated old fool. It's not his fault that the priests got him when he was a child and ruined him for ever, and that now he's busy working the same wickedness on others. I wonder if he's ever read *anything*. I wonder if he's read any Darwin or Huxley or Buckle or Bradlaugh. I don't suppose so. I don't suppose he's allowed to. And then they put him up to teach little children. And you say it isn't a crime."

Of all the seven le Fabers passing by, only one was interested in this vehement oration. And it was not Beatrice who had heard it too often before; not Justin who was far in front now and chafing at their slowness; not Gerard who was still looking back at the great actor's home and thinking of him; not Hector who, like other fat and pasty children, was of heavy, self-centred, inactive intelligence; and not little Bozzy, swaddled in his muffler and highwayman's coat, for Bozzy, as we shall tell, spoke hardly at all, but smiled at everybody who looked at him, and laughed shrilly at loud noises, and touched his mother's heart with grief and fear. None of these, but only Robin. Robin, in his white sailor suit, was as fascinated by these grey-stone buildings of the priests as Gerard by the grey-brick home of the actor. His long-lashed, soft brown eyes stared and stared at the young priest who ought to be hanged in his girdle, and at the old priest in the doorway who had been ruined for ever as a child. They stared at the children who were being marched to mutilation, and at the church doors which were wide open to receive them into its darkness. Looking back, and looking back again, he saw the children pass into the church under the continuing smile of the old priest, and he saw the doors close on them like the doors in the Pied Piper's mountain. He heard the muffled music of an organ behind the high pointed windows. And, unable to leave the fascination behind, he stopped upon the pavement and stood there, staring at the church with a thrilled and guilty interest because of the wickedness that was practised within. He stood there till the family was almost out of sight and he realized that his mother had turned round and was anxiously calling him.

§

Meanwhile Justin, that tall, dark, and somewhat flamboyant child, his hands in the pockets of his Eton trousers, was leading them on, with fretful, impatient steps, towards the river. He loved the river, as he loved all places where the houses ceased and there were wide green tracts and the whole of the sky. All the way up Hammersmith Bridge Road he walked in front, hungry for the wet, briny air that came up these tidal reaches and smelt of seaweed in rocky pools and of holidays by the sea. He longed to hear the seafowl mewing above the sliding water, and to watch them striking like birds of prey on the sodden crusts that drifted under the wall. Their cries were like the complaining of a ship's rope, and to Justin they seemed like the voices of a wholly different world that had won a narrow tract for itself right through the midst of London. When the family turned out of Bridge Road on to the Lower Mall, he was already leaning on the parapet of the river wall and gazing at that narrow stretch of wildness and freedom. He was watching the flow of the steel-grey water, patterned under the sun like a damascened blade, and listening to the quiet chuckle of the lifting tide.

CHAPTER TWO

THESE are the generations of the le Fabers. The family of le Faber, or Le Fèvre, as it was in the beginning, came originally from a village perched on a hill in the heart of the Vosges, but by the time they were of any importance, in the fifteenth and sixteenth centuries, they were merchants with large interests in Germany, Flanders and England, and either the German or the Flemish connection, it seems, had gradually modified the name into le Faber. Most of the merchant le Fabers had the reputation of being hard, unscrupulous men, but that is the

way to wealth and power, and wealth and power was what they
had in mind until one of them, the head of the family in his
day, determined to be a great gentleman and, for this purpose,
bought the estate of Châtillon in the valley of the Haute
Marne on the borders of Lorraine. His château was not a
hundred miles, as a bird flies, from the village in the Vosges
which still sheltered peasants of the name of Le Fèvre, but
there were many hills and mountains in between. At what
point in the two centuries between 1590 and the Revolution
one of their descendants acquired the title of Comte de
Châtillon is no longer known, nor in what way the le Faber
family became connected by marriage with the family of the
great Bossuet, Bishop of Meux, and most famous preacher,
controversialist and apologist of his time, but they were
proud of their great kinsman's name and appropriated it for
themselves. Had not this celebrated divine been the favourite
preacher of Anne of Austria, Queen Mother of the Grand
Monarch; had not Turenne, Saint-Evremond, the Prince of
Condé, and Madame de Sevigné sat under him enraptured
(when sleep did not overpower them); had not Le Roi Soleil
himself, on going to hear him, in a surge of curiosity rather
than of piety, been so deeply moved for an hour or two after
the sermon that he had felt compelled to send a message to the
preacher's father, old Bénigne Bossuet, *"pour le féliciter
d'avoir un tel fils."* No wonder the name of Bossuet came
down the generations of the le Fabers like an heirloom. And
it is strange to think that now it was housed only in a small,
muffled boy who smiled sweetly but foolishly at all who would
look at him, and about whose development hereafter wise men
were dubious and grave.

In 1756 was born Honoré Jean Bossuet le Faber who, as
Comte de Châtillon, figured so conspicuously as an ardent,
and later a violent, royalist in the France of Louis XVI, and
was accordingly marked down for the guillotine. He escaped
to England in 1791 in the same hour as his royal master, also
attempting to escape, was arrested at Varennes. Honoré Jean
Bossuet never returned to France but remained in England and
married a few years later, when he was nearly forty, an English
wife, daughter of a small Oxfordshire squire. The le Faber
name had been at the height of its fortunes, at the summit of
a pass, when the Comte de Châtillon was strutting and preening
himself in the favour of Louis XVI, but from the moment of
his and his master's fall its glory narrowed and dwindled till we

find some of the last of its English bearers dwelling in a tiny red and white house in Pemberthy Road, Brook Green.

The Count and the squire's daughter had a dozen children, and somewhere among them the title of Count got lost or carried away. So did the greater part of the family capital which was at no time very large. One of the dozen children was Charles le Faber, who became a tea merchant in the neighbourhood of Tower Hill, but his scale and his profits were small. A very small merchant, Charles le Faber, compared with the great le Fabers of the sixteenth century. He too had many children, fourteen of them, born between 1820 and 1845 when his wife was nearly fifty and past bearing any more. The only one of his children who is of any interest in this tale was Harry le Faber, born in 1823, who became a soldier, went to the Crimea, and earned there a reputation for fearlessness with the enemy and ruthlessness with his men. Both aspects of his reputation pleased him. That his men called him a slave-driver and a bully and declared that one of these days he'd find himself shot in the back he told with a high satisfaction to all. His name was clouded for a while, after he had struck and injured a soldier who was improperly dressed and whose expression he considered impudent, but he redeemed it in the battle of the Alma by leading his company in a wild charge up the slope of Kurghane Hill and bringing them triumphantly on to the crest, though he himself had been hit in shoulder, leg, and face. He died seven months later in a dingy barrack at Scutari, but not of his wounds. Most of the patients in that hospital were suffering from frost-bite or cholera or typhus, which they had contracted in the trenches and camps before Sevastopol, and Harry died of typhus; a fact usually suppressed by the le Fabers, who thought it more picturesque that he should have been mortally wounded, leading his men. That hospital was Florence Nightingale's, and, for all we know, she came one evening with her lamp to look at him as he lay dying, and shook her head sadly, and passed on.

This Captain Harry le Faber, because of his charge, and because of Florence Nightingale, became something of a legend to Augustus and Beatrice le Faber and their sons. He was only a little over thirty when he died, and he left behind him three children, a boy and two girls. The boy was Augustus. (In those days the name Augustus was not a source of laughter but was thought of rather well. It was still good currency at the time this story opens, though Justin was beginning to find its abbreviated form, "Gus", exceedingly amusing.) Augustus was but six when the Captain died, and his mother had all she could do to provide him with some education for another ten years. At sixteen, through the influence of an uncle, he was apprenticed to a firm of West Indian merchants and began work as an office boy, affixing stamps, copying letters, and discharging small commissions in the firm's London office in Gracechurch Street. He earned twenty pounds in his first year, and this rose by stages to a hundred pounds during the five years of his apprenticeship. He did well enough with the firm, for he was one of the orderly le Fabers, and if there was a peculiar le Faber violence, and if some of it had trickled down to him, it erupted only in hot arguments with his friends—especially those who would defend the churches and the priests. Before he was forty he was a head book-keeper, and by forty-five, when we see him walking to the river with his string of sons, he was chief cashier and office manager. His income was now four hundred and fifty pounds a year, but, with five children to feed and educate, this allowed for no more than the little house in Pemberthy Road.

He had begotten six children in all, but one of them, a girl, born between Gerard and Hector, had died of diphtheria at two years and three months old. These children had arrived with a monotonous regularity, and in a kind of cosmic rhythm, at intervals of twelve calendar months, so that Augustus, who could be hearty and coarse with his city friends, would speak of Beatrice's "lambing season" and maintain that you had only to look at her affectionately and she conceived. "Upon my soul," he would say, laughing till his eyes were wet like over-ripe grapes and his paunch was a trembling mass, "there are times when I can believe that there's something in this bunkum the parsons talk about parthenogenesis. What's parthenogenesis? Why, virgin birth, old boy. Giving birth to children in the absence of any father. Upon my soul, old man, I don't feel perfectly certain that Beatrice couldn't have a child just by sitting down and wishing hard enough. But I've put a stop to it now. I can't stack any more of them in my little house. As it is, I fall over children all over the place. And they're all twice the size of any normal children, as we le Fabers always are. Five's enough for any man—especially when the last——" and Augustus lifted sad, helpless shoulders, and spread an impotent palm, as he thought of little Bozzy

So there they were, these relics of the once successful but

never really distinguished family of the le Fabers, in their little kennel of a house which stood among a million other houses in the endless ranks of Outer London.   We have descended from the top of the pass, represented by the Comte de Châtillon at the court of Louis XVI, to five young boys in a London suburb, each carrying his unsought but inescapable inheritance of instincts and cravings and dreams, and march‑ ing with this load towards the future.

CHAPTER THREE

THE years that saw Robin grow from five years old to twelve, and Justin from nine to sixteen, saw also the growth of a notable companionship between these two. The constituents of the companionship were Robin's admiration of, and devotion to, his tall, handsome, eldest brother, and Justin's pleasure in this admiration and his royal acceptance of the devotion. Justin's preference for Robin as a companion is easily ex‑ plained. Gerard, only a year younger, was too close to him in age and size, and therefore liable to be critical and disputatious, and Justin did not want an opponent but a disciple. Hector, the next eldest, he thought a fat and pompous fool, which, for once in a way, was a fairly accurate appraisal of a brother, and his contempt for him amounted to a galling dislike. Bozzy, of course, was quite impossible as a companion. He was far too young, and, besides, he was "not all there". Bozzy was best left to his mother and put out of mind. So Gerard, Hector, and Bozzy being no use, there was only Robin left for Justin to enjoy as a squire and friend. But Robin suited him very well. Four years younger, and four years smaller; weaker, more ignorant, and less skilled, he made a splendid audience. Let Justin swagger and boast as he liked, and Robin would swallow it all. Let him parade his wit or play the buffoon, and Robin was ready with rich laughter. Let him say irreverent and outrageous things, and Robin was at once shocked and delighted with the shock, his eyes spark‑ ling with appreciation.   Happy to be the king's favourite,

Robin was always uncritical, corroborative, admiring, and adoring.

And there was another thing whose exact power over Justin it is more difficult to assess. Robin, in Justin's eyes, though Justin never said this to anyone but himself, was "rather beautiful"; and Justin had a restless hunger for beauty. He liked to escape from the dusty streets and to wander by the river or anywhere else where there were trees and grass and birds, and the tall, grey houses were as far away as possible; and for the same reason, since he needed a companion to listen to his outpourings, he was glad to have one whose face was a pleasure to look at. As a matter of fact, Robin was not "beautiful." It might have been said of him that, just as Justin was the handsomest of the le Faber boys, so he, Robin, was the prettiest, the "most attractive." But he was far from strictly beautiful. He had dark eyebrows which nearly met over his nose, giving him an expression half worried, half wistful, and the nose itself, though regular, was slightly upturned. The eyes beneath the thick eyebrows were large and brown and pensive, and the lashes that veiled them were long and soft and dark. His hair was as dark as Justin's and as plentiful, and his figure, on its smaller scale, as graceful and strong. It seemed, in fact, when they walked side by side, a small copy of Justin's. He had shy, dreamy, gentle ways, though the temper which could arise in his father and Justin and Gerard (but not in Hector, who was ponderous and passive, nor in Bozzy, who smiled on all the world) was near the surface in Robin too.

By his quick appreciations, his instant and teeming laughter, his inexhaustible supplies of enthusiasm, and, above all, by his devotion, Robin gave Justin perhaps the only experience that in all his life came near to satisfying him. If there was anyone other than himself whom Justin could be said to have loved in his life, it was Robin, the playmate and friend of his childhood. Mainly in fun, but not without affection, he would call him "Robs" and "Robby", as he might a dog, and this was as near as he ever got to showing affection to a member of the family.

In the memories of both Robin and Justin these last years of the century seemed full of the long, straying happiness of childhood. What walks and talks they had together; what games. Their favourite walk was always along the river malls and over the creek and away on to Chiswick and perhaps to

Strand-on-the-Green and Kew. There was a freshness up the
river and by Hammersmith Creek in those days which is hardly
to be found there now. Indeed the creek with its sailing barges
and its overhanging trees and its swans is no longer there. The
malls were far enough then from the mass of London to receive,
unpolluted, the air flowing in from the highlands of Surrey
and the breeze that came riding up from the sea on the broad
back of the tide. And when the tide ebbed, it drew off the old
air down the channel of the Thames, leaving the riverside free
to take again the new air from the hills. Justin, striding along
the malls, with Robin at his side, would cry out, "Isn't it
wonderful to feel the west wind in one's face? D'you know,
Robs, old ugly-mug, I sometimes think I must hate men and
love places, because I'm never so happy as when I'm somewhere where there's not a human being in sight, but only the
birds. I can just stand you in sight, and that's about all."

Because he longed for beauty, he loved the birds, and he and
Robin would go bird-hunting and bird-watching all along the
river, proud to discover new birds and to give them their
right names. Are the birds there now that these two boys
used to see? All the birds that are the friends of London can
still be found there, of course: the sparrows and starlings, the
thrushes and tits; but are there sandpipers and sedge warblers
and red shanks and swifts, and on the water and among the
reeds, barnacle geese and mallards and great crested grebes?
Justin and Robin found all these, and many others.

One afternoon by the river Robin always remembered. The
tide was slipping up the centre of the stream, but so quietly
that the water under the walls lay basking in the sun; and
Justin and he stood on that curved bastion of the wall which
they say Queen Catherine of Braganza built that the coaches
might turn about before her house. On either side of them, as
they leaned on the parapet, were the elms which the Queen
planted and were grown now into some of the noblest trees in
London. It was a Saturday in spring, and a racing eight,
from one of the boathouses on the Lower Mall, was paddling
up towards Chiswick Eyot with full, easy, even strokes. So
still was the afternoon that you could hear the long sus-
suration of the feathered oars and the dripping of the water
from their blades. In all the world and throughout the ages
men have created nothing that comes nearer to the flawless
beauty their poor souls crave than this unison motion of eight
young oarsmen, over the diamonds of a sunlit river; all of

them in the first flowering of their strength, and all of them surrendered to a single dream. Justin watched them for a few seconds: then suddenly took his arms off the parapet and stood straight and rigid as a figure in stone. And so he gazed at that crew in their racing Clasper eight till they were round the basket willows of the eyot, and the last of their long, shining craft was gone from view. Even then he did not speak or move. He seemed lost; tranced; and Robin watched him in a faint dismay, while a childish courtesy whispered that it would be unwise to speak. To the end of his life he never knew what Justin was thinking or feeling then, but in later days he believed he could understand.

§

The best of their talks were when they lay side by side in one of those broad green spaces that lie among the press of London's houses: in Ravenscourt Park perhaps, or Kensington Gardens, where they could find a solitude among the trees, and the voices and footsteps of people seemed far away. Once, at about three o'clock in the afternoon, they were lying on a rich mantle of grass under the elms and sycamores of Ravenscourt Park. And as they talked the long blue shadows, thrown by the April sun, moved round like the shadows on the sundials, because Justin was pouring out his aspirations for the future, and Robin was listening with a child's rapt eagerness, and time was nothing. They heard no other voices and heeded no other people. The only thing they heard was the scream of the peacock by the pool, which ever and again, as Justin laid bare his hopes, cried its disquiet. So insistent was its melancholy squall that Robin, ever afterwards, if anyone made mention of Ravenscourt Park, heard that cry in his memory and saw two boys, himself and Justin, lying under the trees.

Justin at that time was thirteen, and Robin nine, though the one was as big as a muscular boy of sixteen and the other as a child of ten or eleven. Justin had been at St. Paul's for about a year, and Robin was at a smaller private school with Gerard and Hector, for it was only the eldest son that Augustus could afford to send to a famous school. Justin was not distinguishing himself as a scholar at St. Paul's, but very greatly as an athlete. In his first winter term, because of his size and speed, he played for the Colts and in the First XV of his club, which

was, and probably still is, a school record. At Colet Court he
had been a risky and erratic, but usually successful, hitter in
the Cricket XI, being taller than anyone else in that team of
prep-school boys, and most of his contemporaries prophesied
that he would one day play cricket for St. Paul's.

And now, because this early success was effervescing in his
blood, he expounded to Robin his future career.

"No city life for me. I don't see myself going to the City
day after day like Gus. Oh no, Robs, old snub-nose. I'm not
one of those who's going to sit on a stool in a stuffy office and
take what salary other people are pleased to give me. No,
I've quite made up my mind about that. I'm going to have a
job that'll enable me to play cricket and rugger every day of
the week and have long holidays at Easter, summer, and
Christmas. And what do you think that is?"

"What?" asked Robin obligingly, suspecting that Justin
wanted to answer his own question. Robin was chewing a
long blade of grass, partly because he liked the sweetness of it,
but mainly because Justin was playing a blade at his lips.

"What would you say?"

"A schoolmaster, is it?"

"You're nearly right. Try again."

"A professional cricketer."

"Good night, no. I couldn't be a professional. I'm a
gentleman."

"Well, *I* don't know. What is it?"

"You were almost right first time. You're a bright kid,
you know. Funny you should be like that, with Bozzy what
he is. I suppose you only just missed that."

"Missed what?"

"Being daft too. You see, you were next before Bozzy, and
the daftness must have been beginning to set in, but I can't
see that you're loopy at all. In fact, I think that you're the
brightest of them all."

"I'm two years older than Bozzy," reminded Robin, his
heart rejoicing, as always, at Justin's praise.

"Yes, that's true," mused Justin over his blade of grass.
"But what about Hector? He's older than you, and he's a
pretty first-class fool."

"But he's not *daft*. He's only a silly idiot."

Justin, chewing his grass, ruminated over this distinction.
"No, he's not *daft*," he allowed at last, "but I often think
some of his superfluous fat has got into his brain. I mean, it's

a fat sort of brain. All his ideas are fat and heavy and suety. An appalling ass. But there's nothing wrong with Gerard . . . nothing much . . . and certainly not with *you*. In fact, I should say you were above par. . . . A little."

Robin, delighted with this valuation, suggested, as was incumbent, that Justin was obviously above par.

"Yes, I think so," agreed Justin. "I can't help thinking so when I see others. Most people seem awful fools when you look around. The way they just do what everyone else tells them! Just obey like sheep. Even Gus, who's no fool, mind you, seems to have gone tamely to an office when his people told him to. Very different from his father who made things hum in the Crimea. *He* cared for nothing and nobody, as far as I can see. I reckon he was a man, my grandfather. Still, he's not a bad ole cuss, Gus. Nor's Beaty in her own way. But they're rather ordinary, don't you think, which is curious in Daddy, considering his father. But there you are: that sort of quality usually skips a generation."

Robin nodded wisely, perceiving the implications of this remark, and wondering if the quality had alighted on him too.

"Nobody's ever going to dictate to *me*," pursued Justin. "Nobody's going to tell me what I shall do and what I shan't do. Not even God Himself, if there is such a person, which I doubt. In that matter I'm inclined to agree with Gus."

Away by the pool the peacock screamed, as if he had heard a blasphemy.

"That's one reason why I intend to be a headmaster. Yes, you were almost right, but you should have said *head*master. I intend to have my own school. I'm going to be boss and no one else. The headmaster of his own school seems to be the one person in England who's absolutely his own boss. I shall start my own school somehow, just as soon as I can. And not only shall I be my own master and have plenty of time for cricket and rugger—we're playing rugger at my school, I don't mind telling you—but I shall make money. There's plenty of money in a school if it's your own and a success. Look at Colet Court. It began in a small way, and now it's an absolute gold mine, they say. And I can promise you that my school'll be quite as big a success. I generally make a success of anything I want to do."

"Oh, I think that's a ripping idea," said Robin, already enthusiastic about it. "Couldn't I be in it too?"

"Oh yes, you're going to be in it too," assured Justin, with that unquestioned preference for Robin which kept the smaller boy's loyalty alight. "I shall want you with me. And what's more, you'll be assistant headmaster. You might even be a partner in the business, but I don't know. I haven't thought that out yet. In fact, I dare say I should hand the teaching over to you, and look after the games myself. And when I've made enough money, do you know what I'm going to do?"

"No."

"I'm going to live in the country, miles from any town, and have a little farm of my own. Not a large one because I shall only want it for a hobby, as I shall have heaps of money then. And whenever I can leave the farm to my steward, I shall wander all over England with a pack on my back and nothing else. I think I shall wander all over the world like that. I shall go where there are forests and mountains and miles upon miles of moors, and where I shall meet nobody except a few dear old shepherds or some jolly woodmen cutting down the trees. Gosh, it'd be rather wonderful. I might take you with me sometimes, but generally I should go quite alone."

And so they talked on, while the shadows swept the grass and lengthened, and at rhythmic intervals the peacock sent his harsh cry from the pool.

And now they had a new pastime for the long evenings, after homework had been hastily done. They would walk the pavements between the sweeping ranks of gaunt, grey houses that stretched in endless array from the borders of their green, and they would choose this house or that as a place where Justin could start his school. Like a pair of officers inspecting a regiment they would halt before at least one house in every rank and consider its appearance from foot to head, and then take a pace forward to peer through its windows. If the house was occupied, they would be bright windows; if it was to let, they would be uncurtained and dingy, and the two boys would tip-toe down into the area, and up the front door steps, to study in detail the empty, dusty rooms in the basement and on the entrance floor. Stepping back into the roadway, and estimating the number of rooms in the house, they would assign to each its function. This would be the Common Room, those would be classrooms, that one up there would be Robin's room, and the best room at the back would be the head-master's study.

§

Justin had not exposed to Robin all his reasons for wanting to be a headmaster. One he had kept back in the shadowed places of his mind. At Colet Court he had seen the headmaster come into a classroom with a cane in his hand and command a boy, who had been reported to him for disobedience, to come out before the class and kneel against a bench. And when the boy had bent his body over the bench, he had given him six sharp cuts with the cane. And always, when the headmaster came in with his cane like that, a curious excitement had stirred in Justin's heart. He had seen, too, small boys going into the headmaster's study for a whipping, and had stood among the excited crowd outside, listening to the swish and impact of the cane. At St. Paul's all the masters had their own canes, and some were quick to use them. They would command an offender to come out before his classfellows and bend over with his hands on his knees. And always when Justin saw a boy coming forward to be caned, the same excitement stimulated his breathing and extended his breast. And now when, brooding alone and apart, he imagined himself whipping one of his pupils just like that, the curious, breathless ecstasy troubled his heart. He determined that, when he had his own school, he would reserve for himself the secret pleasure of the cane.

So strangely exalting was the trouble in his heart, when he dwelt upon this thought, that he resolved at last to relieve it by caning Robin. An element in this decision, which he could not understand, was the fact that Robin's "beauty", as he would describe it to himself, added a keen pleasure to the thought of whipping him. He bought a pliant cane, ostensibly for a walking stick, and as they strolled in the parks together, brought it swishing down upon grasses and reeds, as if they were his pupils, or Robin, who had erred. And he waited for Robin to err. He longed for him to err, that stern action might be justified. And when one afternoon Robin dallied by the lake in Ravenscourt Park to see the peacock spread his tail—an event for which he would wait in a dream without any sense of time or of people passing by—Justin called to him to come along, and called a second time, and a third time, and was not obeyed. So, wilfully inflaming his anger, he returned to

Robin's side, seized him by his elbow, and marched him along with his left hand, while his right gripped his cane.

"I'm not going to be disobeyed," he said. "If you're coming out with me, you've got to obey me. Now I shall have to punish you. I don't want to have to punish you, but you give me no choice."

And he marched him into a shrubbery by the old refreshment room, which he had previously selected as a good place for this execution, and as he came into its quiet, and the overgrown shrubs and the great overarching trees screened his actions from the world, all the life in him seemed to rise up and seat itself in his throat.

"Bend over and put your hands on your knees," he ordered.

"No!" shouted Robin.

"Do as you're told!" Justin slashed the cane across his calf. "Bend over."

The pain was so great that Robin screamed and closed with Justin, hitting and kicking him. And Justin slashed him again. shouting, "Don't do that! Don't try that on with me. Come on. Bend over. At St. Paul's they do it without showing a sign of fear. Don't be a little coward. They take their punishment without a murmur. Stop it, I tell you!"

Robin, struggling to get out of his grasp, had kicked him savagely on the knee-cap and crashed a fist on the side of his chin, and now, reverting in his fury to an infant, was biting his wrist and yelling between bites, "Let me go. Let me go, or I'll kill you. Let me go, or I'll kill you." He yelled it loud enough, Justin thought, to bring all the people in the park hotfoot to the shrubbery. Greatly frightened by the frenzy he had provoked, Justin pushed him away from him, after slashing at him once more, in anger at his defeat.

"Shut up! For God's sake stop that row. All right, I'll do no more to you. I'll let you off this time. Only for God's sake stop roaring. Anyone would think you're mad. I've never heard anything like it. Shut up, old chap . . . do . . . I won't do anything more to you. I *won't*, I tell you. . . . Robin. . . ." He called his name, as if Robin, insulated by his fury, were incapable of hearing him. "Robin. . . . Listen. . . ."

"I'll kill you." Fists clenched, teeth set, breast heaving, feet firmly planted on the ground, Robin stood before his brother, and there was a wild, alarming light in his eyes.

"All right, all right, but don't do it here," soothed Justin. "Don't do it just now. And, my God, don't look so mad, for heaven's sake. You look absolutely mad. It's all over, old man; it is really. I didn't want to punish you; I told you I didn't; but what else could I do? No, I won't do any more. I said I wouldn't." He repeated this, because he thought for a moment that Robin was going to step forward and start the appalling business all over again. "That's right; take it easy, old boy. My, you've got some strength! I should never have thought you'd got the muscles that you seem to have got. And you've got some guts to take *me* on. I must say, I rather admire you for it; I do, really."

This flattery was the one perfect febrifuge. Robin's breath quietened, his fists unclenched themselves, his feet moved from their grim stance, and the stormy light faded from his eyes.

"Come on," encouraged Justin; and he led the way out of the shrubbery.

Robin followed, rather pleased with himself now, and ready, after a few more sobs, to be friends again.

"That's right," said Justin. "Blessed are the peacemakers. But my, you've got a temper, haven't you? You must get it from old Gus. Or perhaps it comes from our grandfather, who seems to have been able to lay about him pretty savagely. I don't blame you for it, mind you, because it's fairly strong in me too. I understand it only too well, Robby, because I can do a lot in that line myself."

§

It was not only along the open stretches by the river, or over the green plots in the parks, that they went straying together in a tranquil content; they liked also to wander along the crowded streets of Hammersmith and "see life." Their favourite hunting ground for this kind of life was the narrow and dangerous channel of King Street, where the costers' barrows lined the gutters, and the bargain-seekers crowded the pavements, and the shopkeepers shouted their wares from their open counters, and in the roadway the horse-trams grated and clanged along, between the buses and cabs and tradesmen's vans. They loved King Street on a Saturday night after rain, when pavements and roadway, under the lamps and paraffin flares, were shining streaks of blue, and there was a gleam on the harness of the horses and a sheen on their sleek, wet sides. They would stroll from shop to shop and from stall to stall, in and out of the struggling people, and listen to the salesmen spieling and the women chaffering and the blind man playing his whistle in the gutter and the drunkards singing at the public-house doors. There was ample life for them to stare at, and listen to, in King Street on a Saturday night.

Once or twice they saw things in King Street that were nearer death than life. There was an afternoon when they saw a policeman wheeling a hooded stretcher towards the West London Hospital, with a string of children following behind him. Instantly Justin and Robin became two of those children, and Justin, declaring that he wasn't afraid of any bobby, walked up and asked the policeman what it was in his stretcher. "It's an old gent who was thrown from his pony cart right under a Derry and Toms' van," said the policeman, not without pride. "Yes, just where King Street becomes the Chiswick High Road." Justin hurried back with this information to Robin whose thumb was at his mouth, in alarmed admiration of Justin's daring. "It's an old cove who's been run over," he explained. "A pity. I hoped it was someone who'd been murdered." Robin grinned, as he always did when Justin deliberately said a shocking thing; and together they followed the stretcher right to the doors of the hospital in King Street East, and watched it disappear within; for they always saw a stretcher home, just as they always followed an arrested man, whose cuff a policeman was holding, to the doors of the police station and the last of his liberty.

Both were fascinated by punishment and sin. In Great Church Lane, behind the Latimer School, was a house of the Female Philanthropic Society, devoted to the reformation of young women convicted of a first offence; and often, about fifty years ago, you might have seen two boys, one rather taller than the other, standing and staring up at this building, in the hope of seeing a first offender or a reformed young woman. So too in the Fulham Palace Road, where the Sisters of the Good Shepherd kept an Asylum for Penitent Women, these two would stand on the opposite side of the road and gaze up at the windows, while they meditated upon the penitence within; and if a young woman emerged and walked down the street, they watched her for a long time. Indeed they could not take their eyes from her till she was lost to sight. On the whole it would be fair to say that Justin watched her because she was being punished, and Robin because she was a sinner.

They committed crimes themselves, and not for the sake of gain, but for the thrill of being criminals. They had a game which they called "Turping". One of their heroes at this time was Dick Turpin, and Turping consisted in petty robberies along the highway. Wandering along King Street, they would walk into one sweet-shop after another and snatch chocolates from the counter while the shopwoman had turned round to look at a bottle of sweets of which Justin had most courteously inquired the price. Or they mounted one bus after another, each of which had its horses' heads directed towards Kew, and they stood on its platform till the bowler-hatted conductor had finished punching tickets inside; when they asked of him politely, "Is this the right bus for Kensington?" Learning that it was going the opposite way, they apologized for their mistake, waited on the platform till the next stop, and there alighted. In such a way they got from Hammersmith to Kew without paying a penny, and back again in the same style.

Justin's pleasure in these games was because they were a defying of the Law, and an assertion of his superiority to lesser men who were frightened by the Law. Crime for its own sake had a lively appeal for Justin.

"This is fine," he would say. "I'm enjoying this."

"But it's stealing," Robin would submit.

"Who says so? Only the coppers, and they're only men like me. If I say it isn't, why isn't my assertion as good as theirs? *I* say that if people can't look after their property properly, it's there for anyone who's got the skill and the guts to get it. *I* say that property's only for him who can keep it."

"But what if you get caught?"

"I don't get caught," said Justin proudly.

All these were merry times, but perhaps not so completely happy as when they sat by the gas stove in their little bedroom at the back of the house, and it was winter without. The little red house had only three bedrooms; their parents had the large front room with the big double bed, and Justin, who refused to sleep in the same room with Gerard, Hector or Bozzy, had insisted on having the tiny back room and taking Robin as his partner there. Here were their two beds and their books and a gas stove in the grate, whose broken asbestos was like the bones of long-dead men. There was also a gas trivet on a flexible tube, and this could be brought, for all manner of purposes, into the midst of the room. And here, when it was dark at four o'clock, and the wind was whining outside, or the rain was rattling on the window, they would boil a kettle on the trivet and make toast at the stove; and when the toast smoked, filling the room with a splendid smell, they spread dripping on it abundantly, showered pepper and salt on the fast-melting dripping, and munched and munched the savoury mess, sitting bowed over the fire. The darkness gathered around them, for they allowed themselves nothing but the firelight, and both became silent, hypnotized by the golden glow where the asbestos was entire and the sickly, blue flame where it was broken. And of a sudden Justin would say, "I wish I were an outlaw." And when Robin asked why, he would answer, "Because it's the only free life, my young Cock Robin. Yes, the only life that's really free; the only life where you can really call your soul your own. But there it is: they don't have outlaws these days, so we shall have to think of something else." And they began exchanging their dreams again.

CHAPTER FOUR

GERARD was nearly as fine a figure as Justin, but his face had not the arresting perfections, the almost unnatural accuracies, of his brother's. His nose was rather short, leaving his upper lip long, so that Justin, one morning at breakfast, after studying these features and deciding that they were simian, said, "Old Gerard's rather like an anthropoid ape, isn't he, Mum?" and thenceforward addressed him as "Monkey Brand". But this nickname was unfair to a face which, if not handsome, was made attractive by large, bright intelligent eyes and curling, brown hair that was the fairest in the family. And for adults, if not for children, he had considerable charm because of a courtesy and a grace of manner which were quite remarkable in a boy of his age. Someone had once said in his hearing that his manners were exquisite, and that he had the grace of an old aristocrat; which had pleased him very much, so that, from that day onward, he strove to cultivate and enlarge this natural courtesy.

In character, too, he was very different from Justin, though there was only a year between them. He hated cricket and football as much as Justin loved them, and in consequence was as bad a performer with a ball, of whatever size or shape, as his brother was good. And just as his brother dreamed of a time when he would have his own school and play cricket every day, so Gerard longed for the time when he wouldn't have to stop hard-hit cork balls with his hands or stand up and be bowled at by fast bowlers. Justin despised him for this, and deduced from it that Old Monkey Brand would never be good for much in life; but it was not any lack of manhood that made Gerard dislike the unnecessary pains and twinges and dismays of the cricket field; it was, in his judgment, mere common sense; and when on one occasion, as the family played on the green, he let a cricket ball, which Justin had hit with all his force, pass between his legs because of an invincible resistance in his hands to the notion of stopping it, and Justin jeered at him and called him a coward, he rushed at his mocker and fought him; and there was no fear in his eyes but only rage; and his blows, though murderous in their design, were technically admirable. It took three strangers on the green to part the combatants.

Gerard was much alone in his childhood, but was happy to be alone. Justin and Robin were a partnership on which his courtesy forbade him to thrust himself; Hector seemed as pompous and foolish to him as to Justin; and Bozzy, poor, smiling Bozzy, was of no use to anyone but his mother. So Gerard found happiness in his books and in secret meditations on the great career he was planning for himself. Gerard's head was charged with an aspiration which will hereafter appear.

§

Hector had the height of the other boys but not their lithe, graceful, narrow-hipped figures. Nor had he their lambent, restless, easy intelligence. His tall body had a soft casing of fat around it, and this quilted and comfortable coat was the very picture of the protective covering of complacency, self-satisfaction and pomposity with which he met the jarrings and thrustings of the outer world. Justin would often refer to him as "Pompey" or "Old Pompey", and this was a much apter nickname than "Monkey Brand" for the graceful Gerard.

No one had ever seen Hector in one of those tempests of hate that hurled Robin at Justin, or Gerard at Justin. Hector would have stood looking on at such a broil and pronounced a ponderous comment on it afterwards. Nor was he in the least jealous of any distinctions won by his brothers, on playing fields or in examination rooms, even though he won no such distinctions himself. On the contrary he collected the achievements of his family as other boys collected butterflies, and exhibited them to his friends. As long as the family was glorious, he was satisfied. And if there were not enough of these distinctions to make a satisfactory show—and indeed there were lean years when none such appeared—he invented them. He was an unlimited liar and romancer.

Laertes said of his sister that she changed affection, passion, and hell itself, to favour and to prettiness, and similarly it may be said of the plump Hector that he changed the affections, passions, and high quarrels of his family into favour and personal decoration. The wraths and combativeness of his brothers were inevitable, he explained, in old Norman blood like theirs. (There was no Norman blood in the le Fabers, but that didn't matter to Hector. A name so French as le Faber was something to boast of; it was a fat, warm, Southern soil in which lies could proliferate.) "A nine-hundred-years-old name," Hector would call it to his schoolfellows. "Yes; and probably older. We are the original le Fabers, and there were le Fabers in France long before they came over here with William the Conqueror. Strictly speaking, my father is a Count, and my brother Justin should succeed to the title when Father dies. If Justin and Gerard were to die, I should be a Count one day. If Justin makes a fortune—and I don't see why he shouldn't; he's dazzlingly brilliant, and makes a success of everything he attempts—I think myself that he ought to assume the title again. It's a shame to let a great name like that die." Bozzy's affliction provided him at first with a shame that was really an inverted pride. "It's dreadful about Bozzy," he would say, shaking his head. "It does one no good with the other fellows to have an idiot in the family. Not quite an idiot, of course, but pretty barmy; and I must confess I don't fancy having anybody like that bearing the family name around. And what's worrying me is that the day will come, after the pater's dead, when we shall all have to keep him." But later he saw Bozzy's condition as something that enhanced the family's distinction. "After nine hundred years the le Faber blood is running a bit thin—that's what I think," he would explain to one classmate or another, walking home with him from school. "You nearly always get at least one idiot in really ancient families. It's a result of too much intermarriage in the nobility. The royal families are nearly all tainted like that, and I don't see why it should be any different with the le Fabers."

§

At three years old Bozzy had not spoken at all; at five years old he spoke but seldom, and then only as a child of two. When people spoke to him, he frowned as if trying to understand, but soon abandoned the strain and smiled at them instead. Sometimes he repeated things said to him, but with staring, only half-comprehending, eyes. He would say, "Clever Bozzy," and "Thank you, Bozzy," after he had successfully handed to his mother the object she had asked for; and he would take the object back to the place it had come from, and bring it to his mother a second time, so as to hear her say "Clever Bozzy" again, and to repeat it after her. When he was six and seven he began to talk a great deal—too much indeed, as if in his small, clouded mind, he was proud of being able to talk like everybody else and was eager to be doing it all day. If his mother was not there to hear him, and his brothers would not listen, he would talk to himself by the hour. But his words were often fluffed and unintelligible, like the lines of an actor whose mind is not in command of what he is saying. He still frowned and gaped when people said to him things that he couldn't understand, but the frustration did not seem to cause him pain, for he smiled immediately afterwards and appeared to like anyone who would talk to him. Perhaps the life in him was too low for the passionate excitements that troubled Gerard and Robin, but he was always good-tempered and always ready to laugh and play with all who would play with him. There was love somewhere in his rudimentary and inarticulate soul because, if Beatrice or Augustus invited him, he would run and fling his arms around them. As might be expected, Beatrice loved this unfortunate and despised one best of all her children.

There was an afternoon when four of the boys were on the green. It was a Saturday in summer, but the clouds were lying so low that they filled the streets with an ominous twilight. Everything was very still, and sounds and voices, even from far away, seemed to be heard with an unnatural clearness. Justin, his cricket bat tightly gripped, was standing on an imaginary pitch in the middle of the grass. Robin, ball in hand, was about to bowl to him. Hector stood watching these two. Bozzy, unwanted by any of them, hovered at a little distance behind.

"Ready?" inquired Robin, tossing the ball from one hand to the other.

"Yes," shouted Justin, but not before he had cast a glance at two nursemaids seated by their high-wheeled perambulators and at two little girls in pinafores who had stopped bowling their hoops to watch.

Robin, taking a short run, bowled a short-pitched ball. Justin, lips compressed, ran forward and hit it with such power that it shot over the trees towards the windows of the houses facing the green. What was a smashed window or damage to a pedestrian on the pavement compared with the admiration he desired from the people watching? Robin, his thumb at his mouth and his shoulders lifted to his ears, watched the flying ball in an exquisite transport of alarm. The ball hit a house wall and bounced back into the road, and Robin, dropping his hands to his knees and drooping his head, acted in humorous fashion the collapse of a man whom relief had undone.

In Hector a quiet pride was engendered. "That's my brother," he said to a youth at his side whom he had never met before. "They say he's one of the biggest hitters St. Paul's has ever had. Everyone thinks he's certain to play for Middlesex one day, and probably for England."

Bozzy, who had let loose a shrill cry of delight every time the ball was noisily hit and had run after it like a puppy after a thrown pebble, did the same now and recovered the ball from the road. He tried to throw it to Robin, but it shot up into the air and fell behind him. Hector returned it to the bowler and, putting his hands into his pockets, prepared to see further distinction accruing to the le Fabers.

Gerard, it will be noticed, was not present; and his absence was as characteristic as the presence and the activities of the others.

Suddenly the game stopped. Justin, holding his bat, looked at the road on the southern side of the green. A plumed hearse, drawn by sleek black horses, and a long chain of blue-black carriages, had drawn up before the gates of an ivy-hung mansion. For days past the owner of the mansion, old Sir Bertrand Lysaght, had been dying, and the doctor's brougham had been moving to and fro before his garden wall. Now he was coming out, feet first in his coffin, on the shoulders of the undertaker's men. Justin watched the coffin sliding into the hearse, while the silky black horses tossed their heads. He had paused in his play, less out of reverence (though reverence and courtesy had played their part) than out of interest—a rapt and piercing interest. The funeral cortege moved slowly away towards the Hammersmith Road and the cemetery, and all watched till the last of the carriages had disappeared beyond the trees. Then Justin cried, "Come on, Robs. Where's the pill? Bowl us a swift one—the swifter the better." And life on the green went happily on.

CHAPTER FIVE

WHEN Justin was twelve and Gerard eleven, the new people came to the house next door. On a fine March afternoon a pantechnicon backed against the kerb, and disgorged its furniture on to the pavement, while its horses with their muzzles in their nosebags chased the bags about the roadway in an effort to arrive at the last of their food. The younger boys, Hector, Robin and Bozzy, watched from windows in a bubbling excitement, and the two elder boys with more restraint but hardly less interest.

A very small man, with short legs, large head, and the dark eyes of a foreigner, bustled about between the threshold of the house and the tail-board of the van, talking fluently, gesticulating often and widely with shoulders, hands, and head, and sometimes clicking his tongue in despair and muttering "Dio Santo!" or "Santa Madonna! What do we do now?" Since he was directing the men where to take the furniture, and since he addressed a plump and stately woman, much larger than himself, as "darling", the boys concluded that he was the new tenant, and she his wife. His large head was bald and lustrous at the crown, but a profusion of limp, grey hair hung around it like a halo which had collapsed; his nose was large and straight; his black eyes bright and smiling; and his skin like a fine vellum which the sun and the years had

tinted to a pale mocha brown. Had his height matched the
size of his head, he would have made a handsome figure even
in a parade of handsome men; but he was small, very small in
the English scene, and he was made to look even smaller by
the ample figure of his wife. This woman, in tight corsets
that threw her bust well forward, and in a bell-shaped skirt
that threw her hips well back, sailed up and down the tiled
garden path like a ship well-braced; and if she wanted to
summon her little husband from indoors, she pitched her voice
high and called in accents that were plainly English: "Domenichino! Domenichino darling, where are you? Domeni-*chee*-
no!" From this Gerard, who had recently been turning over
the pages of a *Don Quixote*, deduced that he was Spanish, and
Justin, who alone enjoyed the advantage of a classical education at St. Paul's, that he was Greek.

The house, exactly the same as the others in the row, was
small, and the drama took on an excitement when the men
were carrying into the hall, or trying to, an ebony grand
piano, half as big as the house. It was like trying to force a
bison into a kennel; and the little man danced about the difficult manœuvres, sighing often and muttering: "Corpo di
Dio!" and "Sacramento!" whenever his beautiful black instrument struck the walls. But so as not to hurt the feelings of
the men, who were doing their best, he added with a shrug:
"Non importa," or "Che cosa importa? We shall all be dead
one day." After a crash against the lintel of the door, the men
retreated a step or two to begin the assault again; and the
little man shrugged anew and, spreading his hands with a
gesture of impotence, said, "Oh, do not mind. The door will be
big enough soon. Avanti. Avanti, my friends, and God go
with you." The piano struck the jamb of the door this time,
and he sighed and addressed himself: "Pazienza . . . Pazienza
. . . Nothing endures for ever."

After the piano certain white busts, of plaster or marble,
and representing men with long hair, were lifted out of the
van and carried into the house by the men, with affectionate
caressings of their remarkable hair. Beatrice, summoned by
the children to see and explain these objects, said, "Those
are Beethoven and Bach, I think. And that's Mozart. He's
evidently very musical;" and this opinion was justified when,
a minute afterwards, they heard him playing elaborate scales
and chords on the piano to see if it had suffered during its
baleful journey from the van to the drawing-room.

Just then the woman returned from pavement to house, calling out in her high-pitched voice: "E vicino l'u ficio postale, Beloved?" and Justin turned away, for he began to think that Gerard must be right about the man being Spanish and didn't want to be reminded that he had scoffed and declared he was Greek.

The five-roomed house did not take long to fill, and before the sun was down, the pantechnicon went rolling out of Pemberthy Road with its men, their task accomplished, smoking in peace upon the tailboard. The house door was shut upon the small foreigner and his large wife, and all that remained of the afternoon's entertainment was some wisps of straw on the pavement and some shreds of sacking in the gutter.

But the arrival of Mr. Domenico Mario Morgari at the house next door was an event of some importance in the lives of the le Fabers. It would be an exaggeration, but it would not be wholly untrue, to say that he was an envoy of the outer world who had come for two of them.

§

Next morning they saw him standing in the cold sunlight, his grey hair ablow in the wind, and affixing a plate to his garden rail. When the fixing was done, he stepped back, his large head on one side to appraise it; and he nodded his head twice with satisfaction and returned indoors. As soon as politeness permitted, they strolled out in a body to walk past the plate and learn what was engraved on it. "Mr. D. M. Morgari, Teacher of Music and Singing," they read; and Hector was shocked. "Good lord!" he commented, when they were out of hearing. "It's a bit of a come-down for the road, isn't it? A teacher of music isn't a gentleman. I always thought this was a road of gentleman's houses." In the evening they saw him leaving the house in a black wide-awake hat, beneath which the grey hair moved in the wind, and carrying under his arm some enormous instrument in a bag of shining black leather. Justin, conceiving it to be a trumpet of some sort, suggested that he played it at public house doors and that he probably did a good trade in ice cream during the summer months. He called him thenceforward "The Hokey-Pokey Ruffian" and "The Alien Immigrant Next Door" and "Our Neighbour the Dago".

In the following days they became aware that little Mr. Morgari was quite as interested in the five boys next door as they in him. He would approach and smile at them over the back garden wall, or the front garden hedge, as if he longed for them to like him. If he passed them in the street his black eyes beamed his goodwill. And sometimes he would say, "Buon giorno," in what they now knew to be Italian, and "Where are we off to this morning, my dears?" And he would look down upon Bozzy and shake a compassionate head and say, "Poverino bambino." They would answer politely, since they were gentlemen, but coldly, since they had never been introduced to him, and when he was some distance away, they would deplore the fact that he could speak to people without an introduction. And Justin was greatly annoyed by the "my dears" and inwardly upset by it.

They did not know that he loved them. Mr. Morgari had no children of his own, nor hope of any now, and he would have liked a dozen to romp around his music room like the innumerable children of Johann Sebastian Bach. His heart had sallied out at once to the five handsome boys next door, and especially to the little one who was simple, and therefore dear to God. His heart had embraced all five of them as a single unit. He longed to put sweets and pennies into their hands and to take them to places of amusement and watch their delight. And when with perfect politeness they withstood his advances, he rejoiced in their English courtesy and their English coldness.

It was a month and more, and the warm days were on the green, before he breached their strong defences. But then, one afternoon as he was coming home along the diagonal path that led straight to Pemberthy Road, he saw Gerard lying beneath an elm, his chin cupped in one hand, and his other turning the pages of a huge leather-backed volume. Very straight and beautiful he looked to Mr. Morgari, like the statue of a recumbent boy, happily reading, which he had seen in a palazzo in Florence.

He stopped. He stopped because he could do no else. Beauty had laid an arresting palm upon his breast.

"Buon giorno, capitano," he said. "And what have we there? What are we doing now? Reading in the Book of Doom?"

At once, with his perfect manners, Gerard rose to his feet and stood facing him. And Mr. Morgari's heart was melted by his courtesy and by the beauty of his youth. This boy was lovelier than his elder brother because his face, though less handsome, was less hard, less firmly set, less strangely over-powering, and it was full of passion, full of soul. His eyes were the eyes of an artist.

"Ah no. Don't get up," he begged. "I did not want to disturb you. I just wondered what it was that you were studying with such earnestness that all the world was lost to you. It is a large enough volume. Is it one of the sibylline books? Yes, I feel sure it is."

"It's a Shakespeare."

"Well, that is good. But I didn't know that English boys read Shakespeare."

"I wasn't exactly reading it. I was looking at the pictures."

"May I see them too?"

"Yes, certainly." And Gerard stooped to pick up the book.

"Thank you. Thank you." But Mr. Morgari's heart hurt him. The lovely boy was exquisitely polite, but grave, and cold. He was showing him the pictures, one by one. They were engravings of old actors in great, tragic scenes: Hamlet at the graveside with the skull of Yorick in his hand, Lear and his fool on the storm-darkened heath, Othello before the bed of Desdemona, and Brutus in his tent with the ghost of Cæsar behind him. "They are nice. Very nice. You like Shakespeare?"

"Well, I've only seen one of his plays."

"And which was that?"

"*Julius Cæsar.*"

"Ah, Julius Cæsar, my countryman. Eccelente! And you have seen it acted. Whom did you see in that noble play?"

"I saw Beer-bone Tree and Lewis Waller."

"Did you now? At Her Majesty's Theatre. I see you are interested in the theatre. I see it in your eyes. Very interested. That is so, is it not?"

This question, touching Gerard on a sure spot, pierced his cold, steel armour, and something like friendliness came gushing out. "Oh yes. Yes, very. Actually I'm thinking of trying to produce *Julius Cæsar* now."

"Really? And where? At the Lyric Opera House?" But immediately, lest he were hurting the child, he changed his tone. "And why not? Of course produce it. I'm sure you would produce it very well. I only hope you have a stage large enough for your ideas."

"I'm afraid I only meant in our drawing room. And only

two scenes of it: Mark Antony's scene in the Forum, and Brutus's quarrel with Cassius in his tent."

"They are two very good scenes. And which parts would you play?"

"I thought of being Mark Antony in one scene and Brutus in the other."

"Why not? You are the Actor Manager. Yes, those are clearly the parts for you. Do you produce plays often?"

"No. It's so difficult producing with children. They try to be funny. Especially Justin. And Justin's a year older than I am. I've written more plays than I have produced."

"Dio mio! You write plays?"

"Yes, but I'm afraid they are all historical plays because I can never think of a plot."

"Ah, I think you will be an actor, not a writer."

"I want to be an actor."

"Then that settles it. An actor you will be. And now why not come to the theatre with me sometimes? I could take you often."

"What? I beg your pardon?" A brilliant hope gleamed before Gerard, but it dimmed and went out. His mother had said that they were on no account to let Mr. Morgari spend any money on them, and Gerard could not question the propriety of this. "Oh, thank you very much. It's most kind of you. But you mustn't trouble."

"Trouble! It's no trouble. I should just take you in for nothing."

Now Gerard stared; and the brilliant hope gleamed again. "For *nothing*?"

"Yes. I am a performer in the theatre too."

"Are you an actor?"

"Oh no. My art is a step lower down. In fact it is several steps lower down. It is in the orchestra pit. I play in the orchestra. I have played in nearly all the greatest theatres in London. And I could take you to sit with me in the orchestra well. Sometimes the musicians bring their sons to sit with them, but I have no sons. I take you instead."

The green had no existence then for Gerard. He saw only Mr. Morgari, and in a haze behind him all the theatres of London. "Do you go in by the stage door?"

"Ma si. Certamente. And I will take you on to the stage and show you everything behind the scenes. I will take you whenever you wish. Perhaps we will even talk with the actors. And we will sit in the orchestra, in front of those who have paid ten and six for their stalls. And later on I will take you to other theatres."

At that point Gerard deserted the family fortress and joined the enemy at the gate. The terms were too good. He resolved that whatever his father and mother said, and whatever that cocky ass, Justin, said, he would go with Mr. Morgari through that stage door, even if he had to do it in secrecy. And he walked back along Pemberthy Road with Mr. Morgari, talking happily with him as with a friend.

Justin saw them. He saw them standing at the gate, Mr. Morgari radiant with his conquest and nodding and smiling and gesticulating, and Gerard plying his questions and shaking hands with Mr. Morgari. He disapproved, and disapproval can be a pleasant, a life-quickening, sensation. Well charged with it, and therefore happy, he hastened to meet Gerard in the hall.

"You were chatting with the Dago," he said. "I saw you. Don't you think it's a bit idiotic to go and encourage him like that? Now we shall never get rid of him. He'll give us no peace at all. What an assinine thing to go and do."

"He's going to take me to theatres. To heaps of them. He says he can take in anyone he likes for nothing."

"What's that? What do you say?" asked Justin, and his defences tottered.

Gerard explained. Justin said nothing. He listened, and, having heard all, walked thoughtfully away. He was deciding that he must reconsider his attitude to Mr. Morgari.

§

At first Mrs. le Faber refused to let Gerard go to the theatre with Mr. Morgari and sit in the orchestra well. She wasn't sure that it would be "quite nice", she said, and they could perfectly well afford to pay for a seat for him. Besides, the Charing Cross Theatre was not a theatre with a very good name, and its present play was a stupid melodrama of the hunting field. No, Gerard must decline the invitation as politely as he could. But to this decision Gerard opposed such an outburst of tears and stampings, such a demonstration of door-slamming and sulking in bedrooms and refusing to come to tea, and at last such a sudden and purposeful rushing from the house (possibly to commit suicide) that she was shaken. Beatrice was a little frightened of Gerard and Robin as well as of Justin: they had tempers too like their father. Gerard did not return, and the dusk came down upon the afternoon like the thunderstorm before the death of Cæsar, and Beatrice, her anxiety mounting, and pictures of the river appearing and reappearing in her mind, told the other boys to go out and find him for heaven's sake. Justin was more than ready to organize and lead a search party. "All right, Mum," he said. "Leave it to us. He's probably dead by this time, but if he's to be found alive, we'll bring him back. If not, we'll drag the Thames and bring back whatever's left. Any reward? No? Not even a tanner? Well, I don't suppose he's really worth it. Come on, Hector. Hurry your fat stumps. Come on, Robs. Rescue!" And he led them out into the dusk.

They did not have far to look. They found Gerard hidden deep in the shrubbery at the eastern end of the green, seated upon the earth and sobbing. The intermittent sobs rent his body as he sat there, and between the sobs he snuffled and swept his nose with his sleeve. Justin and Hector stood and looked at him with a detached interest, but Robin felt a pang of pity like an arrow twisted in his heart.

Gerard lifted his wet eyes to the search party. "Go away," he commanded. "Go away."

"Gosh, he's still blubbing!" exclaimed Justin, studying him with an interest that did not abate. "And he's wiping his nose on his sleeve."

"It's pretty bad for us all, going about crying in public like that," said Hector. "I must say I don't like it at all. People know he's my brother."

"Go away!" roared Gerard, and the roar seemed to shake the plane trees above him. "Go away. Don't stand and look at me. Go *away*!" And he beat upon the earth in a passion of hate.

"It's like a kid of six," continued Hector. "Why, not even Bozzy goes on like that. Bozzy never cries."

"I wanted it more than anything else in the world," sobbed Gerard; and the shaft twisted in Robin's heart more painfully than ever. He would have liked to stretch forth a hand and lay it upon Gerard's shoulder comfortingly, but he was too shy to do anything of the kind. And he could think of nothing comforting to say. He just stood at Justin's side with his heart torn.

"Come on home, Gerard, and don't be an ass," ordered

Justin, some pity stirring in him too. "Mother says you're to come home. And Gus'll be back soon."

"I'm never coming home again," said Gerard.

"Oh well then, stay." Justin's pity was instantly dispersed by opposition. "It won't worry us. Come on, you chaps. Let him sulk if he wants to."

And the three of them went from the shrubbery. It was Justin's idea to make a pretence of walking home, and then to return on tip-toe and keep the fugitive under view, "lest he really does try to kill himself." He would have enjoyed the command of such a tactical exercise. But Gerard, tired, hungry, and shivering with sobs, got up and followed them home, a long way behind. If they paused for him to come up with them, he paused too, that the full distance might be left between himself and those he so bitterly hated.

At home Justin argued with his mother that Gerard ought to be allowed to go with the Dago. His main reason for arguing thus was not pity for Gerard; it was a desire to take advantage himself, at a later date, of Mr. Morgari's powers. But there was certainly some pity in his heart too, and he was pleased on this occasion to give play to it, since it subserved his main purpose. He followed Beatrice about the house, canvassing his brother's case. He followed her out of rooms and up the stairs and down again to the kitchen. "It isn't often I agree with Gerard, Mum," he submitted. "Generally I think him rather an idiot, but I must say I think he's right this time. I think it would be rather swine-ish not to let him go. And it's not only Gerard I'm thinking of; it's Mr. Morgari. I'm afraid we shall hurt his feelings. And I don't think we ought to hurt his feelings, do you? The very fact that he's a Dago means that we oughtn't to hurt his feelings. But we shall. Yes, he'll be cut to the quick. And you don't want to cut him to the quick, do you, Mum? A poor little man, only five feet high! A stranger in a strange land. Oh no, Mum. Far be it from you to cut him to the quick. I must say that if he were to invite me, I should be inclined to go, for his sake."

And Hector inquired at what age they let boys sit in the orchestra pit, since he wanted to know if his support, given now, would yield him a dividend in a reasonable time. And Justin said, "I don't suppose they want kids messing about," but Hector calculated that Gerard was only two years older than he, and that the months would pass, and that if he cast his bread upon the waters now, it would return to him after not so many days; and, having calculated thus, he added his own ponderous arguments to those of Justin.

And against this pressure of the family Beatrice gave way. And Mr. Morgari's delight, when Gerard told him of his parents' consent, was as real as Gerard's and much more demonstrative. He was stirred to the depths, and his whole surface was in commotion. And on a Saturday afternoon he marched off with Gerard, the other boys watching from the dining-room window. Gerard was in his Eton suit; and Mr. Morgari was in a black coat, large bow tie, and wide-awake hat, with his huge French horn, black shrouded, under his arm; and the boy in the Eton suit was but an inch less tall than the grey-haired man with the horn.

Together they walked across the green towards the Broadway and the District Railway. The day was fine after a clouded morning; the sunlight sparkled on the young summer leaves; the children played on the grass; the flowers bloomed above the window boxes of the houses; and everywhere the late May blossom made nosegays of the shrubs and trees. Beauty, so generously spread, was too much for the soul of Mr. Morgari, which swelled with inspiration till its burden was so heavy that it halted him in the middle of the green.

"Do you not feel it, my Gerard? Do you not feel a strange atmosphere in this quiet village in which you live? You must, I think. Oh yes, yes. You are an artist."

Gerard, not liking to say No, since Mr. Morgari thought him an artist, inquired what he meant.

"How shall I say?" Mr. Morgari raised helpless shoulders, spread helpless hands and, unable to explain what he was feeling so deeply, began to walk again. "I cannot explain it, but it is there: a difference; a difference from all the places around. A few steps to the north—a few steps to the south—and you will no longer feel it. You will no longer feel it because it is no longer there. No, I cannot describe it, but I can tell you why it is here—why it is all around us now. It is because artists have lived here and dreamed their dreams, and their dreams have sunk into the ground. Yes, that is it. I felt it directly I came here. I said to your Auntie Ursula——" so he always spoke of his wife to the boys, much to Justin's annoyance—"I said, 'Do you not feel it, my dear?' and she pretended to, but I do not think she did. She is all that a wife should be, but she is not an artist. It is different with you. And when I speak of artists, I do not mean only the great and famous ones—your Charles Reade and Alphonse le Gros and Henry Irving—I mean also the little ones like me who have failed in most of the things they wanted to do. Their dreams may never have been fulfilled, but they have sunk into the ground and permeated the bricks of the houses and the trunks of those old trees, and they are a part of what we are feeling now. And because of this I like to think they will have their share in inspiring other and more successful men one day—men who can really achieve things. You, perhaps. I like to think that nothing which was so good in its time is wholly wasted. . . . Yes, your Uncle Domenico had his visions once, just as they did, but he has achieved very little, my Gerard . . . very little. . . ."

Gerard did not know how to answer this. There seemed no need to demur at such modesty because Mr. Morgari, smiling as he spoke, was obviously happy in this description of himself as one of those who had failed. He was proud, as it were, of his failure and of the pathos of it. So Gerard said nothing, but he listened with great interest because he was applying much of it to himself. He had been surprised to hear an actor called an artist, but he was determining to be an artist, and one of those who were successful and famous, not one of the ineffectual and obscure like Mr. Morgari. And he was feeling glad that he was different from his brothers, who were not artists. He was feeling superior to Justin with his cricket, and Hector with his complacency, and sorry for them.

"Sometimes I think I might have done more," continued Mr. Morgari, "if I had had a little, just a little, more luck. There is no one who can do without a little luck. Not even the greatest. They need money for leisure to think, to study, to experiment, to create work and to destroy it and to begin all over again. Good luck to *you*, my boy. With a little money I might have done something. Who knows? Ecco——" they were now in Brook Green Road, with the traffic from the Broadway hammering past them, and Mr. Morgari stopped Gerard with a touch of his hand and stood still himself. "Ecco. I have it here," he explained, touching his head. "And I have it here." He touched his heart. "But I have never had it here." And he patted his trousers pocket. "That is all. Come on. I do not know that I greatly mind. I have learned to be content. I am content to provide a little music for those who stand in the limelight. No one notices me at all down in the orchestra well, but I am a part of the pedestal on which

they stand. And when they need me no more, when they
kick me away from them, I can always sell hot chestnuts at
the corner of some kindly London street. It is a fragrant trade
of which no man need be ashamed. Here we are. Here is our
celebrated Broadway."

You would have thought it difficult for Mr. Morgari to be
lyrical about the clamorous and vibrating Broadway. But it
was not so. He looked up King Street East and down King
Street West, which were as one artery sweeping across the
Broadway; he flung out an open and appreciative palm towards the West and said dramatically, "The Great West
Road. The Great West Road, my boy. It goes on and on to
Staines, Windsor, Bath, Bristol, and the Americas. The road
that thousands have taken to fortune, and many thousands
more to failure. A road across the world is a terrible and
beautiful thing. I hope you think things like that sometimes
as you cross the road to the station. You must if you are to be
a great artist, with a head full of imagination and a heart full
of feeling. None of these silly people, hurrying about their
business of money-getting, are ever visited by a thought like
that. They are blind, blind. So! Here we are. The station.
Now we go down into the sulphurous smoke. No, no; I pay, I
pay. From first to last, this is my little treat."

A train steamed into the station, as they reached the foot
of the stairs, and they ran beside it, Mr. Morgari holding on
to the handle of a door; and when it stopped, he cried, "In
vagone!" and bundled Gerard in, and himself, too, so that they
both secured corner seats. It was well done, because soon
the compartment was as full as a packed crate, five seated on
each side and five standing. Nevertheless, as the train roared
into the tunnels under London, Mr. Morgari, nursing his
French horn on his lap, and leaning round the loins of the man
standing between them, told Gerard all about the play they
were going to see. This he did to enhance the boy's excitement
and his enjoyment of the day. Then he enlarged with fervour
upon the famous actors for whom he had played, and promised
to take Gerard to see some of them; and this he did to make
the boy love him. Irving, Hare, Wilson Barrett, Tree, Haw-
trey—they all played before Gerard in the tunnels between
Earl's Court and Charing Cross, he bending forward to listen,
untroubled by the smoke leaking in through the windows and
unaware of the stations they were passing.

At Charing Cross the two of them emerged above ground

again, and now Gerard's heart was a lump of excitement, rising and falling between breast and throat, as they walked behind the Embankment Gardens and up an alley to the stage door of the Charing Cross Theatre. "There it is," said Mr. Morgari; and there it was, a dingy and blistered door that was as romantic to Gerard, and as resplendent with promise, as the entrance to a treasure house or the pleasure dome of Kubla Khan.

The stage door-keeper in his office, a melancholy man with a beard, gave Mr. Morgari a perfunctory " 'Afternoon," and said nothing at all but just nodded when Mr. Morgari explained the boy at his side. They passed in, and Gerard's breath was quick with anticipation. It was nothing to him that the brown walls were bare and harsh and the stone steps grey and cold.

"You want to see the stage first, do you not?"

"Oh yes, please, Mr. Morgari."

"Good. You shall. It is down here."

And they went down the steps and down again, for the stage was well below the level of the street. The air became close and musty; it smelt of dust, grease paint and gas. A dark door was before them, and Mr. Morgari, pushing it open, led the way through.

"Eccoci," he said.

They were in an immense and mysterious cavern, whose roof and sides were lost in a darkness like the night's. Gas battens, row upon row of them, were alight, high above the scenery flats, but they had been turned down and were spluttering and whining at this humiliation. The wings of a set were in place, and a cleaner, holding her pail and broom, was tossing some impudence up to a man who stood aloft on a spotlight perch. On the other side of the wide proscenium arch two men were discussing a script at a prompt table. It was a real stage, and it clasped its fingers round Gerard's heart.

The old plush curtains, faded with time and dust, were down upon the boards, and some of the light from the battens lay upon their folds. Not a sound came from the front of the house beyond them, because the public doors were not yet opened; and with Mr. Morgari's consent Gerard parted the "tabs" (so Mr. Morgari called the curtains) an inch or two and peeped through. There was the auditorium, vast and dark and empty, except in remote corners where the exit lights laid patches of cream and gold on the circle walls.

So it remained before Gerard's eyes, but he was no longer seeing it like that. He was seeing it crowded from parterre to gallery with people in fine clothes, all waiting to see him, Gerard le Faber, in the most successful play of the year. His heart shook with fear of the great audience he saw there, but he quickly overthrew this fear. He was never going to be defeated by stage fright. And then, even happier spectacle, he saw all these people clapping and cheering at the play's end and waiting for him, producer and principal actor, to take his curtain. Up in a box were all his family: father, mother, Justin, Hector, Robin and Bozzy. Ever so slightly —not enough for Mr. Morgari to notice—he bowed to these playgoers of the future.

§

"Come on, Gerard. Now we will find you a seat."

They returned to the side of the stage and went down more stone stairs, lit by a single gas jet whose yellow flame sang like a canary in its round wire cage. At the bottom of the stairs was a doorway framing a broken and unhinged door. Through this they passed into the space beneath the stage. In this crypt, on benches that ran between the stout wooden stanchions, some twenty men were seated with bundles of property costumes at their sides. The costumes, once brilliantly coloured, were now dirty and dimmed and tarnished. Some of the men were old and sat humped and dumb by their tawdry bundles. The daily clothes of all were shapeless and frayed, and their boots flattened and crumpled like those of tramps. A sweaty smell from this quiet brotherhood filled the low-roofed and unventilated vault, and it was heavier than the smell of grease paint and dust.

"Who are they?" asked Gerard in a low voice.

"Hush. *Supers*," whispered Mr. Morgari. And in an even softer and more mysterious whisper he added, "And sandwichmen too. Yes. They have just come in from walking up and down the Strand, and going to and fro in it, with advertisements of the play. And now they're going to be huntsmen and heavy dragoons and farm labourers and, what's more remarkable, my dear, visitors of great distinction at the Squire's ball. Some of them are old actors who were quite well known in their day. And they're glad enough to get their shilling a night now. And so the world turns round. We are all sinners, and need our punishment."

Disquieting words these, like a sudden chill in the air. But Gerard refused to be perturbed by them. Not for him the cold warning. Just as young soldiers before the battle know that many will be killed, but do not believe that they will be among them, so Gerard in the high buoyancy of eleven years old, felt completely confident that the end of his day in the theatre would not find him under the stage like one of these, a casualty. He knew, he *knew*, that he was going to be a success, and not only a success but the greatest success of his time. Even, possibly, of any time.

"This way." Mr. Morgari led him up some narrow steps, and behold, they were in the orchestra well, among the music stands and the instruments; and the auditorium, fully lit now, was before their eyes. Gerard swept his gaze round the cream and gold walls and the gilded sweep of the circles and the red plush seats on the broad, raked floor. The people with shouting and shuffling were streaming into gallery and pit, and those already seated had begun a facetious applause for someone in the vicinity of the stage. For a moment, a bashful moment, Gerard thought it was himself they were thus honouring, but no: he turned his head and saw an attendant in a faded green tunic, braided and frogged like the uniform of a Hungarian hussar, walking before the curtains and putting his long taper to the footlights. The gas footlights flung their orange glow on the bottom of the old red tabs. No wonder the people applauded and waited for entertainment.

"This is your royal box," said Mr. Morgari, placing a cane-seated chair against the red curtains that enclosed the well, and beginning to unpack the splendid arabesque of his French horn. "No one in the house will see as well as you."

"Oh, thank you," said Gerard.

But he did not at once sit down. He stood in the centre of the well and faced the incoming people that they might see him as someone different from themselves, a performer; a part of the theatre; one of the privileged persons who entered by the stage door.

CHAPTER SIX

NEXT the loving Mr. Morgari laid his hand upon Robin. He was as much attracted by Robin as by Gerard, and as eager for his love. He spoke of him to his wife as "the wistful one" and "the spiritual one", and when the expansive and picturesque mood was upon him, would go so far as to suggest (for he loved the English Bible) that God had chosen Robin for His servant, just as He had chosen David from among the sons of Jesse. "You will see, my dear; you will see. There are love and compassion in that boy's eyes, and a light that is not of this world. And sometimes when he is standing alone in a dream, there is a bewilderment on his brow as of one who will never be content with the surface of things. He will never be content with the things that are temporal—no, no, not that boy. He will only endure by seeing Him Who is invisible. I may be wrong; I may be wrong; but I don't think I am. I think I know the chosen of God when I see them."

Perhaps he thought that he might well act as God's messenger in this business, for Mr. Morgari had a great admiration for all saints and servants of God and every willingness to bring a recruit to their ranks, so far as was possible in one who was not himself of their company. Mr. Morgari's native city was in Umbria, and though the mountains and fields of Umbria had seemed ordinary enough in his boyhood, and though in his youth he had sinned often enough among them, and had been but a faithless and frivolous son of the Church, now that thirty-five years had passed since he left them, and he was never likely to return and live among them again, they had become "the land of the saints" and there was a light upon his Umbrian Vale of a brighter and rarer quality than anything that lay over London. And because of his memories and this sad but sweet nostalgia Mr. Morgari loved all saints and was a regular and self-censuring worshipper in the hindermost pew in the Church of the Most Holy Trinity on Brook Green. This church, though smoke-grey outside, was brightly lit and painted within, and it reminded him of his Santa Maria Maddalena at home. It differed only in being much cleaner; its pews and its paint and its brass were always polished and shining; and in this it resembled the Englishmen who shaved every day and his English wife and English mæstros who liked him to do the same. "The Church of the Most Holy Trinity is a Catholic," he would say, "but it is also an Englishman;" and he loved it no less for that.

But, whether he acted deliberately or not, it was in a district railway carriage that he laid his hand upon Robin and gently guided him in the way he should go. He had taken him in his turn to the theatre and seated him beside the orchestra's brass, and now they were on their way home and sat opposite each other in corner seats. Unlike the day when he travelled with Gerard there were no others in the carriage: only the big French horn in its black bag sat at Mr. Morgari's side. And he was leaning forward and dilating with a flashing enthusiasm in his eyes on the beauties of High Mass and Benediction just as he had dilated on the beauties of *Hamlet* and *Pinafore* to Gerard. He had surprised Robin by mentioning that he was a Catholic, which had shocked Robin and pleasantly excited him, since a Catholic to him was a person of ill fame and therefore of no little fascination. Instantly perceiving the shock, though Robin had politely tried to conceal it, Mr. Morgari was moved to reveal more and worse: for example, that he often played in the orchestra in the Pro-Cathedral and in other celebrated Catholic churches. An orchestra in a church! Robin's interest was wide-eyed. He sought to know more. He fished for it with some diffidence because he had a vague feeling that he was asking a conspirator to reveal the secrets of his underground camarilla. But he need not have been anxious, for at every question and half-question the information and the descriptions gushed from Mr. Morgari, like water from a rock, sparkling and spumy and rapid, and Robin was soon as restless to see a Mass as Gerard to see a play.

"But you shall, piccino. You shall come with me one day when I play in the orchestra."

"My father would never let me."

"Why?"

Robin was too polite, and too shy, to say why, so Mr. Morgari, who was longing to be attacked, and had asked his question for that purpose, gave the answer himself. "*I* know. *I* know. He thinks all Catholics are scheming knaves, if they are not poor deluded fools, and that our priests are the blackest knaves of all. But no, no; it is not so, my little Robin. He should meet our Father Madelon and talk to him, and then he would know that, whatever else the father is, he is not a villain. You know Father Madelon, the Rector of our church

on the green? You have seen him—you have certainly seen
him, eh?—an old man with bushy white hair?"

Yes, he had seen him, said Robin. He had seen him at the
door of the church, welcoming the children in.

"Well, let me tell you something, piccino. He is a saint.
He is Love Incarnate. And because he is Love Incarnate he
is like God. And he is like God in this, that all who know him
worship him. It is always so: if you are like God, the people
will worship you. My own country, my own Umbria, has
produced many saints who were like God, and the people
worshipped them when they were alive, and they worship
their memory still. People from all over the world call it
Holy Umbria, you know. And our Father Madelon is just
such another one. Sinners break down in his presence, and
their sins fall away from them, because to come near him is to
know that there is a God, and that His other names are Forgiveness and Love."

And thereupon, lifting his voice to defeat the roar of the
tunnels, Mr. Morgari poured forth a chronicle of Father
Madelon's good deeds, and Robin was as captured by the tale
as Gerard by the tales of the actors; and a desire was fast
possessing him to be a saint, to be Love Incarnate, and to be
worshipped by all. His heart beat fast before this splendid
vision.

On roared the train, and it was an easy transition for Mr.
Morgari, a-sway in it, to pass from Father Madelon to the
Umbrian Saints, and to rehearse the records of St. Francis, St.
Margaret, and St. Clare. From St. Clare and her community
of Poor Clares, it was but a step to the holy women of Hammer-
smith who made beautiful the neighbourhood. Think of the
Daughters of the Cross at Brook Green, and the nuns of the
Sacred Heart on the Broadway, and the Sisters of the Good
Shepherd in Fulham Palace Road, and, above all, the Little
Sisters of the Poor in Nazareth House. Because of these
places Hammersmith to all Catholics was a name to be
revered—which was a new view of Hammersmith to Robin,
whose father usually scoffed at it as "Pope's Corner".

The Little Sisters of the Poor were a subject that flung wide
the gates of Mr. Morgari's heart. Love for the Little Sisters
danced in his eyes. He told Robin how they took in from the
streets the old and destitute people, and went out and begged
food for them, and did not eat themselves till all these honoured
guests had been fed and comforted. And then they sat down

to the remains of the food, "the crumbs from the poor men's table," and gave their thanks to God for these sweet-tasting mercies. His eyes brimmed as he described such sanctity.

"The Sisters of the Poor! What a name! I could weep at the thought of it. I say their presence makes beautiful that whole stretch of King Street West from the Red Cow to the Broadway. As you pass the wall of their convent, if you have any feeling at all for the atmosphere of a place, you must feel their sanctity coming out into the street like a kind of aura, and be the better man for it. There may be many who don't feel it, but I am sorry for them. *You* would feel it; you are the sort. You have the necessary spiritual tentacles, I think. Oh yes!"

Robin was delighted to be numbered among the rarer sort like this. The spark in Mr. Morgari's eyes had long ago leapt across to his own eyes, and was dancing there as he listened. And now as the train steamed into Hammersmith, he begged that they might walk home by King Street West and the wall of Nazareth House. They did so. And they stood together outside the high enclosing wall that they might feel the sanctity of the sisters there on the pavement, and be the better for it.

§

Mr. Morgari had done his work. The following afternoon was Sunday, and when Augustus had fallen asleep after the heavy Sunday meal, and Beatrice was on the verge of sleep too, Robin stole from the house on a secret adventure. He was going to visit the holy places of which Mr. Morgari had spoken. He went to the Convent of the Sacred Heart by the Broadway and stared up at it, and to the Convent of the Good Shepherd in Fulham Palace Road, and stared up at that; but did not stay long at these places because a greater thrill awaited him outside the wall of Nazareth House. It was because this would be the finest thrill that he had kept it to the last. The lesser places visited, he walked to the spot where he had stood last evening with Mr. Morgari, on the pavement before the Gothic door in the high grey convent wall. And here he stood gazing at the door and the wall, and the solemn-looking buildings behind, for a long time. The people passed by him, and they did not notice him, nor he them. A woman came to the convent door, rang the bell, and the placid face of an old nun appeared in the grating. She smiled at the woman and opened the door and let her in. And the door shut again upon Robin as he loitered there, watching. And he remained there in a dream, drifting from pavement to gutter and from gutter to pavement. Happiness was agitating him because in a small way he had fallen in love. He was in love with the Love which Mr. Morgari had so dangerously sung for him.

After fifteen or twenty minutes of lingering and drifting he walked away. He walked homeward by the Red Cow and St. Paul's School and the Roman Catholic institutions at the eastern end of Brook Green. It was nearly three o'clock, and once again the children from the pauper school were crossing the road to the doors of the church. And just as it had been on that Sunday long ago, the black-robed nuns were shepherding them across the road, and Father Madelon, with his bushy white hair and his beaming smile, was standing on the church steps to welcome them in.

Robin stared at Father Madelon because he was a saint. He stood and stared at him, hardly conscious of what he was doing. He strayed a little nearer to him in order to feel, as Mr. Morgari had said was the experience of all who came near to Father Madelon, that there was a God; and to feel further, as a consequence of this, his sins falling away from him. But he did not feel anything remarkable unless it was a mixture of shyness and pleasure when the father turned, saw him, and gave him a special smile for himself. The last of the children went in, with the nuns behind and the father following, and the inner door of the church swung behind them, and someone shut the big outer doors, and Robin was left in the pagan sunlight of a perfect Sunday afternoon.

He dawdled on the pavement, playing with the awful but fascinating idea of pushing at those doors and slipping into the church. Organ music came out to him as he waited, and the shrill, harsh, willing voices of children singing a hymn. And then a man's voice, almost certainly the father's, talking to them, and suddenly a loud, happy laugh from them all, because he had said something funny. Robin could not move. He stayed there, fingering his fingers, till the man's voice ceased and the organ was playing and the children singing again.

Then abruptly—for it was a habit of Robin's, after a period of shy hesitation or puzzled indecision to act, in despair, passionately and abruptly—he walked towards the large outer doors and pushed at one of them. It yielded and he crept in. Nervously, guiltily, he turned the handle of an inner door a very little way. Its click stopped his heart. One does not retreat, however, having adventured as far as this, and he completed the turn, pushed the door quietly, and passed into the church.

And what he saw now was, to him, sheer beauty. It was more beautiful than the sunlight without. White walls; jewelled windows; painted and gilded angels projecting from the walls to support the rafters; a gilded screen across the chancel arch; six tall candles alight on the altar and twenty-two small candles alight beneath them; and before this array of stars Father Madelon in a golden vestment, with boys in white cottas—two holding tall candles—standing about him. On the altar, high above everything else, was a dazzling ornament of gold, all rays like a sun; and it was to this that everything in the church at this moment seemed to be addressed: the inclinations of Father Madelon's head, the lifting of the grey smoke from a golden vessel swung by one of the acolytes, the flickering of the candles, and the singing of the children and the nuns in the nave and aisles.

"O Salutaris Hostia ... O saving Victim, opening wide. ..."

The smoke wreathed above the figures at the altar, and a sweet smell, sweeter than pine-gum burning among the trees, filled the church.

"Tantum ergo Sacramentum. ..."

With profound venerations the people sang, and then all ceased singing, and there was no sound except a clinking of chains as the acolyte swung his golden vessel to and fro, and a low, continuing mutter from Father Madelon.

Everyone was kneeling. The nuns had their heads bowed over their missals; the good children kept their heads bent too; the less good looked about them as they knelt. One, a boy, turned and stared at Robin, who, after a few seconds of that stare, dropped upon his knees on the hard floor of the aisle—not in piety but in a judicious conformity. When the boy, apparently satisfied, turned his face towards the altar again, Robin half rose and worked himself into the last pew of all and knelt there watching.

Now a bell was ringing on the altar steps; three times it rang, and Father Madelon was holding up the golden ornament before the people and moving it in the form of a cross. Three times he did this, and then turned his back upon the people and replaced the ornament in the curtained cupboard on the altar.

"Bendictus Deus, Benedictum nomen sanctum. . . ."

Robin's heart was beating fast with the beauty of it all, and as he knelt behind everyone else, alone with his secret thoughts, he determined upon a dangerous experiment. He had crept guiltily into the church, and now, even more guiltily, he was going to creep a little further into holiness. Just as other children, greatly daring, experiment with idolatry, or a blasphemy, to see if God will really strike them dead, so Robin, in spite of the diatribes of his father, or because of them, experimented with piety to see what it felt like and if any remarkable effects would ensue. What words should he use? He knew the Lord's Prayer from saying it at school, but it was not this that came to his lips. What came was the rhythmic opening to a hymn they were always singing at School Prayers. Its words were memorable because they jingled in his mind. He bowed his head like the nuns, shut his eyes tight, conjured up a vision of God on His throne above the heavens, and said:

> "Thy kingdom come, O God,
> Thy rule, O Christ, begin . . ."

CHAPTER SEVEN

BUT if some of the immortal longings of man were born in Robin on that Saturday and Sunday, with Mr. Morgari for their father (or their midwife), they were for long but a small growth and had to keep incongruous company with aspirations of a much more worldly temper. One of these had been brought to birth in him by Hector, and it was a hardy and restless infant.

Hector, after reading an historical romance about the twelve sons of Tancred of Hauteville, called *William of the Iron Arm*, had discerned many points of similarity between that celebrated and all-conquering Norman family and the family of the le Fabers in Pemberthy Road. And only a little later he read *Lorna Doone*, and here again in the stalwart sons of Sir Ensor Doone he perceived a similarity to himself

and his brothers. He had been much stirred to read how the
outlaw Doones, in their deep, green valley, would make each
of their sons and grandsons, at the age of twenty, stand bare-
foot in old Sir Ensor's doorway, and if he failed to touch with
his head the lintel, which was six foot one from the threshold,
and with his shoulders the jambs, which were two feet apart,
then he was cast forth from the valley as unworthy to be of the
company of the Doones. And because of this stern demand,
said their chronicler, there was not one man in three score
who, standing by the side of a Doone, did not look like a tailor.
No detail in the whole romance of the Doones stuck so firmly
in Hector's mind as this, because it was plain to him, from the
stature of Justin at thirteen, and of Gerard at twelve, and of
himself and Robin at ten and nine, that they would all be able
at twenty, like great John Ridd, to walk off with such a door-
frame on their shoulders. Hector himself might be fat, and for
that reason less agile and powerful than the others, but he had
height and breadth and, in any case, he was always ready, if he
lacked a particular glory which his brothers possessed, to get
his satisfaction and his boast out of their possession of it.
The physical excellencies of Justin had no greater admirer and
praise-singer than the fat Hector, but it was rather for his own
glory than for Justin's that he sang the praises to all who
would listen. He had found no record of the measurements of
Tancred's twelve sons, but he endowed them in his mind with
the splendid proportions of the Doones and with the pro-
portions-to-be of the le Fabers. And of all this he talked much,
in his ponderous way, to the family; and Robin was scarcely
less impressed by it than he. He was the more impressed
because Justin, who as a rule made merry over Hector's
pomposities, was inclined to accept as intelligent this likening
of himself and his brothers to the sons of the Doones and the
twelve sons of Tancred of Hauteville. Justin, to be sure, had
retired into a privacy with *Lorna Doone* and *William of the Iron
Arm*.

So now, by the side of Robin's desire to be a saint like
Father Madelon and to be beloved by the people, there was a
monopolizing desire to be as tall and strong as Justin, the
tallest and strongest of the le Fabers. Perhaps because of the
aspiration to sanctity, which neighboured this other desire so
closely, he was always a little ashamed of it, and it was in
secret that he did exercises on the floor of his bedroom or,
better, in the Children's Gymnasium under one of the railway

arches that strode across Ravenscourt Park. This gymnasium was equipped with parallel bars, a horizontal bar, and a bridge-ladder, and often, forty odd years ago, a boy of ten or eleven, quite alone, might have been seen doing press-ups on the parallel bars, up-starts on the horizontal bar, and short-arm marches along the bridge-ladder. It was Robin le Faber, and he would do these clandestine exercises in this secret place for an hour on end—with intervals of breathless rest. Other boys made no such practice of bodily improvement—at least not with Robin's steadfastness—and thus it came about that at feats of purely muscular strength he was soon able to surpass them all.

In his mind, and indeed in actual fact, he was now Robin of the Iron Arm, and when he was twelve he was proud enough of his muscles to suggest to Justin, then sixteen and six foot high, a trial of strength between them. It was a test in which he had worsted all the boys at his school, to their undeniable chagrin. This was the test. The two competitors sat at a table's corner, one on either side of the angle; they rested their right elbows on the table, laid their upright forearms one against the other, interlaced their fingers and pressed to see which could force the other's forearm backwards. Most willingly, and with the utmost assurance and a tolerant smile, Justin agreed to the competition. He had no doubt that he, with his brachial muscles which he often contemplated with admiration, could force down young Robin's arm in the first ten seconds.

"Come along," said he. "How long do you say it'll take me to get your arm flat on the table?"

"I may get yours down."

"You think so? All right. We'll see."

And they sat down at the little table in their bedroom. They laid their upright forearms together and interlocked their fingers.

"Ready, old cock?" asked Justin, and prepared to teach Robin what muscular power could be.

"Yes," said Robin, setting his teeth and gripping tight with his fingers.

"Rightho! *Go!*"

And each exerted all his strength against the other. Neither arm moved. Then each poured the whole of himself, his will, his dreams, his envies, his jealousies, his needs, into his right arm. And still neither arm moved. The arms vibrated, the clenched hands moved through an inch and back again, but ever the arms stayed upright. They moved no more than two jarred pillars set in a concrete base. Justin's teeth set like a tiger's. Intolerable that he at sixteen—*he* who was one of the hardest hitters in the eleven at St. Paul's—*he* whose strength was the admiration of younger school-fellows—could not push down the arm of a twelve-year-old brother. But he could not. He could not move it, though the veins of his temple swelled and his face flushed crimson with the effort. There was no question, of course, of Robin's forcing *his* arm down, but it mortified him to think that a mere twelve-year-old could resist the pressure of his strength like this. But Robin continued to resist it, and he began to hate him and want to hurt him. More and more he concentrated the whole of himself into his right arm, but Robin's eyes and mouth were as set as his, and his small, white arm stayed upright, trembling. "I won't be beaten," was in the steel of Robin's eyes and in the forward thrust of his jaw. If Justin gained so much as an inch, a kind of fury, almost frightening, almost murderous, invaded Robin's temples, eyes, and mouth, and the grip of his smaller fingers became harder than the grip of a lion's teeth. The ends of his fingers went purple with the strain, as if all his blood and being were directed there. At length Justin realized that he couldn't overcome him in hours, and that, unless they were to go on all day, honours between them must stand easy.

"Rightho," he said, and unlocked his fingers and stood up and breathed heavily.

Robin rose too, even more breathless but very happy.

"Well, I'm damned!" said Justin, panting. "Good lord, I wouldn't have believed it. I don't think there's anyone else could do that. It's marvellous. Quite honestly, I was doing all I could. I was really exerting myself, and it's no good saying I wasn't. I think it's a great credit to you, and I feel quite proud of you. I'll bet Gerard couldn't do that, and as for old Hector, you'd make his fat arm look like butter. Jolly good, Robs! But between you and me, I shouldn't overdo all that exercising, or you'll become muscle-bound. These strong men, you know—Sandow and others—are all muscle-bound. I shouldn't like to be like Sandow, I must say."

This victory over Justin, for it could hardly be called less, was a memorable moment in Robin's childhood. It was like a gateway through which he passed out of dependence and inferiority into a new confidence and a pleasant sense of equality. Thereafter he felt himself Justin's partner rather than his servant. And because he had defeated him and earned his approbation, he loved him all the more and felt all the nearer to him.

§

For their holidays the le Fabers used to go to a little bay among the chalk cliffs of Sussex where there was a shelving beach and, at low water, rocks extending from the two headlands of cliff like harbour walls. It was the seaweed and the pools among these rocks that Justin used to smell, as he stood in a reverie on the mall at Hammersmith, when the tide came crawling under the bridges. One whiff of sea-salt in the tidal wind, and of dank green things in the mud, and the whole of London fell away from Justin and ceased to be—its pavements, factories, and grey gaunt houses—and he was alone among the rocks of a beloved bay, his feet in cold sea-water, his body bent over a still clear pool, and his hands chasing a swift crab or a shy, elusive prawn. The sea-scent of the Thames wafted him back to the rocks and caves and the hills above them, because his hours in these places had been the most serene he had ever known. There he had been far away from all men and alone with nature, and his body had seemed made of wind and joy, and in one way or another, unconscious of worship, he must shout aloud his thanks for the life that was in him and was good. He might have an audience of one to hear his praises, and that was Robin, or he might be quite alone, but in either case the exultation would burst out in song.

There were four bathing machines on the shelving beach, and in two of these the family would undress, and when an old horse had dragged the machines axle-deep into the sea, the family came out and descended the steps into the lapping water. Augustus's big paunch was surrounded by a red-and-white-striped costume, and Beatrice's tall and now rather angular frame supported a black, billowing assembly of blouse, skirt, and bloomers. The boys were in dark-blue swim-suits which had a fringe of skirt for decency. All the family could swim except Beatrice and little Bozzy who were never able to keep their feet off the ground, though they thrashed about vigorously with their arms. There was a long rope attached to the bathing machine, and it was seldom that Beatrice let go of this lifeline. Usually she held it with one hand and Bozzy with the other. Not so the boys. They swam

out into the deep, and Justin, of course, must swim out farther,
much farther, than any of them. He swam on and on, till his
head was but a speck upon the water, and Beatrice in a
growing anguish was crying to him, "Come back, Justin.
Come back."

When they were not enjoying themselves in or by the sea,
Augustus and Beatrice went cycling about the country.
Cycling had just ceased to be "fast" for women and become
fashionable. With the invention of a "Lady's Safety" bicycle,
which had a large open frame, the women could pedal about
the roads in skirts and unashamed. Beatrice on her safety
model wore a straw hat and a tailor-made costume, and
Augustus on his wore knickerbockers, double-seated to with-
stand the wear of the saddle, and high stockings with patterned turnovers which put a frieze round his enormous calves.

The boys, who had no cycles, wandered on foot over the
hills. And sometimes when they were near the cliff edge,
Justin would run, apparently at high speed, to the very brink
and arrest himself one inch this side of disaster, or he would
make a descent of the cliff with Death holding his hand all the
way. He loved such perilous enterprises, and with him it was
a real, not a feigned, ecstasy to come as near as possible to
Death and touch his garment. He would adventure on hair-
breadth hazards even if he was alone, but still more if there
was an audience there to watch him.

§

Later, when the boys were older, and Augustus was earning
more money, they would go for a fortnight to a cottage in
Cumberland and spend their days upon the mountains. And
now the sea was quite outshone by the mountains. What a
day it was, the day before they started, when with much
talk they got out their old climbing boots, packed their rucksacks, stowed the maps in their pockets, and tested the second-
hand compass which was Justin's pride. The little white
cottage was in the tiny hamlet of Deep Langstrath, the most
remote village except Seathwaite in the Borrowdale valley;
and from this starting place they attempted all the great
peaks of the central Cumbrian mass. They would split into
two parties: first, the four boys, fast walkers and pledged to
the summits, and then, a long way behind them, the more
modestly inspired team of Augustus, Beatrice, and little

Bozzy. Needless to tell, Justin strode always ahead of the boy's party; and on the tops of the passes or on the intervening crowns that were but steps to the ultimate peaks, he would stand and gaze upon the wild and majestic view, too lost in love of it, too hushed by it, to be impatient or "cocky" with his brothers. He would be silent for a long while, after he had turned his back upon it to climb higher.

After a time he and Robin would set off on their climbs alone. "Come on, Robs," he whispered one day. "Let's get away from the others. We'll do much better alone. Hector's too fat to climb mountains, and Gerard hasn't a head for heights; that's plain. Would you believe it, he was quite upset when we were on the Lever Face yesterday. He didn't say so, but I could see he was. And the Lever Face is nothing. It's just nothing. But *you've* got the real climber's head. You'll make a mountaineer one day." And Robin, much pleased by this flattery and friendliness, concealed the fact that he too had not been very happy on the Lever Face, and followed after Justin. And thenceforth he and Justin climbed alone. In all weathers—rain, shine, or mist—they did their ten or twenty miles a day, and sometimes they climbed out of the sunlight into the wool-grey mists above, and then emerged out of the mists into the sunlight again, where the peaks were like islands amid a foam of cloud. Scafell, Great End, Bow Fell, Gable, Kirk Fell, Pillar and Steeple—they climbed them all, and the memory of these climbs bound them closer to each other for ever.

They had a game which they called "Head of the River". Justin invented it—he would, because it fitted his nature as close as a skin—and it consisted in catching up with every team they could see in front of them on the slopes, gently bumping the rearmost of these people (as an eight bumps the boat ahead before taking the lead of it), courteously apologizing for the accident, and going on ahead—and thus overtaking everyone till they were foremost of all and "head of the river".

The air on these high places was not air but the stuff of life itself; it was the breath of God that makes the living soul; it was power and life and joy. And there was a beauty in action—in climbing, muscling, aching, panting—that was akin to the beauty of sky and mountain and dale. And Justin, knowing these things with his blood, if not with his brain, led the singing which acclaimed them. " 'Try not the pass,' the old man said," he would roar, five paces in front of

Robin. " 'Dark lowers the tempest overhead. The roaring torrent is deep and wide.' And loud that clarion voice replied: 'Excelsior . . . Excelsior-or . . . EX-CEL-SI-OR!' " Or in a manner most unsuited to a hymn he would yell, "O'er moor and fen, o'er crag and torrent, till The night is gone——" and break off his singing to address a grey-black sheep who was looking down on him from above, "Hallo, Percival. Are we going right for the Gable?" The sheep ran from his words, and Justin resumed his singing. "They climbed the steep ascent of heaven Through peril, toil, and pain. . . ." He, the least religious person on the mountain, had learned these hymns at Colet Court, and now at last was really using them in worship. When they were on the summit, if no one else was there, he would stand and roar:

> "The Saints of God, their wanderings done,
>   No more their weary course they run . . .
> O happy saints, for ever blest
>   In this calm haven of your rest."

They came down from the summits, running and leaping, because they felt more than conquerors and capable of all things. They bathed their feet in the cold running ghylls, and when they were down in the valley, they would sometimes, if there was nobody to see them, paddle homeward along the brilliant water of a mountain stream, the water travelling faster than their feet over the rounded stones of rose and mauve and grey. The stones bruised their feet, the water numbed them, but that was all part of the fun and joy of it. They were irreverent lads, but if there was anything they worshipped, it was the life that was in them when they escaped to the mountains about Deep Langstrath.

CHAPTER EIGHT

JUSTIN was sixteen when, like a ship that had mutinied and purposed to be a privateer in future, he sailed out of the harbour of childhood into the free and open sea. His mother and father, a couple of gunboats lying off the harbour, tried to contest this departure, but he mounted heavier guns than theirs and silenced them and went on his way. The brief engagement with his mother took place in the little bay-windowed dining-room, and people passing along the quiet Pemberthy Road, knew nothing of the significant event that was happening behind those small, curtained windows.

The cause of the quarrel was no more than a gram or two of dust from the playing fields of St. Paul's. It was a Saturday evening in winter, and Justin had returned an hour or two before from playing in the First XV against the Old Paulines. Now Beatrice le Faber was a woman of quick temper—or rather, she had taken this colour, for her character was imitative, from her quick-tempered husband and sons. Augustus, Justin, Gerard, and Robin were all likely to go up in flames, if friction was applied to them long enough, so why should not she enjoy the same exquisite relief? She did. For years now she had been as ready to fly into a passion as any of the others. And this evening, when she observed that Justin, despite her repeated requests, had shed the mud from his football boots on to the carpet of his bedroom, her temper became a furnace within her, and she hurried down to the dining-room, where he, Gerard, and Hector were seated over their homework, to open the furnace doors and pour the heat upon him. Justin listened and, when she paused for a breath, mumbled that he was sorry; but she needed to vent more of her anger and continued to pour it over him. And he, angry that his apology, which he had thought gentlemanlike and, from such as he, generous, had not been appreciated, changed his tactics and resolved that, if she wanted a counter-offensive, she should have it. Gerard and Hector were at the table with him, and he was disposed to entertain them with some skilful shooting.

He sighed. He laid down his pen. "Dear, dear," he said, slightly raising his shoulders. "Doesn't the woman realize that we have work to do?"

"Don't you dare talk like that to me."

"Excuse me, but I wasn't talking to you. I was talking to these gentlemen here."

"You were talking *at* me, and I won't have it. Nobody should talk like that to his mother."

"Oh well, chaps." He leaned back, thrust his hands into his pockets, and extended his long legs under the table. "I don't suppose this irruption'll last for ever."

"You impudent young jackanapes! You——"

" 'Jackanapes' is rude, chaps, isn't it? Very rude. And so

unoriginal. Even in one's most undignified outbursts one should try to avoid the commonplace." Justin was proud of his prose style, when he did battle with words. "What will she say next?"

"Good God in Heaven Above!" Beatrice in her rages would reproduce the very oaths of Augustus, and Augustus swore always by a good God and by Heaven above, though he believed in neither. "I will not have you speaking to me like that. I——" She was speechless and could only stutter. "I—I shall tell your father about this."

"Why not? It's not uninteresting, and he may be amused, but could you reserve it for him, so that we could resume our studies?"

"What did you say?" She stepped close to the lounging boy as if to strike him.

"You heard perfectly well what I said. I see no occasion to repeat it."

She gave him a stinging slap on his cheek, as she used to do when he was small.

He rose. His cheek was red from the slap, but the rest of his face was white. Without hesitating, he gave her a slap precisely the same, except that it was sharper and louder. As she recoiled under it, he gave her a second of the same pattern, and no gentler. She collapsed into a chair at the end of the table, and he stood above her, fists clenched, lips tight closed, and a light in his eyes like the glint of a stiletto. They were the eyes of someone who was determined at all costs to impose his will. They seemed to be trying to hold her down in her chair by sheer power of will. In this moment of a winter evening, while the wind sighed without, he stood there, his quivering mother gazing up at him, a new-grown, stripling man, straight, shining, and terrible.

With a fierce softness like the hiss of a cat he said, "See? Touch me, and you get double what you gave."

"You wicked, wicked boy! You'd strike your mother, would you?"

"Certainly."

"Oh, what's to be done with you?"

"It's quite simple. Keep your dirty hands off me."

"You hit women, do you?"

"Every time. If they hit me."

"Oh, you wicked boy! You dreadful, dreadful boy! You'll come to no good. I don't know what'll happen to you in life."

"One thing that'll happen to me is this, that no one'll hit me and get away with it."

"Gerard—Hector—how can you sit there and let him strike your mother? Have you no manliness? Haven't you a spark of spirit in you?"

Gerard did not respond. This sudden appeal found him at a disadvantage, because he had not supposed that he would be expected to take any part in this encounter. He had been shocked at first by Justin's immediate reprisal upon his mother, but he was thinking now that there was some cogency in his argument. Hector was shocked, both by the unfilial blows and by the unfamiliar argument, because his mind was completely conventional, but, being three years younger than Justin, and much less of an athlete, he had no intention of opening a scuffle in which he would receive contusions and be quickly defeated.

And so, both inhibited from movement, they just sat and watched the battle with a wordless and concentrated interest.

"Your father will be home soon. He'll be home any minute now, and then we'll see what'll happen. He'll thrash you for this."

Justin unclenched his fists and thrust his hands into his pockets. "Don't make me laugh, Mother."

"You'll laugh on the other side of your face, when he thrashes you; as he will."

"What? That excessively corpulent old boy? Oh no, Mother. Oh no, no. He's not such a fool." Did she not realize that he had just come from the football field where he had thrown young men many years older than he, while his schoolfellows cheered from end to end of the touchline? "The old boy'd be on the floor before he got started. Let's try and talk sense."

"He'll thrash you."

"I take leave to doubt it. Haven't you noticed that he gave up that game directly we got big enough to hit back? I did. I noticed it long ago. And very sensible of him too. He's no fool, is our Gus."

Beatrice, palpitating in her chair, continued to gaze up at him like an animal fascinated. Gerard and Hector from the dining-table stared too. To all three, and to Justin too, though he was hiding his agitation, the world at the moment was upside down; and no one said anything because their wits were not yet adjusted to a world which had overturned. And

Justin, feeling that he must break the silence and pretend to be quite untroubled, said in an unstable voice and certainly not in his best style, "If the old boy wants a fight, he can have it, but I shall be sorry. I don't want to hurt him;" and he walked out of the room and out of the house. Ostensibly it was the withdrawal of a conqueror who sees no point in continuing the battle, but really it was an escape from their eyes because he was shaken and they must not perceive it. He would escape into the open places and the cold air, till his heart steadied.

He wandered by force of childish habit on to the green. And there, from behind one of the great elms (like the child he still was) he watched for his father's return. It was not long before he saw him crossing the road and the green in his black overcoat and silk hat. He dodged along to another tree and watched him walking along Pemberthy Road and entering the house. After allowing him enough time to hear the indignant tale he too returned home, his heart beating rapidly, but not so that its behaviour couldn't be hidden. The door was shut, so, not wishing to ring the bell like a suppliant, and have the door opened by either parent, he pushed up a window in the bay and slipped in that way.

"Old boy back?" he asked of Gerard and Hector.

The query was answered by his father's voice. "That you, Justin?" There was a threat of thunder in the voice.

"Yes, Father."

"Come here. Come here at once."

Justin hesitated. He was not sure that he wanted to be commanded by anyone.

"Come here at once, I said!"

"All right. I'll come when I'm ready."

Hands at ease in his pockets, he entered the little drawing, room at the back. Augustus, a huge figure in that little room, was pacing up and down before the french windows.

"Is it true that you struck your mother?"

"Certainly."

"Don't say 'Certainly' in that impudent way. I don't want any impudence."

"You asked a question, and I answered it."

"Are you not ashamed of what you've done?"

"No. Is she ashamed of striking me?"

"Don't be absurd. Good heavens above——"

"She hit me first, and just as hard as she could. I gave her back what she gave me."

"But, good God in Heaven, you can't go hitting women."

"Why not?"

"Well, because—because I say you mustn't." He raised his voice. "Because I say I won't have it. Men don't go hitting women—least of all their mothers."

"Why not?"

"Because—oh, *I* don't know—you *know* they don't. Because women are weaker, I suppose."

"Rightho. Then let her be too weak to hit me."

"Nonsense. It's a terrible thing you've done——"

"I can't see that——"

"Stop interrupting. It's a terrible thing to strike one's mother. And I won't have it, I tell you! I won't have your mother *touched* by you."

"All right, then. You'd better talk to her seriously. You'd better tell her not to touch me again."

Augustus stood, legs apart, before the fireplace. Justin stood, hands in pockets, before him. There was nothing to choose between their height. Justin was an inch shorter than his father, but he looked as tall. He looked ten times as agile and sinewy. There was silence between them, as Augustus, temper hot upon his lips, face, and neck, contemplated his son.

And in that silence Augustus was defeated. He saw that if he struck this quietly waiting boy, he would be struck back as surely as Beatrice had been. He could feel a resolve, hard and tense as fine steel, behind the boy's eyes and mouth and in his hands at rest in his pockets. And he saw that he could use no force to support his threats, because the enemy's strength was larger than his own. He must change his note. There was nothing else for it. He must change from shouted reprobation to quiet reasoning. Slowly the blood sank from his face and neck, and with it his colours were hauled down.

"Oh, come, come, Justin. Let's be sensible about this. You know as well as I do that men don't strike women. It's just not done."

"It is by me."

"What? *Nonsense!*"

"It seems simple to me." And he produced a sentence which he had prepared on the green. "If they claim the right to hit, they must forego the right not to be hit."

"Oh, no, no, Justin, old man. That won't do. You have some sense of decency, haven't you?"

"None, if decency means letting people lam out at me as

hard as they like, and doing nothing about it. That's not my idea of decency."

"*Your* idea! Do you realize that if people knew what you'd done, they'd ostracize you as an unspeakable cad."

"I can't help that. I'm not going to be forced by a crowd of sheep-like people into thinking what I don't think."

"Indeed? You set yourself against the world at sixteen?"

"Certainly. If I don't agree with the world. *You* didn't agree with it as regards religion and churches and all that rot."

"Oh . . . well . . . never mind me. . . ." Augustus, after this thrust, had to admit to himself that Justin was intellectually as well as physically as strong as he. "All I have to say is this —it's this, old man—whatever your original ideas may be, they don't include hitting your mother. I won't have it."

Justin wanted to say, "I don't really see what you can do to stop it;" but he had some wisdom, and some compassion for his father in his present embarrassment, and he decided, as before, that it was unnecessary to continue a battle that was plainly won. So he contented himself with saying, "I've no desire to hurt her, Father, and I promise I won't, if she keeps her hands off me."

Augustus pretended that this was a concession, and Justin was quite willing, and even anxious, that his father should save his face. "That's right, Justin. That's right. I dare say your mother gets irritable at times, but you must remember that she's had a trying time, bringing up a large family on a small income. You pride yourself on your exceptional intelligence, so remember that."

Manifest peace overtures, these, and Justin, who had felt the strain of the conflict, was glad to receive them. "Gosh!" he said boyishly. "I think that's the first intelligent thing anyone's said on this matter." This was his peace offering to his father.

Augustus was pleased with it. "Good, good. You're not a bad boy, I'm sure."

Justin smiled, and his smile could be very pleasant. "Well, I must get on with my ghastly homework which this little contretemps interrupted," he said. And he walked out of the room. Apparently he walked out of a small drawing-room into a dark passage where Gerard, Hector, and Robin were all standing that they might hear the sounds of battle. Actually he walked out of childhood into an adult's freedom.

§

That night, in their little bedroom at the back, when each was in his separate bed, and the light was out, Justin, in whom the recollection of his victory had been working like the fumes of a rich wine, must brag and boast a little to Robin, his best audience. Their talk that night Robin never forgot. Never *wholly* forgot, that is. It sank into his subconsciousness, but only to be recalled with a startling clarity many years later. No sound came from the house around them, except the heavy breathing of Hector in the room next door, and the occasional creaking of his father's armchair in the room below. A cordon of silence seemed to surround the house, insulating that most secret talk from everything but itself. So is a maturing seed hidden from the world. But beyond the silence the traffic murmured in the Shepherds Bush Road, and the wind moaned and rose at times into boisterous gusts, and these continuing sounds were like the rumble and the reverberation of a world that was going on without halt or heed.

"I had to adopt strong measures with the woman," Justin bragged, delighting to divert Robin with outrageous phrases, "but the old man had too much sense to stir up trouble. Yes, I think Mrs. le Faber has had her lesson, and I'm glad of it. I never did like the woman."

"Justin!"

"What's the matter? What are you getting excited about? I'm just telling you the simple truth. As far as I can see, I've never loved anyone. I'm sorry, because I should quite like to; but it's no good pretending to feelings I haven't got. You're the only person I've ever been able to get on with, and if what I feel for you is love, then it's a damned overrated business; that's all I can say, ha, ha, ha! Do *you* love the woman?"

"Who? Mother? . . . Yes . . . yes, of course."

"But why?"

"I don't know."

"What is there to love in her?"

"She's my mother, I suppose."

"Listen: don't you think it's just because people say you ought to? Do you really think there's such a thing as natural affection? I don't. I've no experience of it at all. I like Father, but no better than I do old Morgari, say, and I've

no feeling for Mother and Gerard and Hector at all—except
to think that Hector's the most pompous ass in creation, and
that Gerard's quite a lot of a fool too, who's being particularly
silly just now about wanting to be a famous actor. Gerard'll
never be a famous anything."

"Don't you think so?"

"Of course I don't. He hasn't got it in him. Only one in a
thousand becomes a famous actor, and why in the world
should that one be Gerard? He's quite unoriginal. In fact,
he's one of the most commonplace people I've ever met. He
never thinks his own thoughts or refuses to be bamboozled
by the crowd." Here the obvious but unstated contrast was
"as I do; as I'm doing now". "He just wants to imitate others,
Sir Henry Irving or someone. You've got to be original, a
new force, to be a famous anything."

Justin was not the only one in that darkness who was inclined to refer all talk to himself. "Do you think *I* should
make a success of—of what I told you?" asked Robin nervously, dubiously. One day when discussing their future,
during a walk by the river, he had shyly revealed to Justin—
after a long hesitation, and then only in one of his sudden,
desperate resolves—that he was troubled sometimes by a
desire to be a saintly parson like Father Madelon and to be
loved by all.

Justin prided himself on speaking his mind. "I doubt it.
Quite frankly I doubt it. In fact, I see no hope of it at all.
What chance would you have? Father can't afford to send you
to St. Paul's or Oxford, so you have to go to your present
rotten school, and when you leave it at about seventeen, you'll
have no public school or university behind you. You might
be as good as Father Madelon, you might be the complete
and howling saint, but don't tell me that goodness alone ever
got any man anywhere—What a hell of a row the wind's
making! It's blowing up for a gale. No, you've got to look
after yourself and shove like hell, if you want to get on. Sorry,
but I'm afraid I'm not an idealist like you. I won't even
pretend to be, as most of the hypocrites do. I think it all
sounds very pretty, but I don't believe a word of it. I believe
in looking after myself. I dare say that sounds awful to you,
but I can't help it: I say what I think, and not what people
want me to pretend I think—unless, of course, ha, ha, ha, it
suits me to pretend to think what they want me to think. Are
you still awake, Robs? Good. No, I'm not the kind that steps

aside nobly to let other people get ahead of me. It's they who get out of my way."

"But, Justin——" Robin's brow was creased in the darkness, as he puzzled over this conscience-free egotism, and over the recoil from it that was instantaneous and invincible in him—"surely you think *some* things are wrong?"

"Do I? I don't know that I do. I should think it wrong if in doing something technically illegal I made a mess of it and got found out and put in prison. I should think it wrong because it was stupid."

"But would you—say—*steal*?"

"Rather! Not half, if I could get away with it. We've done a little already, haven't we? It's all a question of who's the stronger. Unfortunately one's got to admit that the great mass of people with their police and their prisons are stronger in some ways than one is oneself, and therefore there's no sense in butting up against the cops. It'd be like butting your head against a steam-roller. But if I could outwit the cops and the crowd——"

"Go to sleep, you boys. Go to sleep." It was their father's voice on the stairs. He and their mother were going up to bed. "It's after eleven o'clock."

"Justin, do let Robin go to sleep." Their mother's voice now. "Do remember he's not as old as you."

"All right, Mum." Justin waited and then dropped his voice. "If I could outwit the cops, I would. Don't you ever think for yourself? If you did, you'd soon see that the Law and the police are only for the little people. Did any of the big ones, who got on top of them—the Napoleons and Cromwells and the rest—ever hesitate to take anything they wanted from anyone? It's comic how it ceases to be wrong to steal, directly you're too big for the police. The Law wasn't for those lads! Well, no more shall it be for me, if I can dodge it."

No answer came from Robin's bed, as he pondered this heavy problem in the darkness. There was a silence except for the sough and wail of the wind and the quiet breathing of the two boys. Then Robin began, "Well——" and coughed and cleared his throat to begin again—"say murder. What about murder? You wouldn't murder, would you?"

Now the silence wrapped Justin's bed, as he mused upon this challenge. And at last, with a deliberate cheerfulness, he replied, "Oh yes. Yes, I can imagine myself murdering someone if I had to. Once again, which of the big ones, given the power, have ever hesitated to put their opponents out of their way? It's only the little people who are solemnly told that it's wicked to murder."

"But it *is* wicked."

"Who said so? Only the people it suited to say so."

"Something inside one says so."

"Only because they've carefully put it inside you. I may choose to cut it out."

"But you couldn't do a murder, unless you were a Napoleon. You'd just be hung."

"Would I?"

"Yes, of course you would."

"Only if I was found out. And I shouldn't be such a mug as to be found out."

"Murders are always found out in the end."

"Don't you believe it! Remember Mathias, the Burgomaster. Really, Robs, for a clever kid, it's amazing how you just produce the stock remarks one after another. I bet there are hundreds and hundreds of murders that are never found out. I can think of heaps and heaps of ways of getting rid of someone without anybody suspecting a thing. I've often thought of them."

"What are they?" Robin's heart began to hammer under his blankets. The darkness added a terror to Justin's words, but a terror that was fascinating.

"Well, what's wrong with taking him in a boat far out to sea and then accidentally overturning the boat? You can swim and he can't. Or if he can, you hurry to his rescue and when he struggles, you accidentally keep his head under the water a second too long. You're found supporting his body with one hand and hanging on to the upturned boat with the other, and you get a medal for heroism and wear it on great occasions for the rest of your life. Or you go for a family trip on a liner—it's probably one of the family you're bored with and want to get rid of—probably your wife—and one dark night there's a 'Man Overboard!' and you raise the alarm, absolutely distracted; you plunge to the rescue but, alas, with no success because the spray is in your eyes and you swim the wrong way; and they lower a boat and drag you out from your work of rescue protesting and weeping; and you're the ship's hero for the rest of the voyage. Or you dare him to peep over the edge of the cliff and accidentally tumble against him and, good gracious, he's gone. You yell for help and try to climb down after him but most unfortunately stick half-way; and every newspaper in the land writes you up as a hero; but, alas, alas, that's no consolation to you, because you're inconsolable. You've lost your best friend, and you weep as you haven't done since you were a child; and everyone is touched by the sight of a strong man's tears. Asleep, Robin?"

"No."

"Almost?"

"Yes, I suppose so."

"All right, I won't yarn any more. Night, night."

"Good night." Robin was tired and yawning now. He tried to excogitate upon these difficult words of Justin, but he couldn't do it for long, and soon they were dragged down and engulfed in his sleep.

PART II

CHAPTER ONE

A DOZEN years later, on an afternoon in midsummer, a young man stood in a coach of an underground train that was travelling up from the tunnels into the daylight a mile or two west of Hammersmith. This was a very different compartment from those in which Gerard and Robin travelled with Mr. Morgari, where five persons sat opposite five, in carriages that were the direct descendants of the coaches on the turnpike roads. This compartment had broken with the past. It was a long tram-like chamber in which the passengers sat lengthwise or stood in the gangway holding on to loops that depended from the roof. The District Railway was an electric railway now, and its old steam trains were forgotten.

The young man was among the people who stood in the middle of the compartment near the doors. He was tall, and his hatless head was some inches above those around him.

More than one of the seated passengers gazed at him standing there. They did so because his face attracted them. Some were moved to whisper among themselves that it was a charming face. Perhaps it drew their eyes and held them because, though it belonged to a young man who could not be more than twenty-two or twenty-three, the hair was already iron-grey and there was a touch of grey in the dark eyebrows that nearly met above the large, soft brown eyes. Long brown lashes increased the softness of the eyes and accentuated the contrast between their youthfulness and the iron-grey hair. The nose was a pleasing rather than a handsome feature, since it was not very long and tried to turn up at the end. But it may be that it was chiefly his expression which engaged the glances of the people. It was shy, wistful, and kind: one felt that if strangers addressed him he would be embarrassed at first and then very polite to them; he would stutter for a moment and then smile shyly and get a pleasure from helping them on their way. He was standing now because he had given up his seat with a diffident courtesy and a broken smile

71

to an old lady hung about with parcels and bags. At present
the wistfulness was in full command, for it was obvious, as he
swayed on his loop, that a dream was enclosing him in its own
private haze. But since all wistfulness has a look of sadness it
would have been difficult to say whether this haze that en-
wrapped him was clouded and heavy or lit with a secret joy.

The train ran into Hammersmith, and the young man
stooped and picked up a gladstone bag and stepped out. Those
who had been studying him were sorry to lose his company
and to think that they would never chance upon him again.
They watched till his dark, iron-grey head was out of sight.

§

The young man ran up the steps, making light of his sur-
charged and swollen bag. He emerged from the station, and
there was the old Broadway: there was King Street, narrow
and thronged; there was Brook Green Road. The old circus,
the old converging highways, the old cavalcades, the same
wide sky-space above—and yet how different it all was
from the scene of his childhood. For once, thought he, an
epoch had ended as a century ended; for once a movement of
history had fitted itself comfortably to Man's arbitrary
divisions of time. From all the six roads whose confluence was
the Broadway the motor buses had chased away the old yellow
and green horse buses, the taxis had dismissed the four-
wheelers, and the private touring cars had crowded out the
leisurely victorias and broughams. In King Street the long cars
of the London United Electric Tramways had succeeded the
old two-horse trams; and as the young man looked, a team of
cyclists, bowed over their slight and spidery machines, came
speeding across the Broadway where once the ladies and gentlemen had pedalled on their heavy "safety" models. The
costers barrows had gone from King Street too; they had been
thrust into side streets to let the multiplying vehicles of the
new epoch go speeding through.

The young man walked a few yards along King Street and
then turned into the Grove, that long, wide road that stretched
in a straight line, five quiet furlongs of it, between the noisy
thoroughfares of King Street and Goldhawk Road. It was a
road of tall grey-brick houses which had long ago lost the
high hopes of their youth and were sombre about the loss.
And it seemed to the young man that the sky above the

straight undeviating road was grimier, and the daylight sadder, than it used to be when he walked these pavements as a boy, ten or a dozen years before.

Why "The Grove"? Why that name from the free and unconfined country for this long, regimented road? Did it find its meaning in the two Indian files of plane trees that marched along the kerbs without a swerve to left or right as far as the road's end, five furlongs away?

The young man walked four of these furlongs till he came to the tallest house of all, which stood at a corner on the western side. Except for carrying its cornice some feet higher than its neighbours, it was the same as they: grey-brick with plaster architraves, semi-basement, and high front door above a flight of steps. Above the railing in front of the house was a notice board which said:

ERASMUS HALL

Principals: Justin le Faber, Esq.
The Rev. E. S. Cumberland, M.A.,
Jesus College, Cambridge.

He ran up the ten steps and pulled at the old-fashioned bell. Waiting on the top of the steps, he seemed as youthful and vigorous as the house was faded and worn. It belonged to the epoch behind the traffic in King Street.

Nothing but silence within the house. He rang again; and then a door at the end of the passage opened. To the young man, his perceptions alert, it seemed to open rather stealthily. Again a pause; then, slowly, some slippered footsteps approached. There were panels of leaded and coloured glass in the hall door, and he suspected that someone was peering at him curiously through a lozenge of deep-sea blue. Fumbling fingers turned the handle, and the door opened a little way. In the narrow opening stood a grey, spectacled, slovenly old man in clergyman's dress.

"Good afternoon, Mr. Cumberland." The young man's greeting was full of kindly affection.

The old man swept his spectacles off his nose to see more clearly the visitor on the threshold.

"Ah, Robin! Our Robin! Come in." The old man's welcome was full of affection too, and it sounded like the affection of gratitude—gratitude to someone who had the kindness to be fond of him. "Come in. This is a splendid addition to our somewhat meagre staff. This is great. Justin and Primrose are expecting you. We are all expecting you."

"How are you, Mr. Cumberland?"

"Me, Robin? Oh, well, well—as well as can be expected in an old man nearing seventy. Yes, nearing seventy. In a year or two I shall have reached my span, and my strength will then be but labour and sorrow. So says the Book. But never mind me. Come in, come in."

Now, if the house belonged to the generation before the lively generation that was romping along King Street, then this grey old man was well met at its door. His clerical dress belonged to thirty years before; which is to say that it was more emphatically clerical than anything worn at the present time. The coat was a frock coat and long and cut square at the neck; the vest presented a buttonless front to the world like the breast of a Sarum cassock, and it too was cut square at the neck to reveal a receding instead of an upright clerical collar. The fat face with the sagging chaps was clean-shaven as a parson's should be, but a suggestion of grey whisker was suffered to grow before each ear; and the grey hair was encouraged to bunch at the sides in a way that reminded one vaguely of the portrait of a divine on a college wall. The very seating of his spectacles on his fat, small nose, and the lifting of his eyebrows as he looked over the top of the spectacles, was reminiscent of lectern and pulpit. But the bleaching hair was untidy, the collar was soiled, the frock coat was frayed and shiny, the vest was crumpled and bespattered with the stains of ancient meals, and the trousers were baggy at the knees, and not solely as a result of prayer.

He studied Robin over his spectacles as he shepherded him into the hall.

"Yes, leave your bag there. This is excellent. We need you. You can be the greatest possible help to us. When Justin suggested your coming, I was enthusiastic in my agreement— my assent. I gave my consent at once. And my Primrose is delighted at the idea of your coming. She was saying so this morning; she said, 'Papa, isn't it lovely to think that Robin'll be here to-day?' And dear Justin's been longing for you to arrive, I know. Yes, shut the door. There's a demoiselle downstairs, and I can't think why she didn't come from her tomb and open to you. Peradventure, like Baal, she is talking, or she is on a journey, or peradventure she sleepeth."

Robin closed the door. It was a shock to him, who wanted to think fine things of Justin's school, to notice the musty, mouldy smell of the house as the door shut out the air. The smell provoked an instant perception of the scratches on the paint, the stains on the wall-paper, and a crack in one of the leaded panes of the hall door. And it made the sound of boys' voices reciting in unison in a room above, and the sound of someone practising scales on a piano far away, seem the very music of dreariness and melancholy.

"That's Justin up there with his class. They're giving tongue just now in the French language. *Je finis, tu finis, il finit.* The language of Corneille and Racine, of Ronsard and Pascal. The language of the Pléiade, my dear boy. Ah, Pascal! What a man! What a writer! *Le silence eternel de ces espaces infinis me'effraie.* Yes? You were saying?"

"How is Primrose?"

"Primrose? My Primrose? She is out, I think. . . . *Le silence eternel.* . . . You will go up and see Justin, will you? I must get back to my grindstone. I'm trying, trying my hardest, to teach my young hooligans their first halting steps in the humanities. But I don't think it has pleased God to visit my labours with any success. I have planted and watered, but God, alas, has not given the increase. Not yet. Not yet. In His own good time, perhaps. I had just set them a Latin exercise to write when the door bell rang, so, as the demoiselle did not issue from her catacombs, I just came to see who it might be."

An insight less sensitive than Robin's might have conjectured from all this parade of French and biblical knowledge, and all this show of humour and self-assurance, that the old man was insecure in this house and in the world. Not for nothing had he mentioned his "consent" that Robin should come to them. Not for nothing was his language as deliberately clerical as his dress. Because of a fear in his heart and a wound in his memory he had to impress upon all that he was a clergyman and a scholar and a gentleman. And a yet subtler perception than Robin's might have divined that he used Justin's Christian name with an exaggerated ease because he was afraid of him. And perhaps a similar but smaller fear could be heard when he spoke of his daughter as "my Primrose".

"Go you up and find Justin. I must get back. I must get back to my strange exhibits in there. It would not do to leave them to their own devices or the place might be wrecked.

Didicisse ingenuas artes in their case *non emollit mores*, I'm
afraid. But it's good to see you, my dear boy. Very good
indeed. Good to see you looking so young and fresh and to
think that you'll be a parson soon. How soon now?"

"Next Trinity, I hope."

"Trinity. I was ordained at Trinity. Forty-four years ago.
And with what hopes, what hopes! . . . Forty . . . four . . .
years. Nearly half a century, and it doesn't seem so long ago,
really. *Eheu! fugaces, Postume, Postume*—— I translated that
ode of Horace once. I used to love turning Horace into
English verse. 'Ah, Postumus, the swift-gone years recede To
join the Past. No piety can plead Reprieve from wrinkled
brow where Age hath writ The great Death Sentence by the
Judge decreed.' That was a bit of a gloss on the original, that
part about the great Death Sentence, but it made a good line,
and it describes me now, I'm afraid—'a wrinkled brow where
Age hath writ the great Death Sentence. . . .' Yes . . . but it's
good to see you young ones coming along to take up the
burden as we lay it down——"

"Hallo! Is that you, old Robin? What ho!"

" 'What ho, without!' as Shakespeare says. That's Justin.
That's our Justin." And instantly Mr. Cumberland fled into
his classroom, his enlarged slippers dropping their heels as he
hastened along. It was like the flight of a limping old roebuck
who has heard the roar of the young lion.

And down the staircase in his "scholar's gown", which was
all he was entitled to wear, came Justin; and Robin thought,
as always on seeing him after a long absence, that he was the
finest man he had ever seen. Certainly he had never seen a
finer. Though he himself was six foot two Justin was three
inches taller, and his wide shoulders, deep chest, and slender
flanks made up the perfect figure of a man. His clothes were
always good, for he was proud of his appearance; and to-day
his dark blue suit sat as well on his tall, shapely figure as Mr.
Cumberland's clothes sat loosely on his slack, lapsed body.
His silky, black, waving hair was parted in the middle, and
this, which might have looked effeminate on a man of smaller
frame and features, seemed an added distinction above his
large masculine nose, his laughing dark eyes, and his strong
jaw.

"Hallo, Reverend," he called, hurrying down. "Who let
you in? The old Duke? He would, interfering old devil.
Awful old man, isn't he? No wonder he's doubled back into

his room. It's as much as I can do to keep him there. I have to keep leaping out of my classroom to chivvy him back. He's as lazy as hell, and if I were not around, he'd do nothing to earn his living. A thoroughly bad old man. The baddest old boy ever. Come along up. Your room's the same old room. Primrose is about somewhere, I think." He lifted his voice. "Mrs. Justin le Faber, where are you? Here's your young brother-in-law. Damn the woman, she must be out. Extraordinary woman that, Robin; never anywhere where you want her to be. She's probably standing outside some shop in King Street, talking her head off to some other woman who's got nothing better to do. I suppose Primrose was a bargain, on the whole, but I don't know. There are times when I doubt it—doubt it very much. And the worst of it is, I've got her for keeps now."

They were going up the stairs together, and Justin was really happy. It was good to have young Robin here and to be saying monstrous things to him.

"How long before you're a parson, your Reverence? How long before you've done with that dam-silly Theological College? Next year? Crikey! Pity old Gus isn't alive. I'd like to hear his views on your becoming a parson, and a high-church parson at that, and me being married to a parson's daughter. A rather rascally old parson, granted, but still, a parson. And me walking the boys to church every Sunday and singing the hymns like one o'clock. You can hear me all over the church. And teaching 'em Divinity, old boy, every Monday morning. Any Divinity you want to know, ask me. I'm a dab at it. Confound it, my dear chap, we're next thing to a Theological College ourselves."

"Don't trouble to come all the way up. I know my way."

"Oh, I'll come up. I've nothing to do. I've set my kids an exercise to work at, because I can't teach 'em any more to-day, for the simple reason that I've come to the end of what I know. Never did know any French. I'm going to mug up some more to-night to teach 'em to-morrow. That's why I'm such a fine teacher, Robs, because I'm always only one pace ahead of my pupils. I always know their difficulties because I was wrestling with them the night before. Damned difficult language, French. Beyond doubt, I'm Britain's most ignorant headmaster, and therefore one of the best."

§

The shock of disappointment that had been Robin's, as he entered the worn, abraded, time-dulled house, increased and hurt more as his first days within it went by. Wandering dreamily about the place, he perceived things now to which he had been quite insentient when Justin was enthusiastically starting his school four years ago. He remembered Justin's happy and excited interest as he laboured with saw and hammer, gimlet and chisel, paint-pot and brush, making shelves, fixing hooks, painting classrooms, painting the stairs, and generally creating, decorating, and giving beauty to his ancient dream. "I don't think I've done badly, Robs," he had said, "to be headmaster of my own school at twenty-three. Wasn't long about it, was I?" And his mother, infected by his excitement, had declared that everything he touched seemed to succeed, and Hector, willing to believe this of Justin since it was glory for himself, had announced to the clerks in the bank where he worked: "There's no doubt that my brother, Justin, is destined to do very big things in the world. He's a kind of Cecil Rhodes, I think. Everything he touches succeeds. He won't stay as a schoolmaster, you mark my words. The scope won't be big enough. This is but a first step. Just wait and see." In the next year or two parents had sent their boys to the school in fairly good numbers—probably because of Justin's fine presence—and Robin had still thought of that tall house in the Grove as the birthplace of a success. But now, not having seen the school for many months, and having grown in perception, he suddenly saw it for what it was. A film had dropped from his eyes, and he was seeing things which Justin was mercifully withheld from perceiving because the artist at the time of enthusiastic creation must believe that his work is good.

Robin was a student now at Lavant Theological College, Sussex. He had completed five of his eight terms there and, if he passed his examinations in the spring, would be a parson this time next summer. So the old purposes were working themselves out. The le Fabers had very little money when Augustus died, and Beatrice needed all her small pension to keep herself and Bozzy (whom nobody would employ, let him smile as he liked) in the little house in Pemberthy Road.

But Holy Orders is a profession you can enter by side doors even though you have no money and no university degree. You have only to be a devoted member of a vital and vigorous parish church, preferably one of an Anglo-Catholic colour, and the vicar and congregation, with help from the diocesan Ordination Candidates' Fund, and perhaps from party funds, will ensure your two years' training at a Theological College, if you covenant to pay back some of the money when you are ordained and earning a stipend.

It happened so with Robin. He was about sixteen when, wandering in search of the beauty that had visited him long ago and was troubling him still, he found his way into the church of St. John the Divine, Kensington; and there the splendour of an Anglo-Catholic mass had simply thrown its jewelled arms around him and won him for a devoted son. Within a few weeks he was a word-perfect disciple of the Anglo-Catholic Movement, an eager proselytizer, a warm critic of the bishops, and an impassioned apologist for Keble, Pusey, Machonochie, Stanton, and lesser priests who, up and down the country, had suffered persecution or imprisonment for the Faith. (Had something of the great divine and controversialist, Bishop Bossuet, come back to the world in Robin le Faber?) The rest followed with the years. Five years he spent as a clerk in his father's old firm, saving what money he could out of his salary, and spending long nights in the study of Greek and Logic and Church History, and when he was twenty-two the vicar and congregation, who all loved him— the vicar with the reservation that he had yet to get shut of much youthful preciosity, and the women, for the most part, with no reservations at all—sent him to Lavant.

Now in the cheaper Theological Colleges such as Lavant there were four terms in the year so that the students could compress into two years a course of studies which at the universities would require three years or more. The summer term ended in mid-June and the Michaelmas term began in mid-August, so Robin was able to accept Justin's suggestion that he should spend the rest of June and July helping him in his school "on mutual terms"—which was a phrase of the scholastic agents and meant that he should give his services in exchange for board and lodging. This he was glad to do because he had no money and didn't want to be a burden on his mother.

But if Robin stood thus at the very door of his dream, Justin was well inside the house. After leaving St. Paul's at eighteen he had managed, doubtless on account of his size, appearance, and reputation as an athlete, to get an assistant mastership in a private school at Bath. His salary was sixty pounds a year, resident, and this was good money in those days for a young man with no academic qualifications at all. At St. Paul's he had not sat for a single examination that would yield him a certificate: he had just advanced from form to form with leisurely step and no pushing, reserving all the best of his intelligence for the playing fields outside. But a mastership in a private school was a blind alley unless he had a degree or, failing that, money enough to start a school of his own, which in England one is allowed to do without any qualifications at all. And he had no intention of dawdling in a blind alley. So at twenty-three he had promptly married an available widow, eight years older than he, but the possessor of a few thousand pounds and a houseful of good furniture. This Mrs. Rossiter, at thirty-one, was a tall, heavy woman with a small face and small, hooked features which looked odd at the top of her large-boned and bosomy figure. Her face must have been pretty once, but now it was red and shiny, and the powder which she applied to it seemed always too much or too little. Her hair had become lank and flat and likely to escape in wisps from the chignon at her nape. Her brow was puckered with a chronic anxiety and the carriage of her shoulders was limp and weary.

"But what would you?" Justin had said at the time to Robin. "One needed the few thousands accumulated by her late husband, the engineer. And his furniture will be distinctly useful. It's not at all bad, some of it. The enormous great woman will do very well as a matron, and I shan't have to pay her anything. The parents like them large and substantial and a bit on the old side. I'm thinking of growing a beard myself, so as to look a bit older; and if I don't, she probably will."

They had not been married three months before her father, the Rev. Edwin Sowerby Cumberland disgraced himself in a manner that resounded throughout his West Country but fortunately did not echo in the metropolis. He had long been a widower, and now that his widowed daughter could no longer look after his rectory, he advertised for a young working housekeeper "under thirty", and when a girl of twenty-five wrote applying for the situation, he wrote back and told her that it might involve other and more intimate duties than keeping his house. He was immediately prosecuted for criminal libel, and the noise of it was all over the West Country.

And at once Justin saw his opportunity. Mr. Cumberland could write after his name, "M.A., Jesus College, Cambridge, Honours in Classics, Philology, and Languages", though no one would have supposed it who looked upon the rusty, relaxed and slovenly old man. And when he stood trembling in the dock at Exeter Assizes, the defending counsel in his "speech in mitigation" and a detective inspector in his "information about the accused" both informed the judge that the prisoner had a son-in-law who was willing, if his lordship saw his way to being lenient with him, to give him a home and occupation and look after him. And Justin went into the witness box after the inspector and stated that this was so; and the people admired him for this fine rescue, and were much moved by it. The judge commended him for his piety, and urged the old man to take advantage of it and be grateful for it. Then he bound the prisoner over to be of good behaviour for a period of two years, and to be under the care of his son-in-law.

A splintering and slowly rotting old timber before this disgrace shivered him, he was quite broken up after it. But Justin did not mind about that. He believed he could furbish him up a little, give him a coat of paint, and use him, for a while at any rate, as a figurehead at the prow of that good ship, Justin le Faber's Career. "Principals: Justin le Faber, Esq. and the Rev. Edwin Sowerby Cumberland, M.A., Honours in Classical Tripos, Philology, and Languages." It was perfect. He immediately gave his headmaster notice, and next holidays hurried up to Hammersmith to choose a house for his own school. The lure of his childhood, and memories of happy walks with young Robin looking for a likely house to hold his dream—in fact, the old days and the old dream—drew him to Hammersmith like the twin horns of a magnet, though he justified the choice on other grounds. And he found this tall house in the Grove. A fact that pleased him about it was that it was a few feet taller than any other house in the road.

He took it, and here he set up his play-booth, with the Rev. E. S. Cumberland, M.A., as the chief attraction on the bill, whatever his role on the boards inside. That was four years before Robin came with his bag to the door, and Erasmus Hall was now an academy of forty-one boys, six of whom were boarders.

§

But now Robin, who in the beginning had been as enthusiastic and excited and delighted about it as Justin, was seeing it with clear eyes. He was seeing it as a grey place of little promise; disappointing, depressing, disquieting. The shadow of mortality lay over it. The school would grow to a certain stature but it would never know robust health because there was too much wrong with its organs; and as the climate of the neighbourhood changed, it would probably die. For the first time he was really feeling the wrongness in this house and being offended by it. The old worn house offended him, with its large dusty rooms of a fashion that was dead and its unfitness for the part it was playing. The school furniture, scanty, cheap, and out-moded, the cold in the large rooms, the coarse food at dinnertime, the poorly paid visiting teachers whose purpose was mainly to decorate the prospectus, the fact that Mr. Cumberland was but a window-dressing figure of sawdust and straw and that Justin himself was a false pretence—not so much because he was without academic qualifications as because he was in the work solely for his own advantage—all this was disturbingly wrong when you thought of the young, growing pupils and their needs. How could a man so exploit the needs of children? Robin furrowed his brow over this, wandering alone about the house.

He felt a wrongness too, oppressive and threatening, in the relations of the three persons who dwelt in this house as a home. Two were unhappy, and the third was happy only because he was still young, engrossed in himself, and indifferent to the opinions of others. On the night of his arrival Robin went down the basement stairs to supper. The family had to eat in the boys' dining-room because Justin had taken the best room at the back for his study, and all the other rooms on the lower floors were wanted for classrooms. The boards of this large basement room were bare, and its furniture was a large sideboard and a long trestle table with benches on either side for the boys and three chairs at the top for Justin, Primrose, and Mr. Cumberland. That it was used as a classroom between meals was shown by a blackboard and maps on the walls. When Robin entered, Justin was already in his place at the head of the table, and Primrose was on his right-hand side.

Mr. Cumberland had not yet arrived from his bed-sitting-room on the second floor.

"Come on, Robs," said Justin gaily. "You'd better sit beside Primmy."

"Yes, you come and sit beside me, Robin," endorsed Primrose archly.

"But wait: do you think that'll be fair on him?" corrected Justin. "If he sits there, he'll be opposite the old Duke and see him eat. And that's not a pleasant or an appetizing sight."

"Oh, don't be silly! Isn't he dreadful, Robin? Papa isn't as bad as all that. Come and sit by me and tell me all your news."

Primrose, this tall, plump, *passée* woman of thirty-five, was too arch for her age and twice too arch for her size. The archness, like the small bird-like features, seemed absurdly out of place at the top of such height and volume. It was embarrassing to see her put her head on one side or clasp perfervid hands or frisk to her place like a schoolgirl. The whole laughing façade, as Robin could see, was brittle. Like her father, she pretended all day that she was happy and at ease, to deceive herself and any visitors to her home. And like the old man she maintained the same show of affection for Justin though it was obvious that she feared him and would one day hate him.

"The old Duke's got some teeth," explained Justin, "but he won't wear them if he can help it, because he says they hurt. When he does wear them in class, they come tumbling down like a row of guillotines in the middle of his best expositions, so he removes them behind the lid of his desk. The boys love it. I expect they're in his desk now."

"Hush, darling. You're shocking Robin. It's only his fun, Robin."

"Heavens, I know Justin by this time!" laughed Robin, hastily comforting her lest she were more hurt than she pretended. "He'll say the most atrocious things about anybody."

"Not at all, not at all, your Reverence. I merely state the objective truth about people, which no one else ever does. And the objective truth about most people, including myself, is usually shocking. Sad, but there it is."

"*Sh!*" warned Primrose. "Here he is. Here's Papa." The slippered feet were shuffling down the basement stairs. "Come along, Papa."

Primrose was only a dozen years older than Robin, but her "Papa" seemed to thrust her back into a previous generation.

" 'Evening, Duke," said Justin.

"Ah!" Mr. Cumberland spread appreciative hands. "The company is assembled, I see. And now we have our young Robin with us, the future bishop. A most distinguished company. Am I late, Justin? I trust not. But I was deep in a book of some profoundity which the Vicar was good enough to lend me. Don't wait for me, children. Continue. Continue."

He was now at his place, but before he sat down he ostentatiously folded his hands over his food-stained vest, bent his head, and said a grace.

Justin caught Robin's eye and winked. "The old fraud!" his lips whispered.

When Mr. Cumberland had finished his long, private grace and so demonstrated his clerical character, he sat down, washed one hand over the other, and looked at the plate which Justin had laid before him. "What have we here? An excellent slice of beef. Excellent. 'What say you to a piece of beef and mustard?' You would hardly think that was a line from the immortal Shakespeare, but it is. . . . Ah, well, let us not dally. Let us plunge *in medias res*." And he picked up his knife and fork.

It was a cold supper. On the soiled white cloth at the top of the long table were the cold remains of the joint which had been hot for the boys' dinner, and some tomatoes and lettuce. The meat was tough, and at times its toughness forced Mr. Cumberland to remove from his mouth such portions as his teeth could chew no more. Whenever he did this, Justin watched him out of the side of his eye, fascinated by distaste; and his nostrils turned upward, forming a deep, steady fold on either side of his mouth. Once or twice the old man perceived this expression of repugnance and was plainly vexed by it, and then Robin would feel driven by an upsurge of pity to turn to him and offer some remark that was subtly flattering.

"We only have a light supper in the evening," said Primrose, obviously ashamed of the meal. "We have our chief meal in the middle of the day with the boys."

"This is a spread for me," Robin instantly comforted her. "At the Theological College we're lucky if we have an egg and a cup of cocoa. And the egg is usually hard, and the cocoa mud."

"Cocoa, the classic drink of the student!" acclaimed the old man. "Many a great career in the Church has been built on that foundation, which you rightly describe as somewhat muddy. The late Archbishop Temple, whom I knew personally, a great man, a very great man, sprang like a towering sunflower out of a rich bed of cocoa—at least, I *think* he did—at any rate he used to go out into the passage to read his book by the light of the gas lamp there, because he was too poor to have a light of his own. He told me that once when he was talking about his days at Oxford—or Cambridge—I forget which. May I have one of those excellent tomatoes? Do you remember the tomatoes we used to grow at the Rectory, Primrose. And the lettuces? I was proud of my kitchen garden, Robin, very proud."

"I'm sure you were," said Robin promptly. "Primrose always says you had green fingers. She says your garden was the most beautiful in a parish of beautiful gardens."

"Well, I don't know about that, Robin, but——"

"But it's true, Robby," Justin assured him. "The old Duke's a first-rate gardener. He really is." And Robin discerned that Justin needed to believe and state that something at least was first-rate about this old man, his relative. "I was staggered when I saw his garden. But then you must remember that he spent all his time looking after his tomatoes instead of his parishioners. The tomatoes did fine."

"That's very unfair," began Mr. Cumberland, "very unfair——"

"It was only a very small parish," Primrose hastily explained, "and Papa had most of the day on his hands."

"Yes, he never went into his church between one Sunday and the next," laughed Justin.

"But I said my daily office regularly. I said it at home. Primrose knows that. And I do still. I say my Matins and Evensong every day. It's obligatory on all clergy. *You* know that, don't you, Robin?"

Even if it was not true that he said his office daily when he was a country rector, it was true now, since his position as a parson had been shaken. He said the priestly office every day in his little room upstairs, and never a Sunday or a Saint's day but he was kneeling at Holy Communion in the neighbouring church. No one should doubt, not even himself, that he was still a priest of the Church.

"Yes, all his life he's only had to do one day's work a week," continued Justin, his eyes twinkling, "and he's finding it an awful strain, now that he does seven."

"Not at all, Justin. I like my work with the boys."

"More than I do, the disgusting little swabs. But he's a

clever old man, Robin. Wish I had his degree. If it wasn't for him, I should say this academy was a fraud. Actually, of course, it *is* a fraud."

"Oh, oh, really, Justin!" protested Primrose; and, turning archly on Robin, and dancing coy shoulders up and down, she bade him not listen to such rubbish. "He often goes on like this, as you know. Of course he doesn't think his work is a fraud. I never heard such nonsense. Give him another tomato to keep him quiet. Whatever will Robin think of us all?"

"I should be very sorry to think there was anything fraudulent about an undertaking to which I had lent my name," said Mr. Cumberland, shaking his head as he chewed.

"No, you don't like to think so, but you know it is, both of you. Amazing that nobody will ever say aloud what they really know, isn't it, Robby? Not even after they've said their Matins and Evensong. And you're both partners in the fraud; and so's Robby now. Matins or no Matins, you're aiding and abetting me in a shocking fraud on the public."

"Really, Justin! Really!" objected Primrose with an artificial laugh.

"No, no," persisted her father. "I do my best for the boys. I give them of my best. I couldn't be a party to a fraud. I *wouldn't*, as a priest of the Church. I wouldn't." His mouth had turned angry.

"He doesn't mean it, Papa. He's just being absurd."

"I don't like to hear it said. It worries me. I give of my best."

"Oh, don't let it worry you, Duke. It's quite legal, what we're doing. The cops can't touch us, but it's pretty criminal all the same, eh, Robby? The Reverend Robin doesn't approve of it, I know, but then he's a good lad. He's a Holy Man. He was talking to me about it this evening like a father. Still, it's probably no more fraudulent than anything else that cashes in on the weaknesses of mankind. As long as parents are snobs and cowards someone'll come along and relieve them of their money; and I don't see why I should let anyone else get ahead of me in the game. I quickly saw that parents in a third-class neighbourhood like this don't mind where they send their children to school, so long as it's not a board school. That's why I came here and set up my little stall. Do they ever inquire what sort of goods I sell, or examine my scales? Never. The only thing they care about is that the goods aren't state-provided and free. They'll sacrifice their children any day to save what's left of their gentility."

"I do my best for the boys," repeated Mr. Cumberland, looking down upon his plate. His knife and fork were trembling, and Robin saw, to his discomfort, that he had worked up his resentment till he was on the brink of tears. "I think the boys are fortunate to have a scholar of my attainments to teach them. I do, really."

"He's only teasing you, Papa."

"I took an Honours degree. A very good degree indeed."

"Yes, Papa . . . yes. . . ."

"And I might have made a great deal of my life if I hadn't chosen of my own free will the poverty and obscurity of a humble parish priest. I never expected to end up teaching *Mensa, mensa, mensam* to little boys. I have been accustomed to preparing young men for university scholarships, as Primrose knows. When my dear wife was alive, we used to supplement our narrow income by——"

"Yes, yes, Papa. Justin knows that; and Robin too."

"I know it, and it's my only comfort, Mr. Cumberland," laughed Robin, trying to console him. "I know that I know nothing on earth about teaching and that I'm coming to you for advice and instruction. I've been telling myself that if I come up against any difficulties I shall bring them to you." Inwardly he was thinking with pleasure that, however Justin might tease the old man, however impatient he might get with him, he never alluded to his crime and disgrace.

"Some of my pupils did very well, Robin. Very well indeed."

"I know. And that's why I've been hoping you'll give me a little help when I do some reading for *my* exam next year."

"I'll do all I can to help you. All I can. It'll give me great happiness."

"Thank you, Mr. Cumberland. This is a great piece of luck for me."

"For God's sake don't call him Mr. Cumberland, Robs. Call him Duke. Everyone calls him Duke. Even the boys do."

But Robin, of keener insight than the others, suspected that the nickname, "Duke", short for "Duke of Cumberland", was not without its wound for a fallen and necessitous old clergyman; and for that reason he always spoke to him with respect and called him Mr. Cumberland. He smiled back at Justin and said nothing.

"And I can't think—I can't think that these poor little boys suffer through having me for their teacher," maintained the old man, drawing from his tail pocket a handkerchief so soiled and old as to be yellow, and brushing with it a tear from his right eye. "I'm not as young as I used to be, I know, but my intelligence is as good as ever it was, and I give them of my best."

"Yes, yes, Papa. We all know you do."

Justin bowed satirically to Robin and pushed away his plate. "And that's that," said he, referring in part to the end of the first course and in part to the end of a family scene.

After the beef there was bread and cheese, but no one seemed to want any except Justin. Mr. Cumberland dived again into the tail pocket of his frock coat and brought forth an old blackened pipe and an old rubber pouch. He opened the pouch on the table and began to fill the pipe. Justin watched him as one watches a child for a misbehaviour. He contained his irritability for a minute and then rebuked him.

"I haven't finished yet, Duke. Don't light up yet, *please*."

"Oh, I'm sorry," answered the old man nervously. "I beg your pardon, all. I'm forgetful sometimes." And, removing pouch and pipe from the table, he sat with them on his knees and stared sadly at his plate.

"That old pipe of his smells rather worse than an incinerator," explained Justin with a laugh, for to a certain extent he was fighting his rudeness. And he continued to eat.

Primrose sat as silent as her father. All pretences, it seemed, were now intermitted from weariness. Robin was silent too.

Justin finished his cheese and rolled up his table napkin. "Well, come on, Robby. You and I'll have a chat. I shall enjoy that. Primmy, what are you going to do?"

"I have all the boys' mending to do," said Primrose rather sulkily. And, gathering up some plates, she passed out with them to the kitchen.

Justin made a humorous grimace and a mock bow as he watched her sullen departure into the kitchen. "Right. Good. Exit Mrs. le Faber, full of love for her husband. And you, Duke? What's your idea——"

But the old man had already slipped away with his pipe and pouch. He was shuffling up the basement stairs to his bed-sitting-room aloft, where he could be happy.

"Ah, thank God!" exclaimed Justin. "We've seen the last of him for another day. He offends me."

§

The study was a large back room on the ground floor

Justin had laboured with love upon many parts of the house, because it was the framework for his dream, but most of all upon his study. He had made his own bookshelves and stained them a dark oak. With his own pots and brushes he had distempered the walls a pale apple green and painted the woodwork a brilliant cream. While stinting money for the classroom furniture, much of which he had built himself for cheapness sake, he had spared nothing that would make his study beautiful. A carpet of a plain gold pile reached to the skirting; two long, deep easy chairs reclined on this carpet in plum-coloured loose-covers; and curtains of the same colour hung down from the window in graceful folds. The room proclaimed Justin's hunger for beauty. In the faded house it was like a jewel in a tarnished setting.

"Now then, Robby, lower yourself into that chair there: you'll find it sweeter than the embrace of any woman. In plainer language, sit down, old cock. I'm in lamentable odour with the wife just now, I'm afraid. That was a damnably unamiable exit of hers, wasn't it? Still, that sort of thing often happens with husbands of good quality. Sit you down." He himself set Robin the example. He lit a pipe and lay back in his long, deep chair. "Well, I haven't done so badly, do you think, Robby? Forty-one pupils in four years. Of course we're not making much money yet. We shan't do that till we get some more boarders. It's only out of boarders that you can squeeze a large profit. But they'll come all right. Meantime, money or no money——" he extended his long legs on to a footstool—"there's not a single person in the world who can tell me what I'm to do, and what I'm not to do. And to me that's better than a fortune."

Robin drew at his pipe and said nothing. He was contrasting the reality of this school with its creator's glittering fantasy about it. And this from Justin who prided himself on seeing the objective truth of things! Were all artists inhibited from seeing their work with naked eyes?

"I guess it was a stroke of genius, coming to Hammersmith, Rob. Directly they started the Twopenny Tube at Shepherds Bush and electrified the old District, I knew that Hammersmith was the place. I knew that Hammersmith and Shepherds Bush would simply pack up with cheap little parents who'd want a school like mine. So where did I put it? Here in the old Grove, exactly between Hammersmith and Shepherds Bush. And up bundled the parents. I had twenty pupils before the first year was out. It was the name, Erasmus Hall, that did it; I count 'Erasmus Hall' one of my best inspirations. Sounds like some damned place at Oxford. 'Where's your boy at school, old man?' 'At Erasmus Hall, old chap.' 'Oh, *is* he? Is he indeed?' And the inquiring party says no more, because he isn't sure where Erasmus Hall is and supposes he ought to know. One day I'm going to look up and see who Erasmus was."

"Well, I can tell you all about *him*," laughed Robin. "We meet him often enough in Church History. He was one of the greatest scholars of the Renaissance. For a time he was Professor of Divinity at Cambridge——"

"Well, there you are! I told you the name was a stroke of genius. Professor of Divinity! That's excellent. We go in for Divinity here, and I'm the professor. But I'll tell you what my scheme is. As soon as possible I'm taking the house next door. It comes vacant soon. Then I shall throw the back gardens into one and build there a large room for gym. and school hall. I've got all the plans for it in that desk: I drew 'em myself. Then I'm taking a third house, rather smaller, as the Headmaster's Residence. 'Residence', mark you, not 'house'. And into that dignified residence I shall retire, leaving my salaried masters to do the work and earn the money. I shall pop in now and again and see that they're hard at it. I reckon that in ten years I shall be living at my ease, and in twenty—when I'm still only forty-seven—I shall be living in my little clearing among the forest trees, with a mountain or two near by. Somewhere near Deep Langstrath, perhaps; and that's the last that London or any other town'll see of me."

"But, Justin, tell me one thing. If you heart isn't really in the teaching, how will you ever make a success of it?"

"But my heart *is* in it, old chap. Not for the boys' sake, but for my own. I don't care a hoot about the nit-wits but I look upon the really bright kids as so many racehorses I'm entering for the Derby. It's quite fascinating training them up for their Matric. It's like coaching an eight for a boat race. And after I've got several of them through the Matric. I'm going to sit for the damned exam myself. Haven't had time so far. Too many jobs to do about the house. But I'm going to take the Matric. on the quiet one day, and then a year or so later my Inter. and then my B.A. After that I shan't want the old Duke, and I sincerely hope he'll die. I should think he will, don't you? I mean, he's nearly dead now."

Robin grinned, as he always did when Justin was flashing preposterous remarks at him. "How does the poor old boy feel now about—about his disgrace? Is he getting over it?"

"He'll never get over it. They broke him then, poor old devil. It was awful, Robby; it really was. I'm not the softest person in the world, as you know, but even I felt some pity when I saw him in the dock with his face as grey as his hair and his hands twitching. And as for poor old Primmy, she was just snivelling her heart out at my side. The old judge did an extraordinary thing, you know. When the Inspector chappie had said that Primrose and I would give him a home and look after him, the judge went broody for a bit and then told them to bring the girl back into the box——"

"What girl?"

"Why, *the* girl. The girl he'd written to, suggesting that she should become his mistress. She went into the box, all beautifully dressed for the occasion, and stood there and looked at the old Duke, who never once lifted his head. And the judge, after considering him, turned to the girl and said, 'I want to ask you one question.' She lifted her rather beautiful eyes to him and said, 'Yes, my lord?' And he asked her very quietly, 'Tell me. Do you want him punished any more?'"

"Splendid, splendid!" cried Robin, feeling his heart expand at a tale of mercy.

"Yes, but wait. Wait for the end. The girl didn't answer at once. She looked down at her fingers, and then raised her head with a splendidly haughty gesture and said, 'Yes.'"

"Oh." Robin's heart sank again.

"A thrill went right through the court. It was a fine answer, I thought."

"Was it?"

"Don't you think so?"

"No. . . . No, I don't."

"A woman defending her honour, old boy? The old judge was obviously impressed."

"He would be." Robin felt an irrational anger surging up in him. His temples heated; his heart accelerated. The surge forced him to get up and pace about the room. "A judge would be. But I'm afraid I don't admire a cheap vindictiveness. On the contrary, I cease to be rational at the sight of it and become vindictive myself."

"Well, I still think it was rather fine."

"I don't.   I think it was easy, crude, commonplace and immature."

"Good lord!" Justin lifted amused eyebrows at this outburst.

"I can see in it neither understanding nor imagination nor mercy.   A facile vindictiveness is always a sign that you haven't begun to grow up."

"All right, don't get so hot about it.   Sit down again."

Robin sat down again, slowly.   "Her really great answer was the opposite."

"And what was that?"

"You wouldn't appreciate it, but it would have been the right answer, all the same."

"Well, what is it?"

"No, no.   Leave it.   Let it be."

"Not a bit.   I insist on knowing now."

"All right.   She should have said, 'My lord, forgive him, for he knew not what he was doing.'   That would have thrilled the court ten times more, because we all recognize the truth when we see it.   We shiver before it."

Justin pulled at his pipe and smiled.   "Well, I'm afraid that's not what happened.   Not at all.   The judge turned on the old Duke and used his tongue on him like a whip."

"He would.   They always do.   They always pour their salt into the wounds.   Pompous, censorious, hypocritical old fool! I wonder how many women *he'd* had in his life."

"All right, calm down, calm down.   He wasn't as bad as you think. After he'd told him off, he left it at that and bound him over."

"Good."

"But the matter didn't end there.   There was the Bishop to be considered.   The Bishop deprived him of his benefice and put him under discipline for a period of two years, with the promise that if he received a satisfactory report of him after that time, he'd be allowed to minister again.   He got his satisfactory report all right—dammit, I wrote part of it myself—and now he's allowed to officiate in this diocese.   He helps on Sundays now at our church, St. Anselm's."

"I'm glad."

"So'm I.   It suits us all fine.   It's quite a good advertisement for the school, because he doesn't look so bad in his surplice and by artificial light.   I saw its advertisement value at once.   There's him up among the parsons, and there's me, down among the people, with my boys, singing the *Te Deum* and the *Benedicite* louder than anyone else. The Vicar thinks the world of me, you'll be glad to know, and wants me to go on the Church Council. I think I shall. I early saw that religion was the line for us. You parsons still have a good deal of power, you know. The women trust you, God knows why; they go round and ask you to name a good school; and I see to it that the parsons round here name mine. Sometimes they let the old thing preach at Evensong, and then we know all about it. We see nothing of him all Saturday afternoon and evening. He's shut up with his sermon, and you can hear him creaking up and down as he rehearses it. I went to hear him once; and it wasn't so bad, really. In fact, I was rather proud of him. Not that there was any passion for souls in it; his one passion was to show that he was a scholar. He used words twice as long as the Grove, Hammersmith, but it impresses silly people, that sort of thing. The school's stock went up a point or two, I felt.

"He has other uses too, of course. I let him read our School Prayers each morning: it'd break his heart if I didn't. But *I* read the lessons, Robin, and that's the first time the boys really sit up. The Bible's magnificent in places. Then sometimes he teaches me my Latin and French at night so that I can teach it to the boys next morning. But there's one thing I don't let him do. I don't let him interview the parents. Oh, no, because he won't bear a close inspection. I do that job myself. I tell the mammas that the whole aim of the school is to turn the boys into little Christian gentlemen, and the papas that our one purpose is to give them a sound commercial education. The two things are incompatible, but it's not my job to expound that. What do you think of my Primmy?"

"Who?" The question was so abrupt that Robin, who had been half enveloped in a dream, hardly took it in.

"My Primrose by the river's brim."

"Oh. . . ." Still disordered by the abrupt question, and not quite freed from his haze of thought, Robin could only falter, "I like her. I like her very much."

"Do you? Do you, really?" Both hands holding his pipe at his teeth, Justin smiled. "Good lord!"

"Of course I do. I have always liked her."

"Well, now! Marvellous!"

"Why?"

"Well, have you no nerves?"

"Plenty. Far too many."

"You're not all sweetness and light?"

"Heavens, no! Bitter as wormwood sometimes."

"Well, do you mean to say you can stand that awful skittishness? And that ghastly shrill laughter which is simply a kind of advertisement-hoarding with nothing behind it? It goes through me like a two-handed saw. Directly anything appears in trousers, even if it's only you, she goes all coy like that. She goes coy with her head, her shoulders, her hips, her hands— ever seen her flap her hands in kittenish disapproval? I turn my eyes away when she does it, and suffer. She forgets she's five foot eleven, and thirty-five. Still, like the old Duke, she has her uses. Confound it, the school was built on her money, her furniture, and, come to that, her old dad. She has *some* advantages, which is more than can be said for the woman Gerard's landed himself with. Have you seen Gerard lately? He's done for himself, I reckon. A fool, if ever there was one—the wildest ass imaginable. Never knows if he'll have any money next week, and doesn't hesitate to marry a girl who hasn't a penny of her own and is as feckless as he. I never believed much in this acting business of Gerard's, but if he ever really had any chances, I should think they've gone down the drain, now that he's landed himself with Anne. But would he really ever have done anything? It's nine years since he started on the game, and he's done nothing yet. If he'd been going to do anything he'd have got his foot on the ladder before he was twenty-six. Same with Anne."

"What are they doing now?" asked Robin, keeping to himself his thoughts of Gerard and Anne.

"Nothing," answered Justin crisply; and it was plain he was pleased with the answer. " 'Resting.' "

"What are they living on?"

"God knows. I wouldn't live as they do for something. They've got a room in Elsie Road, West Kensington, and probably owe the rent for that. You should see it. You should see the squalour." Unwittingly Justin looked around at his own large and tastefully furnished study; and Robin, watching him, knew that he was secretly pleased that Gerard, his next brother, was so much less successful than he. Besides, he had always prophesied failure for the ambitious Gerard, and it was good to be justified.

CHAPTER TWO

GERARD had been no more than seventeen when, passionately rejecting the appeals of his mother, the scoffs of Justin, and the wiseacre doubts of Hector, he set off one day from Pemberthy Road, went to the addresses of all the theatrical agents in London, climbed their dingy stairs, and entered his name in their books. Nothing came fluttering towards him from all these pigeon-cotes except one small offer: that of a super's part, at a shilling a night, at the old Crown Theatre, Kennington. He pounced upon it. Like Justin with his school he saw it, not as it was, but as a doorway aglow from the triumphs in the chambers beyond. To his mother, appalled at the wage, he pointed out that if he'd sought a clerkship in some business house, as she had recommended, he wouldn't have been offered more than ten shillings a week. "Yes, but that would have *led* to something," she bewailed. "It would have led to a permanent position at a salary of eight or ten pounds a week." At which Gerard laughed. "And this is going to lead to something a lot better than that," he said. "In a few years I may be earning fifty pounds a week."

"Don't be daft," was Justin's comment; and Hector counselled him heavily not to set his hopes too high. "I doubt if it'll lead to anything much," said Hector. "I do, really. If it should come to anything, nobody will be more pleased than me."

The few years swept by and fell behind, and it certainly hadn't led to much. At eighteen he was earning a pound a week in walking-on engagements, or playing tiny parts as a footman, butler, or waiter. At nineteen his earnings had improved by fifty per cent, but fifty per cent added to a pound is still only thirty shillings. He had come now into the full possession of the fine le Faber presence, and this was enough to secure him more conspicuous parts, played a little further down stage. He must still be pronounced much less handsome than Justin: the long upper lip, so often a feature of those who dream of the mimetic art, had denied him Justin's good nose; the space it needed on his face it had robbed from his nose, which as a consequence was brief and truncated. Nor had he Justin's massy black hair and dark eyes. But he was the same height as Robin, six foot two, and gracefully built; he moved well; his eyes were full of laughter; his manners were perfect (except with his brothers); and his voice, since a deep desire to be an actor will sometimes invest a voice with a new quality, was the best in the family.

No doubt because of his appearance and manners he was given the job of Assistant Stage Manager in a touring company, with the chance of playing some quite important juveniles; and it was this that lifted his salary to thirty shillings a week. On this he was able to keep himself, which was more, as he emphasized to his mother, than Hector was doing as a bank clerk or Bozzy as nothing at all. He would pay seven and six for his lodging, and by limiting himself to one and six a day for food he managed to keep enough flesh on his frame and to clothe it with the quiet elegance that he loved. Like Justin he was not content unless he walked among men in graceful, well-cut, well-groomed clothes.

After four years there was a temporary brightening in this rather dim and unpromising sky. Now, suddenly, he got an engagement at the Court Theatre as the understudy of two juvenile leads; the salary was two pound ten shillings a week; the play ran well; and the night came when one of his principals was absent and he played for him; and all, including the management, agreed that his acting was at least as good as his principal's and his appearance much better. The management increased his salary from two pound ten shillings to three pound ten shillings. This was money at last, and he immediately married Anne Cheshire, a slip of a girl in the company, with whom he had been sunk in mutual love for five weeks. Anne called herself Anne Raven on the stage because her hair, as she maintained, was blacker than a raven's wing. She was as sprightly and irresponsible as a flame; and the tip of the flame was a leaping light in her eyes. Like Gerard she was twenty-one and a few months more, and together in their best clothes, each with a white flower at the breast, they ran off to the Register Office and were married, their only witnesses being two excited ladies and a capable youth from the company. No one from either's family had a hand in this rash business. The marriage achieved, they went off to a bed-sitting-room in Westminster, full of happiness, hope, schemes, and hilarity. Anne was earning her thirty shillings a week, Gerard had his three pound ten shillings, and what could not a young couple do with five pounds a week? Five pounds a week was two hundred and fifty pounds a year,

True, but the five pounds did not stay with them in that room. The show at the Court, after playing to good business for several months, suddenly sickened because of the warm weather in the streets and at length, there being no abatement of the summer heat, wasted away and died. And Gerard le Faber and Anne Raven were left mourning this good and indulgent parent. They were out of work again, and nearly out of money.

But not out of hope. Gerard had now played juvenile leads in a West End theatre, and not without some recognition; and he supposed that his name would make an impression on agents and managers. He addressed a circular letter to several managements, informing them that he was now free; he obliged the agents with the same information; and he inserted his "card" on the front page of the *Stage*: "Gerard le Faber. At Liberty." No one was impressed. Few even acknowledged his letters. No one answered his advertisement. And Gerard was compelled to wait at stage doors again, soliciting interviews with managers; to pore over and reply to "Wanted" advertisements in the theatrical journals; to climb the dingy stairs again to the agents' offices and sit in the drab waiting-rooms, looking up at the portraits of actors and actresses who had succeeded, and around him, on the chairs, at the figures of those who had failed. So old, some of them, and so withered! What purpose did the paint on the ageing ladies serve but to stress their age and their failure? And the old gentlemen, whose neckties and suits were as flashy as they were shabby—of what did they remind him? Of what were they making him think? Why, of those old supers under the stage of the Charing Cross Theatre whom he had seen with Mr. Morgari years and years ago.

But Gerard was no more defeated by the sight of them now than he was then. Always he came down the stairs with the words, "Nothing to-day, old fellow," echoing in his ears, but with the knowledge thumping in his heart that one day he would show them all; one day they would sue for *his* custom; one day they would have his picture in their waiting rooms as a proud advertisement.

At last, though no one in their families was ever told the real truth of this matter, Gerard le Faber and Anne Raven, those two West End actors, were reduced to going on a cheap provincial tour again at thirty shillings and one pound a week between them. Once, and none but they two knew of this till years afterwards, Gerard, having changed his name for the base purpose, walked on as a super again.

And so it went on. And now both were twenty-six, and the most they had earned in their five years together was six pound ten shillings a week, and that had been a cause for a jubilee. Generally their earnings were much smaller, and always they had to put something by for the long times when they were "resting".

§

The evening after his arrival at Erasmus Hall, Robin, hardly waiting to eat any supper, hurried off to see Gerard and Anne. There were several reasons why he should long to see them, and one of these was his love of praise. He would go seeking praise in a way that disturbed his conscience in his graver moments; and Anne was one who lavished it over him. She would tell him to his face that she adored him and would announce his virtues at the top of her voice to anyone who was around. Another reason was the knowledge that Anne would be an engrossed, enthusiastic, excited, dancing listener when he unfolded to them his great secret—the secret that had enclosed him in its glamorous haze as he stood in the compartment of the Underground train, and that would recapture and entrance him now, whensoever people turned aside from him and left him to wander alone. This secret was like an engine in his breast, driving him towards Gerard and Anne—especially Anne.

As Justin had said, Gerard and Anne were living in a large bed-sitting-room in Elsie Road, West Kensington. Elsie Road lay but a minute's walk from Brook Green, and the deep-rose walls and towers of St. Paul's School closed its long vista at the western end; for Gerard, after the le Faber fashion, had harked back, in an hour of ill-success and scarcity, to the places he had known as a child.

Robin knocked at the door of their room and, feeling in the highest spirits, called, "Anyone at home? Anyone at home? Come along. Don't keep me waiting."

And Anne opened to him. "Robin!" she cried. "My Robin!"

She appeared to be free of all encumbering clothes such as frock, petticoat bodice, petticoats and stays, and to be clad only in stockings, drawers and chemise, which private garments were wrapped round by a bath robe of scarlet silk. In contrast with this *négligée* her black hair was in flawless order on the top of her head.

"Oh, *Robin!*" It was an intense, almost tragic utterance in her deep stage voice, as if he had been unexpectedly recovered from the dead and the relief were too much to bear. And immediately she rose as high as she could on her toes, flung her arms around him, and kissed and hugged him; and his heart rushed out to her in gratitude.

"Hallo, Anne," he said quite inadequately, during a pause in her kisses.

"Gerard, my loveliest! Here's Robin. Here's the one redeeming feature of your family. Come in, my precious one."

Gerard was sitting on an old Chesterfield sofa in a dressing-gown of blue silk with gold lapels. Justin had said that they lived in squalour, but this was a harsh and unjust word. In disorder, yes, and even in gross disorder: Anne's powder, whose scent had rushed to the door and embraced Robin even before she could, lay scattered on dressing-table and carpet; her skirts and petticoats hung on the door; other costumes and underclothes drooped over the backs of chairs; her hair-pins and hair combings lay in a tarnished silver tray very near to the remains of a supper; and a large-brimmed hat, trimmed with a feather ruche, was stabbed by its hat-pins, like a giant butterfly, to the arm of the sofa opposite Gerard. The room was in disorder, but not Anne nor Gerard; they were merely in deshabille. Anne, twenty-six years old, an actress, and still hopeful of success, could not have let herself become a slattern. Nor Gerard. And to-night both were radiantly robed in the heart of the chaos.

"Hallo, Robin, old thing," greeted Gerard. "This is fine. You're just in time."

Anne stood gazing at the visitor, her eyes lit with pleasure. "Gosh, Gerard, isn't he adorable? How on earth the parents who produced Justin and Hector also produced—however, we've gone into that before."

"Yes, we have. And let's forget it now."

"There's only one of your brothers who's even tolerable, and that's this one who's just walked in. I wish I'd seen him before I saw you. I'd have married him."

"Always supposing he'd have let you. He's got more character than I have."

"Nonsense. Of course he'd have let me. It's plain that any

woman who wanted him enough could have him. He'd be too considerate to refuse. Now put him there beside you—oh, damn that hat!—and fancy him turning up at this moment of all moments. Isn't that nice of him? I'd rather he'd turned up to-night than anyone else in the world."

"Why, what's up?" demanded Robin, now seated beside his brother, and Anne stood before him. "Something special?"

"It's proof that God's behind it all. I said so. It's proof that the whole thing is the work of Providence and bound to be a success. Who shall fight God?"

"But whatever is it, Anne? What's the matter? What's up?"

"What's up? *We* are. Up at last. Look!" She pointed to two champagne bottles and two champagne glasses on the table opposite the sofa. "What do you think that means?"

"He must have smelt the phiz," suggested Gerard.

"You don't mind my being like this, do you, darling? I was determined to be comfy and enjoy myself. Pity there's not another champagne glass."

"I didn't know you had champagne glasses."

"We haven't," explained Gerard. "I borrowed these from the pub, where I'm sorry to say we're quite well known. Freddie, the landlord, and Kitty, his lady, are two of our dearest, aren't they, sweetheart? I told 'em we'd had a spot of good news, stood 'em the top of their fancy, did the same for all the boys in the bar, and came out with the glasses. Wish I'd brought three. Never mind, wash out a tumbler for him."

"But please—*will* you tell me what it's all about?"

Anne looked at Gerard. "Who tells?"

"You, lovely. You'll dress it up properly. It needs a woman's touch."

"No, darling heart. It's your success. You're the little hero."

"Come on, children!" urged Robin. "What is it?"

"It's sixteen pounds a week. Put crudely, that's what it is."

"But how splendid! Go on."

"Yes, sixteen perfectly good pounds," Gerard took up the tale. "And, as far as I can see, a long engagement that may lead to anything. After years of waiting and, I confess, some-what indifferent success, the gates are wide open. So far from my importuning the managements, a management has come to me."

"On bended knee," added Anne.

"Well, that's as it should be," laughed Robin, "but for mercy's sake tell me more. I'm thrilled."

"Now isn't that nice of him?" said Anne. "Isn't that just what he would be: thrilled?"

"You've heard of Wardon Asche?" continued Gerard.

"Don't be silly. Who hasn't? Didn't I see you act with him at the Court?"

"Well, he's gone into management with Frank London at the New Comedy, and in his new play, which he's up in the air about, there's a part which he says only I can fill. He was good enough to send for me urgently and tell me that while plenty of people could act it, no one would *look* the part so perfectly as I would. He says I'm the best piece of casting he's ever done."

"I expect there's another point," reminded Anne. "Wardon's on the tall side himself and, unless he has tall actors around him, he doesn't look so good."

"And what's the part like?" asked Robin. "It it a decent part?"

"*Decent?* It's the fattest part in the play after Wardon's. That's why he couldn't offer me less than ten quid a week. I chanced all and said I couldn't take it unless there was a part in it for my dear wife; and he said there was quite a good part in it for her, and offered her six quid a week. At which point I closed with him before he changed his mind."

"And if you're any good at arithmetic," said Anne, "you'll find that that makes sixteen pounds a week, and that sixteen pounds a week in eight hundred and thirty-two pounds a year. We've just been working it out."

"That's right," assured Gerard; "and look here, old boy, I don't want to hurry you over your drink—we're delighted to have you, and all that—but could you as soon as possible go back and tell His Imperial Highness all about it? My first thought, on getting this offer, was, My God, how can I get this news to Justin? And now here you are and can take it back to him. As Anne said, lt's clearly Providence. The *Bon Dieu* is at work."

"Oh, yes!" Anne danced up and down. "And pile it on to him. Don't forget. Sixteen pounds a week. Eight hundred and thirty-two pounds a year. It'll be years and years before he's making a clear eight hundred pounds out of that ridiculous school. And it's a permanent job, almost certainly. Wardon's idea is that Gerard and I should act with him permanently. So you can safely tell that black-haired devil that it's permanent."

"Devil!" Robin sat smiling at her. "Poor old Justin. He isn't a devil."

"Oh, yes he is. The very thought of him stirs up everything that's wicked and vicious in me. He must be a devil because he raises a devil in me. I hate him. I hate him with a kind of nasty, grim, dark-green hate. It's dark green, I know it is. It feels like it. I want to get my hands intó him." She made claws out of her hands, and her eyes danced. She ground her teeth. "Oh, I shall do him a mischief one day. And don't forget to point out that the New Comedy is not only a West End theatre but a theatre with a famous tradition, and that both Gerard's part and mine are leads. Oh, hurry back and— no, stay a whole lot longer, darling Robin, and have heaps of champagne, but go back in time to tell him all this and spoil his night's rest for him. Just to please *me*. I've made it one of the set purposes of my life to down him—to humble him—to knock him silly with the knowledge that Gerard's ten times the better man than he is, and so am I."

"But why, my darling Anne? Why this slight acerbity?"

"Because he said Gerard would never do anything. Because he scoffed at him for marrying me and said I'd be the ruin of him. Because he's glad we haven't had much success so far. Because he *wants* Gerard to fail. Because he despises everybody but himself and is brutal in his own way to Primrose. And because he's much too good-looking. It's *awful* to be as good-looking as that. It's diabolical. Men should be nice and graceful and ugly like my Gerard."

"Good God in Heaven!" protested Gerard.

"Besides," Anne concluded, "I never trust any man whose black hair is curly and silky and parted in the middle." With that she sank upon a chair before the champagne. But she had hardly sat down before she sprang up again, a glass in her hand, and sailed across the room to the washstand. Robin watched her: he was always captivated by the beauty of her movements, which were the movements of an actress who had played through the hard years a hundred "feminine" and "bewitching" roles. Passing from table to washstand, she did not cross a room, she crossed a stage. She did not actually dance, but it was as pleasing as a dance; it was a willowy, sweeping glide; it sang—the metaphor was not too strong— it sang with the easy sweep of a violin. See Anne walking in the Hammersmith Road, and all other women, even the youngest, seemed to waddle. She was a swan afloat, and they

were geese ashore. From the washstand, having washed the
glass, she flowed to a cupboard in the same unconscious dance,
fetched down a tumbler, and swam back to her chair and slid
on to it. And every movement sang.

She filled up the glasses. She raised hers. "I drink to the
devil," she said. "The devil in the Grove. And I tell you why.
Because he's the most valuable driving motive we've got,
isn't he, Gerard darling? If Gerard and I feel lazy or des-
pondent, we think, 'There's Justin to be downed.' It gets
me up in the morning. I think, 'Will I be beaten? No. Will
I down him? Yes.' And up I leap and start the day's work.
He's changed my character entirely. I used to be rather giddy
and harum-scarum; now I'm a grimly determined character. I
used to be rather selfish; now I'm the completely unselfish
wife. I care as much and more now that Gerard should do well
as that Anne should. I do, honestly." Her eyebrows arched in
surprise at her own goodness. "And it's all that man's doing.
He's just *making* me, and I'm going to make Gerard."

"Hardly sounds like the work of a devil," laughed Robin.

"The devils work good despite themselves, don't they?
Isn't that the Scripture? You ought to know. You're a little
parson. Tell me, Robin, he *has* said to you, at least once
since you came back, 'Look at that woman Gerard's married.'
He has, hasn't he?"

"No!" asserted Robin promptly; and knew that he would
have to argue with his conscience to-night about this round
and unhesitating lie.

"I don't believe you. I know he says it to everybody. I
know it by the way he looks at me. Oh, oh, oh!" She beat
her fists upon the table. "Give me my chance."

"Well, you've got it now." Robin lifted his glass. "To the
new play."

"Bless you, you singularly pleasant person."

"The new play, Gerard."

"Thanks, old toffee." Gerard sipped too. "What do you
think of this bubbly? Is it any good? *I* don't know. I dashed
into the wine merchant's and said, 'Two bottles of champagne,
please,' and he asked, 'What kind?' and I said, 'Good lord, I
don't know. D'you think I've been drinking champagne all
my life? Give me the dearest.' And before I was through with
him I'd stood him a bottle of his own port. On tick. Have
some more?"

"It suits me all right," said Robin; and as he sipped he was thinking of the difference which two opposed environments had worked upon two brothers. Justin had no environment but his own thoughts; he was walled up in them and had become solitary, self-centred, close, his own prisoner. Gerard, moving among a crowd of actors who, however unstable their virtue at times, were always warm-hearted and open-handed, had become gregarious, generous, demonstrative. As he sat there, he was comparing Gerard and Anne with Justin and Primrose. "To Gerard le Faber and Anne Raven," he said, raising the refilled glass. "And may they bring the house down!"

"They're going to," announced Gerard. "They've made up their minds about that, the pretty dears. This is a fat part with immense scope, and I'm going to put everything I've got into it. And, as Anne said, nine tenths of my driving charge will be the desire to knock Justin flat. And I'm going to produce Anne in her part till she's one hundred per cent perfect, aren't I, ducky?"

"Oh, my part's nothing. I'm only a poor little soul. And I don't care. It's Gerard's part we're going to knock him out with."

"You know, she's quite right: our Justin's a godsend," continued Gerard. "It's because he's so awful that she loves me after a fashion. And it's because she dislikes him so intensely that she thinks you divine. That's the only reason."

"That's rubbish. I should have adored Robin in any case. He knows I should." And she got up and put her arms around him and laid her cheek against his, and then held him so that her face, looking into his, was not four inches away from it. And as every movement of her body and limbs when she ran across a room composed themselves into a dance, so now she was unconsciously dancing with her mouth, eyebrows, and eyes. She pecked at him with a kiss. "Oh, Robin, darling heart, you *are* so dear," she said, and traced her finger along the dark eyebrows that met above his nose.

Her actions, answering so fully his deep hunger for love and praise, shot the tears up into his throat. And he put an arm round her and squeezed her to him. And as she tripped back to her seat, he hid his emotion behind the words, "When is this damned play anyway?"

"Three weeks to-morrow," said Gerard. "Three weeks and things will begin to happen."

"And Robin will pray all the time, won't you? He's a little parson, even if he does say damn, and he'll pray for us every

night and morning, and at mid-day when he can manage it.
Won't you, dovey?"

"You bet."

So happy were they with their great news and their great
hope, and so eager for him to return and tell Justin, that he
decided this was not the time to unpack before them *his* great
secret. He came away with it still untold.

§

Being twenty-three and full of life and zest, Robin quickly
forgot the shock which Justin's tall grey house had given him,
and was happy within its walls. After the first day he was
troubled by the musty smell no more; nor were his eyes
aggrieved by discoloration or cracks. Justin's high spirits,
always at their highest when Robin was with him, were there
to counteract any depressing influences that might issue from
the bare, dusty, and inappropriate walls. It was difficult in
the atmosphere of Justin's optimism to recapture that fore-
boding of failure. Justin was forever improving the place and
he was always happy and hopeful when he had his hammer or
his paint brush in his hand. When Robin hinted that the front
of the house was a little cheerless, Justin, who had not seen it
as such, exclaimed, "Good lord, Reverend, is it really so?
That won't do;" and the next night at sundown he slipped out,
carrying his paint brush like a weapon. He crept out with a
great show of stealthiness, in disguise and on tip-toe, since it
ill became a headmaster to be seen painting his front door.
In an old waterproof, an old boater hat, and with his back to
the world, he painted his door and his area railings a lustrous
green since these were his shop-windows on the street. Robin
felt an uprush of love for him when he saw him fighting so
heartily the greyness and unsuitability of his house. And
Primrose, called to admire the work (for Justin often used her
as an audience) could almost feel a love for him too.

Then there was the affection that had flowered so richly
between Robin and Mr. Cumberland. Robin's pity, rushing
out like a tide to the timid and insecure old man, made him
minister, whenever possible, to Mr. Cumberland's desire to be
recognized as a priest, a scholar, and one of the principals of
the school. It carried him up the stairs to the old man's room
with requests for advice, approval, or consent. It carried him
to church on Sunday evenings when the old man was preach-

ing, and to the vestry door afterwards to flatter him about the sermon. It sent him up the stairs on week-day evenings, if he divined that the old man was lonely in his bed-sitting-room, that he might discuss theology and the politics of the Church with him. And then Justin would say, "There are those two parsons together again, like a couple of old rooks on a tree-top."

And soon the old man, feeling Robin's affection, and eager to love someone, gave the best of his love to him and prophesied great things for him as a priest; and now Robin had a new motive for going up to sit with Mr. Cumberland: the same motive that had sent him hurrying to Anne's door—the desire to bask in an atmosphere of praise, admiration, and love.

In his feeling for Justin there was conflict; there was even a polar opposition. The old affection, built of a thousand memories, and the newer affection, born of pity and understanding, had to do battle with a vehement, almost a frantic, exasperation at times—a plain, teeth-setting hate. The very jocosity of the tones in which Justin called him "Rev." an "Bishop" and "Bish", like that which accompanied his salutation of Mr. Cumberland as "Duke" and "Your Grace", spoke of a patronizing superiority that didn't really believe Robin would ever be more than an ill-paid parson, and was glad to think so. No chance, thought Justin, of this young brother competing with him in success. And when Robin perceived this thought in Justin, he would be hardly less furious with him than Anne at her hottest, and a desire would seize him to achieve a great name in the Church and "learn" Justin to feel superior. The frenzy of exasperation, for it was little less, would wear away, and then Conscience would enter with its whips and screws, like that medieval officer, the Tormentor, and Robin would take his punishment for his self-centred ambition and vindictiveness.

A more admirable wrath was stirred when Justin, by word or manner, struck at Primrose or her father. He was never crudely rude to them or vulgarly brutal—indeed he was usually genial with his victims—but his victims they were. He wounded them by a faint derision in his railleries, or he laid them low with sarcastic courtesies. Coldly indifferent to whether they loved or hated him, he held a position of great power and was invulnerable. Often Robin went into battle on their behalf with weapons as pointed and poisoned as Justin's own; and then there was a coldness between them, for Justin was not so completely invulnerable if Robin took the field.

CHAPTER THREE

THE secret that walked with Robin wherever he went, that shrouded him in a glowing haze and shut him off from the voices and events around him, was as follows.

Back in the city of Lavant there was an old priest, Canon Lowther, who had once been a canon of Maritzburg in Natal and was now Prebendary of Estrange in the diocese of Lavant and rector of two tiny churches in that ancient town. Theologian and bibliophile, he was also Librarian of the Cathedral Library and spent much of his time among its massive and dusty volumes. Seventy-five and a widower, he lived with his married son in a flat white house at the corner of West Wall. The son was also a priest in that city of priests, and his flat white house was a staid and discreet residence such as Jane Austen might have lived in or peopled with the daughters of her fancy. There were two women in that house: the son's wife, a woman of much vivacity and excellent clothes and more like a cabinet minister's wife than a clergyman's; and her daughter. There were also, in the vacations, a son from Oxford and another from Winchester, but Robin had seen little of these. His eyes from the first had busied themselves with the daughter. Not that he had fallen in love with her at first sight, but simply that she interested him. When he first came to Lavant, she had been but sixteen, and her pale hair had hung in a long plait down to her waist. This hair was the colour of satinwood, the colour that many English children are born with and their mothers hope against hope will endure. Her small, soft features were appealing rather than striking; so too were her blue, childish eyes. Her mouth was generously modelled and remarkably restless; her face had little colour, but what it had was good; her legs, in their black school stockings were long and slim as a boy's; and she looked no more than fourteen or fifteen. He thought her no more, and his feeling for her at first was but a pleasant, dreamy interest. She touched him as a child; she did not trouble him as a woman. A youth of reflective habit, he perceived for the first time that a long-legged schoolgirl, whose beauty was about to descend upon her like a fire from God, was a deeply touching thing.

A secret interest like this is often a pleasant game for the remote and dreamy, and this child, the canon's granddaughter supplied for Robin the means for such an indulgence. No one and nothing else in that city of Lavant interested him as much as she. At four o'clock each day he deserted his books and went and sat at his upper window in the College Hostel to see her pass by, on her way home from school. He watched her all the way from the Market Cross to the grave white house at the corner of the street known as West Wall; and not till her door had closed behind her could he return to his *History of the Hebrews* or his *Procter and Frere on the Book of Common Prayer*. Almost always her eyes were set in dreams as she walked along, and seemed to be seeing other worlds than West Street, Lavant—probably future worlds—and as people had always bantered *him* about his woolgathering—not wholly to his displeasure—he liked to think that in this respect they resembled each other.

On Sundays, from his place in the choir stalls of the Cathedral, where the students of the Theological College sat in their scholars' gowns, he would watch her in the nave, where she sat with her mother. After Matins, Litany, and Ante-Communion, which were usually enough for those who were not compelled like the College students to stay for more, she and her mother would go out into the sunlight at the West Door, and the high Norman cathedral would seem empty of everything but cold daylight and drifting, luminous dust.

But he was not in love with her. It was still only an idle and very private game.

And then one Sunday morning, the third Sunday in this summer term which had just closed, she walked up the nave of the Cathedral to her seat on the north side, and he gasped. It was she, sure enough, but she wore a long white summer frock whose lace-veiled skirt swept the ancient flags, and long white gloves, and a straw hat as large as the shield of Achilles. The hat was trimmed with a ring of flowers and flopped down towards her hair. The hair, whose satinwood sheen seemed a little darker now, was drawn up on to her head, leaving bare her neck and ears. And somehow, when he saw the girl dressed as a woman, and her neck and ears bare, he knew quite simply that he wanted her. And he felt that she, who, as was plain, had long been aware of his glances, knew that this knowledge had swooped down upon him this morning and was in total possession. Seldom, hardly at all, during Matins, Litany, and

Ante-Communion, did she lift her eyes from her prayer book
and let them appear from under the brim of her large, flopping
hat. For nine centuries the Norman columns of the Cathedral,
massive and cold, had watched such moments as these, when a
mutual knowledge was passing between two ripe young people
of Lavant, while priests and congregation were engaged with
God.

The knowledge that he wanted her was the loveliest thing
that had ever swelled up in Robin's heart. It changed the face
of the world. It was terrible and splendid as a new birth.
It displaced, disordered, and partly dispersed all earlier
aspirations and desires. It gathered the whole of him into
itself. It was at once as selfish as a tiger's appetite and as
selfless as the service of a saint. His studies flew away before it
like piled papers in a wind. Eusebius of Cæsarea, Grosseteste
of Lincoln, the judicious Hooker, Archbishop Cranmer, and
all the other ecclesiastical shadows with whom he had been
living, faded like the ghosts they were before the flesh-and-
blood reality of Bryn Lowther, granddaughter of the Cathedral Librarian. Church, Party, Mankind, and all the other
loyalties, sank into temporary smallness beside her. The
exquisite torture drove him out into the streets in the hope of
seeing her somewhere, and particularly into that street called
West Wall, where he would watch the prim white house with
its door most firmly shut and its windows sedately curtained.
It drove him into the Cathedral Library that he might talk, if
not with the girl herself, with her grandfather. It built between him and the grandfather an agreeable acquaintance.
Together they considered old and valuable volumes, quaint old
maps of Lavant, and heavy old registers which Canon Lowther
himself dragged in from the muniment room. Together they
studied a facsimile of Domesday Book, prepared thirty years
before by a Chancellor of the Cathedral for the Sussex
Archæological Society. Together they deciphered and translated the old Latin text: *"Terra Episcopi. Ipse Episcopus
tenet in dominio* ESTRANGE. . . ."

The Domesday Book was the door through which Robin
approached Bryn Lowther. The old canon was warmed to a
great liking for this serious and well-informed young student,
and within a week Robin received an invitation to tennis from
the house in West Wall. This appeared so quickly that Robin
dared to believe—in fact, he knew, such is the telepathy that
passes between those who have never spoken but are drawn to

each other—that Bryn, on hearing her grandfather speak of
this student with the strong interest in the Library's treasures,
had suggested that he might be invited to their next tennis
party.

And all that afternoon, from three till six, Robin and Bryn
Lowther, as they played side by-side, or face to face across the
net, knew what they were thinking, and pretended they didn't.
And for both it was not the sun that filled the episcopal city of
Lavant that day but the light that never was on any see.

The rest is simple. The wheels ran speedily down the old
trite way. Robin and Bryn played tennis together twice again.
They met in the streets, each pretending it was an accident
and doubting if it was; and, having met, they walked a little
way together and spoke of commonplace things. Once Robin
was walking along North Street in a dream when he felt a
hand touch his elbow more lightly than a drifting leaf, and,
turning, saw her smiling up at him. "Hallo, lonely one," was
her greeting; and she quoted impudently, " 'He wandered
lonely as a cloud . . .' " And then they walked along the pavement together, but so shaken were both by this unexpected
encounter that they were glad of an excuse for parting at the
corner of East Street. Once they cycled in a happy party to a
picnic tea by the sea at Fettering. In the Cathedral they gazed
at each other through the choir screen—at least Robin stared,
and she sometimes caught his eye and blushed warmly and took
a header into the safety of her prayer book. Sometimes, if she
had stayed for Communion (which she seemed now to be
doing more often than before) the one who first left the
Cathedral dawdled in the noon sunlight by the West Door to
see the other pass out and to receive a smile as a ration on
which to live for the next twenty-four hours.

In all they met and spoke together perhaps nine times.

But not till the term's last day, till the eve of the day when
we saw Robin standing in a trance in an Underground train,
did the prospect of not seeing her for many weeks, and of
leaving her for other men to approach, force him to overcome
his diffidence and fears. After hours of pacing about his room,
unable to work or read or even sit, he suddenly, in one of
those desperate, abrupt, and almost furious resolves that
could sometimes seize and drive him, rushed out into the
street that he might loiter near her house and, before the
evening was gone, speak to her. He had contrived, by too
much thinking, to sink himself into the depths of humility.

What was he? A penniless ordinand, with no hope of earning more than one hundred and fifty pounds or two hundred pounds a year for many years to come. An ordinand without a University degree and with little chance, therefore, of ever advancing to a well-paid and distinguished position in the Church. How could he possibly expect her to love him as he wanted and to promise to marry him? The doubt and suspense were such that he was now passionately, angrily, determined to know all—to plunge forthwith into whichever awaited him: an intolerable happiness or a sick despair. "God be with me," he prayed as he rushed out. "God help me now." How he was going to see her, how he was going to speak to her, what he was going to say, he had not the least idea. In one way or another he would see her. He would not return home till he had spoken to her. God would help him. It was then about five o'clock and, vehemently refusing to be defeated, he loitered in and about her street till eight.

At eight o'clock the sun was falling behind her house, and the sight of the sun going down and taking the day with it, turned his impatience into an anguish, and, again in a sudden, blind resolve, he went up to her door and angrily pulled the bell. "God help me now."

The parlourmaid opened the door; an old woman with a rounded back, a nose like Punch's, and a white apron reaching to the ground.

"God give me words." "Can I speak to Miss Bryn? Could I—do you think?—see her for a minute?" His heart hammered against his side, and his brow steamed.

"Why, yes, sir. They're in the drawing-room. They've just finished their dinner."

"Oh, I don't want to see them all. I just wanted to——" He stopped. He dried up as completely as an actor whose memory is suddenly paralysed.

The old maid waited; then, since Robin had been struck dumb and could only stare and blush with shame, she asked, "Did you want to speak to Miss Bryn alone?" And though she had not smiled nor looked knowing nor, indeed, suffered any change to pass over her face, he knew that she knew all about him and had a heart.

"Well, yes, I did."

"I'll try and get hold of her, see?"

"Oh, thank you. Thank you awfully."

"Would you like just to step inside?"

"Oh, no—I——"

"Well, if you'll just wait—perhaps I'd better just shut the door, see, and she'll come out to you when she can."

"Oh, thank you. Thank you so much." He smiled at her gratefully, and she smiled at him a little knowingly now, and "By gosh, one day I'll kiss her," he thought as the door shut.

He walked from the front of the house. The old wall of Lavant is still intact on the city's western side, and long ago the city fathers built up a gravel path along the parapet where once the defenders stood to arms. Steps lead up from the roadway to this promenade, and tall trees spread their ragged awnings over its whole length. Now this parapet and path touched the side wall of the Lowthers' house, which stood next the place where once the old gates stood, and was therefore known as West Gate House. Robin went up the first flight of steps on to the path and leaned against the trunk of an elm. From here he would be able to see Bryn when she stepped from her house into the road.

And there he remained, waiting and staring, waiting and staring, while his heart belaboured his side. "She is coming, she is coming," repeated his heart, unaware that it was plagiarizing any previous poet. And at last she came. Her door opened, and she stepped on to the roadway and looked up and down it, not without alarm.

"Bryn. Bryn." He walked to the top of the steps. "Here I am."

"Oh!" The eyes that looked up at him were embarrassed and hesitant. "Did you want to speak to me? Mossy said you wanted to speak to me."

"Yes. . . . Yes, I do, please. . . ."

She was dressed as if she had come straight from her tennis lawn, for the family had played late this warm June evening. Down the front of her white shirt was a blue-and-white-striped tie like a schoolboy's. Her pale clean skin was tanned by the sun to the tint of a brown egg-shell, and her hair looked the fairer and her eyes the bluer for this midsummer brown. But now the brown was flushing into a ruddier hue. "What is it?" she asked.

"Can't you come up here?"

"I suppose so." She ran up the steps to his side. "What is it?"

"Come further away . . . please. . . ."

They walked across the path to the old stone parapet and

leaned against it. "Oh, God help me now. Give me words, for God's sake"—but no remarkable words were laid upon his lips, and it was only as a result of one of his sudden, precipitate, mutinous resolves that he was able to speak, and even so his cheeks fired to a deeper tint than hers, and his hand, resting on the parapet, trembled like a palsied thing. "I don't know if I'm off my head or not, but there's something I've just got to tell you or I shall go mad. We go to-morrow."

"Yes?" she encouraged.

But like an engine that has started too violently, his speech stalled again. His tongue would not move.

"Yes? What is it?"

"It's—oh, you don't mind, do you?—it's just that I'm madly in love with you. I——" But this was such an awful moment, now that he had put all to the test, that he could not utter another word. He could only stand there, breathless, waiting for what she was going to say, waiting, as it seemed, for life or death.

"Robin!" It was not embarrassment that stood in her eyes now. He knew joy when he saw it.

"You don't mind, do you?"

"*Mind!*"

"I mean you don't mind my getting you out like this to tell you. I felt I couldn't let another moment go by without telling you. I couldn't go to-morrow and endure the suspense of not knowing whether you—whether, by any chance, you——"

"You mean, whether I love you too."

"Yes. Yes, of course."

As an answer she laid her hand on his where it trembled on the parapet.

"Bryn! Do you mean——"

"You know what I mean."

"Oh, my beloved! Oh, Bryn!"

She was in his arms. She was his possession, and his happiness soared into an air that was almost beyond belief or bearing. She might be pale and fair, and look like one of the colder people of the North, but she was hot with love for him too, and more than willing to receive his kisses and to return them, and to press her body against his. She was only unwilling to let him go. To feel her breast against his, and to think that the large, shapely mouth which had so often troubled him was now at his mercy, lifted him to the highest joy he had known. For the first time he understood the meaning of ecstasy and knew it for a simple, exact, unextravagant word.

At last, since one must break such a joy to save it, he raised his head and laid her back against the parapet and imprisoned her there with an arm on either side of her and his hands gripping the wall. Her arms remained in a noose round his neck. He remembered always that the sun was falling behind her, as she stood thus, because he was facing the West.

And while she was thus his prisoner, fettered to the old stone wall, he forced her to tell him how long she had loved him. "You don't go back till you've told me. How long, Bryn Lowther, how long?"

"Since I first saw you, I think."

"Well, that's fine. But why?"

"Because you looked so different from all the other students. Quite different."

"In what way?"

"I don't know. Sadder——"

"Hell, no! Not sadder. I'm not sad."

"Oh, well, not sadder; more thoughtful. And nice and shy. And then you know——" She paused, looking at him mischievously.

"I know what?"

"Well, of course you know you're very nearly frightfully handsome."

"I know nothing of the sort."

"Well, you are, my pet. Your nose is rather snub, but I love it. And I simply adore your hair. How on earth did you make it go iron-grey at your age? It looks lovely on top of a face as young as yours." She ran her fingers through it, and her touch was a delight. "Most men have to wait years and years to get nice, interesting hair like that. And your eyes are always so far away—hundreds and hundreds of miles away—and when they're not, when they've come back to the present again, they're kind eyes. I love everything about you."

To one who hungered for love and praise, what charged, what overcharged, moments were these. He paid for them by telling her how he had been watching her from his hostel window for a year and more, ever since he first saw her coming from school with her hair down her back and her books under her arm. "I must have been in love with you from the first," he said, "but I didn't know it till you put your hair up."

She smiled with tight lips—a half-smile. "Yes, I rather thought something happened that Sunday morning. But I must go now, darling." It was the first time she had called him "darling". "I must go, my heart. They'll wonder where I am."

"You'll not go." He did not move the imprisoning arms. On the contrary, he gripped the parapet tighter. "You'll not go till I let you. Now tell me all about that old maid of yours. Does she suspect anything?"

"Oh, yes. Mossy knows everything. Mossy's the short for Morris; her father was a Jew. She and I have discussed you a lot. And the first time you came to tennis she said she thought you were—well—rather in love with me."

"Wise old woman. But why 'rather'?"

"Well, as a matter of fact, she said she thought you were 'pretty far gone, miss'."

"So I was."

"She's an old dear, and she admires you. She says nobody else looks quite like you. And now I must go, darling."

"No, no, don't go, *please*. Please stay a little longer, Bryn, *please*." Strange quality about this moment of life by the old parapet: it was so perfect as to be timeless and still, and yet it was fugitive, threatened. Time touched it again and again, and it faded at the touch. Now Time had hold of it, and it was fading right away. "Not yet. Not yet, Bryn, you incredibly adorable thing. I shan't see you àgain for weeks. You don't seem to understand that I love you."

"The holidays won't last for ever. We shall be back from the sea at the end of August, and then——"

"And then——?"

"Then we'll do everything together. Everything. Good-bye. I love you."

A last kiss, and she broke from his restraining hands. She ran down the steps and at the bottom put her finger to her lips and blew him a half-hint of a kiss; then fled into her house and very quietly shut the door. And Robin was back in the loneliness of Time.

She had asked him the hour of his train to-morrow, and he had demanded why she wanted to know, because he believed he knew. And the next morning he hurried to the station, believing she would be there to see him off. She was not there. He looked up the platform and down it; he ran out into the road again and peered up South Street as far as the Market

Cross; he stood there, straining for a glimpse of her; but she did not appear, and the train came in, and he had to jump into it with a heart heavier than his bursting gladstone bag. And yet the pain in some way was sweet, and he would not be without it. He sat himself in a corner seat from which he could look out at the spire of the Cathedral and the old walls. He must see again, if it were possible, that place on the wall where they had stood together last night. The train moved out, and he waited for the houses to slip behind and the Bishop's Meadows to come into view. Here they were, the meadows, under the south wall that flanked the palace garden, and there—there was Bryn, running anxiously, desperately, hotly, as if some digusting interference had delayed her, to a place by the railing where she would be nearest the train. Here she swept the windows of the already retreating train in search of him and lifted a handkerchief shoulder-high in readiness to wave. He flung his head out of the window and waved to her. She saw him and waved back violently and smiled and waved again and blew him the shapes of kisses till he and his train were out of sight.

§

That was the memory which drew him back to itself a hundred times a day; which laid a haze on his eyes and shut out all sight of the people in Justin's house and the people in the streets. He was relating all things to his memory of Bryn.

Justin and Primrose. He and Bryn would not be like Justin and Primrose, living in the same house, apart from one another, indifferent to one another, and even at times hating one another. He and Bryn would be lovers to the end. Mr. Cumberland, shambling along the passages, old, widowed, lonely, and unwanted. It would not be so with him and Bryn. By the time he was old he would be a priest honoured and loved by a multitude of people, and Bryn would be a happy and beautiful partner at his side——

But wait: this was all wrong, very wrong. Where had he got to now? He whose haunting vision was of a selfless love for all men, and especially for sinners; whose desire to achieve this had been heightened of late by his studies in the lives of famous churchmen—where was he now? Sunk in wholly self-regarding thoughts. Selfish towards all the world, he was selfless only towards Bryn—and far from completely selfless

there, either. It was plain that he was not really good, but only
wanted to be.

Take this question of telling Justin about Bryn. He ached
to tell him. And he knew that he would tell him soon. He
would have to. But wouldn't there be a taint of unkindness,
of cruelty, in this bragging about the love he had won and
the kisses he had enjoyed, since these were something that
Justin had manifestly missed? Yes, his keen and sympathetic
insight showed him that there would be pain in it for Justin,
and largely because he was Justin's brother.

None the less he told him. He had to. The need to do so
had swelled up into one of those high-pressure and con-
straining desires to which he always in the end succumbed.
One evening as they were walking together for old time's sake
along the river malls and speaking of the days when they used
to discuss their ambitions, he let the whole story go from
him with a rush—and without a trace of pity. (That came
afterwards.) He described Bryn's beauty, even exaggerating
it for his purpose, and her high position in Lavant, exaggerating that too, and the way she had given herself to him at
his first word of love, and her indisputable adoration of him
now. Justin for a time was silent, and Robin, who could see
so much of his brother's heart, knew what he was thinking;
and he too walked along without speaking, because he was
suffering the first pangs of remorse. The remorse increased
when Justin said, "Well, I wish you joy, old man. I hope it
all turns out as you think. With you I suspect it may;" and
when, at supper that night, Primrose having offered him "a
penny for his thoughts," Justin chaffed him, saying, "Ah,
good people, he is not for you. He has no ears for your talk.
Weave a circle round him thrice, for he on honey-dew has
fed and drunk the milk of paradise." Robin smiled, but did
not reply. He was telling himself that he had got a satisfaction
out of hurting Justin that day, and that he was a pretty
hopeless case. And yet he was not without hope, as he continued his meal in silence, after the story had been told and
much persiflage and congratulation showered upon him, that
one day he would be a little nearer to his vision

CHAPTER FOUR

Bozzy was twenty-one now, and the loneliest, and probably
the happiest, of the le Faber boys. Of dim vitality, he was
unvexed by the ambitions that chafed Justin and Gerard, and
unbemused by that glowing vision of the beauty of holiness
which cast such difficult shadows across the path of Robin.
Of dull imagination and quite empty of critical intelligence,
he was unable to put himself in the place of others and see
himself as they saw him; and this is a prime condition for
passing one's time in peace and content. What is yet more
to the point, he was quite unable to hear himself as others
heard him, for he was now an incessant talker if anyone was
at hand to be talked to, and whether that person was listening
or not. He who at two years old had not spoken at all never
stopped speaking at twenty-one, as if there were much leeway
to be made good. His talk when there was company was like
the running of a broken tap: it never stopped, but it spluttered
often, and sometimes spat over you.

That he was very well satisfied with himself was revealed
by his dress. For most of his day he enjoyed the simple,
sensuous pleasure that one imagines to be experienced by a
plant in the sunlight; and just as a plant, for all we know,
may get pleasure out of putting forth its blooms for the
admiration of the bees, so did Bozzy enjoy dressing himself
in what he considered to be an admirable style, and in strolling, thus attired, among the people in the busy streets. He
wore a fawn-coloured lounge suit that was somewhat amor-
phous now, both because it was old, his mother not being able
to buy him many clothes, and because his imagination had
never embraced the notion of having it ironed and pressed.
But it was not in his suit—not on his torso, as it were—that he
gave expression to his desire for beauty. Like the plant, he
put out his blossoms at his extremities. On his hands he wore
wash-leather gloves which, since he never buttoned them,
opened out over his wrists like the petals of a yellow flower;
on his left forearm he hung a crook-handled stick with a
silver band or, if the clouds were low, a crook-handled umbrella; on his feet, in all weathers and temperatures, he wore
grey spats, and very odd they looked at the bottom of his
baggy trousers and over his wrinkled shoes; on his head he

wore a brown trilby hat, turned down at the front and up at the back. Sometimes he smoked a cigarette, and felt a man, and a fashionable man too.

Many a time Robin or Justin or Gerard saw him strolling along the street in this self-pleasing array, alone and happy and smiling. Robin would greet him and chat with him as an equal that he might not feel an inferior; Gerard, having less sensitiveness, would greet him and tease him; but Justin would turn and fly at the first glimpse of that trilby hat and those wash-leather gloves. Bozzy was best forgotten, he would say; the very thought of him was too great an irritant.

In this desire to be well dressed Bozzy was a pale reflection of his brothers; for the same desire was strong in Justin and Gerard, as we have seen; and it was strong also in Robin— stronger than his conscience, when it mounted its rostrum, was ready to approve. But Bozzy's pleasure in his gloves and spats was only a small part of his happiness as he sauntered along the pavements; a much larger part was the pleasure he got from smiling and nodding at as many people as possible in the course of a stroll—and in this too, perhaps, there was a pale reflection of Robin's ambition to be a lover of all men. Bozzy was under the impression that he knew far more of the residents in Hammersmith and Shepherds Bush than he really did. There were scores of these people who had no idea why he smiled and nodded at them so pleasantly as they passed by; but Bozzy's idea was that if he had once smiled at some persons by accident, or had been smiled at by them, this constituted an introduction, and their mutual goodwill must be expressed, and emphatically expressed, on all future occasions. It was a fount of quiet happiness in Bozzy that he had so many friends with whom he was on nodding and smiling, if not on speaking, terms.

It was in King Street on a clouded evening that Robin first saw Bozzy, after his return from Lavant. The sight of him was something of a shock, and Robin stood still and watched him, unprepared this evening to run up and greet him. There was Bozzy, drifting along the kerbs, his umbrella hung on his left arm, his wash-leather gloves ablow on his wrists, his spats, slightly frayed, sitting loosely on his shoes. and the brim of his tribly hat turned down towards his eyes. He was smiling at one acquaintance after another, and to some of them, as they passed, he said, "It's nice, isn't it?" and smiled and nodded again when they agreed that it was

In point of fact it was not nice at all, for there was a low, surly sky, and a muster of sooty, threatening clouds along the west, and a fretful wind that seemed to belong to November rather than to June. But Bozzy was happy. Now and again his lips, when they had no one to smile at, moved up and down in a brief conversation with himself. He came to a corner and stood quite still there for a minute, looking up the side street; then he nodded to himself, crossed the street, and went on along the main road, his umbrella swinging gently on his arm.

CHAPTER FIVE

JUSTIN took the newspaper from Robin's hand. He, Robin, Primrose, and Mr. Cumberland were seated at breakfast, at the upper end of the long, trestle table in the Boys' Dining-Room.

"This is magnificent! Magnificent!" exclaimed Mr. Cumberland. "I am more pleased than I can say. I always believed there was a great deal in our Gerard. And our dear Anne—how pleased she will be. They have deserved this; they have waited so long. I shall go round this evening and offer them my felicitations. God bless them both."

"Where is it?" demanded Justin.

"On the page before the editorial page," said Robin, who, immediately on arrival at the table had opened the paper at the dramatic critic's column; for last night he and his mother and Hector and Bozzy (Justin making an excuse) had been at Gerard's opening performance and witnessed an ovation for the play, for Wardon Asche, and for Gerard himself. "Good old Gerard."

"Oh, I *am* pleased!" repeated Mr. Cumberland over his porridge. "I wonder if I could run round this morning after breakfast and congratulate them. It is not far. I should like to be among the first to offer my felicitations."

"You can't possibly do that," said Justin sharply. "There'll only be about half an hour before school begins."

"Yes, yes, I suppose so. Yes, you're right, Justin. I shouldn't have time. I'll go this evening and take them a little present."

"You wouldn't find them up at this time of the morning,"

said Robin to comfort him. "If I know anything about Gerard, he and Anne have been celebrating half the night and are now in bed."

"And why not? We can be young and hopeful but once. Dear young people! Bless their hearts. I can imagine how happy they were."

Justin was reading. Silently and with lips compressed he read the part about Gerard.

"But Mr. Wardon Asche's was not the only triumph last night. He would be the first to admit that he shared the honours of the evening with a young actor, hitherto but little known on the West End stage. Gerard le Faber, like the author of the play, is a discovery of Mr. Asche's, and we congratulate him on his discernment. This young candidate for theatrical honours has everything in his bag: a fine presence, a good voice, a finished technique, and youth. He is only twenty-six, we understand, and that is an early age to stand where Mr. le Faber stood as the curtain fell last night——"

"Have you come to the part where he calls Gerard a discovery?" asked Robin.

"Oh, let me see it! Do let me see it," pleaded Primrose; and she jumped up and, standing at Justin's elbow, bent over his shoulder to read. He drew away from her as if the nearness of her large, bending body were overpowering; he looked up at her as if to tell her to go away; but he forbore, and went on reading.

"With thirty or forty years of acting before him there is little to which he cannot hope to attain. It is always a hazardous thing to predict a young man's career in a profession that is notoriously the most capricious and cruel of all, disappointing more hopes and breaking more hearts than any other; but we will venture the guess that in twenty years' time, if all goes well, Mr. le Faber will have the English Theatre in his pocket."

"Don't *lean* over me," protested Justin to Primrose. "I hate having people lean over me when I'm reading."

"I'm sorry, dear. I'll read it afterwards."

"Mr. le Faber was not content to stonewall while his more famous partner scored the runs. There was batting at both ends of the wicket last night, and often it was difficult to say which was the more exciting display. The new man scored quite as many sixes as his captain."

The metaphor irritated Justin, who had been a celebrated

cricketer at St. Paul's and who remembered Gerard's timorous cricket on the green.

"The ovation that greeted him at the close of a gallant and dashing innings was richly merited. It was the acclamations of the pavilion for a first-class player who had most convincingly justified his selection."

"Anne won't like this too well," suggested Justin, passing the paper to Primrose. "There's hardly any mention of her."

"Anne will be delighted," affirmed Robin indignantly. "She wanted this to happen. She worked day and night for it. It's her triumph as well as Gerard's."

"H'mm . . ." muttered Justin. "I wonder. . . ."

He hardly spoke again, but sat at the top of his table, reading his letters a second time, or pretending to; and as soon as he could do so without exposing his wound he went from the room.

He went to the study and shut the door on himself. It was only half-past eight, and he had half an hour in which he could be alone. He lit a pipe. He tossed the match away somewhat mournfully. Then he fell into his long, deep chair, extended his long legs before him and, holding the bowl of the pipe with the fingers of both hands, drummed it gently against his teeth. He was the very picture of a man brooding.

Three weeks ago Robin had come home with the story of Gerard and Anne's good parts in a good play, but he had chosen to believe that their optimistic reports were the usual exaggerated stuff of rather silly and frothy actors. Sixteen pounds a week was rather startling, certainly, but probably it was only a temporary spell of luck that would lead to little. Then, two days ago, Robin had told him the story of Bryn Lowther, and this had been a sharper pain than he would have believed—much sharper than the story of Gerard and Anne. To be drawn to the breast of a young and beautiful girl in an enveloping love was something he had never known. Apart from some bought embraces, which always seemed inadequate and therefore displeased as much as they pleased, and some temporary favours which had been given him for nothing, and which therefore he had despised as he took them, he had had nothing in the way of love. Nor did he see anything of that kind before him now. He had only Primrose: Primrose, big and heavy and faded; Primrose, so exasperatingly arch, Primrose, that despair-breeding fool. . . .

Had he missed something? Perhaps. but you couldn't have

everything, and he had chosen success rather than love. He had never set out to compete with Robin in love. But now here was Gerard competing with him in success, and even taking the lead of him. He was not going to be surpassed by Gerard—he who had always been looked upon as the most brilliant of the family. How could he increase, and quickly, his own success?

Always when Justin dwelt upon the future and his success in it, sitting alone in his study and behind a closed and misanthropic door, he found himself contemplating the death of someone. Or the death of several. The death of all those who might stand in his way. How could one help considering the death of people if one would profit by it? There was his mother. Her death would release him from a recurring and fretting expense. The three le Faber sons who were earning money, Justin, Gerard, and Hector, all contributed something towards a home for their mother and the helpless Bozzy; and Justin, determined to be the family's success, contributed most. He sent his mother a pound a week. If she died—but no: she mustn't die before Bozzy, or they'd be left with Bozzy on their hands and have to provide him with a home somewhere else. Bozzy then. Consider Bozzy. It'd be a relief if Bozzy died; a relief to all, and no great loss to Bozzy, since his life, so low-powered, aimless, and drifting, was little good to him. No: people might pretend what they liked, but *he* wasn't going to lie to himself and say that he would grieve much if Bozzy died to-morrow.

Or the old Duke. In a year or two that old man would be no use to him at all. He would be a dead weight in the boat ... he would be a drag on his wheel. Once he, Justin, had got his London B.A. he would not want the Duke as a screen. How long would it take him to get his B.A.? Four years, perhaps. The old man would be seventy-three then. God send he died quickly, very quickly, after his purpose was served. Death would be a happy release for him, surely. It was with him as with Bozzy: Bozzy's life was never properly made; the old man's was wrecked; both were pretty useless, and in their ending there would be nothing for tears. But—and here Justin's lips, already set in a hard line, turned down in dismay—these old parsons sometimes lived till they were ninety. Parsons and old women were the toughest things in the world; they went on for ever. Ninety! Fancy having the old man on his back for twenty years and more! That would be a grim score for Fate. The old Duke, whom he'd used for his own purposes, fixed finally on his back like an old man of the sea! But he wasn't tolerating that. Somehow or other he'd circumvent that. He wasn't the sort who suffered with a bow the smart little tricks of Fate.

Or Gerard. Gerard might die before he had got much further along the path they were prophesying for him. That would put an end to his success. No failure so complete as death.

And then, his thoughts returning to the girl who had taken Robin into her arms, he considered the figure of Primrose. His pipe out, and his chin fallen upon his two joined fists, he contemplated her. Perhaps when he had made a good position and no longer needed her as matron and housekeeper, she would die, and then he could seek the sweetness which Robin had described. He could compete with Robin in that alluring field and beat him.

As he sat there, brooding, calculating, scheming, his expression was heavy and without light. It was as if all the pleasanter lamps in him were extinguished, and all his laughter forgotten. The eyes were dull, the mouth turned down, the cheeks lined, and the chin sunk upon his knuckled fists. His mind was grey, and his face was grey.

§

The irritation was with him all that day. All day it craved action: some action that would seem to minister to future success and at the same time unleash the displeasure on others. Success. Success meant boarders. There were not enough boarders in the school to yield an income comparable with Gerard's. More boarders meant more dormitory space. That idea, long in his scheming mind, of a new dormitory, a model dormitory, distempered and painted by himself in sunny colours and decorated with bright bedspreads—not to be used at first, but simply to be shown to parents—he would begin upon it at once. He would start at once upon his race with Gerard. The only room that could be used for it was the old Duke's room on the second floor. So much the better. He had long begrudged that unpleasant old man his living-room on the second floor. And there were good reasons why he should be moved out of it. He befouled the atmosphere on the second floor with his pipe; he degraded the school before the boys who slept up there by slip-slopping about the passage in a disorderly dressing-gown and down-trodden slippers—or even with bare feet; the recurrent clearing of his throat in a protracted, assiduous, liquescent cough came resounding down the stairs and galled Justin in his study below; and, finally, the room was a front room, and he would sit looking out of his window at the people in the street, a grey and shabby old face that did no credit to the school at all. He was best put away and out of sight. It would be a relief to Justin if he were stowed away as far as possible from his eyes and ears on the attic floor. There was quite a good dormer-windowed room there at the back, larger than his present room, but it was next to the room in which the maids slept, and so far Justin had hesitated to suggest the old man's removal there, just because it was on the servants' floor. He would hesitate no longer. He would set free the front room and begin painting and beautifying it. To do this would be something.

And some evenings later Robin, who had heard nothing of this decision, which had been discussed in private with the old man and Primrose, and which Justin, something ashamed of it, had not cared to communicate to his brother, saw Mr. Cumberland, still in the faded frock coat which he liked to wear before the boys, struggling with a pile of books up the narrow stairs to the attic floor.

"Hallo, Mr. Cumberland. Hallo, sir. Where are you off to with those?"

"This is a *déménagement*, my dear boy."

"A what?"

"Your French is not your strongest point, I perceive. This is a household removal. I am changing my residence—did you not know? The fiat has gone forth."

"But where? Where are you moving to? Let me carry those for you."

"I am going aloft. Like Poor Tom Bowling. 'Faithful below I did my duty, and now I'm going aloft.' Don't drop them. They are precious books, some of them. Thank you. You are a good lad."

"But why this sudden change?"

"Justin wants my old room for a dormitory, and I have consented. Yes, I have given my consent. The boys must come first."

"Which room upstairs is it? The back room?"

"Even so. Justin and two of the boys have moved all the boxes that were bestowed there into the roof-space, and the demoiselle has scrubbed the floor. Justin has already carried up my heavier furniture for me and hung the curtains very nicely. He is excellent at that sort of thing. And he says that one day he's going to paint the room up for me. My few books and trophies, my few *lares and penates*, I preferred to move myself. I know just how I want them, you see. Primrose is helping me. She knows where they go. She remembers them in the Rectory."

"Well, you can at least let me carry them for you." Robin's pity had gone out to the old man like the hurt, hurrying arms of a mother. "Give them to me. I'll be your coolie. You can tell me what to do, and I'll do it."

"It's very kind of you."

"Not at all. Pile them up. . . . Thank you. Now you lead on, sir."

Just then Primrose came from the room he was vacating. She was carrying all the mementoes that had stood upon his mantelpiece: a tobacco jar emblazoned with the arms of his college, two pictures of college groups in which Mr. Cumberland was to be discerned as a young man of twenty, some framed portraits of friends of long ago, a picture of his wife, and a picture of his church in the West Country with the Rectory beside it.

"Hallo, Robin," she said, and it was clear that she was ashamed to be caught in this act, but had been too afraid of Justin to resist his orders. "What do you think of this?"

"I knew nothing about it."

"It's a shame, isn't it?" Her father was now in the room above, out of hearing. "Poor old man. He had grown very fond of that room, and it was all he had."

"But why is this necessary?"

"It isn't. It's just done to spite him. And me."

Robin never knew what part to play if Primrose started speaking against Justin, so he said cheerfully, "Oh, well, never mind. We'll make his new room much better than the old. It's larger, if anything. You and I'll work at it and make it immensely attractive."

"I'm *going* to," said Primrose firmly. She could show her defiance of Justin when he was not there to hear it; and no doubt it was a relief to do so. "He's my father."

"And I'm going to help you. And in a very little time he'll be as happy and comfortable as he was before. We'll make a good job of this."

"Hush!" They were about to enter the attic room in which her father was standing.

They entered in silence. In some ways it was not a bad room. Its ceiling was low but its floor-space was large; the dormer window looked west, and the evening sun was now pouring on to the bare walls and floor. Floor-boards and white walls were clean, for Justin must have everything clean in his house. But it still had the chilliness and the desolation of a room that had not been inhabited for years. Mr. Cumberland's few pieces of furniture looked bewildered and uneasy in the cold, white, unfamiliar place.

Most of his Rectory furniture had been sold after the trial to pay the costs of his defence, but he had kept enough for the bed-sitting-room promised to him in his son-in-law's home. Among the pieces was a small, upright piano on which he would sometimes play (very badly, and much to Justin's exasperation) the hymns that reminded him of the old days and certain Old Scottish and Old English songs that he and his wife and Primrose used to sing in the drawing-room of the Rectory when Primrose was a child. Sometimes he would call Primrose up to his room to sing these songs to him again.

To-night, as Robin and Primrose entered, he was standing near this piano; and he lifted its lid and played with his right hand only, the opening bars of "Christ is risen! Christ is risen! He hath burst His bonds in twain. . . ." Then he laid back the lid and surveyed his new home.

"So! Here we are. Here we are. Well, well, well, *Vae victis. Vae victis.* . . . Still, children, it's not so bad. It might be very much worse. So long as I have somewhere to smoke my pipe and read my book, and a corner in which to lie down to rest at night, what more can I want? *On n'est jamais si heureux ni si malheureux qu'on s'imagine.* Give me my books around me and my tobacco jar on the mantelpiece and a small fire when it's cold, and I am content. Yes, lay those there, Robin. Justin has put up my bookshelves, you see. It is kind of him. I'm afraid I have not the library I used to have, have I, Primrose? Nevertheless, some of these that are left are quite valuable, and all of them are precious to me. *Ronsard.* I went to Couture once, where Ronsard was born, and remembered how he sang, *Quelqu'um après mille ans, de mes vers estonné, Viendra dedans mon Loir, comme en Parnasse, boire* . . . and I gathered up the water of the Loir in my hand and drank of it. *Poetae Latini Veteres.* It's a hundred years

old, that book. I used to be able to read the old Latins as I
read my Byron or my Shakespeare." He opened the thick,
heavy volume. "Catullus . . . Lucretius . . . Virgilius . . .
Horatius—ah, above all, the wise old Quintus Horatius
Flaccus! *Horatii curiosa felicitas*—the exquisite felicity of
Horace." He read from a poem on the page. *Aequam memento
rebus in arduis Servare mentem.* . . . That fits me at the moment : 'Keep a level head, Cumberland, when things are hard.'
Yes, put those on the bottom shelf, Robin, and I pray God it's
not damp there."

"It's not damp, Papa. And I'll light a fire." Having said
this, Primrose turned and whispered defiantly to Robin, "I'll
light one whatever happens."

"Yes, that'll be nice," agreed Mr. Cumberland. "Just for
the first evening a fire is legitimate. We must have a little
house-warming." He walked to the dormer window. "Well,
well, my dears, this is so many steps nearer heaven. And it's
pleasant when the sun's setting. 'Brightness falls from the air,
Queens have died young and fair, Dust has closed Helen's
eye. . . .' And what a view! It must be the best in the house.
Behold the whole wicked world spread below me. This is
fine." He rubbed appreciative hands. "This is a real philo-
sopher's tower. *C'est ma tour d'ivoire.* Arrange those things on
the mantelpiece, Primrose, just as they were downstairs, because, as you know, I get used to things as they've always
been. Yes, I think we can do great things with this room."

All the rest of that evening Robin gave to making Mr.
Cumberland's new home as comfortable and attractive as
possible. He made the old man's first hours in it quite happy,
since it was an agreeable pastime to share with an enthusiastic
and muscular young mate the arranging of chairs, chests,
pictures, and books. "You're a good lad," Mr. Cumberland
would say every time they had achieved some satisfying
effect. " 'Blessed be he that replaceth his neighbour's land-
mark.' That seems better than cursing him that removeth it.
There are curses enough in this world." And Primrose, having
set a fire ablaze up the astonished chimney, went down into the
garden and picked flowers and came back and disposed them in
a colourful display about the room.

"Thank you, children," said the old man, when the room was
complete and there was no more they could do. "I am going to
be quite happy here."

CHAPTER SIX

THE school term ended with July, Robin did not have to
return to Lavant till mid-August, and Justin, all his disappointments forgotten, and all his high spirits in possession
again, suggested to Robin that they should spend this fortnight together in their old childish paradise among the
mountains. And Robin, who, because of the old memories,
would rather climb the mountains with Justin than with anyone else in the world, assented with the excitement of a boy.
And there and then they began their preparations. How
could they hold back from such a delight? Out with the old
rucksacks, the old boots, the old friendly sweaters, the old
compass, and the old frayed maps. Examine the sweaters, test
the compass, dubbin the boots. Try out the boots on the
drawing-room carpet, up and down, up and down; spread out
the maps on the study floor; kneel beside them and plot out a
climb for every day of the holiday. They would go to Deep
Langstrath, as always; and from there, as always, they would
climb the great mountains of the central band. They would
try to find their initials which they had engraved on the cairns
that crowned the summits; and they would look for their own
cairn which they had raised to mark their first conquest of
Scafell, the roof and top of England, and which they had
restored each year that they returned to it. But it was ten
years now since they had gone back to Deep Langstrath and
climbed Scafell. How stood their cairn after the storms of ten
years?

Justin's gaiety, now that this prospect lay before him,
welled up and flowed over all. To Mr. Cumberland he said,
"We're off to your duchy, Duke. Can't you do something about
it? Can't you raise the clans to welcome us?" and to his wife,
"What a holiday it'll be for you, Primmy! A fortnight without
me. Why, you'll be on the Delectable Mountains too. Nonsense, woman, of course you will. What liars these women
are, Robby. Consider, Primmy: you'll be able to live how you
like without anyone to find fault. You'll be able to discuss
my shortcomings all day with the Duke—and that I have a
few shortcomings I should be the first to admit. It'll do you a
power of good, Primmy. It'll get a lot of the more atrabiliar
stuff out of you." And to Robin he said, "Think of the smell

of the middens in the farmyards, that warm, rich smell. Think of Esk Hause and Sty Head with nowhere a hedge or a wall in sight to suggest the presence of men. Only the cairns—only the cairns, my boy—to show where they have passed."

And on one of the last days of July, rucksacks slung, they set off to shake the pavements from under them. The sun shone down to bless their going; and ten yards from the house, Justin said, "Ah, thank God! That's behind me. We're free now, old boy; we're free." Ten hours later they were walking among the assembled pine trees on a fringe of Derwentwater. Above them, on their left, was the carriage road to Borrowdale, and above that the up-ended forest on the face of Walla Crag. On their right, beyond the pines, gleamed the satiny spread of the lake. Beyond the lake Causey Pike and Cat Bells, two well-loved peaks, had their necks in a ruff of cloud, under a sky of speedwell blue.

Happily the two young men walked on, free of rucksacks and bags, and cleaving the good air like swimmers. They had put their loads on the brake at the station, determined to walk the seven miles to Deep Langstrath, since a fortnight was but fourteen days, and every hour must be milked for pleasure. First they had come ringing along the carriage road, but now they had dropped down into Great Wood to find among the pine trees an enchanted path of their childhood. Their feet trod a sodden carpet of pine-needles, twigs, and russet leaves, and drank up delight from it; they paddled through nettles and dog's-mercury, and crunched on cones and shards of bark, and were more than content. Chaffinches, blackbirds, and thrushes disturbed the leaves and, in so doing, pointed the silence; and after a few minutes of this, during which no word had been spoken between them, Justin exclaimed, and his voice was little more than a breath, "My God, Robby, this is better than the Grove, Hammersmith."

At the end of the wood they climbed back on to the road, and now they had a steep blue scree on one side of them, and on the other a lakeside meadow, flushed with clover and pied with hawkweed and buttercups and moonpenny daisies. And there before them were the Jaws of Borrowdale. The Jaws where the valley narrowed between Grange Fell and Castle Crag before opening out again at the foot of its watershed mountains!

The Jaws were the gates of their kingdom. Justin and Robin walked through, and the south wind saluted their coming.

And then there was a sudden quiet. And there, ahead of them, under a low sullen cloud, was the storm-toss of mountains, deeply shadowed, and heavily shawled with old dark green. They were a green and indigo heap beneath the cloud, which housed faint murmurs of thunder, but the ghylls streaking down the defiles glistened with a light snatched from some interspace of luminous sky. There, loneliest of all the dales, was Langstrath, with the high, wrinkled front of Eagle Crag beetling above it; and there in its fold lay the straggle of cottages and barns that was the little hamlet, memory-haunted, of Deep Langstrath.

§

They were days without stain that followed among these hills of proven happiness. Every day, rain or shine (and there was more rain than shine) they left their cottage in Deep Langstrath and went striding over the fells or scaling the peaks. They played "Head of the River" overtaking all who were in front of them on the slopes, just as they did when they were schoolboys. And Justin, six steps higher than Robin, was still given to roaring at the top of his voice, " 'Try not the pass!' the old man said"; to which Robin would respond, no less raucously, " 'Dark lowers the tempest overhead.' " Or they yelled the old hymns as they staggered onward and up, and, whether they knew it or not, this was praise—praise to Whosoever built the mountains and mixed the upland air.

On the Gable they found their initials, J. le F., G. le F., R. le F., 1902, but in an oddly different place from where they had imagined them, and they were nearly weathered away now. They could not find them on Kirk Fell or the Pillar. Either memory had lost their position, or the weather that lived on the heights had erased indignantly their insolent assertion of a triumph.

On the third day they fared forth to climb Scafell Pike. They approached by their own route, the le Faber Approach, which was along the desolate glen of Langstrath. The upper valley of Borrowdale, within the Jaws, forks into two up-slanting arms which grasp, left and right, the huge upheaval of Glaramara. One of these is the pleasant combe of Seathwaite, and the other the long depression of Langstrath. Seathwaite is kind and welcoming; Langstrath is grim, untenanted, discouraging, and apart. There are those who say that at its upper end, where the mountains close in, the air is unnaturally oppressive and sinister, as if the slopes were haunted. It bids one leave it quickly. Few people go further up Langstrath than the foot of Stake Pass; its higher and tapering end is unvisited. And that is why the le Fabers went that way. They liked to go alone into that mysterious silence and to climb up out of it, by their own private track, on to the windy chaos of Esk Hause.

To-day they walked along the west side of the beck, over the humped and bosomy ground that ran beneath the scree and the crags of Glaramara. This blue-green bottom was strewn with boulders and monoliths and loaves of slate-grey stone. Above it the long hem of Glaramara's skirt was covered with a pelt of bracken, so densely packed that it looked, from a distance, like moss. There was real moss between this and the scree, and much of it was swollen with some vegetable sickness into bosses of a sodden yellow. Once the deep dyke of Langstrath had been thick woodland, from the beck in its bottom to the bare crags above, but the iron smelters had long since felled the forest, and there were no trees among the boulders now except a few wind-vexed hollies and thorns.

"A sweet little valley, isn't it?" said Robin to Justin, after they had walked a mile along it, matching its silence with their own. "Inhuman, I think, and just a little malign."

"I love it," said Justin.

Another hour was needed before they were out of it and in the larger air on the tops. Here they met a sudden clash of wind and sunlight; and the clouds bore away; and they saw the mists leaving the crests like spindrift from breakers that have heaved up under a gale.

There was no trace on the rocky crest of Scafell of their own private cairn. It had been dismantled and scattered over that high wilderness of rocks, either by the despoiling hands of men, or, slowly and in His own time, by the dispassionate fingers of God.

"Here we have no abiding monument," said Robin.

And promptly—vain of his Biblical knowledge—Justin added, " 'Some there be which have no memorial; who are perished as though they had never been. . . . But these were merciful men, the le Fabers, whose righteousness hath not been forgotten.' "

Noon behind them, they came down from the mountain, filled with the exultation of achievement and conquest. And, talking and laughing, leaping and exploring, tossing jokes and plunging into argument, they lost the cairns that should have guided them home.

They had been descending what seemed an arrested avalanche of rocks—a catastrophe stabilized in its course for ever —and now they had come upon the first vegetation, which sprang from a slope whose edge met the sky.

"Hell!" exclaimed Justin. "This is wrong."

"We've never been here before," agreed Robin.

"And it doesn't look too healthy either." He glanced down at his shadow. The afternoon sun had laid it on his left. "We've been going east. We ought to have been going northeast *into* our shadows. This is fun. We're lost."

"Out with the maps," cried Robin, unslinging his rucksack.

"Out with the compass," amended Justin. And he fetched it from his pocket and, happy as a child with a toy, turned back the prism and held it to his eye. "Christ!—if you'll pardon the blasphemy, Reverend—the bearing is one hundred and twenty-five degrees. We're actually going south-east."

"And where are we now?" Robin had his map open and was frowning over it.

"God knows."

"We're somewhere on Ill Crag. About here. Seems to me that if we steer due north we shall come to the first shelter just above the Hause. Agreed, gentlemen?"

"Agreed. But it also seems to me, young Robin, that we've got a precipice on our right all the way."

"Undoubtedly. But what of it?"

"As you say: What of it? It'll keep us from straying to the right. If we walk a few yards to the right, old son, we walk into Heaven, and I don't feel they're ready for me there yet, whatever they may think about you." He walked to the brink—or to two feet this side of it. Slowly he leaned forward and looked down. "My crikey! Sheer. Sheer for fifty feet, and then some damned uncomfortable stuff to fall on."

Robin came to his side—or nearly. He, too, and very carefully, looked down. The cliff presented a deep frieze of wrinkled and fissured rock to the eastern sky. Below this was a debris of fractured boulders and split slates, then a steep of stones and scree, and lastly a green and slanting gully, watered by a writhing beck, as if it were a small, sad sister of Langstrath.

"Yes. . . ." murmured Justin, looking down at the precipice again. "I think we'll give this a wide berth."

"The widest, if you please."

" 'Try not the pass,' the old boy said."

And so they returned to the cascade of rocks down which they had come, and they walked northward, Justin using his compass for the pleasure of it, and talking about Magnetic Variations and Local Magnetic Attraction, to display his knowledge.

But this cap of green and stony fell did not allow them to give the cliff edge a wide berth. It narrowed. It narrowed from a cap to a ribbon. And not only did it narrow; it grew steeper, till at last there was only about fourteen feet of herbage and stones between the soaring rocks and the sheer precipice. Neither Justin nor Robin exclaimed or gulped or made a sound of any kind. Neither would admit to the other that his head was unequal to these moments when Vertigo walked between them and the precipice. Robin even went ahead of his brother to suggest that he was unafraid. And Justin, later, did likewise. But they did not speak. They could not spare the courage or the energy to speak. The whole of their will, the whole of their power, was concentrated on getting safely along this narrow and dreadful shelve. Justin was the first to grasp the rocks at his side, but Robin immediately grasped them too. And then, just as they feared a break-down of will and self-mastery, they saw that a little way on, only such a little way, the narrow, tormenting tilt opened out again into a broad and gentle patch of fell.

In silence, step by step, their hearts constricted and yet pulsing and emptying, they reached that broad and easy shoulder.

"H'mmm. . . ." said Justin, when he stood at last on that small Elysian Field where all was exhilaration and joy. "Not so bad. Not to be compared with Lord's Rake or the Eagle Traverse."

Robin did not answer. He could not so lie. And both knew that these last few minutes—first on that incline of horror, and then of a sudden on this shelf of safety, had been the worst and the best they had known together on the mountains. Both knew that when the sharp edge of the horror had become a little dulled in memory, they would begin to feel the mountaineer's ache to return and repeat the exalting experience.

§

Two more days, and this happy holiday would be over. All to-morrow, all the day after, and then they must exchange Deep Langstrath for the London train. It had been a completely happy holiday, Robin was telling himself, as he and Justin sat in the parlour of the white cottage at seven o'clock in the evening. Not once had he felt any of that hot hostility towards Justin which could so distress his heart because it laid waste a partnership that he had loved. Justin away from Primrose, away from Mr. Cumberland, away from humanity, and alone with wild nature and Robin, had been nothing but a vessel packed with animal spirits, high jocularity, and daring enterprise. Robin had been able to rest in his old affection.

In the little low-ceiled parlour, where the table was spread for supper beneath the deep-embrasured window, four people were seated, waiting for Mrs. Huxley, the lady of this apartment house, to come in with her tray. In chairs on either side of the fireplace sat an elderly man and his wife. They belonged to a party of holiday-makers whose younger people were quartered next door. On a sofa against the wall sat Justin, his legs before him. On a chair by the table sat Robin. Both were reading the day's papers, which had not arrived in the morning when they left the cottage to climb. And as they read, their bodies were passive vehicles of pleasure— the pleasure that is in cleanness after sweat and in rest after fatigue.

When Robin had exhausted his *Manchester Guardian* he rested his chin on his hand and looked out of the window. But he did not see the cottages opposite or the woody slope behind them; he was seeing West Street, Lavant and West Wall and the house of the Lowthers. Four days—about ninety hours— and he would be back in Lavant. He would be there by early afternoon. Before three o'clock he would be approaching the house in West Wall. She would know he was coming and be ready to run out to him. Ninety-two hours.

He had received a few letters from her; one a week; but they were long diary letters, fervently added to day by day. The last but one, following him to Deep Langstrath, had told him that they were not going away for August after all, but were going to have a "jolly holiday at home with tennis parties and picnics by the sea. So I shall be there when you return. Isn't that splendid?" The next letter had described the tennis parties and the bathing parties at East Fettering, and begged him to take care of himself on those shocking mountains. Perhaps there would be another letter before he left Deep Langstrath; to-morrow, perhaps. . . . He rehearsed the first words he would say to her, and thought with the beginnings of an ecstasy of her welcoming embrace. He felt sorry for the old couple by the fireplace who had left such joys behind them.

On the sofa Justin had also exhausted his *Times*, but since there was nothing else he desired to read in the brief while before supper, he scanned it again in search of any interest that he had missed. He considered the advertisements and announcements on the front page. His eyes travelled lazily down the first column. And suddenly his eyes rested. His brows met together. He read something. He read it again. Then he gave a quick glance at his brother, unobserved, for Robin was gazing out of the window.

A moment of motionless thinking, and he turned to an inner page. He read something there; he lowered the paper, and with eyes staring over it gave himself to thought.

Only when pursuing his own ends did Justin dispense with pity. In a matter that touched him not at all he would not wish others, and least of all, Robin, to be hurt. He was wondering now how best to act so that Robin should be least hurt. Should he perhaps say nothing till they were home? Or should he say nothing at any time and let Robin learn the news in his own way? Some selfishness hurried to the support of these ideas because, if Robin knew nothing, they could enjoy their last days together.

But no. Old Robin ought to know. He might want to do something about it. He would certainly want to do something about it, and at once. He looked at Robin, and there was a fixed interest as well as pity in his look. One looks so at a condemned man. He looked at the old couple, the woman knitting, the man gazing into vacancy and tapping his wrinkled fingers on the arm of his chair.

"Rob," he said, rising up.

"Yes?"

"Come outside a minute." This was signalled rather than said.

"Why?"

"Come. I'll tell you." Justin led him out of the parlour, taking the paper as it was, unfolded, and gathered up between finger and thumb.

"What the hell . . ?" laughed Robin.

They passed into the passage and through the front door which was open to the evening. Justin went along the stony path to the gate in the garden wall. He opened the gate and stood on the far side of the wall.

This Cumberland cottage, which had held so much of their happiness when they were boys, was a stumpy two-storied place, built of local stone and whitewashed, with two low windows on either side of a gabled porch. A dry-stone wall enclosed a square of garden in front. The garden now was an exhibition of colour: sweet williams, crimson and purple and pink, springing from the beds, ferns and fuschias and dark cotoneasters crowding under the sills, and sweet peas and roses climbing about the porch. Stonecrop, yellow and white, toadflax and parsley fern perched in the crevices of the dry garden wall and lay along its coping like small embroidered cushions.

Justin leaned back against the wall. Robin stood before him, inquiry still laughing in his eyes. "What's all this about?" he asked.

"There's something I want to ask you. And not in front of those old bodies in there."

"Well, what is it?"

"Your girl——"

Instantly Robin smiled, and Justin saw that the mere mention of her was a delight to him.

"——her name was Bryn Lowther, wasn't it?"

"Yes."

"And she was the daughter of the Rev. Alfred Lowther and granddaughter of a Canon Lowther?"

"Yes. Certainly." No hint of alarm in Robin's answers.

"Well, old man, I'm afraid——"

"What?" Now the alarm was on his face like a white flag.

"I'm afraid you've got a shock coming."

"What? Justin, *what*?"

"Sorry, Rob, old man." Justin handed him the paper, pointing to something on the first page.

Hands quivering, Robin took the paper and read.

"LOWTHER. On August 11th after a brief illness, at West Gate House, West Wall, Lavant, BRYN, the beloved daughter of the Rev. Alfred and Mrs. Lowther and granddaughter of Canon Kennedy Lowther. Aged 18 years."

Justin laid a sympathetic hand on his brother's arm.

Robin stared down at the paper.

"There's a brief reference to it here, old chap." Justin turned the pages in Robin's unresisting hands. He pointed to the last and smallest of the notices under the heading "Obituary".

"MISS BRYN LOWTHER. Canon Berring writes: The untimely death of Bryn Lowther, the young and only daughter of the Rev. Alfred Lowther of this city, and granddaughter of Canon Lowther, Librarian of the Cathedral, has come as a shock to innumerable friends and indeed to the whole city. For there was no one to whom she was not known, at least by sight, so young, vital, and happy a figure was she in our midst. A fulminant septicæmia, resulting from no more than a thorn-scratch when she was playing tennis—of which game she was an ardent and remarkable young player—brought about her death within a couple of days, before most of us knew that she was ill. A few hours of high fever that quickly passed into coma, and Bryn Lowther was gone from among us. The whole city mourns with her family which is among the most honoured in this town and diocese of Lavant. The funeral will take place to-morrow in her father's church."

Robin handed the paper back to Justin. "I'm going for a walk up the valley," he said.

"It's she, of course?"

"Yes."

"My God, old man, I'm sorry."

"It's Bryn all right."

"Nothing I can do, is there?"

"No, thanks. . . . It's she. . . . oh!" And, lest anyone should be seeing him, he walked quickly away.

There were trees and walled pastures at this end of the valley, and a wet, stony road under the trees. The road led into the sombre heart of Langstrath and there became a nameless track through the desolation. Robin went up that stony road, a tall, youthful figure; and soon a bend in it hid him from Justin's eyes.

Justin shrugged his shoulders helplessly, looked for a moment at the sun which was sinking between Dale Head and Scawdel, and turned back into the garden. His pity for Robin was still there, but now it was accompanied by a new visitor,

and this was a feeling of relief that a race in which Robin had
outstripped him should have been so quickly annulled.

§

Hidden in the road, because it was flanked by stone walls
and roofed with trees, Robin let his head droop and his steps
flag. But he wandered slowly on, sometimes lifting his head
to see the last of the sunlight resting on Eagle Crag and
Greenup Edge.

"Oh, Bryn, Bryn. . . ."

Bryn was lying dead in that white house. She had been
lying there for two days, while he had been striding along the
high ridges, shouting songs for joy. Why had he felt nothing?
Heard nothing? Why had not a vision of her come to him as
she died?

"Oh, Bryn, are you able to see me where I am now?   I
loved you."

Dead. She had gone from him for ever. Gone before he
knew anything about her. How strange, how heart-searing,
to think that he would never know anything about her now.
Never know what the dreams were that clouded her eyes as
she walked home from school. Never know what her character
was in its depths. Never know—to take a little matter—what
it was that had delayed her on the morning he left Lavant and
obliged her to come running through the Bishop's Meadows to
wave to his train. He knew only that she had seemed very
beautiful to him and that he had wanted her and that she had
come running to him with her love. She would never be more
than a symbol now: the symbol of that which he had wanted
from the world.

"Good-bye, Bryn. Good-bye." He was saying these words
aloud to the road, and deliberately, because they were merci-
less daggers that he was driving into his heart.

Steps and voices on the road. Oh, he could not be seen by
anybody. He wanted no one near him. A gate in the wall led
on to the steep side of High Knott and on to a track that
climbed towards Tarn at Leaves. He went through it, and
up and up the woodland track, away from men.

Why had she died like this? Why had God killed her?
There was no sense in it, and he was not going to bow his head
and say there was. Ah, this was relief, this passion of rebellion.
Was he going to devote his life to a God who had chosen to

kill Bryn in the beauty and pride of her youth, and to kill
her by the playful, cynical, method of a scratch with a thorn?
No, thank you! Not he. Never, never. That was done with.
He was finished with God. If "the President of the Immortals
had finished his sport" with Bryn, then he too had finished
his work for the President. He was no longer his gilly, to aid
and abet him in sport like this. "I don't play. I don't play
any more," said Robin wildly to the side of High Knott. Oh
no: henceforward he was among those who were against God.
Like his father he would hate the Church and its clergy and
all that they preached. Oh, yes, this was settled. This was
settled by the grave of Bryn. And he would not only hate God,
he would fight against Him wherever and whenever he could.

Ha, he'd done with trying to be good! God, yes. He would
be like Justin and pursue only his own aims. Always he had
seen a cogency in Justin's contention that if you believed no
longer in God, or cared no longer for him, or rejoiced to defy
him, the only thing to do was to work for yourself by every
means that was out of the eye of the Law.

"Bryn, Bryn. . . ."

He was far up the flank of High Knott now, in a grassy and
rock-strewn solitude, above the bracken and the foxgloves and
the ferns. Above him was the terrible overhanging masonry
of Herple Crag, dark now that the sunlight had fallen from it.
Why not climb and climb through the evening to the brink
of that black wrinkled forehead and hurl himself down?

But no: he was not going to be defeated like that. Oh, no.
He stopped; he stood still; he clenched his fists and his teeth;
anger gleamed like two steel points in his eyes; all the fiery
hostility he could feel against Justin when he was cruel he
now directed against God. Staring, not upward like a child,
but directly before him like a man who believes that if God
is anywhere, He is everywhere, he said to Him: "I have
finished. I loved her, and I'm not going to accept this. I
loved her. And she loved her life and me. And you've killed
her for no reason in Heaven or earth. I don't bow down under
this. Not I. If I could destroy you, I would. But I can do my
best to destroy your work in the world. And I will. I will.
I'll destroy it wherever I can find it. And you can do what you
like to me. I shan't care. You may have all the power to
destroy me, but you have no power to make me serve you any
more."

By these defiant words he felt eased. He unclenched his

fist and parted his teeth. And in the depths of him, though he would not hearken, he knew that this was a storm that would pass.

"I worship you no more. Oh, *no*. I worship the memory of Bryn who came running to me with her love. And now I shall never see her again. Never, never, never. Not in this world or in eternity because I no longer believe in eternity. We're just here to suffer or be . . . Oh, Bryn. . . ." The relief was ending. His head drooped again and his hands gripped each other behind his back, their finger nails pressing into his palms. And he let the pain rack and wrench him, telling himself, "This won't last long. This won't last for ever."

Then, numbed, indifferent, despairing, and heedless of any path, he came stumbling down through the oaks and stones, through the bracken and moss and old leaves.

How could he go back to Lavant and look at that white house; at that door through which she had come; at that place on the old wall? How could he bear to speak of her to anyone, or hear anyone speak of her? Never perhaps would he speak of her again or stand where her name could be heard. One does not disturb too great a pain. . . .

When he was on the road he walked homeward very slowly because he did not want to meet anyone at the cottage or be spoken to.

What was he going back to, now that he had abandoned all thought of service as a priest?

Yes, what?

The dry-walls that marched with the road were high, but Robin was tall, and he went to the one from which he could overlook the valley and rested his elbows on its olive-green stones. The whole valley as far as the Jaws of Borrowdale was a basin of milky haze, with Castle Crag lifting its pine-burdened shoulder above it.

And Robin, touched by the beauty of it, knew that even in this riot of rebellion he could feel sad at the thought of giving up a desire that had dwelt with him so long and still seemed beautiful. Could he not love his fellows even while defying and hating God? Nay, since they were his fellow-victims, could not his love of them be in proportion to his hatred of God?

Yes—oh yes—and he was *not* going to give up his desire to love and serve them. He had no quarrel with *them*. Astonishing the relief it was to get back to his desire. Clearly he was in love with his desire as well as with Bryn. And now that he had lost Bryn, the more need to keep and hold close the other loved thing.

"Oh yes. Nothing matters but goodness and kindness and love. Nothing else matters in the world. I want nothing else. And never did I long for them more than now, oh, Bryn, Bryn. . . ."

But what was this desire that dwelt so powerfully within him that it could not be withstood for long? What could it be but God Himself? Was it not the God of Compassion and Love Who rises slowly in the hearts of men and, having risen, is not easily put down again?

Robin picked at the toadflax and moss that lay along the coping of the dry-stone wall. Some minutes ago, on the steep hillside, he had said to God, "You have no power to make me serve you any more;" and here, it seemed, was God's answer, offered without anger, "But, you see, I have."

To go back and deal only (so far as was possible to a weak, impatient, hot-tempered man) in kindness and compassion and hope—it seemed very good again, and the only healing. To go on loving and serving, with his doubts hampering his feet, and his hasty and self-centred humours beating him often to his knees.

What now then? His head remained bent for a long time over the wall, and then with a sigh he turned away and walked homeward. "When I have recovered from this, I will begin again."

Thus it was that an immortal longing which is in men rose up again in Robin after he supposed he had slain it. It was bound to do so, just because it is immortal.

PART III

CHAPTER ONE

An autumn evening, sixteen years later, was gathering on Chiswick Mall. It was half-past six, and the roadway between the fine old mansions and the river was empty of all but a few pedestrians. A pair of lovers, interlaced, walked along by the gardens that bordered the river. They were walking straight into the low-hung sun of October, which threw a horizontal light on the gold and sallow leaves of the riverside trees and on the crimson creepers that wrapped the walls of the old houses. The river itself was still and quiet, for the tide was out and the wind had gone with it. It had left behind only a pleasant reek of mud and brine and old tarred timbers. The quiet on the mall and on the remnant of the river was so complete and so tenuous that you could hear the birds moving among the willows of the eyot and footsteps and voices in the green places on the farther bank.

When architects and romantics walk along Chiswick Mall, to please their eyes with the old eighteenth-century houses, they will indicate four that are of the first order of beauty, and four that are less than perfect but very gracious and agreeable. The first four are Walpole, Mount Cluny, Eynham, and Bedford houses, and the other four are Strawberry, Lingard, and Woodruffe houses and the old vicarage by the church. On this evening of which we are speaking the three tall windows on the first floor of Mount Cluny House were full of light, their blinds undrawn, so that the passers-by were able to see something of the people within. These appeared to be many. "That's Gerard le Faber's house," said the girl to her lover as they came along; and, still interlaced, the two paused and looked up at the bright windows on the chance of seeing the famous man pass across them.

"The Beloved would appear to be giving a party," suggested the girl. "Now isn't that sweet of him?"

"Not the first party in that house," said the young man, who was more interested in the two-hundred-years-old house than in its present occupant. "Can't you see the carriages rumbling up to those gates in the old days, and the footmen coming to the door——" A cataract of laughter tumbled down towards him from the tall windows; and in their light, of a sudden, he saw the light of truth. "Why, of course!" he exclaimed. "It's the first night of his new play."

"So it is. So it is. How bright you are, dear. And the Blessed Creature's giving a party to celebrate. Wonder who he's got there. A whole lot of celebrities, I expect. Half the theatre world. Oh, I wish he'd invited me. Come on, darling, we're not wanted here. We're only the public who pay our shillings to go in—his 'dear public' as he always calls us in his speech at the end of a long run. Good-bye, Gerard, my blessing, and all the best for to-night. Come on, darling, leave them to it."

The girl was right about the nature of the party but wrong about the celebrities. The only celebrity behind the three windows was Gerard himself. Possibly you might add Anne, his wife, though as an actress the world was beginning to forget her. She was "Anne Raven" no longer but Gerard le Faber's wife. The rest of the people in that long drawing-room, painted cream and gold and furnished in the Adam style, were merely the members of his family.

Gerard himself stood with his back to the fire, his heels on the fender and his hands in his pockets. His mother, white-haired now, sat in the easy chair on his left, with Bozzy at her side on a hard, upright chair. Beyond them, and round the room on various chairs and sofas were Justin and Primrose, Hector and his wife, Gerard's two daughters, Constantine and Rosemary, aged fourteen and thirteen, in their party frocks, and on the longest sofa of all, with Anne, their hostess, between them (since they were the only ones she really liked) Robin and his wife, Lady Jessica.

Three of the brothers, Justin, Gerard, and Hector, were now in their forties, and the forties sat well on them. Even Hector, though fat, was not without a certain distinction, since he was tall, well-dressed, prosperous-looking, and prematurely bald. His brow, scalp, and occiput were now one continuous shining surface. An air of authority, untroubled by self-criticism, had always hung about Hector, and now that he was Accountant and Deputy Manager of his bank it had increased in weight and was a very palpable concentration indeed. Justin's hair was as dark and plentiful as ever, and

Robin's was the same iron-grey it had been at twenty-two. Gerard, with his brown hair worn rather long but most carefully arranged and set; with his long upper lip, his mobile mouth, and his graceful movements; and dressed in a dinner jacket that was slightly different from the normal since it had a velvet collar, looked exactly what he was: an actor of repute whom women adored.

All the brothers except Bozzy were in evening dress. Bozzy was the one deviation from the general distinction. He had neither the height nor the good features nor the alert, intelligent eyes of the other brothers. And he was not in evening dress because, though he was thirty-eight now, his mother had never bought him one. It had never seemed necessary to buy Bozzy an evening dress because he did not go to dances or dinners, being different from other men, but stayed in his mother's house or wandered about the streets alone. Bozzy was in his best black church-going suit, with spats, and his greying hair was darkened with water and plastered down for Gerard's First Night.

Gerard glanced at the watch on his wrist. He did it surreptitiously. He had done it a dozen times in the last few minutes but only Anne had noticed it. He had also gulped and swallowed many times; and more than once he had not heard what someone said to him but had looked at his watch instead; and all the time his vivacity had been somewhat overacted, and his voice too loud as he ordered them to take more sherry—"More sherry, boys"—or his voice had got caught up in his breath and tripped over his words, and broken down for a second, so that he had to cough and clear his throat and begin again, more jovially than ever. "More sherry, Jessica?" Once or twice he had sighed as if his breathing were out of order, and once or twice he had wiped the palms of his hands with a silk handkerchief, and once touched the nape of his neck with it. But only Anne had remarked these things and understood.

Justin sat on an upright chair with his long legs crossed and his mouth set for silence. He was polite when spoken to, but he hardly spoke at all. He did not seem to be enjoying the party. Anne watched him, but not so that anyone would notice it: she was too good an actress for that.

Suddenly all the chatter and laughter died and there was an inexplicable and uncomfortable silence. Someone must break it, but everyone left this duty to someone else. It was

Primrose who spoke at last and, as was to be expected of that unfortunate and unwise woman, she said archly and with exaggerated gaiety the one thing Gerard hated to hear.

"Aren't you at all nervous, Gerard?" she asked.

"Oh no," said Gerard; and gulped.

"Well, *I* should be."

"I've been at the game too long," explained Gerard; and his voice was inclined to break as he said it.

"I should be dead," pursued Primrose as unwisely as ever. "To think of all those hundreds of people and all the critics and all my family and friends—all sitting and waiting for me to begin—oh, I should die!"

"Damn the woman," thought Gerard; and aloud he conceded generously: "Oh, well, there's always a certain anxiety that things should go off properly." And he gulped again. "That's all."

"Well, I think it's wonderful," declaimed Primrose. "Absolutely wonderful."

"Oh no, just a matter of habit," stuttered Gerard.

Anne put out like a speed-boat to his rescue. "*He's* never nervous. He's amazing. When I used to act, I used to be *sick* with nerves on a first night. My inside used to go up and down like a lift that had gone crazy—and it was the emptiest lift in all the world, I'd have you know. My one consolation was that it would be all over and forgotten in a hundred years. But Gerard never turns a hair."

"Oh, but I'm always a little anxious till things get started," Gerard insisted, as one who was both modest and sincere. "But I don't let it worry me too much and spoil my dinner." The mention of dinner made him feel a little sick.

Bozzy in the meanwhile was explaining to all who would listen to him, and garrulously, his relations with God. The only two who would listen were Jessica and his mother; and as his mother was sitting at his side and Jessica opposite him, he was able to swing about and lean right forward to explain at length the current situation. The rest of the family, wives and all, had given up listening to Bozzy years ago. They just left him talking and continued their conversation with others.

Bozzy had recently found God, and his mother was glad of it because it kept him amused. He had found Him in a Shepherds Bush Meeting House, when he wandered in one evening with his wash-leather gloves and his cane. But the others were not so glad of it because it certainly didn't keep him quiet; it inspired him to preach his gospel and deliver a continuous and spluttering message whenever an opportunity opened before him. And now when Gerard conceded that he could be anxious, and a second silence dropped upon the company, Bozzy felt that a word would clearly be in season. So he proclaimed it in the silence. "You would not have to be anxious, Gerard, if you trusted in God."

"Oh, well . . ." Gerard, not knowing what to reply, looked again at his watch; Justin muttered: *"Tst, Tst!"* and the children, Constantine and Rosemary, thrust their fists into their mouths to stop their giggling.

" 'Cast all your care upon God for He careth for you,' " explained Bozzy.

"Precisely," agreed Gerard.

"Oh hell!" mumbled Justin.

"That's what it says in the Word." Bozzy's voice was a rich and powerful baritone, which always sounded strange, coming from one whose mental development was obviously small. "And it's perfectly true. The only perfectly happy people are those whose life is hid with Christ in God."

"I see," nodded Gerard.

" 'Perfect love casteth out fear,' " Bozzy quoted further.

"Yes, dear." His mother patted his knee. "That'll do."

"Isn't it funny," asked Primrose, dancing her shoulders up and down somewhat kittenishly, "that your father who so hated the Church and parsons should have had so many sons who are religious: Robin a clergyman, Justin a sidesman, and now Bozzy——"

"For God's sake don't couple me with that imbecile," muttered Justin.

Primrose blushed at the rebuke, heard only by her. "And Hector goes regularly to church too," she stumbled on. "Hector is quite a pillar of the Church."

"A very stout pillar," laughed Gerard.

"Hector serves both God and Mammon, I'm afraid," Robin hinted with a grin. "And he does both very weightily."

"You cannot serve both God and Mammon," announced Bozzy, having good authority for this.

"He shouldn't be allowed out," grumbled Justin under his breath to Primrose.

Happily the butler entered at this moment and announced that dinner was served.

"Good! That's fine," said Gerard; and swallowed, since the
idea of food made a cramping in his throat. "I'm hungry.
Lead on, Justin. Take Mum down. I'm sure *I* ought to really,
but damn all punctilio. Lead on, you people. I've something I
want to fix up with Anne."

They all trooped out and down the stairs to the dining-room,
and Gerard and Anne were left alone.

"My God, Anne . . ." began Gerard.

"I know, dear," comforted Anne. "But it's working fine."

"Is it?"

"Yes, he's not liking it the least little bit."

"I know he isn't. I can see that, but, my God, what about
me? I'm in a blue funk. I've got stage fright. Pure stage
fright."

"And he's going to like it still less before the night's out.
There'll be no spirit left in him when he goes home to-night. *I*
shall see to that."

"But, Anne, I'm wishing I were dead."

"Of course you are, you darling. I've seen that for the last
hour, my poor sweet."

"I've never felt so awful."

"Oh, yes, you have. You're always like this. And the
worse you feel now, the better you act once you've got
started. Have you ever failed yet?"

"No, but, Anne—Anne—oh, don't go down yet—I haven't
had *him* there before. I wish now we'd never asked him. It'll
be ten times worse with him in the theatre."

"Nonsense, pet. I've been aching for this night for years.
I've dreamed and dreamed of it. And don't forget to say that
bit about me when we drink your health."

"Oh, what was that? What was that?"

"That I'd simply made you. That you owe everything to
your dear partner and wife. It's none of it very true, but I
want him to hear you say it, because he always said I'd be the
ruin of you."

"All right, all right; but suppose I break down with him in
the theatre? Oh, why did we ever play this damned silly
game? I shall suddenly think of him in the theatre and fluff
my lines or dry up altogether. And all he'll witness'll be my
humiliation, not my triumph. It'll be his triumph. . . . Oh
my God!"

"Rubbish. It'll work the other way. The thought of him
there'll make you act as you've never acted before. Tell

yourself all the time that he said you'd never do anything."

"Oh, why does anyone choose to be an actor?"

"Because the people's applause is worth everything that went before. Because of the ovation that's coming to you at eleven o'clock to-night. Now come along."

§

There was one main purpose in this family party of Gerard and Anne's, and it was the discomfiture of Justin. Gerard was now manager of the New Comedy Theatre in association with Quilter Collins. Quilter Collins—"old Q.C." to the theatrical world—was the financier, and Gerard was in complete control of the productions and policy of the famous theatre. He was also the producer of all the plays and their leading actor. For these services he received an annual salary of four thousand pounds and a quarter of the profits. For some years Anne had played with him, but not often now. She was less ambitious than he, and the memory of her years of drudgery on the stage, and the knowledge that youth had fallen from her cheeks and black hair, leaving lines and grey threads behind, had made her quite ready to retire into home life with her two little daughters and her baby boy. She was content to be the wife of Gerard le Faber and to hope that one day he would be knighted and she become Lady le Faber.

The le Faber-Collins management at the New Comedy had had its failures, but far more successes, and it had now, after seven years, a tradition of success behind it. It was difficult for a new le Faber play at the New Comedy to fail. Gerard's first nights were fashionable London occasions. And to-night promised to be the greatest *première* of his career. He was teamed up with Dora Carlyle in a new play by Floyd Bain, a drawing-room comedy that was wittier than anything this graceful writer had done before and at the same time far more substantial and more moving. It was in the tradition of the le Faber successes and yet it was something more.

Already the rumour had run over theatrical London that Gerard le Faber had a wonderful play with a wonderful part for him in it, and that its first night was going to be a great occasion. The chief part had been written for him and therefore fitted him like a new suit, but while it was a suit that became him well, it was also a garment in a new fashion.

Both Gerard and Anne, but especially Anne, had long wished

that Justin could be present to hear the reception that greeted
Gerard's first appearance on a first night, and the cheers and
applause that beat about him and his company—his young
devotees, chiefly feminine, leaning over the gallery-rail to
roar their hearts out at him—as he stepped forward to make
a speech at the play's end.   But never had he been in the
theatre on a first night; and they liked to think that this was
because an ovation for a younger brother would be hard for
him to bear.   And they determined to get him there.

"We must! We must!" Anne would cry.   "We must while you
still have this enormous public.   I don't mean that you'll ever
lose it, ducky heart, but you never know with the theatre: it
may fall away a little . . . just a little . . . and I want Justin to
have seen you on the top of the wave, God, how I hate him."

And the greater grew their hopes of this present play, the
more they determined that he must be there this time.   And
Anne, meditating on this necessity, possessed by it, conceived
the idea of a family party.   Justin, who was not without grace,
would not spoil such an occasion by refusing to come; especially if Anne honeyed her trap by insisting that he was "the
head of the family."   And when she received his acceptance,
she danced for joy and hugged Gerard and said, "Oh, this is
perfect.   I've waited for this for years.   This is the end of my
darling Justin."

§

Justin could show no success comparable with Gerard's.
He had done one of the things he had boasted he would do.
As an external candidate at London University he had taken
his Matriculation, Intermediate, and Finals, and was now a
B.A.   And Justin le Faber, B.A., Lond., could stand comfortably alone as headmaster.   He no longer needed Mr. Cumberland for his window.   And shortly after this Mr. Cumberland died.   Seventy-four, and lonely and dejected, he had
acquired the habit of slipping guiltily from the house when
supper was done and wandering into saloon bars after the
comfort of whisky—much to Justin's annoyance and disgust.   Wandering carelessly about the streets one wintry night,
not quite sober, he contracted a chill; pneumonia set in, and in
ten days he was dead.   He was lying dead in Justin's own room.

A fact much remarked upon at the time was Justin's goodness and helpfulness during the old man's illness and after his
death.   Once when his chill seemed no more than a severe cold

Justin himself took him out to a public house and gave him some strong whiskies, since, as he said: "a little of what the old man fancied more than anything else might prove the best medicine;" when the pneumonia set in, he gave up his own room to him because it was the sunniest, and went and slept upstairs in Mr. Cumberland's attic; after the old man's death he took all the arrangements for the funeral into his own hands and relieved the weeping Primrose of every perplexity and care. And no one published his goodness to the neighbourhood more fervently than Primrose. Justin was so *good*, she would say, the tears welling up into her eyes. It pleased her to be able, with sincerity, to present Justin as an affectionate husband, because she feared that others gave him a different character, and this fear made her feel inferior in the presence of her neighbours. "He did everything," she would declare. "I can't imagine what I should have done without him. He saw the undertaker and chose the grave and arranged everything with the vicar for a lovely service, and he bought a really beautiful wreath. I thought it was the most beautiful of all."

To Robin Justin pooh-pooh'd this tale of his goodness and avowed with the usual deliberately shocking frankness, "My dear boy, I was hoping devoutly all the time that he would die. And when he did I was profoundly relieved. I'd been beginning to fear that he'd live for ever. These old parsons, once they pass seventy, are as near as possible immortal. Yes, I know you liked the old sinner, but I found him a most offensive old man. Everything about him offended me. I used to run from the sight of him. He was dirty and slovenly and an appalling old hypocrite, and when he took to pub-crawling it was the last straw. I felt it was high time he was gathered to his fathers. Oh, yes, I know I went a bit of a mucker on that wreath, but then I never bought anything with a greater pleasure."

Of course it was only to Robin that he said such things. Before the world of Hammersmith, in the days after the old Duke's death, he maintained the mien of one who was much grieved by the loss of an old friend. At the funeral in the church which Mr. Cumberland had served he followed behind the coffin, with Primrose on his arm, sharing with her the gloom, the solemnity, and the dignity that invest the principal mourners. To the assembled boys and staff of Erasmus Hall he spoke with some eloquence about the virtues of their late headmaster and of his grief at the loss of a good colleague; and at

Matins in the church next Sunday, which was treated as a kind of Memorial Service for a late assistant priest, he read the special lesson with a marked though restrained feeling.

All this was ten years ago now, and in the intervening years Justin had advanced more and more in the good opinion of his neighbours. There was now no more honoured resident in these parts of Hammersmith and Shepherds Bush. He was a prominent figure in the congregation of St. Anselm's, with his parade of small, black-coated boys above whom he towered like a black monument; he was also an audible figure when he sang the hymns lustily. He had never accepted the office of churchwarden, though it had been tendered to him more than once, but he had been a sidesman for the last seven years or so, and regularly at the end of Matins he collected the offerings of the faithful. One advantage of this task, as he said to Robin, was that he never had to put anything into the plate himself. He took an active part in all good causes, provided they were uncontroversial and could raise no hostility among likely parents. He was on the committee of the local branch of the League of Nations Union, which it was almost as wise to support as the Church of England; he had spoken more than once on behalf of the Save the Children Fund; for one year he had acted as Treasurer of the Diocesan Council of Youth; and he was ready to lend his School Hall for meetings of the Council of Moral Welfare or the Diocesan Rescue Society. If invited, he would say a few encouraging words at such meetings. He had the reputation of being a good speaker, but in actual fact his desire to speak better than others and his fear of failure were so great that he would write his speeches out beforehand, learn them by heart, and rehearse them in his bedroom for days before. On these occasions he was an actor like Gerard, and nearly as good a one.

But his school itself was something much less, very much less, than his boyish dreams had made of it. It was no longer in the Grove but occupied a large grey double-fronted house in Vandermere Road and a smaller house adjoining. In the garden he had built the large hall and gymnasium of which he used to speak, but he had certainly not been able to withdraw into the quiet and leisure of a Headmaster's Residence, while salaried subordinates earned an income for him. Even now, after twenty years, the school provided only moderate profits. The truth was, he had been wrong in his estimate of Hammersmith and Shepherds Bush as a good centre for a middle-class school. The great change in the speed of traffic which had marked the changing of the centuries had not filled the district with a vast reservoir of middle-class parents but had carried them right through it and away to the west. He had learned that Erasmus Hall could survive only as a Preparatory School, which it was now; and he had never intended to be the Principal of a school for small boys. After twenty years Justin, though he admitted it to none, was a disappointed man.

Still, only Gerard had surpassed him. Hector was no more than the assistant manager of a bank in Ealing, and Robin no more than the vicar of a poor, and in some parts disreputable, parish in North Kensington. Robin was said to be much loved by his parishioners, and especially by the criminals among them, but beyond the borders of his parish none but a few clergy had heard of him. Justin could persuade himself that Robin's reputation in North Kensington was no wider than his own in Hammersmith.

In one thing, however, Robin had beaten him. Eleven months ago he had married Lady Jessica Christine Seldom, the only daughter and the youngest child of the Earl of Harbury. The fact that she was an earl's daughter, though impressive, was less painful to Justin than the fact that she was young—seventeen years younger than Robin—and dark and slim and attractive and manifestly in love with him. Like Bryn Lowther before her she awoke thoughts in Justin of something which he would have liked to enjoy but had not had the time or the nature to acquire.

This remarkable marriage of young Robin, as it seemed to the le Faber brothers, had come about like this. Two years before, when his labours in his congested and sinful streets had worn him almost to breaking-strain, the Bishop had effected for him a temporary exchange of parishes with the incumbent of a tiny village in Gloucestershire, so that Robin could have a long refreshment in the beauty and peace of the country. The patron of the living, and the most important layman in the congregation (indeed almost the only layman) was the Earl of Harbury, and apart from the Earl's family the congregation consisted of little more than the women servants of the great house. At the end of his six months Robin returned to his slum parish with the love of the Earl's daughter, and her promise to marry him, as his possessions. They were the sweetest possessions he had enjoyed since he brought back the

11

love of Bryn Lowther to the school in the Grove and let it
enclose him in an insulating haze. Jessica had eyes and heart
for nobody but him, though he was nearly twenty years older
than she. She was ready to go with him, not only to a slum
parish, but if necessary to a leper settlement or Dartmoor or
Devil's Island. The Earl, an easy-going man and fond of
Robin (who, as he said somewhat apologetically to his friends,
"is an exceedingly personable fellah, and his bishop thinks
the world of him") consented with the words, "All that I care
for, my boy, is Jessica's happiness. I'm afraid I've had but
one rule all my life: What Jessica wants she must have." So
a few months later Robin took her from the Earl's arm in the
tiny Gloucestershire church, before a congregation that over-
flowed into porch and churchyard, and after a week's honey-
moon in Deep Langstrath, where they often talked about
Bryn, they returned together to his poor and his criminals.
Fortunately, since even the Bishop insisted that it was unwise to be too heroic, the slum parishes of North Kensington
are neighbours to parishes of a very different quality, and the
vicar and his young wife were able to get a very fair house on
the outskirts of their dubious streets near the Portobello Road.

§

Dinner was a splendid meal, and set in splendour. On table
and sideboard, both handsome Adam-style pieces, rose-shaded
candles in tall chandeliers spread their light on silver and
flowers and glasses of many colours and fine white napery.
A butler and two maids moved on soft feet behind the twelve
diners. The dishes were well chosen and tastefully garnished;
wine succeeded wine. Anne had seen to all this, because
Justin had once said that they lived in squalour. And she sat
at her end of the table with Justin on her right and played the
hostess as if she had been born to silver and cut glass and men-
servants and maidservants. She had played fine ladies too
often on the stage not to be able to do it with taste and
accomplishment in her own room.

Even Gerard, though proud of the show, began to feel some
pity for Justin as the shining meal went on. And when it was
over he whispered to Anne, "A bit overpowering, old sweetie,
wasn't it?"

"Oh yes. Yes," she answered. "Certainly. And I haven't
half finished with him yet."

"Have a little pity for the poor old thing, won't you?"

"None at all. The massacre's got to be complete."

"No, no, be a little sporting."

"I'm not going to be anything of the sort. This is war, and I don't believe in any nonsense about being sporting. If I were a general I should believe in having ten times the strength of the enemy, which isn't the least bit sporting. Damn 'sporting'. I believe in making sure. Now be a blossom, my exquisite, and see them into the cars."

Gerard's limousine waited before the gates of the house, its uniformed chauffeur standing by its door. Two other limousines from the Daimler Hire Service stood behind it for the rest of the party.

"Come on, Mother; and Justin, you come in with Anne and me." Anne had made Gerard promise to get Justin in their car, and he knew why. "The others'll come behind."

Soon all were embarked, and the little procession set off. Gerard was still swallowing and gulping, and the jerk of the car as it started for the theatre nearly sent his stomach into his throat. His nervousness was like an imp within him, playing mischievous tricks with his heart.

"I hope we don't look too much like a funeral," laughed Anne.

"If we're a funeral, I'm the corpse," he mumbled to her. "And, come to think of it, I wish to hell I were."

"*Tsh!*" she warned, lest Justin should hear.

But Gerard was too good an actor to let anyone but Anne see his forlorn and hapless condition.

The procession passed along King Street and Hammersmith Road; it passed the entrance to Brook Green—the triumph of one of the le Faber boys, with all his family riding behind.

As the car turned into Lower Shaftesbury Lane Gerard noticed that Anne was leaning forward and peering through the window. He knew what she was hoping to see.

"Look, Gerard!" she cried, as they approached the front of the theatre. "Look, Justin. Look at the crowd watching the people go in. It's enormous. If it's like this now, what'll it be like in a quarter of an hour's time?"

The chauffeur, who'd had his instructions, led the procession past the cars and the crowd at the theatre entrance and, turning into the narrow chasm of Lister Street, stopped at the stage door. And here was another crowd, largely composed of young girls, waiting to see the actors go in, and, above all, Gerard le Faber.

Gerard saw Anne nod to herself with satisfaction.

"Hop out, sweetheart and lovely one," she commanded Gerard, who was nearest the door.

"All right, all right. Plenty of time," he muttered, his voice trembling and stumbling; and he and the little devil within him stepped out on to the pavement.

He was instantly recognized. With a roar of cheering from shrill girls' voices, a drum-fire of applause from sedater persons, and flash after flash from cameramen's flares, the crowd surged towards the car. It was all that a policeman and the chauffeur could do to keep them from its running board.

"Go on, Justin," urged Anne. "You next." And she pushed him from behind into the crowd, as you push a man into the deep end of the baths. Not more enthusiastically did the old witch push Hansel and Gretel into the oven.

Justin was greeted by a silence The crowd did not know who he was. He stood there, a tall sad figure, awkwardly waiting.

His mother followed him, and she too met nothing but silence. Then Anne, gathering her cloak about her, made her exit—or perhaps we should say, her entrance. She stepped on to the pavement, and instantly the cheering and the clapping were renewed for her. Excited women held their hands up high and clapped Anne Raven, Gerard le Faber's wife. She smiled upon them like a queen who had arrived to open a bazaar.

Gerard's car drew away, and the next car came up. Out from its front seats stepped the two girls, Constantine and Rosemary, and they too got an ovation because they were so young, and this was their father's hour. "Aren't they sweet?" cried the women, and clapped and clapped. Their cheeks flamed, and they were as happy as they were abashed.

Anne pressed Gerard's hand and whispered: "It's going well."

"Why does anyone become an actor?" he sighed.

"Come on, folks. Let's get inside quick. Lead the way, Gerard. Go on. Hurry up."

"It's all very fine for you," mumbled Gerard.

"Go on, Justin. Follow Gerard."

"Come on, Justin, old man," invited Gerard, beginning to feel with him a fellowship in suffering.

" 'Evening, sir," greeted the janitor from his office.

" 'Evening, Dick," acknowledged Gerard.

"All the best for to-night, sir."

"Thank you, Dick, old boy."

"Never known more excitement, sir. Telegrams and presents pouring in all day, madam. Good evening, miss. You're going to have a great house, sir. It's almost packed already, they tell me."

"Oh, well. . . ." Gerard walked before them up the stone stairs. So walks a criminal up the steps of the scaffold.

He led the stream of them into his dressing-room.

This was a large room to which, since it was his salon as well as his dressing-room, Anne and he had delighted to add comfort and beauty in the last seven years. On a pile carpet of deep crimson stood a sofa and chairs covered with pale green, a walnut writing-table, a cocktail cabinet, a walnut and satinwood coffee table, and a tall, gilt Victorian screen. On his dressing-table, in front of the big gilt mirror, and on the writing-table, stood large photographs of Anne and the children and of famous actors and actresses (the actresses predominating) who loved him. On the cream walls hung the originals of caricatures of him or of his company that had appeared in illustrated journals. But much of these furnishings was hidden to-night by the baskets, boxes, cartons, and bunches of flowers. And on the dressing-table was a stack of telegrams five inches high.

"Oh, what lovely flowers," gushed Primrose. "I've never seen such a display."

"It's always like this," said Anne. "Anyone in the profession who's ever known Gerard sends him flowers and telegrams on a first night. Quite a lot are from people who've failed themselves."

"Oh, I do think actors are nice! Why aren't we all nice like actors?" continued Primrose, elephantinely arch. "The room smells like a florist's shop."

"Or like a hearse," suggested Gerard. And he walked along the flowers, looking at the cards attached to them. Every card stabbed him like a lance, and his heart died before each.

"Serve 'em drinks, Anne, and then turn 'em out," said he, forcing up some humour. I've got to dress." This last sentence caught his voice and stopped it.

"Oh, I couldn't drink any more," declared Primrose, her head on one side. "I'm just not used to all those wines we had at dinner. I shall start singing, or something."

"That's nonsense. Give her a strong one. Then she can go to sleep all through the play."

"I'm certainly not going to sleep. Oh, Anne, really no! Well, only a little. I shall be drunk." And she giggled suitably. "I do think this is absolutely thrilling. I've always wanted to be one of the favoured ones behind the scenes."

Justin, sitting in an easy chair with a cocktail, muttered irritably to himself. "God, what a fool of a woman," he was thinking.

"Have they seen the Visitors' Book?" asked Anne. "I don't think they have. Justin, you ought to see this." She picked up a leather-bound volume from the writing-table, perched herself on the arm of his chair, and opened it for him.

"Daddy's going to leave it to me in his will," announced Constance. "It'll be frightfully valuable one day. It's absolutely full of celebrities."

"There are certainly some very famous signatures in it," admitted Anne. And she pointed out to Justin, one by one, the signatures of Cabinet ministers, divines, poets, authors, generals, and all the famous actors of the last twenty years.

"What heaps of peers!" cried Primrose effusively, leaning over Robin's shoulder in the way that made him recoil.

"Only the Sporting, Dramatic, and Illustrated Peers," Gerard demurred modestly.

Justin looked at the signatures, one by one. He had to, because his hostess was showing them to him. And he strengthened himself to say something generous. "Well, well, what it is to be famous."

"And now good-bye all," said Gerard, herding them out in a pretence of high humour. "That's all till after the show— excuse me, everyone"—he had patted his fingers over his mouth because the word "show" had caused something like a hiccup—"Time, gentlemen, please. Anne, take 'em round to their boxes. And, Anne——" this last sentence was kept be-hind his teeth—"for God's sake keep Bozzy well out of view— though perhaps it'll be all right. Perhaps they'll think he's some sort of manservant."

Anne led them by the side of the stage to the pass door. "Oh, isn't this thrilling!" exclaimed Primrose, and she did a little skip, as she saw the first set in place and the stage hands standing about, and the men on the spotlight perches. They passed into the front of the house and climbed the stairs to the boxes. Two boxes had been reserved for the party. In the larger Anne placed Gerard's mother, Justin and Primrose, Robin and Jessica, and herself; and Primrose, shaking girl-ishly her large shoulders, trilled, "Oh, isn't this just mar-vellous. I'm not used to moving in such high circles;" and Justin made it plain by a mutter that she had said the wrong thing again.

When all were disposed in the boxes, and particularly Justin, Anne swept forward with one of her lovely swan-like movements to the front of her own box and was immediately seen by the watching audience. Applause sprang up in stalls and circle and spread everywhere till the whole audience was greeting her—especially the girls in the gallery. She smiled as if in surprise—she was a fine actress—bowed slightly and deprecatingly, and withdrew to her chair behind the curtain.

Justin was beside her, looking down upon the crowded house. The scene was everything that she had desired for him: row upon row of brilliant gowns and white shirt-fronts; row upon row of bare bosoms sloping from pearl necklaces, and of tall, costly coiffures, made dazzling by jewelled combs and tiaras; all the boxes filled, and filled with the fine flowers of celebrity, fashion, or money; the faces of the habitual "first nighters" reaching back to the high, dark summit of the gallery; a thousand voices chattering and laughing; a hundred feminine perfumes blending in the close air; the orchestra in its well, and—now—the musical director mounting his rostrum.

It was the audience which the boy Gerard, thirty years before, had seen in a dream, as he peeped through the faded old tabs of the Charing Cross Theatre.

And now Justin was looking down upon it, and Anne, to enlighten him further, brought her chair closer to him and pointed out the celebrities one after another.

Two taps of the conductor's baton.

" 'Overture and Beginners,' " said Anne.

"Poor Gerard," gushed Primrose with a shiver. "He must be feeling *awful*."

"Oh, Gerard's all right. He's never nervous," laughed Anne, as the house lights dimmed.

§

There was one who perceived the whole of Anne's purpose; and it was Robin. And he felt a great pity for the victim, who

was sitting silent and unhappy, but smiling politely to his
hostess and the other ladies. He knew the reality of Justin,
which, behind the laughter and the chronic attacks of high
gaiety, was loneliness and friendlessness and imprisonment
in himself: what must it be for him to see the multitude and
the massed affection of Gerard's friends? And as he watched
him, so quiet and defeated and yet smiling courageously, the
pain enlarged till it was a sharp pain at his heart, and he came
to a final decision. No, he would *not* tell anyone his news
to-night. If he told any of them it must come to Justin's
ears; and the success of one younger brother was enough for
Justin to bear to-night.

It was not a small victory, this, because it was fine news
he had to tell, and, more than all, he longed to tell Justin,
who had always and so obviously supposed that he, Robin,
would never occupy much more than a humble place in the
Church. Robin was thirty-nine and, though he had been
fighting it in secret for years, the self-displaying peacock in
him was not dead. On the contrary, there were times when it
seemed as vigorous, as sensitive, and as irritable as ever. And
the fact was that he had dreamed all day, with no small
pleasure, of exploding his news like a bomb upon the company to-night. He would tell Anne and Gerard quietly and, as
it were, casually, and when they shouted it out to the family—
as Anne most assuredly would—he would receive with modest
deprecations the congratulations of all. But the night was
passing, and he had not done this yet, and now, for Justin's
sake, he was not going to do it at all. He wasn't going to add
anything to the burden of a disappointed man.

Three weeks ago the Bishop had written to him, asking him
to come and see him. And when he had walked into the
Bishop's room at Fulham Palace (how often the le Faber boys
had passed Fulham Palace as they walked along Fulham
Palace Road or rowed on the river between Putney and Hammersmith!) the Bishop had risen to welcome him and said,
"Good, my boy. Sit down. There's something I want to talk
over with you." Robin sat down, and thereupon the Bishop,
both literally and figuratively, got into his stride. He talked
fluently, and he strode about the carpet as he talked. "You
know, of course, my boy, that the living of St. Michael's,
Cunningham Gardens, is becoming vacant?" Yes, Robin had
read that its rector, Archdeacon Beresford-Graeme, was to
be the new suffragan Bishop of Uxbridge. "Well, St. Michael's

is what they're pleased to call a fashionable church. I suppose
you could say it's one of the half-dozen most fashionable
churches in London. In that sense it's the very opposite of
your present parish. But in that sense only, my boy—the
worldly sense. In any real sense all parishes are the same:
just congregations of weak souls needing love. You guess
what's coming, eh? Yes, you're quite right. I'm going to
offer you St. Michael's. No, no, you keep quiet for the present,
and let me do the talking. I've watched your success with the
poor ever since you were first ordained—success in the only
way that matters—and I am quite satisfied that the same
methods must work with the rich and prosperous; because
there's only one method really, as we both know, and it's
love. If a man's got that, he's the best man for any parish.
I've been sure of this for a long time, and I feel I proved it
when I transferred Harry Galton, from St. Benedict's,
Canning Town, of all unsavoury parishes, to St. Anne's,
Great Audley Street. He was a hundred per cent success,
because he loved the people.

"I believe you to be just such another—oh, be quiet—yes, I
know you've got heaps of faults, but I'm not talking about
them—all I know is that you've managed to win the hearts of
some of the dearest and wickedest of my children, and that
they'd go through fire and water for you, just because you've
really loved them and they feel it. You're still young—only
forty or so—thirty-nine, is it?—I'm sorry—not yet forty—
well, so much the better. What an opportunity before you. I
repeat, St. Michael's may be a fashionable church, but it's not
scholarship or noble connexions or wealth that it wants, but
—love."

Robin's vision was quick—at times it was instantaneous—
and at this mention of "noble connexions" he guessed that the
Bishop, when discussing Robin's appointment with the leading laymen of St. Michael's, had employed the wisdom of the
serpent and reminded them with a twinkle that le Faber's
young wife, being an earl's daughter, would be some com-
pensation to the *very* fashionable ladies.

"Of course, I know St. Michael's is not a very high church,
but you've lost a lot of your spikery as you've grown older,
haven't you, my boy? Eh?" The Bishop twinkled at Robin.
"Your Anglo-Catholicism has quietened and broadened down
—I'm right in thinking so, am I not? Yes, it often does in
those who've got the real stuff in them: the partisanship which

divides gives place to the love which unites. . . . Well, go away and pray about it, and I'll be praying for you too. Discuss it with some good priests and with the friends whose advice you value. You'll receive a formal offer from me in a day or so. Answer it in your own time. And for my part I sincerely hope your answer will be Yes. God bless you."

Robin's answer had been Yes. And now, though he had prayed about it, and tried to be worthy of it, he could only rejoice in this signal preferment and long to publish it to the family, and particularly to Justin. How well this weaker part of him could understand Gerard and Anne's longing to display their spectacular success before Justin when he was longing to do likewise with his far humbler one.

But he wasn't going to do it. He wasn't going to. There was no further argument: he had decided, and that was the end of it. "Lord, help me not to."

But even as he decided not to hurt Justin in this way, he hurt him in another, though without design, and the hurting actions sprang in part from the same source. Jessica was very beautiful. She was easily the most beautiful person in this party to-night. She was as dark as Bryn had been fair, but she had the same clean, ivory-brown egg-shell complexion, and in this tinted paleness her brown eyes seemed very large and at once brilliant, soft, and shadowed. When she was dressed for ballroom or theatre she made so beautiful a young figure that all the people turned their heads and stopped their talk as she came in. Robin was more proud of her just now than of anything else that he possessed, and to-night, whether or not he was going to display his sudden advancement in the Church, he had been looking forward all the evening to displaying Jessica to the people in the theatre. To-night she was dressed in a flame velvet gown with an ermine cape (the gift of the earl) and a cluster of white camelias in her hair. And as they entered the box, he laid his fingers on her bare elbow that the people might realize that she was his, and gently guided her forward into their view. And it was just as he hoped: her appearance up here in the box turned all faces in their direction and imposed a moment of silence on the great, chattering audience. It was a moment of quite exquisite joy for Robin—so exquisite as to be almost painful. He sat himself beside her and got as close to her as possible that all might guess she was his wife.

That was the first thing that hurt Justin. But it did not hurt him so much as something that happened a minute or two later. Robin and Jessica were still much in love, and always when they were side by side in a theatre, and the house lights dimmed and darkness encompassed them, she would put her hand through his arm and entwine her fingers in his. She did so now, and Robin squeezed her fingers gratefully and was glad that she should be having this share in Gerard's glory because it was so little that he himself had to give to the daughter of a great house. But as he pressed her fingers he saw Justin looking down upon their clasped hands. And he knew that the sight of them had been a sharp wound for him.

The curtain was up. The opening lines were spoken to a silent house, but the silence did not seem to be for them as much as for something else which the whole great concourse was awaiting. Gerard made his first entry, and the silence explained itself: it burst with delight into its antithesis, a din of applause that swelled into an uproar of cheering. The loyal gallery, mainly feminine, leaned forward on its hard benches and roared its heart out. Robin looked at Anne and smiled. She smiled back and wept. "After that," she wailed, brushing her eyes and blowing her nose, "Gerard will do anything."

And he did. The night was a continuing and increasing triumph. When Anne rushed to him after the show, she embraced him and said, "The thing is done. We've done it, we've done it! He's completely and entirely flat. It's gone better than anything I ever dreamed, and now I can be really happy for the first time in my life. I've never known you act better than you did to-night, jewel that you are. I told you you'd be inspired, and you were. You laid him out completely. Come along and celebrate. They're all waiting for you."

CHAPTER TWO

ROBIN walked fast, and even furiously, along Vandermere Road towards Justin's house. It was the following day, and four in the afternoon, and he was hurrying grimly, purposively, to tell Justin of his appointment to St. Michael's, Cunningham Gardens. His self-sacrificing resolve to conceal it from Justin as long as possible had cascaded into ruin

during the night. Justin had said to him in the second interval
—almost certainly to ease his sense of having been surpassed by
Gerard, "Aren't they ever going to give you a decent living,
Robby?" and his tone had revealed his poor opinion of
Robin's present work. The question had cut Robin like a
jagged knife, and the laceration had ached for the rest of the
evening. But the resolve had held. It had held because it had
been so firmly built an hour before.

In the morning, however, it was a wreck. The wound had
festered and ached in the night, and when he rose from a
wakeful bed, he was determined to give it the healing for-
which it clamoured. And now, at four o'clock in the after
noon, he was hurrying to this work of relief. "It's self-indulgent
and sinful," protested his conscience. "It's unkind and against
everything your vision sees as right;" but he couldn't help this.
The thing had to be done. The need to do it was a smarting
poison that must be expelled. And so, with his purpose firm
about his lips, he hurried along Vandermere Road, dragging
his protesting conscience as a nurse drags a recalcitrant child.

His conscience, following behind, reminded him of the
Bishop's praise, and he was appalled at the difference between the things he could see in himself and those that the
Bishop saw. As he walked on, clouded with thought, he saw
himself as ill-tempered, sour, self-seeking, praise-loving, and
vain. Vain about his sermons; proud of the people's praise;
too solicitous about his appearance and his dress. Of course
he was not always in one or another of these sinful conditions,
but far too often, far too often. He fought the sinfulness
when he could and as well as he could. He would force himself to do unselfish and kindly things when he was feeling
sour and loved no one. At times like this, when he felt completely sunk in sourness, he would pray like a drowning man,
"Oh God, keep me pitiful and kind";—but not this afternoon.
He did not want to be pitiful and kind this afternoon—and
not again until he had overthrown a conceited brother just
as Anne had overthrown him. In short, he was both delighted
at what he was about to do and in the depths of gloom about it.

Vandermere Road is a long road, and he had time to
perceive a truth. He saw that it was because he was in
permanent conflict with his ill-temper, sourness, self-seeking,
and vanity that he appeared to the world and to the Bishop
as kind, patient, forgiving, selfless, and devoted. In his shop-
window, inevitably, was all that he wanted to be. Behind

it was all that he was not. The Bishop and the people saw
only the window; Jessica saw what was in the parlour—or
some of it; but only he himself knew what was in the store-
room.

All this he was seeing and deploring as he hurried along
Vandermere Road—but he went on. Sometimes he argued
with himself that it would be good for Justin to know there
were other men as able as he, and that work among the poor
was as important in the Bishop's eyes as work in fashionable
streets; but he could not distort his vision like this. He knew
there was nothing good at all in what he was doing; and he
went on.

He came to the two dissimilar houses that called themselves
Erasmus Hall. One was a large grey-brick, double-fronted
house with bay windows on either side of the front door, and
the other a high narrow house, the first of a long terrace.
The trees and shrubs in front of the large detached house were
so close to it, and had grown so large, that they seemed to
sadden it with their shadows. The York stone steps, climbing
to the front door, were tinged with green. The other house
had no front garden but a cemented area down a dozen green-
ing steps. Tarnished, depressed, and taciturn they looked,
these two disparate houses of Justin's, after Gerard's beautiful
and happy old house on Chiswick Mall.

But since Justin must always believe the best of his own,
it was not often that he saw them as melancholy. And there
was nothing melancholy or dispirited in the manner in which
he greeted Robin. Apparently the glumness of last night had
fallen from him in the brightness of a new day. His splendid
resilience had enabled him to rise again upon his feet and to
fill up again with self-confidence and laughter. Besides, he
always felt big and successful in the presence of young Robin.

"I want to speak to you about something," explained Robin.

"Come in, come in, old son. Sit you down." He directed
Robin into one of the great chairs and disposed himself in
the other. "Smoke away. And what about staying to supper?
It won't be a dinner like Gerard's. Probably cold meat and
tomatoes. Primrose hasn't an idea above cold meat and
tomatoes. There may be a boiled potato too. You can't stop?
Pity. I should have enjoyed a long talk; I never seem to have
anyone to talk to, nowadays. God knows I can't talk to
Primrose. The woman's a fool. And like all fools she goes on
talking for ever, quite untroubled by any question as to

whether what she says is worth listening to, or whether it could be verified if she gave it a minute's thought. Did you hear her last night? Chirruping like a coy canary, and she's over fifty now. I tell you, it spoils my evening if she's there. It reminds me of some enormous fat owl hopping and peeking about like a sparrow. Not a bad show of Gerard's last night; I rather liked it." So he grasped the nettle. "He's certainly got his public. But I thought the dinner party and the supper party afterwards were a bit overdone, didn't you? And I wish Gerard didn't overdress the part; I mean, that velvet collar is a bit precious, don't you think? What did you think of Bozzy? My God, isn't he awful? What are we to do about him, Rob? Do you know he's taken to asking people in the streets if they've found God and to stopping the children on Brook Green to tell them about Jesus?"

Robin smiled, and Justin, his eyes merry and his pipe smoke wreathing above him, went on, "Yes, and he's even tried to preach at a street corner, but nobody, not even a dog, stopped to listen to him, so after a time some sense came down upon him, and he packed up and walked away, sorrowing. But not before he'd called our poor old Brook Green Whoredom Green just because he'd seen a couple of lovers kissing on a seat and another couple lying together on the grass. He's become most extraordinarily fluent. I can't imagine where he gets all his Bible-punching language from. From his chapels and his tracts, I suppose. He's distributed tracts, Mother says, to the crowds queuing outside the Palace of Varieties because in his eyes they were queuing up at the mouth of hell. The man ought to be suppressed. He always had a cheese instead of a head, and now he's got maggots in it."

"I wanted to ask your advice, Justin, about——"

"And then there's Hector. My God, Hector! We've two fools in our family, Rob, and one of them passes for sane. But it can't be sane to be as self-satisfied as that. His conversation simply reeks of complacency. Would you believe it, he's supremely well satisfied with his job as accountant at that bank? That finishes him for me. Only an utterly common-place mind could be satisfied with an occupation like that. I suppose some men have got to be bank clerks, but that's no reason why they should be satisfied with their job and proud of it."

"What's so wrong with his occupation?"

"Good lord, Robby, surely *you* can see. It's completely

unreal. There's nothing real about it. He's shut up all day in a glass and mahogany box, dealing with nothing more real than figures in a ledger. He's never in contact with reality at all. It's screened from him by a kind of gauze curtain all embroidered with cash-ruled lines and figures and £.s.d.'s, but he's much too dull and heavy to see *that*. Good God, I'd die rather than live such a life as his. My life isn't ideal, but it does enable me for three months of the year to escape into the open air and to get a little nearer to the essence of things. He's handed over his will and his existence to a system of usury without a murmur and without a moment's hesitation. Thank God I've never handed my will over to anybody."

The listening Robin perceived where Justin's thoughts had lain since last night. Ever since that glittering display of Gerard's success he had been proving to himself that he too had not done badly: he had trodden a different path but he had done much of what he wanted to do. "Justin, I wanted to ask you——"

"Why, the old Duke was a better piece of work than Hector. He was an old scamp and a lazy old crocodile, but he wasn't a fool. And he had a fine sense of drama, the old devil. Do you know—did I ever tell you—that when he knew he was dying, he got Primrose to sing the old hymns to him in the Boys' Music Room just across the landing and he made her sing, 'The day Thou gavest Lord is ended, The darkness falls at thy behest. . . .'"

"Yes, you told me that. Poor old thing. Look here, I wanted to ask your advice, old man."

"Oh, yes?" Justin was pleased. To have one's advice sought was to be placed on higher ground.

"I haven't told any of the family this so far. Not even Mother. You're the old person I've mentioned it to."

"Well, that's flattering. What is it?"

"You know St. Michael's, Cunningham Gardens?"

"Don't be daft, old boy. Who doesn't? It's the church where all the débutantes are married. I read my paper *sometimes*."

"And you know that Archdeacon Beresford-Graeme was its rector?" Sin upon sin: there was no need to say this; Robin had said it to show that only men of distinction occupied the incumbency of St. Michael's.

"I didn't know it. No. But I've met the old cove. He's active on the League of Nations Union."

"Well, he's just been made Suffragan Bishop of Uxbridge."

"Lucky old man."

"And the point is, the living of St. Michael's is vacant, and the Bishop has offered it to me."

"To *you*?" The note of amazement was rude enough, but Justin had been trapped into it. It set Robin's wound throbbing again so that he was glad to see that his blow had been as effective as some of Anne's last night. "Why to you?"

"I don't know." Robin could not tell him all that the Bishop had said: he could not drop as low as that. Already, as he saw the glumness seated again on Justin's face, his conscience was rising like a dominie who had been defied, and baring his arm for punishment. "I don't know. But he has. And I want to ask you, do you think I should accept it?" Oh, ever enlarging sin: here was a lie, for Robin had already accepted it. Thus does sin, once you have swum into its undertow, drag you further and further from the shore.

"Of course accept it. Why not? What's it worth?"

"That's hardly the point."

"I suppose it's quite a fat living."

"Oh, I don't know. There are others fatter."

"But what *is* it worth?"

"About one thousand eight hundred gross and a house."

Justin met this with silence. He sat pulling at his pipe as if it were his only comfort. And Robin knew that his answer had been another powerful blow, but he had tried, oh, surely he had tried, not to deliver it.

"It works out at considerably less when you've met certain charges," he proffered in penitence.

"But what's your trouble? Why ask me? One thousand eight hundred a year. Pounce on it; and all I've got to say is, Jolly good, old man. I'm very glad for your sake."

Robin tried to discuss the matter further, but he soon perceived that Justin didn't want to: Justin's own thoughts had built a prison wall around him. And after a time Robin stopped speaking, and Justin didn't appear to notice it. He sat there plunged into depression. And Robin sat opposite him plunged into penitence.

§

Robin went out ashamed. Pity for Justin was heavy within him. And walking back along Vandermere Road, his eyes

clouded with thought, he asked forgiveness for his quick in-
dignations and for his cruelty when indignation seized him.
He remembered an occasion in the war when his tendency to
headlong and precipitate anger had dismayed and shaken him.
Robin was the only le Faber boy who had seen much fighting
in the first world war. Justin had been starred as a schoolmaster; Gerard had been in the navy and run into more discomfort than action; Hector had been a paymaster in India;
Robin, newly priested, after waiting in vain for a chaplaincy,
had burst impatiently through the ban of his gentle bishop
and accepted a combatant commission. And he was remembering now an October dawn in Passchendaele, when the mist
was smoking over the grey-green glistening mud, and he,
infuriated by proofs of German brutality to some of the men
of his battalion, had rushed into the morning's attack with his
revolver in his hand, and his teeth protruding like a wounded
tiger's, and had shot and shot at the surprised enemy, exulting
in punishment. He had shot one in the breast, another in the
face, and a third in the back, exulting to kill. He had justified
his trigger finger as the victims fell, but not afterwards. His
conscience was waiting for him directly the bloody work was
done. It was there beside him in the mist and on the mud. It
waited till his heart had stopped thumping and his breath was
steady, and then it began to speak.

And many times afterwards in the war he had wondered in
the presence of this unforgetting and unforgiving conscience
if he who had been driven more by fury than by duty to that
blind, unrecking slaughter, ought to take up his work as a
priest again. "The hands that lift the chalice," so the saying
went, "must not have shed blood." But when the war was
over, there had broken upon him the same clear light as he had
seen on the dry-walled road by Deep Langstrath, after his
hour of passionate rebellion when Bryn died. "Nothing
matters but goodness and kindness and love. I know it. And
never did I know it so certainly as now when we've all done
things like this." And he had gone back to his work and done
it the better sometimes for the memory of that milky morning on the wastes before Passchendaele.

And now on this much smaller field he found a similar
answer because the factors in the sum were alike. He must
make amends for this latest example of self-regarding pique
and vindictiveness by striving all the more to help and love
others. "Oh, yes, I see it all so clearly—*absolutely* clearly—

but, God help me, I don't seem to be able to do it for any
length of time. I have a long way to go yet."

§

Robin was walking along Vandermere Road towards Justin's
house, and this time, not in wrath, but in contrition. It was
the next evening, and throughout the day his contrition and
pity had been rising to such a pressure that he had felt driven
at last to visit Justin again and be kind to him. The impulse
had become as irresistible as the earlier impulse to go and hurt
him. He went to Jessica and suggested that they should "g
over and see old Justin," but she begged most earnestly to be
left at home. "Oh no, darling! You *know* I'm afraid of him. I
don't know what it is, but to me there's something terrifying
about him. When he looks at me I feel quite uneasy. He's
your brother, and you're used to him. You don't see it. I
think you still see the boy you knew when you were little. And
I expect he was quite attractive as a child. He must have
been very handsome."

"All right, darling," agreed Robin, and kissed her; and he
went and telephoned to Justin and, to flatter and make him
happy, suggested that he would like more of his advice on the
matter they were discussing yesterday. There was nothing in
the least terrifying in Justin's hearty voice at the other end of
the 'phone. "Of course, old man. Come along. Come to supper,
and we'll talk the night away."

And within a couple of hours, while the evening was still
bright, they were sitting together, one on either side of
Justin's fireplace, as they had done so often before. Justin had
built up a fine fire for this pleasant chat with Robin. A chat
with Robin, by a fire or on the hills, was the one and only
form of happy communion that his self-imprisoned life had
secured for him.

But they spoke hardly at all of St. Michael's, Cunningham
Gardens, or of Robin and his problems. From the first moment
Justin talked of himself and of a new plan that had come to
him overnight and was hot within him now. His eyes were
bright with belief in this new plan; and Robin discerned at
once that he had evolved it during the night as an effort to
catch up with one at least of his brothers, Robin himself, and
to compete in success with him; and because he discerned this,
his heart went out to him.

"Listen, Robby: I'm going to start a girls' school. What d'you say to that? Yes, I am, really. The idea came to me last night in bed. I shall run a girls' school in connexion with Erasmus Hall, and I shall make old Primmy the headmistress. God knows she knows nothing about anything, but no more did I when I started as a headmaster, and no more do most headmistresses of private schools. Can't imagine why I didn't think of the idea before. It's much more likely to be a success than a private school for boys. You see, people think twice where they send their sons, but they don't care a damn where they send their girls, so long as the school is called a High School. (What *is* a High School, Rob?) Primrose hasn't a degree or even the education of a twelve-year-old, but who-ever looked twice at the qualifications of the principal of a private school for girls? Lord, it's a racket, isn't it; and I can't think why I didn't weigh in on it before. We can have an intelligent mistress under Primmy. Perhaps two; and the rest can be decayed gentlewomen. It'll be cheap enough to run: governesses are two a penny. I don't see why we shouldn't have fifty or sixty girls in no time. After all, we're greatly respected in the neighbourhood, Mrs. le Faber and I. We don't get as much money out of the people as we should like, but we get unlimited respect. I was calculating in bed last night that if we added together the profits of the two schools, our income would run into four handsome figures."

Four handsome figures. One thousand eight hundred a year. Robin saw what had been directing Justin's thoughts last night; and in his compassion he responded to him with flattering and encouraging words. "I don't see why it shouldn't be a tremendous success."

"It's going to be. I'm so sure of it that I left this damned school to look after itself this morning and walked up and down looking for a suitable house for my new High School for Girls. I shall transfer all the kids under eight to the Girls' School. I never did like having kids of six and seven in a boys' school. It turns it into a dame's school. Besides, I can never see the smallest boys in the passages, and I fall over them. They'll be safer over there. And Primrose can live over there with the boarders, and I can live here in peace. Gosh, it's a swell idea."

Nor at supper did Justin mention St. Michael's, Cunning ham Gardens, or Robin's new distinction, and it was apparent from Primrose's chatter that she had been told no word about it. And again Robin understood: Justin had been quite unable to get it past his lips. They talked chiefly about the new scheme, and Primrose seemed as enthusiastic about it as Justin. But then Primrose always echoed the words of Justin, whose intelligence she admired and feared.

When, after supper, they took their pipes back into the study, Justin said, "Well, thank God, that's over. We needn't listen to any more of her stuff. Dear, oh dear, I sometimes wonder if a woman like that could make a success of anything. What are we going to do now, old boy? Saturday night. I know! Let's go for a walk along old King Street and see life as we used to. We'll walk back by the river. Old King Street isn't quite what it used to be, when all the world was young, lad, but it still has its charm. It's still crowded with the boys and girls. Come on; get your hat; and we'll see if we can see the ghosts of our former selves walking along the pavements. This house oppresses me sometimes."

King Street was a lighted aisle stretching eastward into the night. The butchers and greengrocers, their shops open to the air, were as side-chapels filled with a golden glow. The stream and counter-stream of people might have been worshippers in procession rather than shoppers and wanderers and idle gazers. But it was an aisle no more when one looked at the hurrying headlights on the roadway: then it was a canal, and the large electric trams were houseboats happily alight and sliding along, and the tall red buses were painted galleons sweeping past them.

The throngs on the narrow pavements were so thick that often they cast off fragments into the roadway, and the buses and cars and trams had to hoot and bell them out of the way. Raucous voices declared their wares from the open shop fronts; neon lighting and flood-lit windows did much the same for those more dignified traders whose goods were behind plate glass and swinging doors.

The two brothers had walked only a little way towards the Broadway, on the northern pavement, when they saw, coming along the gutter, at a slow pace and with a dignity that sorted ill with a gutter, a figure holding a placard aloft on a pole. On the placard were some words that cried aloud in letters of red and blue. The first words that Robin noticed, because they were the largest and in a vivid red, were, "Hear . . . Hearken . . ." and he realized that this was one of those zealots for the Lord who adopted this method of bringing His gospel into the market place.

But as the figure strode slowly nearer, surprise and dismay caught at Robin's heart. It was—yes, it was Bozzy. Bozzy in a baggy grey suit and spats, holding his pole on high with hands enveloped in unbuttoned gloves, and giving a smile of Christian love to all who glanced at him and his message. The message, sailing above the crowds, was:

> "Hear, all ye people,
> Hearken, O Earth,
> Have I any pleasure at all
> That the wicked should die?"

Oh, poor Bozzy, thought Robin. Bozzy, so happy and smiling in his new-found faith, had tried to give of his abundance to the people at the street corners but, since they would not come to him and listen, he had come to them where they were to be found in their multitudes—in King Street on a Saturday night. In the service of his Master he had not hesitated, even though he was a gentleman in spats and gloves, to tread the gutters, bearing aloft his Master's words. And when the people had had two minutes to look at one face of his placard, he turned his pole round that they might read the appeal and the promise on the other side.

> "Return unto me
> And I will return unto you,
> Saith the Lord of Hosts."

"Oh my God!" It was Justin's voice muttering. "Come quick, Robin, or he'll speak to us. Come on. I wouldn't be seen dead with him."

But in the same moment Bozzy recognized them and hurled at them a smile of ingratiating love as if he would lassoo them with it. He halted in the gutter and rested his pole on the kerb.

"Hallo, Robin. What are you doing in these parts?" There was a new jocosity in his voice. It was the assertive jocosity of those who are compact of happiness because they have found the Lord and are saved.

They avoided the lassooing smile and hastened on. But Robin, turning round to look again at Bozzy, saw that he was standing there and gazing after them with an expression so disappointed and miserable that Robin was stabbed by it. He had known no such intolerable pang of pity since the evening when he saw old Mr. Cumberland struggling up the attic stairs with his books. He left Justin and hurried back to Bozzy.

"Hallo, Bozzy," was all that he could think of to say.

Justin walked on. He walked on hastily, the furies driving his steps. Soon he was far away, his head high above the drifting crowds and moving fast. Bozzy's eyes followed him.

"I've been having supper with Justin," ventured Robin.

"Have you, Robin?" The smile and the jocosity had fallen from Bozzy. "Why has he walked away like that? Is it because he's ashamed of me?"

"Oh no, Bozzy. . . ."

"I don't mind if he is. Tell him I don't mind at all. I expect to be hated and despised, and I'm happy when I am." But the hand that held the pole was trembling. "I remember what Jesus said: 'Blessed are ye when men shall revile you.' Tell him he has no need to be sorry for me; it is I who am sorry for him. I only wish I could see him to tell him how sorry I am for him. He is a lost soul. Does he know it? He is lost, and he laughs at *me*! He passes me by as something to be ashamed of."

A suppressed anger burned in Bozzy's weak eyes. "He doesn't know that it is *he* from whom the Lord will turn away ashamed in the great day, and that, because of this, I have nothing but pity for him. You must tell him so. Let him know it, Robin." His head was stacked with texts, and he unpacked another for Robin. "The Lord hath delivered me out of temptation and reserved him unto the day of judgment."

"We can't know yet, Bozzy, what God has in store for us. His mercy is very wide."

"We *can* know. It is written in the Word. How can you, a minister of the Word, say that we can't know? It is written in a hundred places. You can read it in Two, Peter, Two, Ten. You can read there what is reserved for the presumptious and self-willed. I don't hesitate to say that he is lost, unless you or I can save him." Again his eyes turned in the direction Justin had gone. Anger diluted with sorrow laid a faint red gleam in each of the dull, weak irises. And, still looking after Justin, he said, " 'He that hateth his brother is in darkness and knows not whither he goeth, because the darkness hath blinded his eyes.' "

"I must go on now, Bozzy. I must rejoin Justin."

"There is no hope for him as long as he seeks his own ends in complete selfishness. He who seeks his own ends stands in an awful darkness, and if he stays in that darkness, it gets deeper and deeper. There is no happiness in that darkness, and that is why he is one of the unhappiest men in the world. I know he is; I usedn't to know it, because he laughs and pretends he isn't; but I've known it ever since I myself saw the light. And I feel a great compassion for him, Robin: I pray for him often. One step out of it, and he'd stand in the light. He'd know happiness for the first time."

Now that Bozzy had quietened down and the fire of religious mania had dimmed in his eyes, Robin was astonished at the simple clarity of his vision. "There is only one vision of the truth," he thought, standing there in the hurrying crowds of King Street, "and it's the same whether the sage sees it or the simpleton."

"You're perfectly right, Bozzy," he said aloud, "but these things are easier seen than acted upon. I can see them all, but I tumble back into self-seeking a hundred times a day."

"I don't find it difficult. I throw myself on the Lord Jesus, and he helps me do all. It is He that worketh in me. I asked on my knees what I could do to help him, and it came to me that I should do this." Remembering his pole, he lifted it up and turned it round, so that the passing people could see the other face of the placard: "Hear, all ye people, Hearken, O Earth. . . ."

"I really must run now and find Justin," said Robin, giving his youngest brother a kind smile.

"That's right, but if he says anything against me, say just this to him; say: 'The foolishness of God is wiser than men, and the weakness of God is stronger than men.' "

"I will, Bozzy."

"Yes, and give——" Bozzy held him by the sleeve—"give him my love."

Robin nodded and ran towards Justin. Not once did Justin turn his head, and when Robin was at his side again, he only muttered, staring before him: "We can't have this. We just can't have it. I can't and I won't. How are we to stop him? He ought to be shut up in an asylum."

"Oh no, he's not as bad as that, Justin. He's harmless enough."

"He's not harmless to me. It's all very fine for you to be generous. You don't live in the same neighbourhood. I'm a prominent man here, and everybody knows he's my brother. A fat lot of good it does my school to have the village idiot for my brother. It was bad enough when he just went about

and smiled idiotically at everybody, but now that he's taken
to walking about with texts on a pole, it's time he was put
away. Let's get out of here. The street stinks of him. I
seem to see him everywhere with his ghastly pole. Let's go
where it's quiet. Let's go and look at the river."

They swung up Angel Road so as to reach Bridge Avenue
and the river. And soon they were walking along the mall. It
was low water, and the stream of Thames was but a slack and
shining ribbon between broad slopes of shingle and slime. It
was a silent stream, forsaken and dark, with no whisper or
chuckle as it lapped the sides of barges, no silken rustle,
from up stream or down, of tugs under way, and no lights
approaching from distant reaches above the eyot or below the
bridge. There was nothing human on it anywhere.

Justin walked on, as silent and sullen as the stream, and as
dark and heavy in mind as the mud beneath the wall.

CHAPTER THREE

ON Sunday, at ten o'clock in the morning, the long stretch of
Vandermere Road was empty. A man, turning out of the
Grove into Vandermere Road would have seen no one before
him and heard nothing except the sound of his own feet. He
would have passed the large double-fronted house that was
Justin's and heard no sound coming from within. If he had
been a man of dreams and curious imaginings, he might have
thought that the house with its scaling stucco, its time-
darkened bricks, and the shadows that fell upon its steps from
its too-close trees, was a fitter home for melancholy than many
another in the long road. If, on the other hand, he had been
a good commonplace fellow, and a Londoner all his life, he
would either not have noticed the house at all or have thought
it just one more old-fashioned house, large and heavy and
grey, and perhaps a little more shadowed than its neighbours,
in a part of London where a thousand such houses were to be
seen in rank behind rank, like a brigade on a barrack square.

Had he looked at the broad bay window of the front room
on the left, behind the leaves of the sycamore, it would have
seemed as silent as any other of the broad dark windows. It
would have seemed the window of an empty room.

But that room was not empty. It was Justin's study, and

Justin was sitting there in his deep easy chair by the fire-place. His legs were stretched before him, his elbows were on the chair's arms, and his chin rested upon his interlaced fingers. Alone in that room, with the door shut, he had let himself drop like plummet into the depths of thought.

The house was silent, because the few boarders were writing their Sunday letters in the Lower First Room, under the supervision of Mr. Chase, his youngest and cheapest assistant master.

In the long stretch of Vandermere Road on that quiet Sunday morning there may have been other men as lonely as this figure in the front room of Erasmus Hall, but there could have been none lonelier, because he was sitting there in the company of his disappointments. He had gathered them around him that he might consider them, and like a ring of dull, indifferent watchers they shut him in. This morning he bodied forth, as in a still tableau, all that his mad brother had said of him twelve hours before.

Gerard. Gerard had a host of friends. How ample and interesting a life was his. Think of that Visitors' Book, those flowers, those telegrams. He, Justin, hadn't a friend in the world—unless it was Robin. And whom did he ever meet except a few sheep-like people who huddled together in the fold of a dying church and a few parents who must be dull and brainless or they'd never send their children to a school like his? They'd never let him hoodwink and impose upon them in the way he did. No, there was no one with whom he cared to exchange an idea, so little intelligent were they all. He walked about the world, silent and alone. Even Robin's intelligence he did not hold in very high esteem.

Robin. Robin, they said, was loved by the people of his parish, and no doubt this was true. Robin was that sort: softer than himself, and needing love enough to labour for it. Robin had innumerable friends in his own sphere, and now he was going to meet many more in the circles of the wealthy and powerful.

Even Hector, that fat and complacent fool, was better furnished with friends than he. In the first place he met interesting and important people among the larger customers of his bank, and in the second, being a fool, with a completely ordinary and uncritical mind, he could be easily satisfied with, and enjoy the companionship of, other men, however stupid and empty-headed they were, and being a gossip and gadabout, with some natural heartiness, he had, in fact, a large number of cronies among those who were too unintelligent themselves to be bored by his ponderous prattle.

"Yes, they all have their friends. And I? What have I? I have the respect of the people of the neighbourhood because I've chosen to nurse it, but what else? Exactly nothing. Nothing and nobody."

His chin on his knuckles, his eyes on the floor, he considered the causes of his solitariness. Gerard, though no more altruistic than himself, had all the bonhomie and the free and easy prodigality of his profession, and in proportion as he gave out goodwill to his fellows they returned it to him. He hailed them all by their Christian names, and they responded by calling him Gerard and Gerry and Jed. Whom, outside the family, did Justin call by his Christian name? Robin was really altruistic—or he tried to be—and it was the same story with him: the devotion he gave to his poor people and his gaol-birds he got back in good measure. Himself, he had pursued his own aims, giving affection to none, still less devotion, and because he had given nothing to the outer world, no response had come from it. Oh yes, he could see it all. Think of that point where the outer world was nearest to him: his wife. Think of Primrose, loving him not at all, enduring him only, and sometimes hating him. And then think of Jessica. Think of Jessica slipping her hand into Robin's as the theatre darkened. Or think of Anne: what a partner she had been to Gerard. And Hector's wife. Hector's wife, though as conventional a shadow and as dull an echo as you'd expect him to choose, yet appeared adequate to his simple needs.

Gerard, Robin, and Hector all had wives who helped them in their careers; he had—Primrose.

Now he heard the boys trooping out of the house in the charge of Mr. Chase. It must be half-past ten, and they were leaving for church. He himself had been in no mood to take them to church this morning. Their voices went diminishing into the distances of Vandermere Road.

And the voices were hardly lost when a knock sounded on the front door. Who was this? Who would come to the door of Erasmus Hall at half-past ten on a Sunday morning? The maid opened his study door.

"There's a gentleman to see you, sir."

"A gentleman? Who?"

"He says he's your brother."

"Not Mr. Robin?"

"Oh no, sir. Not Mr. Robin."

Was it Gerard then or Hector, neither of whom the maid had ever seen? Justin was interested. "Show him in."

"Come in here, sir," said the maid to the visitor in the hall.

And Bozzy walked in. Bozzy in his best Sunday black, with spats and gloves and a cane.

Bozzy! It was the first time in all his life that Bozzy had come alone to his eldest brother's home. It was the first time that he had set foot in this house in Vandermere Road.

Justin's first response was surprise; his second, anger. He didn't want Bozzy anywhere near his school, and he determined to show him this by his reception. He rose; he remained standing; and without asking Bozzy to sit down, he demanded what he wanted.

Bozzy's face wore its deliberately loving smile, but to-day it was a forced smile, and his hands were trembling.

"You won't like what I'm going to say," he began in his oddly powerful voice. And he tried to sweeten the coming words with his smile.

"I can't imagine that anything you say will seriously perturb me, Bozzy."

"I'm afraid it will, though. I haven't come in anger, Justin, though you did hurry past me last night and refuse to have anything to do with me. But it isn't that that made me come to see you. It isn't, really?"

"No?" Justin had perceived at once, from Bozzy's very insistence, that it was precisely his soreness at last night's incident which had brought him here so early this morning. "All right then. It has nothing to do with that. Well, what is it, please?"

"Truthfully it hasn't anything to do with that. Did Robin tell you all I asked him to tell you?"

"I haven't the slightest idea. I can't remember what he said. If you want to know, I was so horrified at what you were doing that I didn't want to hear anything more about it."

"Did he give you my love?"

"Your what?"

"My love."

"I tell you I don't know."

"I asked him to. I told him to. And it's in love that I have come."

"Thank you very much." Justin bowed satirically. "And no doubt that is what you think. Well, what is it you have to say? I am busy."

"You're not working on the Lord's Day, are you?"

This incensed Justin not lightly. "Never mind what I'm doing on the Lord's Day. The Lord's Day's nothing to me. Don't try forcing it on me. Please say what you have to say, quickly."

The two brothers stood facing each other, Bozzy not having the courage to sit down, since he had not been invited to do so. There was a pause while Bozzy gathered courage to speak.

"I have only come because I feel that God has guided me to come. He showed me last night that you were my brother, and I ought to try and save you from yourself while there was yet time."

"Hell!" For a moment Justin was speechless and could only stare at Bozzy. In the same dumfounderment, perhaps, did David the King receive the visitation of Nathan the prophet.

"So I came along first thing this morning, and when I saw your boys coming out to church with some other master, I knew that you must be at home, and I felt certain that the Lord wished me to speak to you."

"I see. Well, I shall be pleased to hear the Lord's message, but will you kindly put it in the fewest possible words and then leave me to my work?"

"Yes, Justin. . . . Yes. . . . This is what I think He wants me to say to you. Don't be angry; but it's just what I told Robin to tell you. You are walking in an awful darkness, Justin, because you care nothing for other men and seek nothing but your own ends. That is a very dreadful path. Unless you turn away from it in time, you will find yourself in the utter darkness of hell. I think something of hell is around you already. I have thought it for some time. I can even feel it in this house."

Still bereft of words, Justin stared at Bozzy, and not without wonder that he should be standing there and pronouncing something that he himself had been half-perceiving in the darkness of his thoughts two minutes ago.

"You are clever, Justin; ever so much cleverer than I am—I admit that—but in this matter you are a fool, you are, really, and I am the wise one. There is no happiness but only misery and disaster along the path that you are following. There is no loneliness like the loneliness of those who love no one. I am happy. I love everyone. I love those that hate me. I have never been so happy in my life as I am now, and I want you to be happy too, like me. I am sorry for you. I pity you."

Justin saw at once that, whatever the Lord might have suggested to him, this was what his festering aggrievement had insisted he should say. "You think you are worldly-wise, but Justin, the worldly-wise are wells without water; they are clouds carried with a tempest, to whom a mist of darkness is reserved for ever. If you stay as you are, there is only one thing than can happen to you—and I say it in love: you will perish in your own corruption."

"Will you get out?" shouted Justin. He shouted it, careless who heard him in the house or the street.

"But the Lord is long-suffering," pursued the trembling Bozzy, determined to get out all the texts with which he had provided himself—the texts which he had heard so often in his Gospel Meeting House or read in the tracts which he issued to the people, "and He is not willing that anyone should perish, but that all should come to repentance. That, I know, is what he wants me to say to you."

"Get out of my house!" Justin advanced a step as if to cast him out.

Bozzy flinched. "I'll go, Justin. I was afraid you wouldn't listen, but I'm glad to have spoken, because I think you'll know the truth of it one day. And it *is* the truth. Your soul is dying in you—oh, yes, it is—and soon it will be dead——"

"Get out!"

"All right, Justin, but remember——"

"How dare you talk to me? How dare you advise me about anything on earth? *You!*"

"It is not I who am speaking to you. It is the dear Lord."

"Get out, then, you and the dear Lord." He laid a hand on his shoulder and began pushing him towards the passage.

"I'm going." And indeed Bozzy walked quickly beneath this touch. "But remember what Jesus said of those who rejected his messengers. He said, 'Shake off the dust of your feet on that house——' "

By this time, and appropriately enough, Bozzy was on the threshold, and Justin slammed the front door on him and on the dust of his feet.

But he had not shut out the wisp of truth that had dropped from Bozzy's threadbare texts. Bozzy had left this in the room behind him. And the very fact that it was Bozzy who

had brought it into the house meant that Justin must sweep
it out. He did so, striding up and down and telling himself
that he was not going to turn weakly from the path on which
he had set forth. He would go his own way, with grim-set
jaw, even if it led straight into hell. He would go his own way
even if it meant an absolute loneliness. It might be that his
way did not produce the love of friends, but he was not going
to be one of the weak ones who needed to be loved. Was he
going to admit that he had been wrong all his life? He wrong,
and open to instruction from Bozzy! Not he. He had not
failed yet. He had built much that he had said he would build.
What had he wanted in the beginning? Success in the form
of applause and comfort and power and freedom. And he had
achieved much of it. He had won the applause of his own
neighbourhood. He had made himself his own master at
twenty-three. He had had his own large home since he was
twenty-three. He had a position of some authority and power,
and, above all, of independence. And he was not finished
yet. No, he was still young: forty-three; and he had the
vigour of a man of twenty. Even it he could not catch up with
Gerard, he could build a success comparable with Robin's
in his new parish, which was nothing so very much, after all.

Justin refused to be melancholy any more. As a demonstration to himself that he was done with melancholy, he
seized his hat and stick and went from the house into the
sunlight, cheerfully humming.

§

When Bozzy, cast out, went down the steps of Erasmus Hall,
he was a little shaken and hurt by the violence of his eldest
brother, of whom he had always been afraid. But, walking
along the quiet Vandermere Road, he comforted himself with
the Master's words: "Blessed are ye when men shall revile you
and persecute you. Rejoice and be exceeding glad, for so
persecuted they the prophets that were before you." The
Master walked along the pavement of Vandermere Road,
saying these words to him. And Bozzy tried to rejoice and be
glad, though his heart was bruised and quivering.

He was not only afraid of Justin; he was fascinated by him.
This youngest and weakest of the le Faber children had always
been fascinated by Justin, the eldest, so tall and dark and
domineering and successful. He had been as fascinated by him

as Robin, the next youngest, had been. But that fascination
had remained hidden within him from the time he was three
till now when he was nearly forty. In childhood it had shown
itself in nothing more than a watching, gaping, interest, and
in manhood it had stayed withindoors, never declaring itself
to Justin, because of his fear of him, and only emerging to tell
others at great length (they not listening) of the gifts and
achievements of his eldest brother. This was the first time—
now when he was thirty-eight—that the Spirit of the Lord,
and another less admirable but unperceived ally, his soreness,
had enabled him to go forth and visit his brother's house and
there assert himself as his lover, his equal, and even, in
spiritual things, his superior.

But it was an experience that had strained and shaken and
shivered him, like a violin string that had been sharply
plucked.

§

A few mornings later there went a letter through the letter-
flap of Justin's door, and he read it at his breakfast table;
and it brought more than a little healing to his suppressed
disappointments. It was from the Secretary of the local
branch of the League of Nations Union. After reminding him
that the whole district was combining in a Mass Meeting to be
held on Sunday week in the Shepherds Bush Orpheum "to
celebrate the signing of the Kellogg Pact and the tenth birthday of the Union"; and that all the churches had promised
their support so that they could expect an audience of three
thousand or more; and that the new Bishop of Uxbridge was
taking the chair and Lord Lammle would be the chief speaker,
it invited him to second the vote of thanks, which would be
proposed by the Vicar of St. Oswald's, Shepherds Bush. "We
think it desirable," wrote the Secretary, "that after this
representative of the local churches a representative of the
local schools should be heard, and we very much hope that
you will consent to say a few words."

Justin was pleased and flattered. Here was something to
tell Robin; something to tell his mother and Hector; something that he must get to the ears of Gerard and Anne. Thrust-
ing from thought the idea that the seconding of a vote of
thanks was but a small part in the play, and that, judging by
the shortness of the notice, they had asked others before him
to fill the role, he told himself that it was doubtful if either

Gerard or Robin, for all their success, had ever been asked to perform before an audience of three thousand.

But, as he read the letter, he had also felt, and this was secret indeed, a throb of fear. And more than one throb: a series of throbs; a pulsing of the heart as if it were pumping air instead of blood. He liked to think that he was afraid of no one, but the truth was that he was never quite free from nervousness if he had to make a public speech. Three thousand . . . and he had never spoken to more than a few hundreds. The throbbing of his heart was almost distressing enough to decide him to decline the invitation. He could still contrive that Robin and Gerard and Hector should hear that he had been invited.

But he would not have been Justin if he had bowed before his fears. He frightened of a few thousand people! Not for a moment. Was there one of them he would be frightened of as an individual? Was there one he would think superior to himself? Not one. Then why should he be the least frightened of them when they were massed together? He was not going to retreat before them. He'd despise himself if he did. No, he was going forward with this. He was going to compete with Gerard and Robin.

It was a decision. No sooner had he left the breakfast table than he sat and wrote to the Secretary accepting the invitation. But his heart beat quick, and his stomach sank, as he drove his pen.

And in the next few days he gave much deliberate labour, and much involuntary emotion, to this five-minutes speech. He wrote to the Secretary asking "for a few pamphlets on the work of the League of Nations Union." He was obliged to do this because, though he had been a subscribing member for many years, he was very vague about the Union. He was vague about it because he was quite uninterested in it, and in the League of Nations too. His real attitude to the Union was one of alternating indifference and annoyance. "That damned Union" annoyed him once a year when he had to pay his subscription, and once a month when its magazine, *Headway*, arrived through his letter box instead of something more interesting. Invariably he tossed the magazine, unopened, into the wastepaper basket. "A few pamphlets to refresh his memory," he said to the Secretary, but there was really nothing in his memory to be refreshed. He went to the Public Library and searched for books on the League of Nations. He went into the Reference Library and asked for the back files of the *Times* to learn something about the Kellogg Pact. He read several speeches on this Pact for the Renunciation of War and made some valuable notes. And one afternoon, still dissatisfied, he went all the way to the Union headquarters in Grosvenor Crescent and, entering the Literature Room, made a selection from the swarm of pamphlets there. He went into the Library and made a selection from the books. And he came away, encumbered with pamphlets and books: *The League of Nations, What it is, The Pact of Paris Explained, All about the League, The League of Nations and the Churches, Spiritual Fathers of the League, Further Sunday School Lessons on the League,* and *Roads to the City of God.*

Nor would he have been Justin if he had not been amused by this burden of high-minded books. "When I do a thing, I do it properly," he told himself with a grin. By this time he was beginning to get a great deal of humour out of this business of an address to three thousand supporters of the League of Nations Union.

When he reached home and had piled this hillock of information on his desk, it looked so rich in mineral content that he began to have hopes, and quite excited hopes, of building a speech that would surpass Lord Lammle's, the Bishop's, and the Vicar's, and be the speech of the evening. Nothing else but this literature did he read for the next night or two, and by dint of stealing a point here and a point there, and now this phrase and now that, he did assemble a witty and effective speech. Reading the literature, he became quite interested in the League of Nations.

But the more he dreamed of a great success, the more he decided that he must learn the speech by heart. In no other way could he be certain of delivering it just as he had shaped it, with all its fine phrases in position. And as his ambition soared, he determined to use no notes so that the three thousand people might imagine that the brilliant speech was extempore. He committed it to memory, and each evening, the manuscript on his study table, he rehearsed it, declaiming its stronger points to the closed door or the fireplace. And each morning, the manuscript in his dressing-gown pocket, he rehearsed it again while he was shaving.

More and more pleased with it, and with his delivery of it, he made an excuse for visiting Robin that he might tell him he was going to address an audience of several thousand people.

"I was in your parts visiting a prospective parent," said he, lying briskly, as he sat himself down in Robin's room. "So I thought I'd come along and see how goodness was thriving."

"It's at rather a low ebb just now," said Robin.

"Is it? Well, the tide's right out, so far as I'm concerned. Always has been, I'm afraid. But you're thriving well in the world, old boy. When are you going to your new parish?"

Robin told him. He told him all his plans; he described the new vicarage and Jessica's schemes for its decoration; but Justin wasn't listening—he rarely listened to other people's talk about themselves—and while Robin was still in the middle of a sentence, he broke in, "Seen Gerard lately?"

Robin said no. No one saw anything of old Gerard in these days; he was sunk over head and ears in the success of his new play. It was far and away the biggest success he had ever had.

Justin wondered how he could direct the talk towards the League of Nations. And suddenly, while Robin was describing a visit that he and Jessica had paid to Hector and his wife, he saw a way which had been open to him all along.

"By the way," he interrupted. "Didn't you say that it was your predecessor at St. Michael's, Cunningham Gardens, who'd just been made the new Bishop of Uxbridge?"

"Yes. Archdeacon Beresford-Graeme."

"I thought so. Well, he's presiding at a big League of Nations meeting which I'm addressing."

"Really? Are you?" Robin was surprised and interested. He begged further information.

"It's to celebrate the signing of the Kellogg Pact, and it seems it's going to be a real monster meeting. Three or four thousand people. They've secured the new Orpheum for it."

"And you're one of the speakers?"

"Yes. . . . Yes, they invited me to speak. . . . I'm not the chief speaker, of course," he added with modesty. "Lord Lammle is top of the bill."

"When is it?"

"Next Sunday at eight-thirty, so that the churches and chapels can tip their congregations into it. There's no doubt it'll be a packed audience."

"Eight-thirty. I can make it. I shall come along and hear you. Of course. And I'll bring Jessica too."

Instantly Justin felt again that throbbing of the heart. He had accustomed himself to the idea of speaking to three thousand strangers, but not to the picture of Robin sitting in their midst. Robin before whom, most of all, he needed to excel.

"Sunday at eight-thirty." Robin jotted down date, time, and place on his engagement block, as Justin repeated them to him rather uneasily. "Yes, I wouldn't miss this for something. Have you told Mother? She'll be there, of course. And perhaps Gerard too. After all, it's Sunday. The whole family ought to be there."

Justin did not stay long after that. He said, "Good-bye, good-bye, old man. *Ne mentez jamais*," and hurried home to rehearse his speech again.

CHAPTER FOUR

THE Orpheum was but a few months old when Justin spoke in it. Built and owned by an independent company, it was the newest cinema in West London, and its management declared it was the finest. The management, seeking the good-will of the district, were making a point of lending or renting its auditorium for all good local causes, if they believed they would gain more than they would lose thereby. Any such cause was proclaimed most generously on its screen. There were those who said that Mr. Lasker, the young manager, was displacing all the local vicars and ministers as the real leader of the laity, since it was he who really had the people in his temple, and the cinema screen was the altar at which the modern world worshipped.

Certainly the great temple of the Orpheum was built in the most modern manner. It was a square, flat-topped mountain of warm, reddish bricks, fronting the bus stop in the Uxbridge Road. The only breaks in its high, blank façade were the line of foyer windows on the first floor and, above these, the name "Orpheum" in gigantic letters surrounded with neon lighting. Almost the whole width of the ground floor was occupied by the swing doors that led into the vestibule. In frames, between these doors, were the "stills" of the week's pictures. But this week in late October a double-crown poster board leaned here and there between the doors and stood on an ornamental easel in the vestibule. It said:

THE PEOPLE APPLAUD THE KELLOGG PACT
NO MORE WAR!
The Rt. Hon. Viscount Lammle of Keith
will speak at the
SHEPHERDS BUSH ORPHEUM
on Sunday, Oct. 28th at 8.30 p.m.
supported by
The Rt. Rev. the Bishop of Uxbridge
The Vicar of St. Oswald's, Shepherds Bush
and
Justin le Faber, Esq.

The auditorium was one vast floor and one vast circle
sloping towards the organ casing on either side of the proscenium. The walls and ceiling were painted a soft coffee-
cream, touched with gold; the curtains within the proscenium
were gold; and the carpet everywhere was a mosaic of reds,
browns, and yellows, an autumn tinting that was as soft to
the eye as the pile was soft to the feet.

At nine-thirty on the Sunday evening not a single plush
seat was visible since the audience occupied them all. It was
an audience with a strong Sunday character about it: there
were far more elderly people than young ones and far more
women than men; most were dressed in church-going attire;
and, sprinkled over the dark assembly, there were almost as
many faces above clerical collars as there are ox-eye daisies
in a meadow. On the stage the gold curtains were drawn in
a becoming modesty across the irreligious screen, leaving
but a shallow stage for a platform. On this platform the
Bishop sat in the centre before a small table, a vase of flowers,
and a carafe of water, with Lord Lammle on his right hand
and the Vicar and Justin on his left. Behind these speakers,
in a single row of chairs, sat some persons of weight and
influence who were supporting them.

Justin had given hardly less preparation to his appearance
than to his speech. He had granted himself a new morning
suit for the occasion (telling himself that he had long needed
one) and since a new suit deserves a new shirt, his linen was
white and glossy from the makers. His dark, waving hair,
punctiliously parted in the middle, shone from ointment and
the brush. As Lord Lammle was a small, attenuated, round-
backed man, and the Bishop and the Vicar were plump little

ecclesiastics, and the persons of weight and influence had become merged into a general mass, it was beyond doubt that Justin was the most impressive figure on the stage.

At half-past nine Lord Lammle had concluded his long discourse, and the Vicar was on his feet proposing a vote of thanks to him for coming amongst them and to the Bishop for his conduct in the chair. It was very near the moment when Justin must rise.

Justin's legs were crossed, and his eyes roamed over the field of faces on the deep, raked floor, and over the hanging garden of faces in the circle above. He was not listening to the Vicar any more than he had listened to Lord Lammle. Why listen, when he was not the least interested in the Kellogg Pact or in the L.N.U. or in the views of either of these gentlemen on either? He was interested only in the speech that he must shortly deliver. He uncrossed his legs and crossed them again, anxious to begin. This anxiety to begin was the only symptom of nervousness left in him now, and it was almost quite as much eagerness as nervousness. His speech was excellent, he knew, and incomparably better than that which old Lord Lammle had just concluded. And it might well be excellent, thought he, since it was the cream of fifty other men's speeches and pamphlets. Its phrases were the best they had achieved, for he had been content with nothing but the best. Old Lord Lammle's phrases, on the other hand, had been worn-out tags from the ready-made shelf, dusty and dull and formal, and they had evoked only formal applause.

The Vicar was being much less dull. He was racy at times, as rotund men often are, and trenchant at times, as preachers can be, but he faltered and stuttered a good deal, and Justin, grinning inwardly again, guessed that the number of the Vicar's rehearsals compared with his own were as the half of one to fifty. In fluency and grace of delivery he would leave the Vicar nowhere.

Still, the Vicar was whipping up the audience to bursts of applause, and on the whole, Justin decided, this was a good thing. It would warm the audience for *his* speech, and he wouldn't have to speak to a cold house. "Go on, old boy," he thought. "You're preparing the river splendidly for me. This is excellent ground bait. Wonder how many people there are in the theatre. Over three thousand, I should say. A magnificent piece of publicity for Erasmus

Hall and Erasmus High School for Girls. I still don't know what a High School is, but the high moral tone I'm taking in my speech should fetch the parents along. Yes, I should have been a fool to decline this invitation."

When would the old Vicar stop and let him get going? What was he saying now? Justin turned his face to listen for once.

"There are only two further points I desire to make," the Vicar was saying, and Justin was glad there were no more. "The Covenant of the League of Nations did not completely outlaw war. It allowed two quarrelling nations to resort to war in the event of its council being unable to arrive at a unanimous decision on the dispute between them. That was the agreed position between the nations till they signed the Kellogg Pact. But what now? Now for the first time in the long history of man the honour of all the great powers of the world is bound up with their signature to a pact which states quite simply, quite directly, that they condemn recourse to war for the solution of international controversies and renounce it as an instrument of national policy. I wish I could read you the names of the nations which have adhered to the pact or announced their intention to adhere. What names they are. Some sixty of them. What records of war they recall. What blood-stained centuries lie behind them. But now they say, 'It is enough.'" Applause, " 'It shall cease.'" Louder applause, which the Vicar, lifting his fat palm, both blessed and silenced. "My second point is this. A great American, President Wilson, a century and a half after his people had drawn up a Declaration of Independence and a Constitution of the United States, drew up for the world, in the League Covenant, a Declaration of *Inter*dependence." Applause again. "But then his people rejected him; and the second great historic gap in the League Covenant is the absence of the United States from its fellowship. But now—now, ladies and gentlemen—a second great American, the Hon. Frank B. Kellogg, has come a second time to the fight and brought his people with him."

Prolonged applause filled the theatre here, and Justin began to wonder whether he was pleased any more that the Vicar was doing so well. The Vicar's business, in Justin's design, was to warm up the meeting for *him*, not to walk off with it like this. He mustn't speak so well that anything after him was in danger of being an anticlimax. A faint nervousness attacked Justin again, and he swept his eyes over the steppe of faces on the tilted floor, to where Robin and Hector were sitting with their mother and Jessica and Hector's wife. That was all of the family who were there, and it was quite enough, he thought. He was used to the idea of Robin and Hector being there with their women, but the fact remained that that little posse of relatives worried him as much as the whole nameless multitude put together, and he was glad that Gerard and Anne had not joined the little company.

As for Bozzy, he did not give him a thought.

§

But Bozzy was there. He was in the theatre. Some evenings earlier he had wandered along the gutters with his placards on high to present them and their message to the long queue waiting outside the doors of the Orpheum. On one face of his board, in red and black lettering, was, "What must I do to be saved?" and on the other the answer, "Believe on the Lord Jesus Christ, and thou shalt be saved, and thy house"; and when he reached the gutter before the queue, he stood there and presented the people with the question first and then, swivelling the pole round, with the answer. Twenty times he did this, and the people smiled. But though he may have seemed to them a laughable figure it is likely that he was happier than any of them. He was completely at peace in the love of the Lord and in his own love for all men, and in the thought that he was trying to give to them of his abundance and to win them to the happiness that was his.

And as he stood there, he saw of a sudden another double-crown placard leaning against the wall. Wondering for a second if it was placed there by the Jesus Shall Reign Mission, from whom he got his own placards, he walked forward to look at it. It advertised a Peace Meeting, and to his surprise he saw Justin's name upon it. And because in his view it was the poster of deluded people, still in error, whose way to peace was heedless of the Lord and could therefore lead only to confusion, but still more because it announced Justin as a speaker—Justin, his brother, who had cast him from his door—it pricked into his memory as might a rusty nail and left there a sore place that soon became slightly inflamed. And though he did not perceive and admit it, the pin-point centre of that inflamed spot was Justin. There is none so argumentative as a new convert, and as the day of the meeting drew nearer, Bozzy, ruminating upon it, became conscious

of a call. It was a call such as came to Amos, the herdman
of Tekoa, to go and sow the true seed in so large and rich a
field. He must take the true Word to the people as they
poured into the meeting. Peace through the League of
Nations? Peace through the Kellogg Pact? There was no
peace in such things. There was peace only in the blood of
Christ Jesus. Peace only when his saving health should be
known among all nations. This was the only peace, and he,
Bozzy, must take the Lord's controversy to these people—
and to Justin. "Woe to them that are at ease in Zion, and
trust in the mountain of Samaria."

With the joy of an artist at work he went to the Mission,
selected two appropriate posters, and pasted them on the
front and back of his board. It was a happy hour he spent
doing this in the back garden of the little house in Pemberthy Road. And at eight o'clock on the Sunday, holding
his board aloft, he walked along the gutter towards the
swinging front doors of the Orpheum, and took up a position
there, face to face with the large doorman in his uniform of
coffee and gold who was guiding and regulating the inflowing
crowd. Bozzy directed the front of his board towards the
stream of people. It assured them, "When they shall say
Peace and Safety, then sudden destruction cometh upon
them." After allowing them time to absorb this, he turned the
pole round that they might read, "Peace from Him Which is,
and was, and is to come." Sometimes he lifted his fine deep
voice and cried at them: "Peace by Jesus Christ, Acts, Ten,
Thirty-six. Peace by Jesus Christ, Acts, Ten, Thirty-six."
To those passing through the doors, and therefore passing
beyond his help, he would shout ever and again, as a last
warning, "They were defiled with their own works and went
a-whoring with their own inventions," but would add, that
they might know that he loved and blessed them, even in
their darkness of error, "Peace be with all in Christ." And
those who laughed at him he reminded without anger, "Whosoever is not written in the book of life shall be cast into the
lake of fire. Revelation, Twenty, Fifteen."

Justin, entering by the stage door in Gibbon Street, did not
see him. The others, Robin and Jessica, and Hector and his
wife and their mother, saw him and hurried into the vestibule
before he could see them. Bozzy, his mind concentrated on
his creative work, his vision impaired by a haze of love and
blessedness, did not observe them in the throng.

A clock struck the half-hour; the stream of people was now no more than a trickle; and Bozzy decided that it was time to go into the meeting. He walked with his boarded pole into the vestibule. He laid it against the side wall between the pictures of two film stars. And there it stood like the austere message of God between the portraits of women who, most vividly and colourfully, had declined to renounce the pride of the flesh. The large doorman, after Bozzy had passed from sight, studied its message: "Peace from Him Which is, and was, and is to come," and supposed that it was something to do with this strange religious invasion to-night. He studied it a second time and wondered if the manager would wish it to be there. He decided to turn its face to the wall. He did so, only to read: "When they shall say Peace and Safety, then sudden destruction cometh upon them." This defeated him, and he left it there.

And there it stayed, to warn all who should yet come in, and all those who should come out after hearkening to the speakers and being comforted.

Bozzy walked up the soft-carpeted stairs to the circle. He stood in the dark gangway, but nowhere could he see an empty seat. The eyes of all were directed upon the lighted stage where a bent and scanty little man was speaking. Concealed lighting around the proscenium arch framed the scene on the stage in an halation of alternate pink and green. The only house lights were the illuminated clocks, the illuminated exit signs, and a few shaded lamps in the roof and on the walls. Bozzy went down through the dim gloaming for the whole length of the gangway, looking for a seat. Finding none, and ignorant of the Lord Chamberlain's rules, he stood leaning against the wall immediately behind the rails of the parapet. From here he stared at Justin sitting with his legs crossed, in the box of light which was the stage.

He did not listen much because he had long lost the habit of listening to talk which he did not understand. Like Justin he studied the audience in the stalls below and in the circle behind him. And everywhere, scattered among the people, he saw the priests and ministers who were leading their flocks into error by teaching them other ways to salvation than by faith alone. His religion nowadays being the fixed spectacles through which he assessed the world, he was able to distinguish the Anglicans from the Romans and Nonconformists, and the high Anglicans from the low Anglicans, by their collars or their stocks or their moustaches, just as a small boy, interested in motors, can distinguish their makers' names by the shapes of their radiators. There they all were, and which of them had really seen the light? On the stage, behind the Bishop, was the Rev. Father Hogben, notorious as a Romanizer who would undo the Protestant Reformation in England. The Truth swelled in Bozzy. The Spirit of the Lord, as he conceived it to be, was filling him with the conviction that he must speak aloud to this great gathering, and with the power to speak. It worked his heart like a pump as it filled him with power; it set his whole body vibrating.

But whether or not it was the Spirit of the Lord which was astir in Bozzy now, it is certain that another spirit, unrecognized by his simple mind, was also pumping power into him, and this one might be called the Dangerous Spirit of the Family. There on the platform was his eldest brother. There sat Justin who for nearly forty years had stirred in Bozzy a strange blend of fascination and fear, of admiration, affection, and hostility; Justin who but yesterday had spurned him from his door. The Dangerous Spirit whispered that it was Justin whom he must interrupt with his testimony; Justin whom he must denounce for his error; not the Vicar or the Bishop, but Justin; because Justin was his brother whom before all others he must save. And Bozzy nodded Yes to the whisper, supposing it to be the voice of God, and he waited for Justin to begin.

§

Now the Vicar had finished, and they were applauding him, and the Bishop had risen to introduce Justin.

"I have much pleasure now," he said, "in calling upon——" and here he looked down upon his agenda paper—"Mr. Faber." He looked down again for further information because Mr. Faber's activities were unknown to him. "Oh, I beg your pardon—Mr. *le* Faber, Headmaster of Erasmus Hall."

Justin rose. He braced back his wide shoulders and thrust the fingers of both hands into his waistcoat pockets. He smiled pleasantly at the audience, and there must have been few who did not think, as he rose to his full height, that this was as fine a man as they had seen. Applause welcomed him from a portion of the floor. It was from the congregation of his own church who admired and liked him because he was their officer and because he was always ready with a jest for

those whom he met in the street. His fingers remained in his
vest pockets, for he had no notes. No notes meant no rein-
forcements once he had advanced; no repair services or
supplies; but he was confident now that he knew his speech
so perfectly that he could not flounder in it or stray. Now
that he was upon his feet he was happy in what he was doing.

"As I sat here, looking over this vast audience, the thought
came to me," he began, in a sentence which he had written a
week before, "that it must be something unusually righteous
that had brought together such a concourse of people, most
of whom would disagree on all other subjects." Some laughter
greeted this opening sentence, and he was pleased, and thought
of Robin sitting in his place. "It must be something very
good that has banded us together like this, something so in-
disputably right that 'we needs must love it when we see it.'
And that is just what it is, for in applauding the Kellogg Pact,
ladies and gentlemen, and demonstrating our will to peace,
we are merely giving voice to Man's instinctive belief in
fellowship, in justice, in humanity and mercy and love."
This drew its applause from the half-darkness, as such a procession of abstract virtues was bound to do; and he continued,
"In all men there is, I suggest, a deep desire for peace and
lawful behaviour——" (That should amuse Robin, he
thought, coming from me)—"and if this is so—if no men anywhere wish to suffer the brutalities of war, and few, very few,
desire to inflict them—what is it that so hampers the work of
the League of Nations? I will tell you what I think it is. It is
not people's lack of desire for righteousness and peace, but
their lack of faith that their desire can be achieved. And that
is why those of us who belong to the League of Nations Union
—and I have been an enthusiastic member of it since its in-
ception ten years ago—should address our efforts, not to con-
verting the people to the hideousness of war, because they need
no conversion, but to organizing the universal desire for peace
and righteousness till it has become a demand so loud and
insistent that they themselves can believe in its triumph."
This was a good sentence—he had forgotten from whom it
came—and it drew as loud applause as any heard that evening.

"When they believe in that, they will have their way. The
statesmen will yield when they see that the common sense of
the world—or, if you like, the essential morality of the world
—can tolerate their wars no longer. People say that this
Pact for the Renunciation of War makes too great a demand

upon human nature. Ladies and gentlemen, it is not upon
ordinary men and women, but upon our statesmen and their
habits of thought that it makes too great a demand." Much
applause. This was fine; and he was glad that Robin and
Hector were there. "But let us not put all the blame on them.
The fault is ours too because we will not demand, we will not
insist, on a higher moral standard in our public men. Let us
make it known to them that we want no cynical vision in high
places. Let us demand a moral greatness in those who pre-
sume to lead us—"

A voice rang out from the dim golden twilight of the
auditorium. "Peace through the blood of His cross."

Three thousand pairs of eyes swung from Justin towards
this sudden cry. And there in the corner of the circle by the
organ casing, they saw a figure standing with an arm outstretched and a finger pointing upward. Like a clock in the
church tower Bozzy had assembled his strength and struck.
People rose to see him better. "Peace only in Christ Jesus,"
he called, and his voice was deep and strong. "Why do you
seduce the people saying, Peace, peace, when there is no
peace? There is no peace in any pact among unconverted
men, but only in the submission of the nations to Christ
Jesus."

A hurrying steward touched him on the shoulder to encourage him to sit down. By now more than half the audience
was standing to watch any contention or, better still, any
active belligerency that might develop between this interrup-
ter and the steward.

Bozzy did not heed the finger of the steward. He was full
to the lips with some texts that he was determined to deliver.
"Therefore thus saith the Lord God, You have built up a
wall and daubed it with untempered mortar——"

Another steward, much pleased at this sudden accession of
interest in a hitherto monotonous task, and at this shining
opportunity to exercise his power, came running down the
gangway to lend an authoritative hand to his colleague; and
men in the seats near by, pleased to impress their women,
got up, as responsible burgesses should, to assist the officers
in an arrest. But the Bishop down on the stage, who had also
risen, saw a better way.

"No, no," he called. "Let him say what he has to say. Go
on, sir. We will listen to what you have to say. After all,
we all desire the same ends." And he sat down again, and all

followed his example. But he leaned forward over his table as if he did not intend to remain seated for long. "Now, sir?"

Justin was still standing. His face was dark with wrath, and his jaw was thrust forward. He did not look in the least like a man who believed in peace and mercy and love. Bozzy began to speak again, and now the only two standing in that crowded theatre were these two brothers, Justin on the stage and Bozzy behind the circle wall.

"Peace through the blood of His cross." Bozzy stretched out his arm again, and his eyes were flashing as if his own courage were inspiring him. The texts that he had assembled burst from him in a rapid sequence, and now and again he had to knock the spittle from his lips. "You have spoken vanity and lies. Therefore thus saith the Lord God, Because you have spoken vanity and lies, I am against you. And mine hand shall be upon the prophets that see vanity and divine lies; they shall not be in the assembly of my people. . . . They have seduced my people, saying, Peace, peace, when there is no peace. . . ." He wiped his mouth on the back of his hand. "There is no peace in the works and imaginations of men. You are defiled with your own works and go a-whoring after your own inventions——"

"Yes, yes," said the Bishop, feeling that one word in this last quotation was infelicitous, and that he had better prevent the delivery of any other such. "Yes, that will do. There is real truth in much that you have said, and we thank you for it." He waved to Bozzy to sit down, and Bozzy obeyed. "Most of us here are agreed, I think, that we can achieve little without the help of God, but we are grateful to you for reminding us of it."

Bozzy rose again. "Jeremiah, Six, Fourteen, and Ezekiel, Thirteen, Ten," he explained.

"Yes," agreed the Bishop. "Thank you." And, having smiled at Bozzy and soothed him, he turned to Justin. "Now, Mr. Faber." The Vicar on his left corrected him. "Oh, yes, I'm sorry. I beg your pardon: Mr. *le* Faber. Now, Mr. le Faber, the floor is yours."

Justin had been standing all the time. And now the silence was given back to him, and all the thousands of faces too. He saw them gazing up at him. He tried to remember what he was saying when Bozzy interrupted him. In horror he found that he could remember nothing; and the people were still staring at him. There was silence in the theatre while they

waited. What had he been saying? What was he talking about?
That silence came towards him from the auditorium like a
dark storm. When he realized that there was nothing in his
mind but a void, and a void that nothing would fill, the
silence gripped his heart like a deathly hand. In panic he
cried to his memory to give him back his speech, but because
it had been learned by heart, because it had been entirely
uninformed by any real interest or feeling, because it was a
false and ill-fitting garment, it had gone from him. Bozzy's
voice had blown it away like the paper trappings of some
cheap disguise, and he was naked. He could remember
nothing. He could not even remember what the meeting was
about.

The silence was still there, but now it was covered in
places, as breath covers a mirror, by embarrassed whisperings and rustlings. And that silence, and those whisperings,
smiting upon him, completed the stunning of his memory.
In all his forty-three years he had known no such moment of
horror as this, when he stood before thousands, humiliated,
empty, stunned, and an object for pity. He tried yet again
to recover the lines of his speech, and so drive this moment
away from him, as one forces a nightmare away while one is
still asleep, but no recollection of any kind came out of the
white emptiness of his brain. Without a word, knowing nothing else to do, he sat down.

A low murmur of sympathy swept over the audience, and a
few applauded to comfort him and show that they understood. Perhaps they were his own congregation—his own
congregation before whom he had been shamed. He knew
that that murmur and that applause would ache in his mind
for the rest of his life.

The Bishop had risen. He was saying a few words to close
the meeting, but Justin's brain, beating and throbbing, did
not hear what he said. In his despair, seeking further tor-
ment, he looked towards Robin and his mother and Hector.
He saw Robin staring at him, and that fixed, pained, wondering stare was like a bayonet turned in his heart. He wished that
Robin who had witnessed this humiliation would die to-
morrow. He wished that all these thousands of people who
had witnessed it could be annihilated.

The meeting was over. The people on the platform, the
prosperous, distinguished, and unashamed men, were passing
him as they left the stage. The audience was filing from the

auditorium, chattering as they went through the doors.
Chattering about him? With the others he went to a room
beside the stage. Some spoke to him, but he hardly knew
what they were saying. One idea was mastering his mind:
to escape from the theatre before Robin and the family could
find him. A minute later, having slipped out through the
stage door, he was hurrying home through the welcome darkness, his face burning and his temples beating.

CHAPTER FIVE

IT was between eight and nine at night in Brook Green Road,
and Justin was walking slowly by the high grey garden wall
that bounds its eastern side. He came to the corner by the
green, where, looking obliquely across the grass, he could see
in the darkness the mouth of Pemberthy Road—that mouth
out of which, when he and his brothers were boys, they used
to come running for their games on the green. He turned the
corner and walked along this side of the green till he could
look straight down the little road. It was empty. There they
were, that little string of red-brick houses, with their lighted
windows and their closed doors and their seemly quiet; and
there was No. 7, as quiet as the rest, and full of childish
memories. Nearly fifty years now since his father came to
that house; and his mother and Bozzy had not moved from it
in all the years.

No sign of Bozzy coming out of the house, and he, Justin,
must not be seen lingering in the darkness here. He crossed the
green diagonally and walked up Shepherds Bush Road. He
walked slowly, very slowly, and looked back often. He was
keeping in view the exits out of which Bozzy would come if
he left Pemberthy Road to go wandering, with his stick and
gloves, or his pole and board, among the crowds in King
Street or in the Uxbridge Road. When there was a danger of
these exits fading into the dark, he slowed his step and stopped
and stood dawdling at a street corner.

Bozzy had not appeared. This was the fourth night that
Justin had come to these streets to watch and wait for him.
But on none of the previous nights had he appeared. Surely
he would come to-night. Surely he would: it was Saturday;
and on Saturday, so Justin had learned in the last few days,

Bozzy, if he did not carry his message abroad on a pole, would ramble along the lighted thoroughfares looking for prostitutes so that, when they beckoned him with their eyes, he could go up to them and say, "Christ will save you yet," or "Christ does not condemn thee. Go and sin no more." He *must* come to-night, for everything was at its best to-night. To-night it was high water at eleven fifty-two. To-morrow the water would hardly be high enough till after midnight. The moon was new, and the river was brimming with the spring tide, but the swell of the river would sink as the days passed and the moon enlarged. Come to-night, Bozzy. Come, oh come.

As he thought these things, lingering at the corner, Justin's mind became a kind of dark theatre in which he sat alone and watched his own performance by the river a few days ago. It was midday then, and low water, and he saw himself, a solitary figure moving along the Lower Mall. The figure was walking to a point by the boathouses. Here he stopped and, leaning an elbow on the parapet, looked down upon the un-covered mud and then out at the narrowed stream. His eyes returned to the embankment wall beneath him, and he studied the highwater mark along it. The moss was still soaked and the long weeds lank where the tide had drowned them. Seven foot was full flood depth here, he estimated; and eight foot, deepening to twelve, beneath the wharfs on his right; for the river bed sagged upstream. Eight foot was more than enough for a man who could not swim. He con-sidered the brickwork under the weed-grown and neglected wharf at his side: no mooring rings there, or hanging chain at which desperate fingers might clutch. No skiffs or dinghies afloat at their moorings nearer than two wharfs away. Lifting his elbow from the parapet, he examined that wharf more carefully. It was more like a little garden of weeds now than a wharf. It had an old grey wall on either side of it and a newer concrete wall along its back to shut it from the footpath. Its fourth side was open to the river. The concrete wall was broken by a wooden tidegate, made of heavy horizontal planks which could be lifted, one by one, out of their grooves. There were only two of these in the grooves now, and he walked towards them, stepped over them, and stood among the weeds. A glance to see that no one watched him; and he walked to the wharf's brink and looked down at the broad, deep emptiness between the river walls.

The mud was green beneath the wharf and so soft that the

fallen bricks, the broken chains, and the old castaway tins
were sunk in it almost from sight. Even if the water were not
eight foot deep, a man's foot would sink into that slime as
into a shallow quagmire. He lifted his eyes a little. Farther
out the mud was ribbed and sandy, and its shingle glistened
in the sun: it bore easily the sodden driftwood and the cor-
dage and the old iron that were strewn upon its surface.
Farther still, and it was a silken carpet seamed with shining
rills that ran down the shelve to the low river laughing in the
sun. Justin brought his eyes back to the stagnant bottom
beneath him. Dank and luminous and grey, with a sickly
opalescence or an evil green filmed upon it, and the stark
grey wall falling starkly down to it, it would serve as a picture
of the very bottom of despair.

Now he turned about and looked at the boathouses behind
him. They would be empty at night, and blind. No one
would see what was happening in this little space between
the walls. . . .

Justin left this picture of himself in the weed-grown wharf
as he left the corner where he had been standing in the
Shepherds Bush Road. He strolled back towards Brook
Green and, doing so, noticed that the wind was touching his
right cheek. Then the wind must be a few points north of
west and would be blowing downstream in the face of the
inflowing tide. That was good; yes, that was good; the water
would be distressed and fractious; it would mutter and com-
plain against the sides of wharfs and dinghies, and the air
would be full of sounds.

He passed again the base of the green and looked again
towards Pemberthy Road. No, so sign of Bozzy. Ah, well . . .
better so, perhaps . . . yes, better so. . . . Still, he walked more
and more slowly, unwilling to leave behind him a scheme so
well considered and so favoured by circumstances to-night.
Abruptly he stopped. There, in Brook Green Road, twenty
yards ahead of him, was Bozzy, walking by the old grey wall,
his crook-handled stick hung upon his arm. How he came to
be just ahead of him like that without his having seen him
before was difficult to understand: presumably there were
times when one's brooding was so deep that one's eyes ceased
their office and saw nothing.

Justin followed, keeping him in view. It was too early to
accost him yet. He followed him as far as the Broadway
and when he crossed to the southern pavement of King

Street, kept pace with him on the opposite side. A tepid mist had been oppressing the city all day, but now it had withdrawn before the wind, and stars were breaking up the clouds, and the shop windows were slowly losing their moisture like eyes that have been comforted at last. Lamplight gleamed on the chromium of the modern shop-fronts and laid a sheen on the pavements whose flags were still greasy from the heavy footsteps of the fog. The new wind played gently with the paper tumbled into the gutter or beneath the people's feet. Bozzy, his simple mind keeping him in the rut of habit, took exactly the course he was accustomed to take with his board on high, except that to-night he walked along the kerb instead of in the gutter. He walked as far as Beavor Lane and here crossed the road to come back on the other side. And as he stepped on to the opposite pavement, Justin stepped into his path.

"Hey, Bozzy." There was a mask of merriment on Justin's face. "How's things with Bozzy?"

Bozzy started as at the challenge of a footpad. Recognizing Justin, he became embarrassed, for he had not seen him since that night at the Orpheum. "All right, Justin. How are you?"

"Fine. Glad I've met you, Bozzy. I've been wanting for some time to say I was sorry for being so rude to you that Sunday when you came to my house. I know you only meant to be kind, and I don't want to quarrel with a brother. You've forgiven me for that, eh?"

"Of course, Justin." Bozzy put out a smile for Justin— one of his sweetest. "And you're not angry with me for interrupting your speech?"

"No!" Justin ridiculed the idea. "You bowled me clean out, but there it is! My middle stump flew right out of the ground and was never seen again, but what does it matter? The meeting was a great success even if I scored a duck. That's all forgotten, Bozzy. Don't you worry about that."

"I didn't want to bowl you out, I didn't really, Justin. It wasn't done in spite. You didn't think it was done in spite, did you? As a matter of fact, I've been praying for you ever since."

"Well, this is the answer to prayer, old son." Justin kept up the bantering tone that one adopts with a child, a sick person, or a simpleton. "Here we are! Friends again. Here we are, full of love."

"I'm so glad," declared Bozzy, and his smile was yet sweeter.

" 'The prayer of a righteous man availeth much.' You see: I know my Bible almost as well as you. And that reminds me, old boy: we'll go on one day with that pious talk we were having, when I so rudely escorted you to the door. I want you to tell me some more about my sins."

"We're all sinners."

"Not a doubt of it, Bozzy. Not a doubt of it as far as I am concerned."

"But I'm just as bad——"

"Oh no, Bozzy! No, no!"

"Well, I was, until I was saved. And we can all be saved if we want to be."

"That's what I want you to tell me about. I think it's time I was saved. To tell the truth, I fancy I'm beginning to see the light. I'm impressed by the happiness that religion seems to have brought to you and Robin."

Bozzy shook his head at Robin's name. "Robin is a sincere lover of Jesus, but he is wrong about many things."

"What? Hasn't he got the truth?"

"No. Not yet. Not the real truth."

"Good lord! It's all more difficult than I thought. Old Robby's been sniffing up the wrong tree, has he? No salvation up there? Well, well! Dear, dear! Think of that now. You must explain all these complications to me: there's no doubt I'm lost in the outer darkness. When shall we have another talk about it all?"

"Whenever you like? To-night, if you like. It's still early."

Justin pretended to consider this.

"It's always a mistake to put it off," said Bozzy. 'Don't put it off if the Lord is touching your heart at last. '*Now* is the accepted time. *Now* is the day of salvation.' "

"I don't know that I can talk to-night. I've got a man coming to see me, a fellow in difficulties whom I'm trying to help, an old pupil who's got badly off the tracks. You wouldn't have me disappoint him, would you? But I'll tell you what: he won't take up the whole night. Could you wait for me somewhere?"

"Certainly, Justin. I'll wait for you just as long as you like."

"What's the time now? A little after nine. Suppose we give this lad an hour. He'll want all that time to pour out his woes: one gets very fluent if one's telling a hard-luck story, especially if half of it's lies. Say I meet you somewhere as soon as possible after ten, eh? That all right? And wait for me, won't you. Wait for the lost sheep."

"Of course I'll wait for you. But where?"

"Somewhere where it's quiet and we can walk up and down. What about the old river? It's quiet enough along the malls after ten o'clock. Shall I meet you by the door of the Quaker Meeting House. That seems a suitable place—or are the Quakers all wrong too? It's all very difficult. Who was the man in the Bible who came to someone to ask him questions by night. I feel rather like him, ha, ha, ha. Nicodemus, wasn't it?"

"Yes, Nicodemus." Bozzy, proud of his biblical knowledge, added some more information. "He was a man of the Pharisees."

"Well, that's me all right."

"And he came to Jesus by night——"

"Well, we won't pursue *that* parallel. But Nicodemus and I are a pair. And like him I don't want anyone to know that I'm asking for help. I'm still too soaked in pride, Bozzy. I know I oughtn't to mind, but I do."

"I quite understand, Justin. We always understand that sort of thing. You are as a babe that has need of milk first, not of strong meat."

"What's that?" Justin found it difficult to pretend he liked this.

"It's the Epistle to the Hebrews. 'Strong meat belongeth to them that are of full age.'"

"And that's you, I suppose. Well, I expect you're right. And perhaps I shall be better when you've done with me. Perhaps I shall stand at your side and proclaim to all King Street that I'm your son in the faith. You never know what you'll start doing, once you start being religious. It'd be fine if that happened, wouldn't it, Bozzy? Promise me you'll tell nobody about to-night." Justin held up a humorous but warning finger, as one might to a child before he goes out to play.

"Who should I tell? I shan't see anyone."

"But what are you going to do for the next hour?"

"I shall walk about. I love walking about among the people."

"All right then, Bozzy, old man. The Meeting House as soon as possible after ten. I'll come just as quickly as I can."

Bozzy smiled in agreement and farewell, and the two brothers

parted. Bozzy had intended to return down King Street, but
now that this most wonderful thing had happened, this
miraculous answer to prayer, he went back across the road,
full of excitement and joy, and walked rapidly up Beavor
Lane towards the river, as if he would go to the place of meeting straight away. The joy heaved and brimmed in him. For
some months he had laboured in his Master's vineyard, carrying His message like a seed along the highways or scattering
it from the street corners, but never had he seen any fruits of
this ministry. He had been obliged to comfort himself with
the thought that, though most of it fell by the wayside and was
trodden underfoot, a seed here and there might have found
good earth and be germinating in the darkness, unseen of all
but the Lord. But now the Lord, in His love and bounty, had
vouchsafed him the knowledge of one soul saved for Him—
and that of all people in the world, his brother Justin—Justin
the brilliant and powerful, Justin whom he'd always admired
and loved and whom in this hour he loved more than ever in
his life. Here was proof that he *had* been called to speak
the Truth aloud at that great meeting of misguided people,
and in confutation of his own brother. Here was the justification for that bold but heart-shaking deed. Oh, the depths
of the riches both of the wisdom and knowledge of God.
Bozzy lifted his eyes to the stars. "Oh God, I thank Thee.
I thank Thee that Thou hast been pleased to use me, the
least of all Thy servants, for the rescue of my erring brother."

But not love and humility alone were present in Bozzy
now: there was also a surge of triumph in the thought that he
whom all had despised was the one to whom Justin—Justin
who had despised him most of all—was coming for help as to
a man wiser than he. But this way lay pride, and he did not
want to feel pride about Justin, but only love. Again he
lifted his eyes. "Oh God, save me from pride."

In his happiness he went straight to the meeting place and
was there an hour before his time. But there was no point
in waiting by the Meeting House door, so he walked along the
walled lane that led to the open embankment. And there he
leaned upon the parapet and, looking down upon the river,
watched the tide rising.

§

Justin at the same time was sitting in his room, waiting for
the slow minutes to pass. He was quite alone, with the door

shut. There was no visitor there: no man in difficulties, no old pupil who had got badly off the tracks. . . . He was not reading; he was just sitting in his deep chair, with legs outstretched, waiting for the hands of the mantelpiece clock to complete an hour.

Upstairs Primrose was moving about her room on heavy feet and singing in a low toneless voice, but happily, as she undressed for bed. Strange! He had not heard her singing at night for a dozen years, and she had looked nothing but miserable for the last few days. But this low voice was like the voice of one who must sing to herself because she has been given good news. He could not hear the words, but he could provide them, because it was one of the Old English songs that she used to sing to the Duke, as he accompanied her on the piano in his room under the roof.

> "Early one morning, just as the sun was rising,
> I heard a maiden singing in the valley below,
> 'Oh, don't deceive me, oh, never leave me;
> How could you treat a poor maiden so?'"

At last the song ceased, and the bed creaked, and the house was silent, except when a wayward gust troubled a window-sash or moved an unlatched door.

And still Justin waited. The long wait was a disquieting experience because it gave time and occasion to those thoughts that tried to unseat his resolve. He had to keep them at a distance minute by minute, and all the time he was seeing pictures of Pemberthy Road and the green and the old houses on the green. In this hour of waiting his resolve was like a rock that was repelling every wave, and he like a man sitting in the heart of the rock. The sea was not heavy around the rock, but there was a swell in it that sent the waves slapping against its base or fingering in its crevices and cracks. But sooner or later the impermeable parts of the rock stopped each particular wave, and Justin sat on, immobile.

Half-past ten. But he was not going yet. He was not going to arrive till eleven. Bozzy would wait. If he didn't . . . if he were *not* there, well, perhaps, better so. . . . But he *would* be there. Justin had baited the river bank too well.

St. Anselm's clock struck the three-quarters. "Well, here goes!" and Justin sprang up with a deliberate cheerfulness.

That part of him which was derisory was diverted to think that the church should call him to his present business. "To work!" he said, and laughed a harsh, contemptuous laugh. He opened his study door quietly, listened, heard no sounds above, listened again, and went quietly from the house.

All the side streets were empty now. Even King Street was almost deserted. Pavement and roadway stretched east and west with little moving upon them. He crossed the road and walked along Creek Place by the side of the creek. The water in the creek, usually so slack and dreary between its imprisoning walls, was high and murmurous and astir. It was like a prisoner who shuddered and sighed in his sleep. It stroked and slapped the buttressed walls and squabbled with itself in the secret places behind the barges. There were two barges tied to their quays: old sailing barges a hundred years' old at least, and the mast of one was erect, but the mast of the other was down, and its canvas stowed. These barges also were like captives who shifted and groaned in a troubled sleep. Their timbers complained, their ropes whined, and their blunt sides struck moodily against the wall.

There was no other movement on the water. The swans that swam among the barges in the daytime had retired to their rest on some islet in the stream. But something rustled in the trees that spread their branches over the creek, and Justin's heart leapt and laboured. Then he realized that it was only the fitful wind that, coming from the west, would buffet the swelling tide and be a friendly traveller on the river to-night. Looking up, he saw some poplars gently sweeping the sky like tall birch brooms. The wind in their leaves made a sound like rain.

Rounding the bend of the creek, he came to the little Quaker Meeting House. It was at the mouth of the walled lane that ran from the creek to the embankment and the boathouses. The walls on the north side of the lane were the garden walls of houses that had been turned into factories and offices; those on the south side enclosed factory yards and small wharfs, and these last defied all intruders with broken glass or revolving iron spikes along their coping. Bozzy was not by the meeting house door. Nor was he anywhere in the lane. Justin strained his eyes to see a figure in the lane, but there was none. It stretched before him to the river, its lamps marching down it in single file. Was it disappointment that Justin felt at the sight of that empty lane, or relief? He hardly knew. Disappointment at first; then relief; and now disappointment again.

But look: someone had entered the alley at the far end. Yes, a figure was coming towards him, and it was Bozzy. That was Bozzy's loitering walk, the crook of his stick hung over his forearm, and his hands fiddling with his unbuttoned gloves. One could imagine in the darkness the set smile on his face. Slowly Justin advanced to meet him.

"Hallo, Bozzy." Justin observed that he had spoken in little more than a whisper. He cleared his throat and spoke louder. "Sorry I'm so late. The man went on talking for ever. You know what these people are who are down on the ribs and can show good cause why you should help them. I listened as long as I could, and then got rid of him with a pound note whose loss I've been regretting ever since. What have you been doing all this time, eh? Just walking up and down?"

"Yes, I've been walking up and down the malls, or leaning on the wall and watching the river. It's beautiful to-night. There's a bit of a wind, but I like the wind on my face."

"Well, come for a walk by the river now."

"All right, Justin. I knew you'd come sooner or later. Which way shall we go?"

"I don't mind. I'd like to go somewhere quiet. Let's go back the way you've come. I should think the Lower Mall'd be the quietest. Found anyone to whom you could preach the Word while you were waiting for me?"

"No, the mall's been deserted for some time. There were a couple of lovers under an elm, but they've gone home now."

"I don't wonder. It's after eleven. Won't Mother be upset at your being out as late as this? Won't she be running to the police and dragging the river, or something?"

"Oh no. No, of course not, Justin." Bozzy always resented these teasing suggestions that he, a man of nearly forty, was treated like a child by his mother. "She's quite used to my being out late, especially on a Saturday night. She knows I've got my work to do."

"Work?"

"Yes. My work." For here again Justin had touched him on a sensitive place. Bozzy was always chafed if he suspected that his work as an evangelist was misprised or mocked. "My work for Jesus among the people. I'm out much later than this sometimes. I try to keep the Word of God before their

eyes as long as there are people to see it. One mustn't weary
of well-doing."

"And what does the old lady do? Go to bed?"

"Yes. Of course."

"Well, that's a good thing, because you've got a lot of
work to do to-night, if you're to save my black soul. It'll
take you all your time, because it's in a shocking condition,
Bozzy. It's a mass of corruption and lies. So come on! Say
all you've got to say. Show me how to believe all that you
believe and to be as holy as you and Robin are—oh, but I
forgot: Robin isn't all that he ought to be, is he? He's a
few points adrift. A pity. A great pity. But perhaps you
and I'll be able to lead him into the narrow path, when you've
done with me. So out with it all, Bozzy."

Bozzy began his exposition. He talked fervently about
making one's surrender to the Lord, about letting Him
break one's life before making it anew, about cleansing heart
and mind from every sinful desire and withholding nothing,
because it was only to a heart swept clean that God would
come and reveal Himself. There was no half-way house between salvation and death; no escaping the law of the spiritual
world, which was as unalterable and as certain in its effects as
any law in the natural world. And the law of the spiritual
world was just this: "To be carnally minded is death, but to be
spiritually minded is life and peace."

" 'The wages of sin is death,' " said Justin, to show that he
could quote the Bible too, and to pretend that he was listening.

But he wasn't listening. He was peering ahead to make
sure that the mall at the end of the flagged lane was really as
empty as Bozzy had said. He could see no one moving there.
The windows of the boathouses were lightless and sightless.
Once he turned round as Bozzy talked, and peered behind.
No, no one. He must act promptly, while conditions were
with him. He quickened his step, and Bozzy, thinking only of
his exposition, quickened his too. They came to the end of
the lane, and Justin's glance swung to the little weed-grown
wharf between its grey walls. It was just as he had seen it
last. The tidegate by the path was but two planks high, and
one could step over it into the weeds.

"But what I want to know is this, Bozzy. You say that all
men are sinners and need to be saved. Well, I'll agree with
that all right. But you go on to say that you know every
detail of God's plan for their salvation. And then I immedi-

ately think: how can you—you, Arthur Bossuet le Faber, of Brook Green, Hammersmith, know with such assurance the private thoughts of the Lord of all the universe?"

"I have been trying to tell you. That's what I've been trying to tell you for the last five minutes. In His mercy He reveals Himself to us."

"He reveals Himself to you. And how?"

"One has to experience it to know."

"But how do you know that the whole experience isn't a self-flattering delusion. Don't you think you believe in it because you long to believe in it? There's no proof anywhere that the whole thing isn't illusory."

"Oh yes, there is."

"Well, what is it?" ("We're getting near the wharf now.")

"Jesus came in person to tell us all about it."

Oh dear, oh dear, how simple the fellow was. "But how can you know that he, a small tradesman in a little one-horse town, wasn't deluded himself? How can you know that he wasn't a religious fanatic like—like scores of others who've imagined themselves God or Allah or the Messiah or someone?"

"He *was* God."

"Who said so? Only himself, and that might merely mean that he was crazy."

"Hush, Justin. You don't know what you're saying. You mustn't talk like that——"

"But I've every intention of doing so if I want to."

"He rose from the dead and proved that He was God."

"H'mmm, that takes some believing. How do you know that all those who say they saw him weren't suffering from delusions too. Come in here and let's have a look at the river. The tide is high, you say?"

"It must be very nearly high."

"Come on then."

"But isn't this place private?" Bozzy halted timidly at the tidegate.

"No. It's derelict. It's nobody's. Look at the weeds." Justin stepped over the gate and stood among the weeds. "We can feel private here. Come along. I want to hear some more."

Bozzy followed him. Justin threw a last glance up the mall and down it. There was no one anywhere. He walked to the edge of the wharf and looked down upon the water. It was swirling upstream, thick, heavy, in full flood. The breeze,

opposing its onward sweep, crimped its mid-stream surface
and sent long oblique shivers towards the banks. The water
flopped and protested among the rafts a few yards farther up
and sucked and blubbered at the sides of dinghies and skiffs
moored to unseen chains. As he had foreseen, the river in the
darkness was full of low, distressful sounds.

"Come along, Bozzy. Come and look here."

Nervously Bozzy came forward, but halted some inches
from the edge.

"Oh, come on!" urged Justin. "You're not frightened to
stand on the brink, are you? The water isn't three feet
below us, and I doubt if it's any great depth just here. What
on earth is there to be afraid of?"

Once again Justin had touched Bozzy where his vanity
hurt. He didn't like people to think he was less than other
men, and afraid. So he came forward and stood at Justin's
side. And in that moment Justin wondered whether after all
he would do it—whether he *could* do it. But he braced himself by stirring up the aching, the deathly, memory of his
humiliation in the theatre—that dark misery which was like a
pain suffered in silence in some deep solitude of an Inferno—
and by telling himself that he, Justin le Faber, had the
courage and the will to do anything; that he was no weakling
or slave-mind to be defeated in the last minute by other men's
consciences and to let the night's heavy work go for nothing.
"Conscience is made for slaves. Scruples are the fears of the
timid." For thirty years he had been driving his will against
his conscience, and it was a habit with him now. His lips
came tightly together.

"There you are, Bozzy," he laughed. "Now shall I give you
a push?" Let him make a joke of it so that if anything went
wrong—if Bozzy by some chance survived, or if people
appeared on the mall—he could jump in, swim out, and save
him, and then declare, as the people praised him, that they
had been fooling together on the brink.

"No, don't. Don't, Justin," cried Bozzy, as he felt Justin's
fingers in the small of his back.

"I can't agree with you, Bozzy. There's nothing we can
know to be true. I should like to believe there is something,
but I can't. We just wake up and find ourselves in this world,
completely alone and lost. We know that we've got to live
out our lives here, and then die. And that's all we can know.
According to you, we are born broken and bidden to get whole

if we can; and if that's your God's idea of a fair deal, you can keep Him, for He's no use to me. I do not respect Him. . . . What are you nervous of? We're not doing any harm here. . . . He may have power to punish me hereafter for my recalcitrance, but He will have no power to make me worship Him, even then. No, Bozzy, old man, if the Lord God bungled me when He made me, I'm doing precisely nothing about it. I shall remain broken as I am."

"But you won't, Justin; you won't remain as you are. You'll break worse; you'll break into pieces. That is the inevitable law."

"Then I'll break into pieces. If that is the law, it can take its course. I didn't make it; I'm not to blame for it; and I've no intention of inconveniencing myself trying to dodge its consequences. See, Bozzy, old man? I've said my last word." And he slapped him cheerfully on the back.

The slap was enough to push him into the water. His arms flew forward as he fell, and he cried aloud. Instantly Justin cried, "Bozzy!" in an acted dismay, lest any unseen eye were watching him. "Oh my God! Bozzy!" And he pretended to be pulling off his jacket before diving to the rescue. And he looked around as if for help, but really to be certain that no one was near.

The mall was silent. No footstep sounded, even in the distance. The windows of the boathouses were blank and dark, or they had their blinds down, like sightless or like lidded eyes. Some cars slid along the bridge behind its openwork parapet, but they were too far away to have seen or heard anything. He looked out at the river again. The flooding tide had already swept Bozzy into the silence of midstream. And it bore him on till he was too far away for Justin to see his last struggle in that loneliness.

With tremulous hands Justin rearranged his jacket and pulled down his sleeves, as a man does who has finished his work. His heart trembled in sympathy with his hands. He left the wharf and walked to the parapet where, days before, he had studied the river bed and the depth at high water. There was nothing to be seen on the river now except the tide hurrying on against the buffeting of the breeze.

He walked quickly out of the mall and into Bridge Road; and his heart ceased its trembling when he had his back to the river, because he hoped he had left it and its secrets behind him.

PART IV

CHAPTER ONE

ST. MICHAEL'S Church is a grey temple standing on the east side of the square called Cunningham Gardens. Built in Regency times, it has a lofty Corinthian portico, a circular tower surrounded by Corinthian columns, and on the tower a circular steeple. The Rectory is a house of the same date, the first in the Regency terrace on the north side of the church. Designed in the generous days when John Nash was building in the west of London, it is a tall, spacious house with a long rectangular garden behind it. In the garden are trees as old as the church: an elm, a plane, a weeping ash, and four tall poplars which are now as high as the steeple. Grey walls frame the garden, and a hundred years' growth of ivy muffles the walls. It is a pleasant garden to sit in and take tea when the midsummer sun is high above the church; and on such an afternoon, a year or so ago, the Rector, the Rev. Prebendary Robin le Faber, Prebendary of Medwelle and Orde in the diocese of London, was sitting in the shade of the elm with his wife, Lady Jessica, and his children, Denys Honoré and Esther Beatrice Bossuet. The parents lay back in their hammock chairs, and the children were disposed upon the sun-dappled grass, Beatrice with her legs drawn under her, and Denys with his legs thrown before him and his arms behind him, bearing the weight of his body.

Robin, though within a month of his fiftieth birthday, was as slim as when he was twenty-three, and his hair was the same iron-grey hair, more sable than silver. Only the meeting eyebrows were thicker and greyer, and the large brown eyes beneath them seemed to have withdrawn a little into the shadows. His forehead was scored with lines, and it was these lines alone which made him look his age. They were the incisions left by years of thought; this was a man, one guessed, whose thoughts turned inward for most of the day and were sometimes perplexed in the extreme. His young wife Jessica, was over thirty now, but she looked very young by her husband's side. Her children too, so tall for their age, stressed her youth rather than her years.

Denys, at nine, was as tall as his Uncle Justin had been, though his slimness was rather that of his father. This slimness caused him some disquiet, for his private ambition was to be as broad in shoulder and chest as his Uncle Justin, and not only as tall, when he should be full-grown. He told no one of this rather shameful desire, so Robin was unable to tell him that he was reproducing, forty years later, an ambition which had cost his father much thought and labour and had desolated parts of his childhood. Robin had told him, however, all about the twelve famous sons of Tancred of Hauteville and the tall sons of the Doones who must brush with their heads and shoulders the doorway of Sir Ensor Doone or be cast forth from the valley; and Denys had immediately taken into the secrecies of his breast the family desire to attain a height worthy of a le Faber. Were not his father and his uncles, Justin, Gerard, and Hector, all over six feet? On a doorway in the Rectory which secured one privacy and time, because it had a bolt which people expected one to push home, there were certain scratches which indicated Denys's height last year, last month, and probably yesterday, and the height of his hopes in the future. To judge from his long limbs and his long feet and fingers, as he lay on the grass this afternoon, it did not seem likely that he would fall short of his ambition.

But within Denys's breast there were not only some of his father's vanity but also his father's conscience, austere, persistent, and punishing; and it would harry him unsparingly after he had told a schoolfellow, as a great confidence, that his second name was Tancred (which it was not) and that he was a direct descendant of Tancred of Hauteville, through his second son, Drogo, Count of Apulia, but that he didn't want to boast about it before the other boys.

Esther's chief worry—not at all a secret one because she would uncover it often to her mother and to anyone else who would listen—was the exact opposite of Denys's. Ever since a girl at her school had said that it was ghastly for a woman to be big because men didn't fall in love with big women, she had lived in dread of being over six feet like the men of the family, or even as tall as her Auntie Primrose, in which event she would be a sight and loved by no one. While Denys measured himself against the bolted door and strained upwards, Beatrice walked about with books on her head, both to

discourage her body from growing and to give her lovely
movements like her Auntie Anne's. But in her case, as in
Denys's, there seemed little reason for worry. Esther, at eight,
was a small reproduction of Jessica, black-haired, dark-eyed,
small-faced and slight, and that surely should have put her
mind at rest.

Posed thus beneath the trees, the le Fabers of the Rectory
made a picture of a happy family, such a picture as Ramsay or
Raeburn might have painted, and the picture did not belie
them. Where father and mother are lovers there is always a
happy household, and gushing ladies of the parish would
sometimes say to the Rector, "You two lovers! You are the
ideal couple;" and the words did not hurt him, as they would
hurt a man who knew them to be far from the mark; they
merely wounded him with their keen pleasure because he could
believe them true. They might remind him of many an irritable passage, and many a time when an outburst of temper
(and not always *his* temper) had laid a day in ruins before they
came together again in penitence (and Jessica in tears) but
when he considered his life as a whole he could tell himself
that, in his marriage at least, he was a man completely fulfilled. Jessica, because her love, if less demonstrative now,
was as tender as it had ever been, and because she was so much
younger than he, and because people spoke so often of her
beauty, was the completion of a desire. His heart filled with
affection when he was away and thinking of her; and sometimes, if he had been away a long time, his thoughts mounted
to something like the ecstasy he had known when he was
twenty-two and in love with Bryn Lowther.

To this family in the garden came a pleasant maid in a
shapely brown frock and frilled yellow apron, bringing a
letter on a tray.

"Thank you, Frances," said Robin carelessly, and took it.

He glanced at the typed address and at the postmark, but
could deduce nothing from them. Then he turned it over and
saw on the envelope-flap that which jolted his heart and made
it slam against his side. But it was not in alarm that it beat so
fast, though there was something of alarm in it. It throbbed
with pleasure—but with a pleasure that must start its own
fears.

He had no doubt what it contained. The Archbishop, when
he summoned him to Lambeth recently, had hinted that there
was a chance such a letter would come. A chance, no more;

and Robin had said nothing of it to Jessica, partly because he
had regarded the Archbishop's words as confidential, and
partly because he wanted the letter, if indeed it came, to
overwhelm the family in surprise.

"H'm . . ." he murmured at the envelope now, and that was
all.

In some trepidation his fingers opened it, and he read:

"My dear Prebendary le Faber,

"As you are aware, the Bishopric of Lavant is vacant, and
I should be happy if I might propose your name to His
Majesty the King as Dr. Welling's successor. Most of your
labours in the past have been in urban parishes, I know, and
Lavant in the main is a rural diocese, but I have heard from
the Bishop of Gloucester and from the Earl of Harbury that
your ministrations in the quiet country parish of Harbury
Grace some years ago were as acceptable to its people as they
have always been, in the knowledge of us all, to the people in
your London parishes, and, having in view that there are
large urban areas in the diocese of Lavant, and that these are
likely to increase rapidly and largely with London people,
and furthermore, though this is a much smaller point but not,
I think, inconsiderable, that Lavant is well known to you as
your *alma mater* and is, in its turn, proud of you as one of its
alumni, I am satisfied that there is no name that I can lay
with greater confidence than yours before His Majesty, and I
very much hope that you will agree to my doing so."

And it was signed by the Prime Minister.

The sun had been bright in the garden before, but now there
seemed a new quality in its light. Joy and fear were still
sparring in his heart, as he prepared to tell Jessica and the
children.

"Ah-*hem*," he muttered, staring at the letter; and the
family perceived that he was about to be facetious. "Do you
know, my good woman, what this is?"

"No, darling," answered Jessica. "Is it interesting?"

"Yes, I think you might call it interesting."

"What is it? Who's it from?" demanded the children.
"Has it a valuable autograph?"

"Peace, peace. All in good time. It has an autograph of
sorts, certainly."

"Oh, *whose*?" Esther jumped up to read it over his shoulder.

"Oh no, you don't, miss!" He turned it face-downward on
his knee.

"Oh, come on, Daddy," urged Denys, as though he thought his father had been allowed playfulness enough and should now come to the matter. "Is it from anyone important?"

"He's quite important in his way."

"Is it the Arch?"

"No."

"Denys," rebuked Jessica, "you're not to call the Primate of All England the Arch."

"Daddy always does."

"Well, he shouldn't."

"He certainly shouldn't," agreed Robin.

"Is it the King of England, Daddy?"

"No."

"Is it the Queen?"

"No."

"Is it the Princess Elizabeth?"

"No."

"Is it the Prime Minister?"

"Yes."

"*What?* It *isn't.*"

"I tell you it's from the Prime Minister."

"He's being funny," averred Esther.

Bending the paper over so as to conceal the words of the letter, Robin showed her the embossed address, "10 Downing Street."

"Coo, he's right! It *is.*"

"Has he signed it?" "Oh, do let's see." "Can I have his autograph?" "No, let me have it this time." "It may be worth thousands one day." "Oh, show us, Daddy, show us."

It was difficult to say which child was saying which. Both were now standing by his chair, one on either side. The letter lay face-downward on his knee.

"I'll leave you his autograph when I die."

"But that won't be for ages yet," bewailed Denys.

"Another ten years," suggested Robin. "Ten years, and you should be free of me."

"No. Twenty at least," said the pessimist. "You're only fifty."

"Is that all? Good gracious. But fifty years of labour and sorrow are as good as a hundred. All the same, let me tell you that I'm firmly resolved to live till eighty."

"Golly! I shall be thirty-nine then, and I don't suppose I shall want it any more."

"Is the autograph the only thing that interests you? Don't any of you want to know what the letter is about?"

"Yes, yes. What's it about?"

"I don't know that I shall tell you now. You should have asked before."

"Oh, go on, Daddy. Don't be a swine," begged Esther.

"Hush, Esther. What is it, Robin?"

"It's an offer of a Bishopric."

"Daddy!"

"Robin!"

"It's *not*!"

"It is. The Prime Minister invites me to be Bishop of Lavant. He is, I may say, very polite about it. Very polite indeed."

"He isn't." Esther was incredulous, knowing well, from long experience of her father, that the masculine sense of fun was a curious growth, of unpredictable habits.

"Read it, child."

She read it and exclaimed, "My hat, Mummy! It's the truth. He's telling the truth for once."

"Robin, show me, show me," commanded Jessica.

"Pass the trifle to your mother, Esther darling."

"Bishop of Lavant." Denys savoured the title on his tongue. "The Bish of Lavant. You'll be a lord, won't you? Everyone will call you My lord. Good lord!"

"That's if I accept it."

"Of course you'll accept it. Don't be silly. Why shouldn't you?"

"Not being you or your sister, I might not think myself good enough."

"Oh, that's rot," said Esther. "He's as good as any of the others, isn't he, Mummy?" She began to skip at his side. "Oh, how soon can I tell everybody, Daddy?"

"You'll tell nobody. Let that be clearly understood."

"Oh, heck! Yes, I will."

"Yes, you *won't*. It's only because you're the family that I told you."

"Shall I be an Honourable or anything?" asked Denys.

"Certainly not. Nor will you inherit the Bishopric when I die."

"There you are!" cried Denys in a triumph. "You're going to accept it. You've practically said so."

"Oh, Mummy, isn't it thrilling?" said Esther, rushing to

her mother, who put an arm around her. "Daddy a bishop.
Do hurry up and accept and let me tell everybody."

When the children had run indoors, Robin and Jessica
stayed talking together about the brilliant event till the sun
was down behind a bank of clouds and the garden grew cold.

"Lavant! I'd rather Lavant than any diocese in England,"
he said; and he spoke of the Bishop's Palace with its old
grey battlemented face and its broad and lovely gardens
whose wall, along their south border, was nothing less than the
old bastioned wall of the medieval city. He spoke of the
Bishop's Meadows under the wall, where Bryn Lowther had
waved him good-bye. Strange that she should have stood
there nearly thirty years ago and waved him good-bye. He
said that the thought of her staid white house on the West
Wall and of her grave in her father's churchyard only added a
tenderness now to his memories of Lavant and a certain
sweetness to the idea of returning there. And Jessica nodded
and smiled and understood.

After two hours of such talking, when it was past six
o'clock and Jessica had returned indoors to the children, he
could stay no longer in the garden but must walk out into
the streets. His exultation was distending him like the air
on the heights. He must walk and walk and keep asking himself, when his thoughts had been momentarily diverted, what
was the happy, the incredible, thing that filled with a warm
glow the inmost chamber of his mind. The le Faber craving
for success, though controlled—or partly controlled—by
Robin's conscience, was as strong in him as in Gerard or
Justin, and when it was fully satisfied like this, it was like a
mettlesome steed that wouldn't be held; it galloped and
pranced, and to ride it was a rapture very near to pain.

It galloped him now towards someone he could tell the news
to. Why was he walking so rapidly westward? Why had his
feet taken this course before his mind directed them? Because all his brothers lived in the west, and the need to tell
one of them was a compulsion past resisting. There was
nothing episcopal, nothing prebendal, nothing even Christian,
about this hunger to display his new distinction to the family,
but he couldn't deal with that question now. To-morrow,
perhaps. . . .

To which of his brothers was he going? Not to Justin. He
must not hurt Justin with a tale of success, as he had done,
very deliberately, once before, when his anger had galloped

him to this self-healing work. To Hector? No. Although
Hector would not be hurt because he was well satisfied with
himself and with the family, and would only place this new le
Faber triumph to the credit of his account, still, he and his
wife were a rather heavy metal, and they would not resound
so loudly and so ringingly to the news as would Gerard and
Anne. Oh yes, Gerard and Anne. They would suffer no
jealousy because they had had all the success they could
desire. Gerard had been knighted six years ago and now sat
at the top of his own chosen hill. He was at the head of his
profession, and there was no further he could climb.

Yes, old Gerard and Anne. Robin hurried towards the bus
that would take him to Chiswick. He would be late for his
dinner, and Jessica knew nothing of this sudden sally into the
streets, but what matter? Nothing mattered in this hour
except the longing to tell Gerard and Anne. As a schoolboy
runs home to tell the household that he has been given his
cricket colours, so did the Bishop-designate of Lavant hurry
to the home of Gerard and Anne, heavy with news.

He came upon them in their long drawing-room overlooking
the river. There they were, these two who, according to
Justin had lived in squalour and would come to nothing:
Anne leaning back on golden cushions, and Gerard standing
with a foot on the fender, both dressed with the perfection of
characters in a drawing-room comedy and both sipping a
golden sherry in the few minutes before they dined.

"Robin!" At the first glimpse of him Anne sprang up, ran
forward, and swept him into her embrace. She rose on her
toes and kissed him. "Now isn't that nice of him to come and
see us?"

"Just in time for a little one," said Gerard, walking towards the decanter on the coffee table. "Have you come to
dinner? If so, we don't mind."

"Certainly he's come to dinner," announced Anne. "Don't
be stupid, Gerard."

"No, I mustn't stop to dinner. Jessica's expecting me to
be at home for dinner. As a matter of fact, she doesn't even
know that I'm out of the house."

"What? Have you broken loose for a bit?" asked Gerard.

"Of course he hasn't, Gerard," said Anne. "He's wearing a
clerical collar. He doesn't wear a clerical collar when he's
really worked loose."

"No, I just came along . . ." How was he to tell them?

Why not admit the truth about this incursion, and come straight to the point? Gerard and Anne were the sort who would understand. "The fact is, I'm afraid I'm giving my lower nature an evening out."

"Excellent," said Gerard. "Treat it to this." And he passed him the glass of sherry.

"You see, I've just had a rather nice compliment paid to me, and I want to brag about it to someone."

"And he's chosen us," explained Anne. "Isn't that attractive of him? What's the compliment, my precious?"

"I've just been offered the Bishopric of Lavant."

"Robin! You a bishop! Oh, my darling heart and lovely one! Oh, my angel soul! How wonderful. How marvellous. And how sensible. Who's the really sensible person who thought of that?"

"The P.M."

"The what?"

"The Prime Minister."

"The Prime Minister. He was at our show the other night. Do you think that can have influenced him, Gerard? Oh, I do hope so."

"More likely to have made him think twice," said Gerard. "Hell, I must have another sherry on this."

"So must I. So must we all. Give Robin another one. Do you remember how we all drank champagne together—just we three—when Gerard and I first got a break? That's nearly a quarter of a century ago. Doesn't seem like it. Bishop of Lavant. Gerard, that standing there is the Bishop of Lavant. Oh, I must kiss him again. I've kissed hardly any bishops."

She did so, very thoroughly, and when he had emerged from the embrace and was rearranging himself, he said, "She has some agreeable qualities, this wife of yours, Gerard."

"She's not bad," consented her husband. "Not now that I've got used to her. One can get used to anything. What does the P.M. do on these occasions? Summon you to his presence?"

"No, he writes a letter. It came this afternoon. A rather nice letter . . . really. . . ."

"And he brought it straight to us. Oh, Gerard, I do love him. I think that's the nicest thing he's ever done, to come straight round and tell us. Thank you, Robin."

"But you mustn't tell anyone else."

"Why ever not? Nonsense. I'm going to tell everybody. Why can't I?"

"Because you mustn't. I'm not supposed to discuss it with anyone except just the family and a few close friends, until the P.M. makes his own announcement."

"Well, I sincerely hope you've told the All Highest in Vandermere Road. It'll do him a power of good."

"No, I haven't. And I'm not going to. You don't seem to realize that I haven't accepted it yet."

"But you're going to accept it, that's certain. Of *course* you are. I insist."

"But it's not as easy as that. It's got to be thought over."

"It hasn't. You'll write and accept at once. I'm not going to have any nonsense about it. He'll write to the P.M. at once, won't he, Gerard?"

"If he's not a perfect fool. But you never quite know where you are with Robin. He had qualms about taking his present job, I remember. What I've been thinking while you've been talking, Anne—not being able to get a word in, myself—is that this should be useful publicity for us. This is going to be News, isn't it, Robin?"

"Well, it'll be announced in the papers, of course. . . ."

"Look at him being all modest, Gerard. Look at him blushing. Oh, he'll make the loveliest bishop, he really will. What did the P.M. say in his letter, ducky?"

"I've got it here."

"Oh, show me, show me!" She snatched the letter from him and read it with impatient speed. "Now isn't that instructive?" she commented, this being an adjective that she was applying to most things of late. "Isn't that immensely instructive? 'Your ministrations were as acceptable to its people as they have always been, in the knowledge of us all. . . .' How nice. 'There is no name that I can lay with greater confidence before His Majesty the King. . . .' Certainly not. And *alma mater* and *alumni*. Do Prime Ministers always write like that? Oh, bless him." And she kissed the Prime Minister's letter in approval and gratitude.

"The old le Fabers aren't doing so badly, Robby, are they?" asked Gerard. "Even old Hector has achieved the management of quite an important branch. Funny that Justin should really have been the least successful of all. Except Bozzy." There was a brief fall in the atmosphere at this mention of Bozzy. "But we never expected anything from Bozzy. We expected great things from Justin."

"*I* never did," assured Anne. "He was too vain. You're

shut off from learning anything if you're as vain as that.
You think you've nothing to learn. But never mind him.
Let us talk about something more pleasant. Aren't you aw-
fully young to be a bishop, darling?"

"I'm fifty."

"But what's that for a bishop? They're usually about
eighty."

"I suppose it's younger than usual. But some have been
appointed even younger."

"Perhaps you'll be an archbishop before you've done.
Gerard, he'll be an archbishop. Oh, I do hope so. I'd rather
have him for my archbishop than anybody."

"*Your* archbishop," scoffed Gerard. "And she's never once
been to church since she's lived with me."

"Oh, yes, I have. I've been to heaps of weddings. And
if he's Archbishop, he'll be the first peer of the realm, won't
he? Gerard, oughtn't you to stand? Do you think you
ought to just sit like that in his presence? Take your hands
out of your pockets."

Gerard rose and lifted his glass. "The Bishop of Lavant."

"I'm not Bishop yet," laughed Robin; but even as he said
it, he felt that he'd be incapable of declining so great an
honour. And as they sipped their wine, he could only believe
that they were really drinking to the new Bishop of Lavant.

"If only Dad could look down from heaven," said Gerard.

§

It was midsummer now, and the darkness did not deepen
till ten o'clock; but at ten o'clock, two nights later, the moon
was high, and the warm darkness was heavy with stars, and
Gerard, looking from his window, said to Anne, "It's a perfect
night, as warm as hell, and the tide's coming in fast. Let's go
for a walk along the sea front and smell the sea. It's absurd to
seek the rank sweat of an enseaméd bed on a night like this."

And Anne cried, "Oh yes, precious. Let's;" and they went
out together and walked eastward along the mall between the
old houses and the small gardens that lay along the river.
The air was so soft on their faces, and river and road and
roofs drew such washes of beauty from the moon, that they
walked on and on, arm in arm, till they came to the Upper
Mall, Hammersmith, and the open space where the old
Creek lay buried under concrete and gravel. And since
this wide area was floodlit by the moon, they could not turn

round but walked onward along the walled lane from the
Quaker Meeting House to the Lower Mall. They walked between the boathouses and the derelict wharfs, but not a
breath from the past troubled them as they went by. And
having come to these places of Gerard's childhood, they could
do no other than turn towards Brook Green, and in a few
minutes they were strolling along the south side of that little
triangular green, where the moonlight lay in splashes beneath
the planes and the elms. And Gerard was telling Anne the
tales of forty years ago and recreating for her the old mansions
that stood here then. When they passed the big red and white
School for Girls, he built again on its site the old Grange
where Sir Henry Irving had lived, and replaced its curtain of
trees before it, and then placed himself as a small peering
boy on the pavement by its gates.

It was a Sunday night, and some hours earlier Gerard and
Anne had played host and hostess at a reception in the foyer
of the New Comedy Theatre, and therefore both were very
well dressed in morning *tenue*. Gerard was in a morning coat,
high white collar and black cravat; a costume which he liked
to wear on ceremonial occasions and which had earned for him
in his club, not at all to his displeasure, the nickname of
"Squire". There was something concordant and appropriate,
perhaps, in his return, wearing all the livery of success, to the
haunt of "The Chief " and the place where he had first begun to
dream.

They had just crossed the side road and left the school
behind when they observed a tall figure walking along the
pavement towards them and recognized it as Justin's. He too
was well dressed, because it was Sunday, and a fine, sad
figure he presented, with his lonely eyes, his lined face, his
black and grey hair, and the neat pointed beard, black and
grey, which he had grown since he entered the fifties.

"Good God! Look! Himself!" whispered Anne. "Oh,
thank heaven we're well dressed. Thank heaven we met him
to-night. We must be looking a distinguished little couple to-
night."

"Good lord! Old Justin on the wander too. But how worn
he looks in these days, and how sad."

Gerard greeted his brother with much good humour, and
Justin acknowledged it with a smile, but Anne perceived that
he was wounded by the sight of Gerard, as he always was,
since he had achieved such celebrity and become a knight, and

by the sight of Gerard's wife hanging affectionately on his arm. And therefore she brought her other hand over and linked it into the one on Gerard's arm, that their affection might be even more palpably demonstrated.

"We're walking back into the Past," explained Gerard.

"Revisiting the glimpses of the moon," said Anne.

"Are you on the same pilgrimage?" Gerard asked.

"No." Justin turned his eyes from theirs. "I've been out somewhere, and I was obliged to return this way."

Something in the quick words and in the manner that accompanied them told Anne that this was a lie. Justin's walk had been slow and aimless, and this was not his natural way home. He had come out in his melancholy, she guessed, to wander among the scenes of childhood, and he had lied because he didn't want them to think him a disappointed man who lived in the past.

Gerard cast his eyes through the planes and elms to the far side of the green. "I wonder what became of Old Man Morgari."

"He's playing his French horn in Heaven," suggested Justin. "Been doing it for the last twenty years at least, I should say."

"Not a bad old man. But he was responsible for a lot."

"Gerard's been telling me stories of you all as boys," said Anne. "I think you must have been a rather delightful family."

"I think we must have been rather awful," Gerard dissented.

"Oh, Justin." Anne had seen a point where she could wound him, and she drew her falchion—the falchion of Judith which slew Holofernes. "Heard about Robin? Isn't it splendid?"

"No. What?" Justin's eyes were instantly hers.

"Tut, tut," murmured Gerard. "How utterly unscrupulous women are. Robin told her in confidence. In absolute confidence."

"Don't be ridiculous, Gerard. Justin's one of the family, and Robin expressly said he could discuss it with the family. I distinctly remember his saying he could discuss it with the family and a few close friends. I'm certainly going to tell Justin." And she told him all, omitting nothing that could deepen his wound. "Isn't it too marvellous? Bishop of Lavant! And he'll have the most wonderful palace to live in. It's like a young castle, with battlements and Heaven-knows-what, and its gardens are like a park. Fancy Robin with his own palace and park. And he'll be in the House of Lords one day. Fancy our little Robin in the House of Lords."

"It's very fine news," said Justin. But his eyes did not say the same thing. His eyes were hurt and sick. "I wonder why he told me nothing about it."

"He only told Gerard and me two nights ago. He came and told us directly he got the Prime Minister's letter. Oh, you must see the Prime Minister's letter. It's so sweet. I do think Prime Ministers can be touching. It's obvious he thinks there's nobody quite like Robin—and nor there is. Oh, isn't it all marvellous? It's just like when Gerard was offered his knighthood. I could have screamed with delight. Darling Robin. I'd rather this had happened to him than to anyone else in the world."

"Has he accepted it?"

"No, but he will. Of course he will. Why in the world shouldn't he? Oh, I'm longing for it to be announced in the papers. Our Robin's going to be News. Gerard says its bound to be quite big news because Robin's so young and they've always given Lavant before to someone who's at least a dean, and Robin's only a prebendary, whatever that is. What *is* a prebendary, children? Robin's tried to explain it to me sometimes, but I'm still in a state of confusion about it."

"Good old Robin!" said Justin. "I'm glad. Yes, this is great news."

And soon after that, strangely, uncomfortably soon, like a man driven, he made an excuse for escaping from them. Anne turned and watched his figure receding into the shadows thrown by the moon. "My God, Gerard," she said. "It hurt him even more than I thought. It was a knock-out blow. Well, I don't mind. I'm glad." She gathered Gerard's arm in hers again, almost as if she needed its comfort and support. "I hate him, and he deserved it. This has been a good night's work, my sweet, and we can now go home." So she said, but she was protesting too much, because, greatly to her surprise, a pity for Justin had leapt up in her heart.

CHAPTER TWO

THE Armour Street branch of Hector's bank was an important branch, and its manager's office an imposing room. Hector sat no longer in a cage of mahogany and glass within the

banking hall, but at a large desk-table in a panelled room
with a thick-pile Turkey carpet under his feet and leather-
seated chairs around him for the accommodation of visiting
customers.   On the table at his side was his microphone-
telephone, and in front of him his large writing-pad and,
beyond that, on the other side of the table, a similar pad for a
customer when documents were to be signed that were good
business for the bank. Between the two pads was a handsome
pewter ink-stand.   Seated in his swivel chair before this
well-dressed table, Hector filled out very well the role of
trustworthy, informative, weighty, and hearty bank manager.
In appearance, at fifty-one, he was much like Augustus, his
father, except for his bald head; he was tall and fat, and
his eyes were quick to laugh, but there was that about his
mouth, his heavy chin, and his thick neck that could best
be described as argumentative. Like the table before him,
he was always well dressed, having a good opinion of his position
and of himself as its occupant, and when he could excusably do
so, he smoked a small and fragrant cigar, because it made him
feel a person of substance and prosperity.   Witty women
sometimes spoke of him as "an enormous man with a tiny
cigar."

He was indeed a well satisfied man. He was not at the
top of his profession like Gerard, and nowhere near it, but he
was a boss in his smaller field, and it was no insignificant
field, either. This Armour Street, Westminster, branch was
referred to in banking circles as one of the smaller "plums";
its staff from chief clerk to typist were a picked staff; and he
was their master. He had liked his work as a bank clerk from
the beginning, and because he liked it, he had done it well.
Liking it still better as he rose higher, he was always at ease
in it, and efficient and jovial, and popular both with customers
and colleagues. And now that he sat in this fine room, and
important people came to interview him, he would not have
changed places with any man in the world.

More than anything he liked being interviewed and con-
sulted in the privacy of a closed and handsome room, and no
one could enjoy an occupation as much as he enjoyed this,
without making a success of it. Directly his customer entered,
he rose and arranged a chair for him and, seating himself in
his own chair, extracted from his table drawer a silver cigarette
box and offered him a cigarette. Or he offered him one of his
own small cigars and, glad of an excuse to smoke in working

hours, lit up one himself. Then he discussed his visitor's
business with a fine gravity and show of knowledge and in
good, round, sonorous terms. Their business concluded, he
discussed his visitor's family: the girl at college, the boy in the
army, and the young one at school. Having dealt with the
visitor's family, he spoke of his own children, or of his brothers
and their children, and often told romantic lies about them.

He made much play with the fine-sounding names of his
brothers, Sir Gerard le Faber and Canon le Faber. Robin
he always spoke of as Canon le Faber, because Canon sounded
better than Prebendary, and he would say of him, "All
the previous rectors of St. Michael's, Cunningham Gardens
have gone on to gaiters, and, if you ask me, young Robin
hasn't gone yet as far as he's going." He was still proud of
Justin, mainly because this pride had become a habit with
him, and he would refer to him as "My brother, the Headmaster of Erasmus Hall." Westminster was in another world
than Hammersmith, so no one was likely to know what
manner of school was Erasmus Hall, and Hector, like Justin
thirty years before, thought that the name carried an aura
of academic distinction. He was proud too, in a different
way, of Bozzy. He had been proud at first of his most interesting affliction and later of his mysterious death, which
had been a small sensation in its time—Bozzy's one success,
you might say—and he had paraded before the people his
own shock and bereavement. It is hardly necessary to add
that he was proud of his sister-in-law, Lady Jessica, and of
"her old father, the Earl."

Never jealous hitherto of any of his brothers, he was less
likely than ever to be jealous of them now, in the first place
because of his great content with his present position, and in
the second because he had just added to himself a new and
notable honour in the shape of a weak heart. There was now
an abnormal sound in his heart and an irregularity in its
rhythm, with both of which he was extraordinarily pleased.
He exaggerated the damage to all and hung around it a neck-
lace of decorative lies. It meant that he might "go off at any
moment," he would admit in confidence to a circle of friends,
his lips pursed up and his head nodding solemnly. On the
other hand, the old pump might last him a dozen years or so,
but, whichever happened, he wasn't letting the matter worry
him. There was no better way to die than suddenly and
quietly in one's chair. He knew what was the cause of it; oh

yes, he knew the cause all right. It was a legacy of the old war. He'd been buried alive under a mountain of débris on one occasion, and it was hours before they extricated him. He'd never been quite the same after that. Who *would* be?

Always anxious to make an impression on the branch in which he worked, he had long ago suggested to Gerard and Robin that they should "bank with him", and they had readily consented to do so, Gerard because of his easy good nature, and Robin because of his desire to help anyone and to be liked. This family connexion had followed him from branch to branch and was with him now in Armour Street. Gerard's was a particularly valuable account, since he maintained an overgrown balance, being too careless and easygoing to trouble about investing it till it had reached an inordinate size. Anne, however, had slightly more sense, and she drove him out every now and again to "go and see Hector and do something about it." And so it happened that on the Monday after their meeting with Justin in Brook Green, Gerard walked into Hector's room to ask him what stock he should buy and to instruct him to buy it. Since Gerard always accepted Hector's advice without argument, this business was quickly done, and the conventional talk about their families began. Hector said what he had to say about his children, and Gerard provided some information about his, and then Gerard, for something to say, and remembering that Anne had declared there was no harm in discussing it with the family, told Hector all about Robin and his offer of a bishopric.

"Why, that's fine!" exclaimed Hector. "That's magnificent!" And he was truly delighted because it was more credit for him, and because it was a piece of private information that he could tell in strict confidence to his friends. "Bishop of Lavant! Old Robin! I say, Gerard, have you ever thought this—it's coming home to me more and more of late—that the old governor must have been a pretty good sire?"

"What on earth do you mean?" asked Gerard, his eyebrows contracting in amused surprise.

"Well, the old thing produced a rather remarkable series of sons, didn't he? I mean, Justin, at any rate, is superb to look at. There can't be many men like him about, and in my opinion he gets more and more distinguished-looking as he gets older. *You've* got to the top of your tree all right, you can't deny that. And now Robin's practically a bishop, and he may be more before he's done. And I haven't done too

badly, I don't think, though I don't pretend to be as successful as you two chaps. Of course there was Bozzy, poor old
Bozzy, but there's generally one weakling in a litter, who
has to pay for the rest."

"No, I hadn't thought of any of that," said Gerard with a
smile; and as soon as possible he got out of Hector's room
to go home and report these refreshing comments to Anne.

§

At the head of his long dining-table in his basement dining-
room Justin sat alone, the prisoner of his thoughts. He was
still in his gown, for he was so given to thought these days that
he had forgotten it was on his back when he came down to his
meal. This basement dining-room in Vandermere Road was
much the same as the one in the Grove: a large bare room with
a long trestle table in the middle, a Victorian sideboard from
the old Duke's rectory against one wall, and a blackboard and
some chairs against another, for use between meals when the
room did duty as an extra classroom. Justin's eyes gazed
before him. The boys' dinner was over, and the table had
been cleared, but he had not moved except to turn his legs
sideways and rest his forearm on the table. He was like a
figure whom events had left stranded. Sometimes he raised
his fingers, but not his forearm or even his wrist, and beat
them on the wood.

He was a fine figure still, though certainly not as fine as
Hector had suggested, for there was that about him now
which spoke of caducity and decay. The skin of his face was
a pale greyish brown everywhere, and his expression, once so
bold and bright-eyed and confident, was now wan, as of a man
who had failed and was always sad. Sadness seemed to have
chiselled a place for itself under the cheek-bones and round
the eyes. And from out of the strained eyes a melancholy
captive would sometimes look at you—a captive who no
longer desired to escape. The neat Van Dyck beard which he
had grown of late differentiated his face from most other faces
of his time, and it was for this that he had grown it. Having
achieved by the time he was fifty nothing that marked him out
from other men, he had made himself this beard, giving it in
secret much creative care. It was a substitute for success.

His frame seemed a little shrunken beneath the good clothes.
Whereas in the old days it had seemed moulded in marble,
now it seemed hewn out of wood. The wrist on the table was

bony, and the beating fingers had the pale fawn colour and the knuckled thinness of an old man's. He was only fifty-four, but when melancholy sat upon him like this, he looked like a man of sixty who was tired and defeated.

He lifted the melancholy eyes and scanned the room. There was much in the room also which spoke of decay, and it was always on these things that his eyes fell. Smoke had grimed the walls, the linoleum was worn and split, one or two of the chairs were broken, and the bookshelves, which he himself had carpentered in such gay hope all those years ago, were unstable and listing. And many of the school books that lolled about them were disintegrating into ruin.

"Ha!" He let loose a laugh at his own disappointment.

It was not that his school, in any eyes but his own, was a failure. Established for thirty years, and functioning now as a preparatory school for day boys, it had some sixty pupils. Many of them dined in this room, and a few of them were boarders. But sixty day boys and a few boarders, if they were to yield an adequate profit, provided little with which to repair and refurnish and make beautiful his house. His house was not and never would be beautiful. Compared with his hopes his school was a failure so humiliating as to be a daily sorrow in his heart. The girls' school had failed in every sense, because Primrose's health had failed: the girls' school had just died. Primrose was now a permanent invalid, her disease, diabetes, precariously controlled by insulin, and complicated by cataract, which left her wandering in a haze of partial blindness. All the fullness of her flesh had fallen from her and she was now a tall, emaciated woman of sixty-two, flitting about the upper rooms like a lost bat, a figure from which he turned his eyes away, as he had turned them from her father twenty-five years before.

"Ha!" He laughed again at the empty room and rattled ironically a merry drumbeat on the table. And he sighed: "Ah, well. . . ."

He had been unable to move from the table when everyone else went from it and the servant cleared it, because he could not shake off the shackling news he had heard from Gerard and Anne last night.

Irrational, mad, that he should be suffering like this because of it; that it should seem more than he could bear. His intelligence revealed the irrationality to him and, in so doing, mended it not at all. The news was like a tiger that no wisdom could appease. That it was Robin to whom this unforeseen and immeasurable advance had come, and to whom this wide fame was promised—this was the fact that he could not bear. To Robin his youngest brother (except for the negligible Bozzy) who had looked up to him as a hero; Robin before whom he had always played the part of a superior; Robin whose lordly instructor and august patron he had been! Robin whose faith in unselfishness and love he had scoffed at as attractive but sentimental and weak! That Robin's altruism should have succeeded where his own scheming selfishness had failed! That Robin should suppose himself proved right and he, Justin, pitiably wrong! The more he pondered the news, the more his sick, mad anger fermented within him.

For a moment, and a moment only, the thought occurred to him: would not Robin's preferment, when it was announced in all the newspapers, bring some good to his school? But no, he would not listen to that; such a thought only aggravated his bitterness and pricked it into fury. He wanted no help from Robin. To be beholden to Robin was an idea as unbearable as to be outstripped by him.

When Robin accepted the Prime Minister's offer, and the King's appointment was announced, it would be "news", Anne had said. And she was right. It would be news more prominent than Gerard's knighthood had been. If only Robin's acceptance could be stopped, if only the appointment could be prevented, if only that news could never be issued— that would be the one healing for this savage bitterness. And to ease the virulent and consuming ache he brooded upon ways in which, even now, the onrushing event could be arrested. Could not a man whose pride was that he stopped at nothing, one who scorned the weakness of conscience, conceive and execute something that would outmanœuvre the malignance of fate?

What would stop a priest being made a bishop? His disgrace. To think this was to remember the old Duke. Of course it had all been true about the old Duke: he really had acted scandalously and like a fool, and the scandal had been brought home to him. It was unlikely that Robin had done anything that could be brought home to him. But who so vulnerable as a parson? Who so easily compromised? Could a man of much ingenuity, perhaps . . . ?

Time with its sounds and voices passed overhead while

Justin sat here, brooding for his own relief on ways to ruin his brother. Above him time travelled onward; down in this basement room, it did not move; it deepened.

Disgrace? No. He did not drill this surface very far. Even in his cankered and festering anger he had the intelligence to see that Robin's reputation for goodness would defeat him. That same reputation which had raised Robin higher in the world than all his own cynicism would now spread its breast-works around him. Robin, at least, was not vulnerable.

Not that way. What else? How arrest this last blow of fate if he was determined not to take it?

There was another way. There was another way, of course; and it healed him to consider it, sitting there.

§

His eyes were resting on his smoke-darkened basement room, but now he was not seeing it. He was seeing a lofty room with large windows and walls painted green, though some of the green paint had blistered and fallen, leaving white lep-rous sores. At one end was a dais and desk like the bench of a magistrate. Opposite it, at the other end, were some long pitch-pine seats like church pews. On the left, as you looked towards the upraised desk was a witness box, and on the right a long stall for a jury. Between these two was a table for pressmen and solicitors. One large policeman, of a kindly countenance, stood by the witness box; another by a private door on the dais; and a third by the public door into the room. The jury box was empty; and this was significant to those who understood: in cases of simple drowning a jury was not considered necessary; they were empanelled only when there was suspicion of foul play. On the hard pitch-pine benches sat a few witnesses: Justin himself, his mother, a working man from the riverside, a police surgeon, and a pathologist, nursing his file on his knees. Two reporters sat at the press table, and they were the only representatives of the people. Outside, beyond the tall windows, you could hear the people going about their daily business, this way and that, on pavement and roadway.

Two knocks sounded on the door by the dais, and the police-man standing there called, "Rise, please, to His Majesty's Coroner. O'yea! O'yea! O'yea! All manner of persons who have anything to do at this court touching the death of Arthur Bossuet le Faber, draw near and give your attention."

The Coroner had entered, as the policeman cried the pro-
clamation, and he was now seated on his high-backed chair,
a grey-haired man of comfortable shape, formally dressed in
black jacket, wide-winged collar, and grey butterfly tie.

"Pray be seated," cried the policeman.

And the Coroner, turning over a page on his desk, called,
"Mrs. le Faber, please." He said it softly and gently, because
this was the mother.

Justin watched his mother stepping into the witness box
and taking the oath, while the policeman at her side guided
and helped her.

The oath administered, the Coroner in the same gentle
voice asked, "Is this your son lying dead?"

And his mother nodded, her lips pressed together.

And then, one after another, the Coroner plied his questions,
soft-voiced and sympathetic and nodding. What was his state
of health at the time of the tragedy? "Quite good? I see.
Thank you." He wrote the answer down. And when did she
last see him alive? "About nine o'clock that night. Thank
you." And it was his habit, was it not, to wander about alone
at night? "Sometimes. I quite understand." And where
would he wander? By the river, sometimes? "You don't
know. You can't say. Very well, Mrs. le Faber, I quite understand." Had he ever done anything to make her think he
might take his own life? Nothing? She would say, would she,
that he had all he wanted in life, and was happy. "Very
happy. Thank you. What was that? He was particularly
happy just then because of his religion—happier than he had
ever been. I see. But you would agree, would you not, Mrs. le
Faber, that he had always been somewhat—shall I say,
somewhat mentally retarded?"

His mother nodded and with her head bowed, answered,
"He was a little simple, yes, but always very good."

"And you know of nobody who might wish to do him an
injury?"

"Oh no. No one at all."

"It was improbable that he had any enemies?"

"It was impossible."

"Thank you, Mrs. le Faber. That will do. Dr. Bartholomew,
please."

Dr. Bartholomew, the police surgeon, described how on a
November morning, at fifteen minutes past nine, he had been
called to examine a body recovered from the Thames. He had

found the body in the police van where it had been placed
after being picked up on the foreshore. All the indications
were that the man had been dead several days. No, there
were no signs of ante-mortem violence. None whatever."

"Thank you, doctor. I am much obliged."

The pathologist, Dr. Lamb. "You conducted the post-
mortem examination, doctor. What did you find?" Reading
from documents in his file, Dr. Lamb stated that the body was
that of a man between thirty and forty years of age. As Dr.
Bartholomew had said, there were no marks on it of ante-
mortem violence. There were wounds on the shoulder and hip,
but these had certainly taken place after death. The condition of the body was in keeping with a clean fall into the
water. There were no traces of natural diseases in the organs,
nor any traces of alcohol; the heart was in a normal condition.
The brain, however, was in an advanced state of decomposition
when he saw it, and the lungs presented all the features of
someone who had been totally immersed for several days.
From the condition of the organs he had no hesitation in saying
that the cause of death was asphyxia by drowning."

Next a police sergeant to say that he had been summoned
to a point on the embankment just below Barnes Bridge and
had seen the body of a man lying face downward on the foreshore. The divisional surgeon, on being sent for, had pronounced life extinct and given his opinion that the man had
been dead some days.

"Who first gave information to the police?"

"Mr. Lionel Street."

"Was there any clue as to what point the body got into the
river?"

"No, sir. It had probably been moving up and down with
the tides."

"Thank you, sergeant. Mr. Lionel Street, please. . . . Mr.
Street, your name is Lionel Street, and you live at 13 Bear
Lane, Barnes. What can you tell us?"

"Well, sir, I was walking along the embankment approaching
Barnes Bridge on my way to work at about eight in the morning, when I saw a body floating in the river not far from the
bank. I immediately telephoned to the police from the Grey
Goose Inn, and then waded out a little way and got hold of the
body to prevent it drifting. When the police came they put the
body on a stretcher and carried it to an ambulance. That's all
I know, sir."

"Very good, Mr. Street."

And that was all the evidence. The Coroner completed his notes, considered them, arranged them in order, and, keeping his eyes on them, began to speak. He spoke quietly as if in a private room with a few people.

"Now this is an inquiry into the death of one, Arthur Bossuet le Faber, aged thirty-eight, who lived with his mother at 7 Pemberthy Road, Brook Green. It is a tragic story. This man was not employed in any gainful occupation—he had never been so employed—but in the months before his death he had devoted himself very happily to some evangelistic work of his own devising. Indeed I think it is common knowledge to many in this neighbourhood, for he had become a familiar figure in the streets, that he was of somewhat weak intelligence, though quite harmless. He would often go for a walk at night, his mother has told us, and he would often remain out till a comparatively late hour. He was last seen by her at about nine o'clock on the evening of 3rd November and she heard no more of him till some mornings later, when the police informed her that a body had been recovered from the Thames, and she identified it as that of her son. We have no evidence that anyone saw him fall into the water, or saw him drown. We do not even know where the accident—if accident it was—took place, though we may suspect that it was somewhere along the river malls where, perhaps, he was walking alone. They are often deserted at night, and it would be quite possible, I imagine, for a somewhat dreamy-minded man to fall into the water unperceived by anyone. As we have heard from the doctors there were no signs of violence on the body except some indubitably post-mortem injuries. The only question for me is: How did this man come to fall into the river: by accident or design, his own design or another's? What I need on this bench is definite evidence, and unfortunately there is no evidence in this case that will enlighten us on any of these points. There is no evidence to suggest suicide and none to suggest foul play. In the absence of such evidence, therefore, I state as follows: that Arthur Bossuet le Faber came to his death from asphyxia by drowning, the actual day uncertain, and I record an open verdict."

The Coroner picked up his papers and rose. The policeman on the platform called: "Rise, please," and all in the room stood up.

The Coroner bowed to them, and the policeman, lifting up

his voice again, cried, "All manner of persons who have nothing further to do at this court before the King's Coroner may now depart and take your ease."

And Coroner and policeman departed through their private door; and the few persons in the body of the court strolled out through the public door. Justin picked up his silk hat and drifted out with the others, his mother on his arm. Sympathetic glances followed them.

And thereafter the world had taken its ease. It had troubled itself no more with the death of Arthur Bossuet le Faber.

§

It had been as simple as that.

And there were other ways as simple. Ways that would leave no man suspecting anything. And even if people did suspect, even if they discovered his part and published his name to the world, he wasn't sure that he'd mind very much now. Gerard had made a great name for himself, and now Robin was going to do the same, and he wasn't sure that he wouldn't like to leave a name equally celebrated behind him. He was in a humour to smash the fates that had arrayed themselves against him and humiliated him, while giving all to his brothers—fame, wealth, and the love of their women. And because Robin's goodness had succeeded as conspicuously as his own ruthless realism had failed, he hated all goodness and was in a humour to strike at it when he could. And at that word, "humiliated", he remembered that Robin had seen his ghastly, his unthinkable, humiliation in the Orpheum Theatre, and that ever since that day he had wished that all who had seen it could die, and Robin, perhaps, more than any of them, because he'd heard his boasting all his life, and because he was the audience whose admiration meant most to him.

CHAPTER THREE

AFTER that upsurge of excitement and joy which had burst the dykes and rushed out in the form of self-display, Robin experienced a sinking into shame and self-distrust. Conscience, which he had temporarily driven aside, returned in power. So complete was the dominion of conscience now that his days were harried by the thought that perhaps, after all, he ought to decline the Prime Minister's offer. His spiritual vision, always keen, became a strong white light, and he saw the choice before him as a perilous thing. Was he able enough —more important, was he good enough—for this great charge? If he considered the Church's advantage rather than his own, would he not shake a regretful head and insist that this great and important see should go to a saintlier, a stronger, and a cleverer man? Let nothing but the sternest voice answer this question for him now. He alone knew the truth about himself, and how much worse he was than Archbishop, Bishop, and Prime Minister thought him. Oh yes, he knew. His will was a poor thing compared with his vision. He could always see the right thing to do; he always longed to do it; sometimes he did it. Often, too often, he did not. And his character did not seem to be improving as he got older, but rather the reverse. His will, something worn and tired in middle age, seemed slacker than it used to be. It had less control than ever over his irritability and hot temper, and over his tendency to rush impetuously towards some self-gratification and to argue with his conscience afterwards. That rushing out with the Prime Minister's letter to show it to Gerard and Anne was a small thing, no doubt, but it was a symptom of something much bigger. And surely he was more irascible now with Jessica and the children than he was only a few years ago. Sometimes he would raise his voice and shout at them now, and he never used to do that. They loved him, because he was more often loving with them than angry, and because Jessica was sweeter than he, and because children always forgave, but there were times when he endangered their love.

As a man of saintliness, then, he was poor enough. As a scholar he was nothing. How could he sit by the side of such great episcopal scholars as Gloucester and Durham, Birmingham and Oxford and Truro? As an organizer he was worse than nothing. Always he had entrusted the organizing of his parish to his senior curate, chosen for his administrative gifts, and to his most capable secretary, Joan Routledge. Because he really loved his people, and the sinners best of all (since they were so like him) he had had some success with them, but all this success had been personal and pastoral, not impersonal and administrative. By build and temper and choice he was a minister, not an administrator. Where was the substance of a bishop here? A Colonial bishop, perhaps, or a

bishop of some small rural see; but Lavant! To be the
guardian and chief officer of one of the most important dio-
ceses in England—this was a vast and portentous future into
which he must not lightly step. Oh, no. For the moment his
decision could only be that he must not decide at once.
There must be no trace, no, not the smallest, of self-seeking
in his final word. Already he could see that, were he to turn
away from this opened door because he was sure it was the
only right thing to do, such an act would be one of the best in
his life and, in all that mattered, one of the happiest. "For
once in a way let me do a perfect thing."

And so he wrote to the Prime Minister: "I have the honour
to acknowledge your letter proposing that you should submit
my name to His Majesty the King for the vacant Bishopric of
Lavant, and to thank you with all my heart for the goodwill
and the good opinion which such a proposal implied. It lays
so great a decision before me that I am sure you will understand my reluctance to answer at once and my earnest request
that I may be allowed some days of grace in which to deliberate further on a suggestion of such gravity and consequence. . . ."

And when he had written this, he laid his hand upon it, and
knelt at his desk before it. Then he rose and sent it away
before any weakness could stay his hand. When it was gone
beyond recall, he walked up and down his study for an hour,
sometimes standing at the window and looking up at his tall
church behind the trees.

Once as he stood there he said, "O God, guide me in this
hour. Save me from myself. Save me from my love of admir-
ation and my craving for success in the eyes of the world.
Destroy all ambition in me except to serve Thy people.
Strengthen my love of them till it enables me to see my course.
Thy will only—only—be done."

And, wandering up and down, he saw that not all of this
self-distrust was a good thing; some of it was just fear. The
man whom the leaders of the nation had selected for a great
command had moments when he was but a timid and frightened creature, and he smiled somewhat ruefully at the thought.

Che fece per viltà il gran rifuto—what was this that had
sprung into mind? "Who made through cowardice the great
refusal"—ah, yes, it was Dante on Peter, the hermit of Monte
Morrone, whom they made Pope because of his goodness, and
who, in his goodness, abdicated after a few months, because he

did not believe he had the qualities or the strength for the
task. And for this noble withdrawal Dante consigned him to
a circle of hell among contemptible spirits "who never were
alive." And Dean Milman had written of him—Robin took
down the book and found the place: "A few months showed
that meekness, humility, holiness, and unworldliness might
make a saint; they were not the virtues suited to a pope."
How crude was Dante; how crude the Dean. In a bishop
scholarship, statesmanship, organizing genius were useless,
and worse than useless, without the one thing needful, which
was sanctity; which was precisely humility, holiness, and
unworldliness. The whole history of the Church for two
thousand years proved this to be so.

"O God be with me, be with me. Help me. Forgive me the
selfish aims and the heedless errors of all my past years, and
let them not rise now to cloud my vision and disable my will.
Save me alike from the sin of self-seeking and from the weakness of too much self-distrust. 'If Thy presence go not with me,
carry me not up hence.' "

These last words, which had come unsought into his memory,
expressed so exactly the whole of his thought that he went to
his desk and wrote them down. And having written them, he
laid his hand upon them, as if they were his act and deed.

§

All this was on the Saturday, the day after he received the
letter from Downing Street. On the Tuesday morning, the
duties of a full Sunday and Monday being now behind him, he
went into his study and shut the door that he might take up
his debate again. He took those words from the drawer of his
desk and knelt down before them. Then he rose and wandered
up and down and round about the room, thinking. And it was
while he paused for a minute at the window and looked out at
the garden that the maid announced, "Mr. Justin is here, sir."

"Justin? What? At this time of the morning? Bring him
in, Frances, bring him in." He said it merrily, because he was
glad of an intrusion which would relieve him for a while from
the harassing argument, and he called, "Come in, come in, old
man," and ran to the door to welcome Justin. "What brings
you out at this hour? My gracious, old chap, you're not
looking too good. Anything wrong?"

For he was shocked to see Justin looking so drawn and grey
in the face. He looked like a man whom long solitude had

dried up and long sadness wasted. His face was deep-chiselled and shadowed and wan. His eyes disturbed you. It was as if, behind them, someone was looking at you other than he who spoke.

"I'm all right," he declared with a laugh, refusing pity. "I need a holiday, that's all. That's what I've come about." He sank into a chair and accepted a cigarette from Robin's case. "I want you to come to the mountains with me."

"The mountains?"

"Yes. I no sooner got the idea in my head than I decided I must come and see you about it. I couldn't wait. Robin, old boy, I want you to come."

"To Deep Langstrath?"

"Sure! If they can have us."

Robin lit a cigarette for himself while he thought, "This is odd. Why should he come so early in the morning with this talk of a holiday? He must be shaken and upset if he feels driven like this. And he looks it. He looks like a man whose mind is sick."

"Well?" asked Justin, as Robin tossed his match away.

"I'm not really taking my holiday till August."

"Oh, but I only mean for a few days. A few days in the middle of the week if you like. Or a long week-end. It'll do you good, and it'll do me good."

"But when exactly do you mean?"

"Now. To-morrow if you can manage it. Or the day after. Or just as soon as you can fit it in. But come while the weather is like this. It may break soon."

Robin drew at his cigarette and did not answer. And his lack of an answer showed that the idea was too pleasant to be immediately rejected. And Justin, perceiving this, pursued his advantage with a smile. But for most of the time he was not looking at Robin. He was looking at the daylight in the large window and frowning at it.

"I want to go to all the old places. I want to see the Langstrath valley again with Eagle Crag hanging over it and Greenup Gill twisting down from the mountain. I want to see Stake Pass and Esk Hause and the top of Scafell. I keep seeing Angle Tarn and the shelter on Esk Hause and the cairns leading up to the Pike. And I'm in the mood to throw everything up for a little and go there again. And whenever I think of it, I know there's only one companion for me on such a holiday, and it's old Robin."

Robin was touched. Moreover Justin's words had stirred in him both pity and a kind of excited thirst: pity for Justin who in his loneliness had longed for a companion and a thirst for the old loved places. Always this excitement came alight at any mention of these mountains and fells, and most of all when it was Justin who spoke of them.

"Wouldn't I just love to come!"

"Oh, well, come on," urged Justin, and now his eyes were fixed upon Robin. "Why not? Oh yes, man! Think of the Gable and Wind Gap and Kirk Fell. Think of our own private route from Langstrath up to Esk Hause. Think of scrambling over the upturned rocks on the top of Scafell."

"God, yes!" whispered Robin. And he saw again that splendid desolation of up-ended rocks, bare, green-grey, and cold, like a scene on a planet from which all life was gone. He saw the pale marks scraped on the rocks between cairn and cairn by the feet of climbers who had gone this way before them. And he saw the boundless prospect of mountain, valley, lake and sea that rolled away from the summit of Scafell, which was the very roof and tiling of England.

Justin, his eyes still fixed upon him, seemed to be seeing his thoughts and knowing, in consequence, exactly what to say. "And think of standing on Brandreth and seeing Buttermere and Crummock Water in one deep fold and Ennerdale Water in the next. Think of scrambling down from Dale Head by Lobstone Band and recovering over a huge tea in Rosthwaite. Think of striding along the ridge from High Crag to High Stile and Red Pike. Remember it?"

"Do I not?" Oh yes, old Justin knew how to tempt him. Every name inflated the heart and was a temptation.

"Well, come on then, man. You can't resist it. You can get off for a few days, and so can I. That's the advantage of being our own masters. I've heard all about the Bishopric, and I'm sure you ought to have a holiday before you start on a job like that."

"Yes, but I'm not going to Lavant to-morrow—if at all. How did you hear about it? It's supposed to be a secret."

"Anne told me. You know what Anne is. If you want something published to the world, tell it to her as a secret. By the way, let me congratulate you. It's terrific news. I was overjoyed when I heard it, but I don't think it's any more than you deserve."

"Thanks, old man. But I haven't accepted it yet."

"Not accepted it? But you're going to, aren't you?"
Justin had swung his eyes to Robin again in a sudden surprise.
The brows above them knit and unknit themselves nervously.
"Of course you're going to accept it."

"I don't know. I'm not at all certain."

"Why not?"

"Because, to put it quite plainly, I'm not sure that I'm
good enough or clever enough or——" he shrugged his
shoulders, unable to find the right word—"well, the right type
for it. I can't see myself as a disciplinarian, for instance.
Everyone seems to have a natural level, and I suspect that
I've reached mine. I can manage a large parish fairly well,
but not a great diocese. As I tell myself, I can do a captain's
job, but not an admiral-of-the-fleet's. I've been happy here
—though I still think that I prefer a parish of the very poor to
the very rich. They're a softer soil to work in. I shall always
think that I did my best work, and could do it again, among
the poor. They seem to have my heart in a way that these
good people ought to have it, but——" Robin smiled self-
depreciatingly at his brother, and shrugged again. "No
doubt one ought to love all men equally, but there you are:
the heart of man is desperately wicked."

"When will you decide?"

"I must decide in a few days. I can't keep the Prime
Minister waiting for ever."

It was very curious, the way Justin was staring at him. He
seemed to be thinking of what they were saying, and of something else too. After a minute he repeated, "When will you
decide?" as if he had not heard Robin's answer; and Robin
repeated the answer; and for a little Justin was silent.

Robin could not know that when, most surprisingly, he
expressed a doubt as to whether he would accept the Bishopric,
a hope had flooded into Justin's mind; but it was so, for
there was that in Justin which would be glad to be set free
rom a dark and terrible compulsion. Justin did not yet
know what he was going to do if he got his brother to the
mountains. So far he was resolved upon no more than to get
him to the place of opportunity, and to see what happened
there. At one time he would doubt if he could do the thing
he had in mind; at another, when the bitterness of defeat
made his heart a stone, his lips would set together, and the
fhing would seem a grim and fixed determination—dead to
the touch, inflexible, impermeable. Then, as in the hour

before he went to meet Bozzy, he seemed to be seated within
a rock of iron that resisted thought.

But if Robin, after all, did not accept the Bishopric, then
everything was as before; and this sudden hope, for which
Justin had not looked, was as sweet as the hope of a reprieve.
But the relief evaporated quickly. This hesitancy of Robin's,
what was it but the natural assault of doubt and diffidence
before a momentous change? It was no more than the wedding-
eve hesitation of a bridegroom, and it would be as transitory.
Robin would accept in the end; of course he would. Let them
be in the place of opportunity, then, when Robin's decision
came—and Justin's.

"Well, my dear chap, you've provided me with a conclusive
argument now." Justin's eyes lit up with something of the
old laughter. "If you've got a tremendous choice to make,
surely the thing to do is to come somewhere where it is peace-
ful and quiet, and think it out. Isn't that what Elijah used to
do? Didn't he go climbing up Mount Carmel or Mount Horeb
or somewhere when the Lord had told him to do something he
didn't want to do? Didn't he go a day's journey into the
wilderness and sit down under a juniper tree—or was that
somebody else?"

"Yes, he did." And it was what a greater than Elijah did,
thought Robin, when He was tempted or in doubt or needed
renewal. Everything was driving him to say Yes to Justin:
the desire of a tired man for peace and silence and nature's
beauty, his thirst for the beloved hills in Justin's company,
and more than all, because it was the least selfish of all, his pity
for a brother who looked so haggard and spent, and who needed
so plainly the comfort of a friend. He had firmly resolved to
answer the Prime Minister's call only from the best in him;
and he knew that if he was to do the best in this great business,
he must be doing it—or trying to—in every smaller thing
every minute of the day. Only by keeping himself within the
best, these next few days, would he answer from the best.
God's ways were strange, and often as simple as they were
unexpected. Was he answering his bewildered and wondering
prayers with the simple words, "Do the task immediately to
hand, which is to help and heal a brother who needs you; do
this first, and leave the rest to me." He looked at Justin
again; and again the drawn, sad face and the dark, sunken
eyes distressed his heart.

"All right, old man," he said. "I'll come."

§

And so delightful was the contemplation of this brief holiday
that Robin, the next morning, though he could not start for a
few days yet, hurried over his breakfast, leaving most of it,
and went to a cupboard and sought out his climbing clothes:
shorts, shirts, sweaters, oilskins, and the old boots. And a
pair of spare bootlaces. And a bit of rope. And a small first-
aid outfit, in case, in case . . . And the old map, Jessica—
what are we thinking about: the old map. A guide book?
Pshaw! Justin and I don't deal in guide books. We could find
our way with our eyes shut. Don't be absurd, woman. Guide
book! He made Jessica assist in the packing, ostensibly to
assemble socks and underclothes, but really to attend to his
joyous babble, and to hear descriptions of precarious climbs
that he and Justin had accomplished in the old days, and to
have her ears startled when he burst into the songs they used
to sing together in the maddening mountain air. " 'Try not
the pass,' the old man said. . . ."

His prattle and singing were stopped by a ring of the hall
door bell. He was on the landing as it rang, passing from
linen cupboard to bedroom, and he halted to listen. The ring
was followed by a fumbling on the door and a knock—a
spoiled knock, as of an infirm or irresolute hand.

Jessica came from the bedroom to listen too; and when they
heard the maid in conversation with someone, she went down
to see who it might be. She was curious, because it was still
only half-past nine. She returned to Robin and said, "Robin . . .
it's Primrose."

"Primrose! Primrose at this time! Why, she's even earlier
than Justin. What's up?"

"I think something's the matter, Robin. She especially
wants to see you. Alone."

"But is she alone herself? Isn't that girl with her who
generally guides her about?"

"No, she's found her way here alone."

"Good gracious, what *is* it? Did she say anything?"

"No, but I should go down to her. She looks rather strange."

Robin went down. He went into the breakfast room where
they had placed Primrose because the drawing-room was still
in the servants' hands. Primrose was seated on the single
easy chair, but her posture on it was plainly temporary. She
was sitting upright on its edge. Her half-blind eyes were

turned towards the window, and by her side was the white-enamelled stick with which she tapped her way about the streets.

The moment he entered she rose upon the stick and turned her opaque eyes towards him. Now that sight was partly withdrawn from her eyes there was a greyish tint in the fading pupils and a red-brown light in the dimmed irises. Robin, never quite sure whether she was seeing him or not, would be as embarrassed in her company as one is with the deaf. But he wanted to be kind to her, and he said genially, "Don't get up, Primrose. Sit down and be comfortable."

Obediently, like one bemused and therefore responsive to a clearer mind, she sat down again, laying the stick by her side. It slid to the carpet, and he picked it up for her and put it into her hand.

"Well, how are you, Primrose?"

A formal question, largely answered by her appearance. Primrose, once tall and plumply fashioned, was now as gaunt and lined as some fever-worn old colonel from the East. She held herself erect, and with her stick had something of a masculine appearance—she who was once so big-bosomed and archly feminine. Her hair was shingled in a last flicker of the old archness, but it was grey now and dank and wispy. The skin of her face and dried-up neck had an even sallowness. Her short skirt and cardigan hung slackly and glumly on her raw-boned figure, and her stockings fitted loosely to her thin legs. But most noticeable of all this morning was the fear at play upon her face and even gleaming from the dulled eyes.

"Oh, I'm as well as I can ever hope to be," she answered, and the self-pitying tears welled up and washed her eyes. "I can never hope to be anything but a wreck any more. But it's not about that that I want to talk to you. Robin, I'm so unhappy. Can I talk to you? I must. I must talk to someone, and when Justin came home yesterday and said he was going for this holiday with you, I suddenly saw that you were the one person I could confide in—a clergyman and his brother and so good—everyone says how good and kind you are. I often wonder how anyone so good and kind can be *his* brother. Can you spare me a little time? I know how busy you are, but I don't know what I shall do if I don't speak to someone about it.

"Of course I can give you all the time you want. I was only indulging myself when you came in—playing at packing.

Come into the study and be really comfortable and tell me
everything that's worrying you. Come along, dear."

His fingers on her elbow, he guided her along the passage
between breakfast room and study. And there he placed her in
one of his deep chairs and put a cigarette into her hand and lit
it for her. She drew at it laboriously but without interest.

"Like some coffee?"

"No, no, no. I want to be alone with you. No one must
come in. Shut the door, do."

He shut the door and, seating himself in his desk chair,
swivelled it round and sat looking at her.

"Well, Primrose? What's the great trouble?"

She lifted the opaque eyes, and he could see her thinking
and thinking behind them before she spoke.

"Oh, it's too awful," she said at last. "You won't believe
it. You'll think I'm mad."

"I shall believe anything you tell me."

"No, you'll think it some dreadful hallucination. But it
isn't, Robin. I'm certain it's not. I only wish it were."

"Well, what is it," he encouraged with a kindly smile.

"It's about Justin."

"Yes?"

Again she halted all speech as if afraid of what she must say.
"Don't hate me if I tell you. You're the only person I can talk
to, and you're so understanding, and I need your help so much."

"It's not my business to hate anyone, and least of all you,
Primrose."

"But you don't realize what I'm going to say. It's more
awful than anything you are imagining."

"A parson hears some strange things," he reminded her,
and he laughed softly that she might feel his smile.

She turned her eyes towards the shining brown tiles of the
grate. And when she had gathered strength she said slowly,
"Justin murdered your brother."

"Primrose!"

"Yes. He murdered Bozzy. And that is not all. He also
brought about my father's death. It was as good as murder.
Yes, he murdered my father. My poor, dear, helpless old
father."

Robin said nothing. His embarrassment in her company
increased, because he could only suppose that some control in
her brain had slipped, and she was now mad. This was a
familiar form of insanity. Her resentment against Justin had

burst like an abscess in her brain and was spilling over in these fearful accusations. Poor Justin. Here was a new disaster fallen upon his house.

"And what I've really come to say to you—what I so terribly need your help about—is that I'm terrified lest—I live in terror day and night lest he should one day murder me."

"Oh, no, no, no, no, Primrose. You mustn't say such things."

"I don't say that he *is* doing so, Robin. I don't even say that he will. I only say that I'm terrified of it. You see, I'm only a nuisance to him now, a burden that he'd like to be rid of: he hates the sight of me, and, Robin, he killed the other two when they were nuisances to him—I know he did. I'll tell you how I know. And why shouldn't he kill me?"

"No, no, Primrose. There's not a chance of that. How *could* he?"

"There are plenty of dangerous chemicals in that laboratory he made for the boys."

"But, Primrose, Primrose, you can't go poisoning people nowadays without being discovered. You just can't do it, and Justin knows you can't. Put it out of your head. Doesn't the doctor see you regularly, and wouldn't his suspicions be at once aroused? Besides, Justin couldn't do a thing like that. He couldn't."

"Well, he might do it in some other way. He's clever, Robin. He's diabolically clever. What I can't understand is that anyone so clever should have done so little in the world. He murdered poor Bozzy, and no one's suspected it in eleven years. I didn't suspect anything myself till a few months ago. He murdered Papa for all practical purposes, and I never realized he'd done it till twenty-five years later. I can't think how I've been such a fool all these years. But I know it now. I know it for a certainty."

"How can you know, Primrose?"

"My dear, he almost *says* he did it sometimes. He so hates me and so despises me that he doesn't mind what he says to me. Sometimes I think that he'd half like to tell me that he'd done it, because he's proud of it . . . or perhaps he thinks I shall soon be dead, and it doesn't matter how much I know or guess. Perhaps he has good reason to know that I shall soon be dead. . . . Oh, Robin, you can do things with him that no one else can do. And you are clever too. Perhaps you could find out from him on this holiday what he thinks about me. . . .

Oh, Robin, when I suddenly thought of coming to you, I could hardly wait. I hurried out of the house directly he'd gone in to the boys. When I'd decided to tell everything to you, I felt happier than I had for months."

"You were quite right to come to me and tell me all that's worrying you. But, Primrose, how can you really believe these awful things of Justin? He may hint at such things to tease you. It's his mischief. He's always liked saying shocking things."

Primrose shook her head slowly, helplessly, and her dim, dislustred eyes stared at the door. "He brought about Papa's death. I'm sure of it. Don't you remember that it was soon after he got his degree that Papa was taken ill and died? Once he'd got his degree he didn't need a figurehead for his school any more, and Papa was of no use in any other way; he was even something of a disgrace to Justin. I can understand that. He'd completely let himself go, poor old Papa. He would walk about the house in his bare feet sometimes, and it used to drive Justin into frightful rages, which he would vent first on him and then on me when the poor old man had run from him in terror. More than once he said to me, 'Why doesn't he die? He's no use to himself or anyone else.' And then—do you remember?—Papa was so unhappy that he took to drinking. He would slip out at night to public houses and sit there drinking whisky. He pawned his gold watch and chain to get money for drink, and he even took some jewellery of mine and pawned it—though I never told Justin that. But Justin knew that he sat in a kind of stupor in the public houses near Erasmus Hall, and he was furious. He roared at Papa that he wouldn't put up with it, but the more he shouted and raved, the more Papa slunk away to his only comfort. So Justin decided to kill him. That's all there was to it. He decided to destroy him like vermin."

"Primrose! How can you say that? How can you know it? If he'd done that, someone was bound to know."

"Oh, it was clever enough. It was terribly cold when Papa died—the coldest February for years—and Papa caught a nasty chill, probably because he would wander half-dressed about the house. Justin seized upon his chance. One evening when the old man was sitting over the fire, wiping his eyes which were streaming with the cold, Justin chose to become very gentle and kind and jolly with him—he's always ready to pretend to be a saint, if it suits him—and he said, 'I know what'll cure you, Duke: a drop or two of the best.' And he told him to wrap up warm and come out to the Watermen's Arms, a public house near us, and he'd stand him all he wanted. I asked him if he thought it wise to encourage the old man, but he told me quite merrily to have a heart and let the poor old thing enjoy himself once in a way. He said that he himself was feeling in an understanding and compassionate mood, and, as this was rare, it should be encouraged. Papa was only too willing to go, of course, and Justin helped wrap him up warm in his coat and muffler, and put his hat on his head, and made him take his arm. And they went off together, laughing and joking. But he didn't take him to the Watermen's Arms, which is quite close to us, but to the Queen's Head on Brook Green, which he remembered no doubt as a boy. I didn't know this till some days afterwards, when Papa mentioned it, and I supposed then that he'd gone some distance away so that they shouldn't be seen in a public house near the school; but I see now that he went there to make the journey through the cold night as long as possible. In the public house he filled him up with whisky after whisky, and because the bar was crowded and hot, he helped him to undo his coat and wraps. Papa was not too steady on his feet when they came away, and Justin helped him into the street. His overcoat and muffler were still undone, and Justin walked him home through a bitterly cold wind with the coat flying open—and of course they could only walk very slowly. Poor Papa hardly felt the cold at all because the alcohol was dilating his blood-vessels and making his skin feel warm. It has that effect, as I know now that Justin knew. When they were near the house, Justin stopped him on the pavement and buttoned up his coat. I only knew this because a woman friend, coming home from New End Chapel, told me she'd seen him in the Grove with his coat flying open. That meant that they must have walked from Brook Green to the Grove with Papa's chest exposed to the cold, and Justin must have wrapped him up outside the house to hide this fact from me. Oh, to think of him walking all that way by the old man's side like a devil, laughing and being merry with him while he was slowly killing him.''

"Yes, mad,'' thought Robin, staring at her, who could hardly see him. An old story: when unhappy wives went mad, they always accused their husbands of unspeakable crimes.

"Of course I never suspected that Justin had done anything

deliberately," Primrose went on. "How could I? How could anybody? I never saw the truth of the matter till a little while ago when I realized that he'd murdered Bozzy."

Yes, mad. Poor, poor Primrose.

"Papa suspected nothing. He spoke often of Justin's kindness that night, and Justin was very kind to him afterwards. The next night he was very feverish, and in a little time he was coughing so that it was painful to hear him, and he complained of tearing pains in his chest. Then Justin couldn't do enough for him. He sent for the doctor, and when the doctor said it was pneumonia, Justin said that the old man must have everything we could afford. He insisted on having two nurses, to watch over the old man night and day, and he did everything he could to help them. But of course there was no chance of Papa recovering. When the nurse saw him, she told me that the fight was as good as lost. He got steadily worse and died in a few days. When he knew he was dying he asked me to sing to him—" the tears flooded into her eyes—"and he would hold my hand and quote his favourite Horace and his beloved Pascal. Once he said to me with a smile, '*Non omnis moriar*,' and another time, '*On mourra seul. . . .*'"

She could not go on till the tears had sunk from her eyes and throat. But she nodded to herself several times, as she remembered it all. Robin kept silence.

Then suddenly she emitted a low laugh like a man's. "Ha . . . and no one could have taken more trouble than Justin did about the funeral. Everybody said how wonderful he was. I remember a maid we had saying: 'I've always said, Madam, the Master's bark is a lot worse than his bite.'"

Primrose stopped. She seemed to have stopped altogether, so Robin was obliged to speak.

"But, Primrose, there's nothing in that story to suggest that Justin was anything more than careless. There isn't, really."

"I know. And so I thought for twenty-five years until I realized that he'd killed Bozzy."

"What is it you are thinking about Bozzy?"

"Think? I *know* that Justin murdered him. It remains a mystery to me how I was so blind as not to see it years ago. He was furious with Bozzy at that time, mad with him, because he said he was disgracing him and his school. He said again and again that he wished to God he would die. And then Bozzy interrupted him in a public meeting and humiliated him

before thousands of people. His vanity was wounded beyond
bearing—he didn't speak for days and he looked deathly all
the time—and after about a week Bozzy disappeared; and it
was only then that Justin began to speak again and be his
normal self."

Robin shook his head, as one who discounts what he is
hearing; and Primrose, either seeing or apprehending the
movement, demurred, "But listen, Robin. Listen. For some
nights before Bozzy disappeared Justin took to going out after
supper without saying a word to me and staying away till
nearly midnight. I couldn't think what he was doing, and I
was jealous. I knew I was getting old and unattractive and
that he recoiled from me, and I wondered if he was going to
meet some woman. At last—I know it was wrong, but I
couldn't help it, I was so miserable, and I had to know—I
followed him through the dark. I followed him twice, and each
time he turned towards your old home in Brook Green and
walked up and down the Shepherds Bush Road. I watched
him from a long way off, expecting to see him meet some
woman and determined to find out who she was. The first
time he met nobody and came home; the second time he met
Bozzy. There are some flats at the corner by the green, and as
I hid behind their gateway I saw Bozzy pass me, and then I
saw that Justin was following him. He was not going to meet a
woman at all. He followed him all the way up King Street as
far as Ravenscourt Park—and I followed too—and there
they met and stook talking together. I was surprised to
see how friendly Justin was with him, because only a day or
two before he'd been too furious to speak of him, but now
he was laughing and joking with him just as he did with Papa.
I couldn't hear what they were saying, but I judged from their
actions that they had arranged a meeting somewhere, because
Justin repeated something and held up his finger as one
does to a child, and Bozzy nodded to show that he understood. Then Justin turned as if to walk home, and I hurried
home another way, running, so that I should be back before
him, and he'd never know I'd left the house. I was so relieved that it was only Bozzy whom he'd met that I got
happily into bed. I remember singing as I undressed, so
great was the relief. But after I'd been in bed about an hour
I heard him slip quietly from the house. Then I was anxious
again, but I couldn't attempt to follow him, because he'd
have been out of sight before I could have dressed again. I

just looked from the window and saw him walking south-ward towards the river. After that I lay waiting to hear him return. He returned about an hour later and went to bed. Bozzy was never seen again after that night."

All through this story Robin had kept his eyes on hers, be-cause a suspicion that she was right had begun to grip him with its fearful hand. Trying to escape its grasp, he objected, falteringly, "But nothing of this *proves* anything, Primrose."

"It proves enough to me. Why did he go looking for him night after night? Where did he go that night? Above all, why did he never tell the police or the coroner or me or anyone that he'd met Bozzy and spoken to him on the very night he disappeared?"

Yes, why? Oh, could it be that she was right? His heart, as the suspicion increased and strengthened, hammered like the fist of an imprisoned truth on its cell door. Shafts of irrele-vant sunlight slanted through the window, and his eyes rested on them because they were the brightest things in the room.

"Did you ever tell him that you'd seen him with Bozzy that night?"

"No. How could I? I couldn't confess that I'd been spying on him."

"Did you ever tell anyone else?"

"No. I couldn't have told them the reason why, I was too ashamed of it. I've never told a soul till this moment."

"But what did you think about his strange silence?"

"I don't know that I thought anything much. I've been a complete, deluded fool all these years. I suppose I just thought that he didn't want to be mixed up in police proceedings."

"Could that be the truth, perhaps——" began Robin, but Primrose hurried on, unheeding.

"You see, however unkind he's been to me, I've always thought him cleverer and wiser than other people, so I told myself he knew best."

"Don't you still think that that was the reason for his silence?"

"No, I do not. I do not."

"Why not?"

"Because in the last few months I've seen everything clearly. Suddenly a hundred and one things about Papa's death and Bozzy's have all fallen into the same pattern. Of late, as I've told you, he's seemed quite indifferent to what he says to me, and I fancy sometimes that he almost *wants* me to suspect something. I think he's proud of having outwitted the world in this matter and wants *me* at least to know of it. It's his one great success, you see: he hasn't been too successful in other things. He hasn't been as successful as Gerard or you."

It was when she said this that Robin abandoned the idea that she was mad. This was a woman to whom suffering had given, not madness, but a cold wisdom. She had been foolish once, but she was foolish no more. He wished—he wished in a kind of helpless pain—that he could have gone on believing her mad instead of wise, but he could not.

"Over and over again, Robin, he's said to me with a curious look in his eyes, 'Those that stand in my way, Primmy, don't stay there long.' Or things like, 'If I've made up my mind to do a thing, Primmy, I do it.' I remember him saying once, 'You see, Primmy, I don't recognize half the moral sanctions in the world. I took those dead weights out of my shoes when I was about fifteen. Ask Robby.' Over and over again he's said things like that to me. He claims to have what he calls a bunk-proof mind, and sometimes I think he has to prove it to himself by going deliberately against his conscience. Once he said, 'If someone injured me enough, I shouldn't hesitate to put him safely out of the way; and for all you know, Primmy, I may have done it.' It was remarks like this that seemed to come together one day and light up everything for me. It was funny, Robin, but the scales began to fall from my eyes just as I began to go blind. The blinder I got, the more I turned inward, I suppose, and began to see."

Robin looked at the disabled eyes and knew that they were not seeing him; they were looking at an illumination within.

"You have never charged him with—with having helped your father to die?"

Now the eyes turned full on him. "Do I want to make sure that he murders me?"

"Oh, Primrose, don't say that. Don't imagine that. Even if these other things are true, what reason have you to imagine that?"

"No reason; only fear; only terror. Up till a few years ago I was of some use to him, as his matron or his housekeeper, but gradually I got less and less so. The balances were less and less in my favour. Now that I'm so ill and so blind that I can do nothing to save him money, but am only an expense and a burden, the balance has tilted down, and I am standing now where Papa stood."

Robin, unable to comment, sat thinking of the daily agony of this gaunt and lonely woman in that house in Vandermere Road. To dwell upon it was to imagine it more and more vividly, and he leaned forward and picked up her hand. "If you feel that, Primrose dear, even if there's no justification for it, I think you ought to leave him at once. You ought to come away from that house. You mustn't suffer like this."

"Where should I go?" Her hand grasped his in gratitude, and pressed it, and the tears shining in her eyes gave them an extraneous light. "I have no other home. And I'm blind and a burden."

"I'd find somewhere where you could be happy. Jessica and I would do that. And in the meantime you could come to us. At once, if you like."

Her fingers were gripping his spasmodically, like those of a person on a death bed. "I don't know what to do. I don't know what to do. I don't think it's time to do that yet. Do you know what I think, Robin? I think he would like to retire and go far away into the country, and my death would be an excuse for retiring, and my little bit of money would be some help. I think he would like me to know first what he did to Papa and to Bozzy, because it was so great a triumph and then kill me before I could do anything about it. But I don't know: I may be mistaken. Mistaken."

Robin nodded, as one who was decrying her fears. But was he decrying them any more? He hardly knew. Perhaps it was in doubt of them that he nodded—or in the hope of doubt.

"Yes, yes, Primrose," he said; and he didn't know what he meant.

"I must go now," said Primrose. "I feel so glad to have told you all. I feel ever so much happier. I feel I have a friend somewhere. I must go home now." She felt for her white stick and rose, tall and angular and blind. "Don't worry about me. I shall be all right. You'll take him away in a few days, and perhaps you'll find out more about him. You understand him so well, and he talks to you as to no one else. Till then I shall be all right. Thank you so much for listening to me."

He drew her to him and kissed her. And when she refused his invitation to stay and rest a little, he went upstairs to Jessica who was now packing his suit-case for the holiday, and said, "Leave all that, darling. Leave it now. I want you to help Primrose on her way home. She's very unhappy."

"Of course I will, darling," said Jessica promptly, and did not even ask the cause of her unhappiness.

§

Robin was left standing in his room, his eyes apprehending nothing while his mind stared at the things which Primrose had told him. And he was appalled to realize that he believed she was right. The realization made his hands tremble and his heart tremble. Everything that she had said or suggested seemed to fit Justin like a well-made garment: Justin *would* hint to her as to what he had done; to Justin success *would* be incomplete unless those to whom he was tied emotionally knew of it. It was conceivable that he could be tempted to hint at it to Robin. Never so far had he done so. And as Robin thought that, he remembered, with a further sickening, that, in these last eleven years, Justin had often spoken of the old Duke but had never spoken of Bozzy. He who used to talk at length, either comically or virulently, of Bozzy! Whenever Bozzy's name had been mentioned, he had turned his eyes and his talk away. Robin had noticed this often, and had supposed that it was the disgrace of Bozzy's death which had left Justin bitter and dumb. But if it were only this, its sting would have worn away with the years. If, on the other hand, it were what Primrose had suggested, when, if ever, could it wear away? There was no such tendency to swerve away from talk of the old Duke, but no doubt he didn't consider his handling of the old Duke so indubitable a murder.

What had he done to Bozzy? Thrust him into the river? Held his head down? Out of the past, up from the tomb where it had lain buried beneath the weight of forty years, rose a memory of Justin and himself in their little bedroom in Pemberthy Road, and Justin, flushed with a triumph over his parents who represented to him the outer world, maintaining that the great ones of history had never been afraid to kill, and going on to enumerate ways in which you could kill your victim and bilk the police. "What's wrong with taking him in a boat far out to sea and then accidentally overturning the boat? You can swim and he can't." Yes, when they were boys, Justin used to scorn Bozzy because he could never learn to swim.

"Oh, Bozzy . . . Poor Bozzy . . . What was done to you on that dark night? He met you that night. Why has he never said a word about that meeting in eleven years?

"Or you go for a family trip on a liner, and one dark night there's a man overboard. . . ."

No doubt Justin had completely forgotten that he had said these things in a bedroom darkness of forty years ago, but they had lain like living seeds in his mind and in the heavy atmosphere of defeat and envy they had rooted and come to flower.

Robin was standing by the window now, his hands clasped behind his back, one hand convulsively pressing the other. He was believing Primrose.

He who could sometimes see into his brother's mind so clearly was now discerning a curious but quite simple likelihood: Justin had always desired to be different from the multitude; to that end, from the time he was young, he had parted his fine black hair in the middle; to that end in later years he had grown a Van Dyck beard; to that end he had murdered Bozzy. He had murdered him, that he might believe himself the equal of Napoleon and the great men.

The more Robin thought about the poor old Duke and poor, simple Bozzy, so happy in his faith and works, the more his wrath rose like a hot flood and he longed to denounce Justin to his face and to punish him; to say, "I loved the old man; and Bozzy was my brother. He had another brother as well as you."

And yet, mixed with the wrath, swelling up with the hot tide, came the old love for Justin, not to be repressed, nay, more irrepressible than it had ever been, now that he saw Justin rotted with his own selfishness like a piece of driftwood floating down the river. Extraordinary that this scalding anger, with its savage desire to hurt and punish, and this pitying and despairing tenderness could be in his breast at the same time. In his rage, when it possessed him, he was impatient to confront Justin with his knowledge and, after castigating him with words, to paralyse him with fear; in his love, when it troubled his heart again, he was in love with the idea of helping him.

"O God, what am I to do? Show me what to do." The hands were pressing convulsively again, and twitching. "If possible, show me that I am wrong. Oh, is it possible that I am wrong? What a relief and happiness that would be. But if not, show me how to learn the truth. No one else must know it—I alone shall know it—and I shall have to act. I shall have to deal with it alone. But what, oh my God, what am I to do? There is Primrose."

"If a man has succeeded once in a premeditated murder, he is likely to murder again." How often had he heard that. And how often it had been shown to be true. Oh, was Primrose right? Was she in danger?—oh, to think that in these last days when he had been filled to overflowing with the joy of success, she had been sitting in that house alone with her fear.

Now all that pity and love which could mount up in Robin till it was a driving pain, was embracing Primrose. The kiss that he had given her just now was the sacramental expression of something that he was really feeling. Primrose had gathered into herself, as it were, and become the symbol of, all those poor and suffering people who had always captured his loyalty, his service, and his combativeness.

Lost from sight now were his doubts and wonderings about his own future. Grimmer and more fatal decisions were before him.

He remained before the window for a long time and in the same position, his body hardly moving, though often his shoulders twitched and his fingers contracted. Now he would fold his arms across his breast; now rejoin his hands behind his back. When he came away, it was with a first decision. He must discover the truth. He must get these dark questions into the air and light. He would go with Justin on the holiday which they had planned, and which two hours ago had seemed so delightful, and in some desolate place—perhaps on a mountain far above the ways of men—he would charge Justin with these things and, taking him unprepared, prise out the truth. How and in what words God alone knew. God, in the form of inspiration, must give him the words.

CHAPTER FOUR

Two men, one behind the other, were climbing the easy slope from Maiden Moor towards the cap of Scawdel Fell. They appeared to be tall men in the good middle of life. The one behind was slighter than the one in front, but both were built in pleasing lines and retained much of the grace of boyhood. You would have conjectured, had you passed them, that they were brothers.

They were Justin and Robin le Faber, with rucksacks slung, bending their backs to a familiar path.

The track that swings up and down between the summits of Cat Bells, Maiden Moor, and Scawdel Fell they would describe when they were young as "a nursery slope" or "a soft climb"; and it is soft in more senses than one. The turf is soft, the slopes are gentle, and the top of Scawdel is only a little way above the 2000 contour line. There is but one thing to distress a head little used to heights, and it is this: between Maiden Moor and Scawdel the track now and again turns away from the soft fledge of heather and turf and becomes a ribbon of stones skirting the haggard precipices which men in the vale below, seeing them black and broken against the sky, call Eel Crags. Sometimes the track is but a yard from these sheer and splintered eaves, and it is then that the novice keeps his eyes averted and laughs to hide his fear.

Justin called back that they must have crossed the 2000 contour line and that the summit, therefore, couldn't be more than a hundred feet higher.

But because this undulating range is high, and yet not of any great height, they seemed to be in the very lap of the mountains. On their left, across the deep of Borrowdale, rose High Seat and High Tove and Ullscarf and, behind these grey and heaving tops, the peak of Helvellyn and the pyramid of Catchedicam, sculptured side by side in the southerly light of the sun. On their right, beyond the unseen glen that lay beneath the Crags, rose Hindscarth and, beyond it, Red Pike and High Stile and High Crag, crowding their shoulders together. Their view in front was blunted by the gradual slope of Scawdel, but if they turned and looked behind, they saw Skiddaw and Saddleback rising in blue, kneaded masses from the glistening sheet of Derwentwater.

They were silent. Neither had spoken much since they had started out on the day's trek, and Justin had tended to keep a long stride ahead, partly because he could never bear to be anywhere but in front and partly because he was looking for something. Care, deep thought, and the wind too, strained the faces of both, and they climbed absent-mindedly as if their thoughts were visiting other places than Scawdel Fell.

Robin was not speaking now because he was wondering how to speak later. "Knowledge, knowledge," he was thinking. "I must have knowledge. But if I ask him straight out, is it likely that he will calmly confess? *Is* it? I don't know. Not likely, perhaps, but not impossible. Not impossible because Justin is Justin, and he has always been ready to say strange things to me. And not impossible on a wild height like this, away from all sound of the world. But if he confesses, and I have my knowledge, what then? What shall I do? I cannot denounce him. That would blast too many lives. Think of Gerard and Anne; think of Jessica; think of Denys and Beatrice and Gerard's children and Hector's. Besides, one does not denounce a brother. One does not. No, that is certain: I do not go to the police with the tale of his confession. But what else can I do? I cannot leave him free. Think of Primrose. Even if I took Primrose from him I could not leave him free in the world. If he has worked two premeditated murders, he is mad. Egotism as extravagant and arrogant as that is madness. It is a morbid growth and madness. He doesn't look mad; he doesn't sound mad; he only sounds bitter and self-enclosed and harsh; but he *is* mad, and I cannot, I must not, leave him free. But how could I get him certified insane? To do that I should have to tell all. And if I told all, and they brought it home to him, he would hang for a certainty. No man who has committed a carefully premeditated murder will ever get a verdict of 'Guilty but insane.' I cannot denounce him, then, and I cannot let him go free. What am I to do? . . . But first . . . knowledge. Knowledge, and then perhaps I shall see a way."

Robin walked on, looking at the figure of Justin, seven paces ahead.

"To-day. To-day," he adjured himself. "I must speak to-day. Three days we've been here, and I've not yet found the courage to speak. O God, give me words. He is my brother. Help me somehow to help and save him. Help me to forgive him if he has really done these things. Show me what to do. I have never needed Thee as I need Thee now."

Seven paces ahead, behind a seamed and puckered brow, Justin was wondering whether or not he would do the thing for which he had enticed Robin to the mountains and, if the answer was Yes, when he would do it, and where.

"Not to-day, and not on this mountain. I do not know enough about it. A man might survive a fall from Eel Crags. If I do it, he must not survive. And this summit is too level and open. There are too many people coming and going, and they can see you from too far away. It must be somewhere where the people do not come and the missing are not easily found. But where? If I am going to act, I must not falter or waver much longer. We have only three days more before we go home. Have I come all this way for nothing? Have I been successful so far, only to turn back and go feebly home? I pretend to myself that I am waiting till he tells me he has decided to accept the Bishopric. But that is a mere excuse for procrastination; a mere cloak for timidity. The old slave isn't wholly dead in me yet. He gets up from his grave a hundred times. Yes, I see that with clear eyes. Just as I see through other men I see through myself. And just as I've always refused to be imposed upon by other men, so I decline to be imposed upon by myself. I shall not wait till he tells me any such thing. It is certain he will accept. Of course he will accept, and I can act as if he had already decided. And I'm not afraid to do it. There's nothing I'm afraid to do."

He walked to within twenty inches of the precipice edge, thrust a foot forward twelve inches, and looked down.

"Thank God the wind's blowing from the west," he said. "It at least blows you away from this. It blows you indoors, so to speak."

Robin came to his side—or nearly—and peeped over too. "H'm . . ." he grunted. "One step into eternity."

The western face of the mountain for some twenty feet was a vertical bluff, cloven and creviced and split, after which it broke up into pinnacles and crockets of dark volcanic slate, and then fell to the valley below in long buttresses of the same rock, which held avalanches of scree suspended between them. At their foot, fifteen hundred feet below, a beck went twisting and tumbling through the wild Newlands valley. You could hear its low roar weaving its way through the silence.

"No, eternity isn't there." Justin shook his head. "You'd strike a rock and roll down the scree."

"What if the scree went with you and buried you?"

"I should have thought you'd done enough scree-running to know that it doesn't move as easily as that. If the storms and winds of a thousand years haven't disturbed these screes, I don't think your body alighting on them would trouble them much."

"That may be so, but I'll confess now what I've never admitted before."

"What's that?"

"If I live to be a hundred, I shall never really like looking down a precipice as perpendicular as this. In fact, I hate it."

"Do you? I think I rather like it."

He came away, and they climbed further, Justin leading.

And now the wind saluted them with a hearty slapping, for they had nearly won to the top. The cairn marking the highest point was but a minute ahead of them. They came to the cairn, and immediately the southern views were spread before them. There, behind the thrumming wind, were the Gable and Glaramara and the peaks of Scafell and, below them, the entrance to the secret valley of Langstrath. Scafell, shadowed by a suncloud, was a flat silhouette in the sky, above some shreds and trails of mist.

Justin looked at Scafell. In that rent and shattered world on the tops of Scafell, that waste of gullies and folds and faults, was there not a place where a man might fall, and none count it anything but an accident in the mist? And immediately he remembered that slanting shelf, between the cascade of rocks and the stark precipices, along which, thirty years before, they had walked in an uneasy balance between exhilaration and fear. Was not that the place? No man would survive a fall from that brink. No one would arrive there in time to save.

A mist was travelling like a tattered curtain across this further valley, and it joined them as they went down the slope. And out of it, like grey figures in smoke, came a troop of young fell-walkers. Alpine boys and girls they looked, with their shorts and open shirts and rucksacks, and the spiked sticks in their hands.

Justin greeted them as they passed. Always he had shouted a greeting to any strangers encountered on the fells.

"Good day."

"Good day, sir."

"Which way have you come?"

"We came up by Lobstone Band," said a flushed and happy girl.

"Well, I hope you enjoyed it."

"Not a bit. I'll never come that way again. It's as steep as hell, and it goes on for ever."

"You're right. Wise men go down it, and not up it."

"You going down that way?"

"I expect so. If we don't go over Dale Head."

"Well, good luck. We're going on to Cat Bells."

And they went on, and Justin thought: How little that bright girl knew. She assumed that if two men came up on to a mountain, they would go down it together. But there might be a time when one descended it alone.

§

This further slope led down into a depression of low, tossing hills. The ground down here was a tumbled quilt of reedgrass, sedge, and sphagnum moss. In places its deep pile was spongy, and their boots sank into a lurking and sobbing moisture. The humps of drenched moss had a yellow and sickly tinge, and the high grasses, shimmering in the wind, were more grey than green. The whole corrie was strewn with boulders, and when they had plashed through its marshy bottom, they wearied of such heavy footwork and ascended the highest of the low hills to find some dryness on its knees or some boulders which the sun had warmed. On two such rocks, as it might be on a couple of Olympian thrones, they sat side by side.

Robin looked over his right shoulder. There on a table-land he saw a small lagoon, staring up like a grey-green mirror at the sky. It was Dale Head Tarn, and behind it rose the blunt mass of Dale Head, with a mantilla of mist on its crown. A cloud shut the sun from the mountain, and its face was a dark featureless indigo, under the lacework of mist. As the cloud, slowly moving, cut the sun from the tarn, its sheet of green glass became a shield of dark steel.

The two of them took their lunches from their packs and began to eat; and their silence sat between them. Robin, looking before him as he munched a sandwich, saw a shelf of path round a haunch of mountain. It was the track they must take to descend by Lobstone Band, and from here it looked no more than a goat-track on a slope too steep for men.

But he was not thinking of that path, though his eyes were resting on it. He knew it of old, and that it was much easier than it appeared from here. Compared with some shelves and traverses that they had cat-walked together, it was a child's promenade. He was thinking, "Now. I will speak now. I must. But how?"

How did one ask a brother if he had contrived the death of two people?

The silence between them oppressed and fretted him; and, tired of casting about for words and discarding them, he did what he so often did: he drove blindly at his problem. Here at last, in this fold of the hills, he spoke.

"Justin?"

"Yes?"

"How did the old Duke die?"

Abruptly Justin turned and looked at him; and in that moment, because of the sudden and unnecessary apprehension in Justin's eyes, Robin closed his hand upon the truth.

Justin, bewildered, repeated the question. "How did the old Duke die?"

"Yes."

Always Robin would remember the scene around him as he asked his question. It was as if the question, like a violent magnesium flash, had given precision and clarity to the landscape on which it broke: the high Dale Head, the tarn in its lap, the falling slopes before them, and their pathway home. Even the birds were fixed for ever upon his memory: a falcon wheeling and swooping above the open valley, a curlew beating its long clean path through the sky, and down on the green flats a whirl of black-headed gulls, screaming fitfully, as if they had come inland from the threat of a storm.

"He died of pneumonia," said Justin. "You know that perfectly well."

"How did he get that illness?"

"Good lord, I don't know! It's a quarter of a century ago. I can't remember what happened after twenty-five years."

Robin looked straight before him at the falling slopes and the green leas of Rosthwaite far below. And he said, "The old man had a severe cold, and you took him out for some drinks. It was a bitterly cold night, and you wrapped him up well. But in the bar of the public house it was crowded and hot, and you undid his coat for him. He drank at your expense far more than was good for him, and he came out into the cold air with his coat still unbuttoned. It stayed like that, and he was chilled through, but was hardly aware of it because of the alcohol in his blood. Next night he was in a fever. The pneumonia had got him."

"Wait a minute!" This was a sharp and angry command, like a schoolmaster's to a pupil. "Are you suggesting that I murdered him?"

Robin kept his eyes on the heights across the valley. "I think you helped him to die."

"*Good . . . God! . . .*" Slowly Justin emitted these syllables, but they were an unreal oath; an actor's line. And for a second or two he could compose no line to follow it. And when he could do so, he stuttered, "My God! You're mad. Primrose has been suggesting something to you. That foul woman. That sickly fool. This is her doing, obviously.

Heaven and Hell, she shall hear from me when I get home. It's time that woman was put in a mental home. She's half mad."

Robin turned and looked at him. "I said you helped him to die. Do you deny it?"

A wrath like a steel rod held Justin's eyes to his brother's. "Of course I deny it. What do you think?"

"Well, then, let us come to Bozzy."

Now Justin's stare was a stabbing knife, and Robin knew that his own anger, taking fire at Justin's, had driven him into the right way. This sharp, unsparing accusation had pierced to the truth. Justin was not answering. He had no answer. He could only mutter, like a man who must thrust *some* word through his lips, "Bozzy?"

"Yes. How did Bozzy die?"

"The fool fell into the river."

"How?"

"How the hell should I know."

"The fall was not aided?"

"Look here, Robin. Will you kindly stop this? You may have gone mad, but I'm not taking these incredible insults from you or anyone."

"You were seen following Bozzy the night he disappeared. You were seen talking with him. And you never told anyone that you were with him that night. You withheld all mention of it from the police and the coroner. You have never told any of us in all these years. After you had met him and talked with him, you went home, but late that night you went out again and were gone for about an hour."

"Who saw me? Who says he saw me?"

"You admit that you were with him that night?"

"I'm not being questioned by *you*. I'm asking *you* something. Who saw me?"

Robin's anger, ever quick to flame up, and more easily lit by Justin than by anyone else, was now out of control and his master. He thought of poor old Mr. Cumberland, and of Bozzy, and he filled with rage and power.

"You *are* being questioned by me. And you're going to be questioned by me. I'm going to know what passed between you and Bozzy that night. Bozzy was my brother."

"It was Primrose. It could only have been Primrose. Anyone else would have spoken. Was she following me——"

"Then you admit that you went out that night?"

"Was she following me? Never mind where I went. Was she following me? Was it Primrose?"

"Did you murder Bozzy?"

Justin, lips shut in a tight line, suffered no answer past them.

"Did you meet him somewhere by the river and push him in? I remember years ago in our little room in Brook Green you suggested some such method of doing away with someone without being found out. No doubt you have forgotten that bedtime talk, but I haven't. I don't remember it all, but I seem to remember that you also suggested something very like the method you adopted with Primrose's father."

"Oh, you say outright that I did it now?"

"Yes."

"Thank you."

"And that you murdered your brother—who was my brother too." Robin was looking straight into Justin's eyes. "That's the truth, isn't it?"

And Justin looked straight back into Robin's eyes. "Yes, It is."

§

When Justin said: "Yes. It is," he knew that Robin was going to die within the next few days or as soon as he could manage his death. The idea which had been unstable before was now set and solid. It had been given that which hardened it as carbon hardens steel. Robin had guessed the truth about those two old deaths; let him have it then from his own lips; and after that he would see to it that Robin did not remain in the world to denounce him. He had little doubt that he could manage his death, and he was the readier to believe this because he wanted—or a part of him wanted, *longed*—to tell Robin that he'd had the strength and courage to do what he'd often said he'd do, and the skill to do it so that no one had suspected anything. His resolve was fixed and secure now, and he was content with it. And because he was content, he no longer felt angry with Robin. Nor did he care a single hoot what he said to him, up here on this high abandoned waste.

"Yes, old boy." He put a new puzzling smile into his eyes. He could almost feel the smile and the glitter in his eyes. "Yes, Robby. The old man expressed a constant wish to be in Heaven, and I helped him a little on his way. That was all right, wasn't it? He was for ever saying he wished it would please God to take him to His mercy, so I did what little I could to ensure that his wish was granted. I consider that I did him a kindness. Of course it happened to suit me well enough because he was quite abominably in my way. I don't regret it in the least, old boy. He was better dead. He was a burden to himself and to everyone else; a dirty, unpleasant, dreadful old man who lacerated every sensibility I'd got. And when he took to fuddling himself every night, and disgracing me everywhere, I really had to do something. If I hadn't, I think I should have gone mad. And you must allow, I think, that technically my work was pretty good. Alcoholic excess is one of the classic predisposing causes of pneumonia; and I merely encouraged the old gentleman to accelerate the predisposing with a few good drinks. If he was too befuddled to button his coat up after he left the pub, well, I wasn't going to do it for him. He got pneumonia; but pneumonia, I'd have you remember, has been called 'the old man's friend' because it gives 'em an easy passage over. I helped him very gently into the mercy of God after which his soul panted. And no one's ever suspected anything from that day to this. Not in twenty-five years."

Robin was just staring at him, so he smiled satirically at his stare, and went on: "And no one would have done, if I hadn't felt driven to open that foolish creature's eyes a bit. Her idiocy irritated me. . . . Well, there it is, Robin. There it is, and you can't do a thing about it. Not a thing."

"Why not?"

"Well, in the first place, because you wouldn't mention it for your own sake and everyone else's, and in the second, because if you did, I should deny that I ever told you, and a wife can't give evidence against her husband. You know that, I hope?"

Robin did not know this, and kept silence.

"Besides, where's any proof that my little effort caused the old man's pneumonia? I don't even know that it did. He might have got it in any case. He probably would, behaving the way he did."

"Well, let us leave the old man for the present. What about Bozzy? Do you think I'm going to do nothing about that?"

"Yes. Yes, I'm afraid that's exactly what I do think, Robby. Bozzy had done me considerable harm for many years, strolling about the streets and bowing and smiling to everyone, whether he knew them or not. And when he decided to become a prophet of God, carrying texts on a pole, I began to find it quite intolerable. He was making himself an object of ridicule, and me an object of pity; and I'm afraid my nature is such that I cannot stand being an object of pity. The wonder is that I bore with him so long. You should account that to my credit. He was getting madder and madder every day; a little more, and he'd have discovered that he was the Messiah, and I had no intention of having a divine brother in the next street. No doubt it ought to have helped a religious school like mine, but I had a suspicion it wouldn't. The last thing he did was to rise up and denounce me before thousands of my neighbours. Yes, that was the last thing he did. No one does that to me twice. At my invitation he met me by the riverside, and we stood talking about my sins and looking down into the water, and before he knew what was happening, he was done with this sinful world. He had accidentally fallen in, and as no one was about, I lacked the courage to jump in and save him. And I don't think I've regretted it for a moment since. Bozzy was what I call human trash and best disposed of. So was the old man, after a time. All the same, I played a pretty handkerchief at both their funerals. There, Robin, that's the whole story; and will you tell me, please, what you propose to do about it?"

Robin could not speak at once. He was white with balked fury. Justin's mocking indifference to what he had done, the inconceivable egotism which it expressed, were tormenting and enraging him—as they were intended to do.

Justin leaned back upon his rock, hands clasped comfortably behind his head. "Can't you tell me what you propose to do about it, old son? It naturally interests me."

"I do not know what I shall do about it."

"The police, eh?"

"No, I shall not go to the police."

"Why not?"

"You are my brother."

"Well, I take that very kindly from you, Robby; and as there's nothing you can do about it——" he got up, bent over his rucksack and began to buckle it up—"shall we get on with our walk?"

Robin rose too, and was silent. He remained silent, because he could find no answer to the question what he was going to do about it. He had his knowledge. He had dredged it up from the river bed. But what now?

They walked across the corrie towards Lobstone Band, their

feet brushing through the shaggy coat of reedgrass and sedge
or sinking into the soaked, peaty soil; Justin leading the way,
whistling to himself, and laughing at all obstacles, and Robin
careless how he stumbled, because he was anæsthetized by
thought.

CHAPTER FIVE

"ARE you coming, Robin?"

"Yes, if you like. The sky is clearing."

"Good. We can't go home without climbing Scafell. It
must be expecting us. Shall we go by our own private route
for old time's sake?"

"If you like."

Justin and Robin were standing on the stony road outside
their hotel in Deep Langstrath, looking up the Langstrath
valley. The new hotel in Deep Langstrath was a long whitewashed building among the barns and cottages of the little
hamlet. It was, in fact, an enlargement of one of the cottages, and the le Fabers could remember well the small white
cottage whose deep winow-embrasures were still to be distinguished in one part of its façade. That cottage had stood
two doors from the one in which they used to stay, and Robin,
standing now before the hotel doors, could see the gate in the
garden wall by which he had read of Bryn's death. And this
wet, stony road which they purposed to take now was the
road up which he had staggered with the weight of that news
about him.

This was the second morning after Justin's dark admissions
in the corrie on Scawdel Fell. Yesterday had been nothing but
clouds and rain, clouds and rain, for the whole of its daylight.
It had confined them to the long sitting-room in the hotel and
kept them within the warm aura of its fire. They had sat with
the other guests, and neither had spoken much to the other,
for Justin's confession stood like a party wall between them.
Justin for his part had affected all the time the scornful indifference of yesterday, and in truth he was unworried by anything that Robin might be thinking or planning, because he
knew that he was going to die very soon.

As for Robin, he had been unable for more than brief
minutes to release his thoughts from the one dreadful, bitter,

and galling field. Tethered there, they had grazed and wandered in despair. His head had been sick with conflict, and towards evening he felt as if he could burst into tears like a child. Against a storm of vindictiveness there struggled like lost and blinded infants the old love and a desire to do right and be pitiful. But it was small headway that love and tenderness could make in such a vehemence of anger. When he thought of Bozzy, so happy in his new-found religion, and how he had been suddenly snuffed out, annihilated, cancelled, in the midst of his happiness, the anger clenched his jaws and grated his teeth. A selfishness so complete that it coldly deprived others of life, a superiority so overweening as to assume such rights—these raised in Robin, the more he dwelt upon them, a hate, a restless hunger to punish them, and a wish, since he craved an issue from his conflict, and rest, that Justin were finished and dead. The pure abstract evil that had come to birth in the heart of Justin's suppurating egotism made him long to stamp on it as one stamps on a snake—and at the same time it fascinated him. There were times that morning and afternoon when, Justin's head being bent over a magazine, he stared at him, trying to believe that he had twice, coldly and deliberately, ended the life of another. He stared at the other people who were sitting in the room, three women and one man, and thought: "What would they feel if they knew that that tall silent man with the fine black hair and neat Van Dyck beard, who offers them coffee so courteously, and caresses the Chinchilla cat on his knees, has murdered a colleague and a brother?"

So handsome, so courtly, and so terrible. Ethically he was damnable; æsthetically he was just as admirable as he was formidable.

Or so Robin thought at times. The child is father to the man; and in such moments the old admiration was astir again.

And as he considered these things, his book dropped to his side, his eyes sought the fire, and he tried by an imaginative effort to see how a man could come to that state in which he could decide on the destruction of another. He tried to experience that state; to create it in himself and realize what it must be like.

Most men could understand the temptation to lie, to pilfer, to embezzle in time of need, to slander an enemy by doubtful witness, and even to injure a friend when one's resentment flamed. All these sins lay close to their doors, and the doors

were insecurely latched against them. But against murder
they were bolted. They did not fear this temptation because the
long generations had rooted in them an absolute recoil from this
ultimate selfishness. How did that rooted recoil die in a man,
or how did he grub it out so that it was almost as easy to kill
as to lie?

Robin, trying to imagine himself into such a state, trying to
become such a man, closed his eyes tight upon the task. And
for short moments his imaginative effort succeeded. Scruples,
filed away like fetters, dropped from him, and he was able to
contemplate the assassination of an enemy or a rival. He was
over a margin. He stood where Justin stood. He could kill a
man who had tried to win Jessica from him, or someone who
possessed such knowledge as would destroy his position in the
world, or someone who had killed a friend. He would say to
such a one as this last, "You are not the only person who can
decide to kill. You took it upon yourself to decide that others
were better dead. Did it never occur to you that someone else
might come to the same conclusion about you? You claim
that the fear of killing dwells only in the weak and slavish.
Very good. I am converted to your point of view, and I have
decided to be weak and slavish no more. I have promoted
myself to your rank, and am about to kill you. Yours is a
meadow in which two can play."

And at night, after thinking these thoughts, his sleep had
been tormented by a heavy and hurrying dream. He and
Justin were walking in Great Wood by Derwentwater, under
the pines and sycamores, their boots sweeping through the
nettles and dog's-mercury and old brown leaves. It was a
memory of their walk through the sedgegrass on Scawdel Fell
and of a walk nearly thirty years in the past, when they took
this track through the wood, coming from Keswick to Deep
Langstrath on the first day of their holiday. In his dream
Justin walked ahead of him as he usually did, but Justin was
not leading him; he, Robin, was driving Justin. Before them,
beyond the lean fir trees, shone the ribbed, silver surface of
Derwentwater, and he was driving Justin towards it, not with
a weapon, but by his voice alone, as a drover guides an ox. He
was saying to him, "To the water, Justin; to the water," with a
cheerfulness that was sinister, because both knew that he was
going to drown Justin in the water. Justin, though aware of
this, only turned his face and laughed—that was one of the
most horrible parts of the dream—he turned and laughed and

said, "*A la lanterne*, eh? Do you remember how proud the old
Duke was of his French? A dreadful old man." And Robin
nodded and guided him on towards the shining water. And the
water in his dream was not shallow, but bottomless. The
ground did not shelve slowly down into the water, but stopped
and fell sheer, like a river wall. But, unlike a river wall, it did
not reach the mud after eight or ten feet; it went on and on for
ever—an everlasting precipice. And Robin was going to thrust
Justin over that brink into that endless abysm. But just
as they issued from the trees and came near the water,
they saw the body of Bozzy floating there, and the ripples
were bringing him towards them. His eyes were closed,
but otherwise he looked like the Bozzy of eleven years ago,
with the smile on his lips that he used to carry about the
streets. "There he is," said Justin, as if this was what
they had come to see. "He has done with this sinful world;"
but just then Bozzy's eyes opened. He was alive. He smiled
at his brothers and said, "Whosoever is not written in the
book of life shall be cast into the lake of fire. Revelation,
Twenty, Fifteen." After eleven years in the water he was
still alive. In the horror of it Robin awoke. He awoke to see
through his uncurtained window the wooded slopes of High
Scale, washed by the moon, and to hear a sheep bleating.

He dropped asleep again; and then he was in a boat on a sea
as level, and as lightly waved by the wind, as the broad face of
Derwentwater. The boat floated serenely within sight of the
coast which they used to visit in their summer holidays, but it
was many miles from the familiar cliffs and the rocks and the
eyes of men. From that boat, one moment ago, he had thrust
Justin into the sea. Was not this the method that Justin had
himself suggested in the little bedroom at Brook Green? He
was leaning over the gunwale of the boat and watching Justin
sink through the pale green submarine light. And as Justin
went down and down he, like Bozzy, opened his eyes and
smiled and said, "What must I do to be saved?" for he was
alive down there, two fathoms down, beneath the crimpled
surface which flowed ever onward—he was alive and smiled
the old sardonic smile—and in the horror of it Robin awoke
again. The sheep was still bleating in the night, its voice like
the plaint of a dumb, suffering world. Frightened by the
nightmare, Robin was seized by the idea that someone was
creaking in the darkness of the room. Justin? Had not his
voice whispered, "Are you awake, Robin?"

"Yes," he whispered to the darkness. "Yes, what is it?"

No answer. His heart packed and pulsing with fear, he fingered a match and struck a light. No one was in the room. The door was shut, and the house was silent around him. His watch stood at ten minutes past three.

That was last night, and now the sun was over the world, and Justin was standing at his side, looking up the Langstrath valley. He seemed to be gazing in the direction of Scafell.

"Well, shall we go, Robs?" he asked.

"Yes, if you like."

"Right. We'd better do it. It's our last day."

And they turned indoors and packed their lunches and waterproofs and maps, and slung their packs and came out. They walked towards the Langstrath valley. For a while the path was the undulating road between the dry walls: a road of gravel and stones, fringed with ferns, shadowed by trees, and as wet after yesterday's rain as a tributary stream of the Langstrath beck. Below it spread the lush water meadows, and above it rose the green flank of High Knott and the first hills of Glaramara.

As they went on they passed the place where, after vowing everlasting mutiny against God because of Bryn's death, he had rested on the dry wall and let his love of love rebuild itself in his heart again.

The road dwindled to a track; it rounded the foot of Bull Crag; and then it was in the valley.

Langstrath, after its fashion, was empty, silent, and melancholy. A long, deep, inland gulf, it pierced into the bosom of the mountains; and the sigh and chatter of its beck, winding tortuously down it, and a roar of many waters far away, were the only sounds in the narrow wilderness. The track, leaving the beck far on its left, went twisting and steeple-chasing among the boulders and the humps, frowned upon from on high, and for all of the way, by the stormy crags of Glaramara. Ahead was nothing but the mountains closing in, and the four ghylls streaking down from Gavel Moor, Esk Hause, and Allen Crags.

Not a bird, not a sheep, not a man disturbed the desolation. There were sheepfolds and lonely byres and dilapidated dry-walls, but where was there a grazing sheep? Where were the rooks that wheeled and cawed over the fresh green floor of Seathwaite on the other side of Glaramara? Where were the black-headed gulls that visited those happier fields? There were birds in Langstrath sometimes, there must be, but the sight of one always surprised you—and that was the difference between this dyke of Langstrath and its sister glen of Seath-waite, that wider and livelier close to the long cleft of Borrow-dale.

Justin and Robin went on and on, and still no human figure appeared before them or behind them. Only the grey boulders lay about the path like the monoliths and menhirs of a fallen world. Somewhere among the boulders the two brothers had changed places, and Robin was now leading. And Justin, following close behind, looked at the writhing path before them and at the trackless scarp by which they would climb on to Esk Hause, and he thought, "There are two of us in the valley now. One may come home alone." Would he return this way alone, the roar of waters his only companion?

"This strath is damnably lang," he said, desiring to hear Robin's voice.

"Five miles of it," answered Robin. "But we'll come home on the other side for a change."

"Yes."

And not once did Robin turn round to look at the things he was leaving behind. Rather did he keep his head bowed, as if it were loaded with thoughts.

Robin's head was certainly crowded with thoughts, but the one thought which had not entered it was the thought that *he* was in any danger. He had so persuaded himself that it was Primrose who was in danger that he could not at the same time consider anyone else in that position: one cannot feel more than one ache at a time. And he was so filled with the question, "What am I to do?" so preoccupied with the problem of *his* action towards Justin, that he had not once turned his mind on to the question of Justin's action to-wards him. And had he done so, it would probably have been a completely inconceivable idea that Justin could contemplate killing *him*, the one person for whom he had always felt an affection. Primrose, yes; Bozzy, yes; but not himself, Robin, Justin's one close, confidential, and intimate friend. And so he walked with Justin to-day towards the Scafell rocks as blindly and unsuspectingly as Bozzy had walked with him towards the riverside. And indeed there was an-other similarity in the two walks, because Robin, like Bozzy, was wondering all the while how best he could save and help Justin.

Their path crossed the beck at Foot of Stake, and now at last, stepping down from Gavel Moor, came two figures. Youthful figures, lithe and nimble; a young man and a girl, as they soon descried, though the girl, in shirt and shorts and with a rucksack slung, was no differently dressed from the man. But her hair was ablow, and she was smaller than he. They were coming down fast, like happy children, leaping and scrambling down the rocks of the watercourse. It was the course of the ghyll that came tumbling down from Angle Yarn in grey ribbons and white tassels; and the ribbons did not run so fast, nor the tassels drop so cleanly, as this youth in full self-display. He was a long way in front of the girl, running down the steeps, jumping from the boulders, shouting encouragement to her, and in general showing off like a lapwing cock before its hen. Soon they were close to the le Fabers, and Justin called out, "Good morning."

"Good morning." The boy's speech had a Northern accent, and so had the girl's, as she too echoed: "Good morning." So often there were Northern voices on these hills.

"Where are you off to?"

"Goin' ho'am."

"It's early to go home. What's it like up above?"

"There's mist on Esk Hause."

"Thick?"

"Aye, it's thick enoof."

"How far can you see?"

"Aboot fifty yards or soa."

"Hell! Is that all? What's it like on the Pike?"

"Ah do'ant know. We decided we worn't goin' oop."

"Oh!" Both Justin and Robin, observing that the boy had a rope expertly coiled, and expertly hung over a shoulder and under an arm, were surprised that he should have turned back from the ascent of Scafell, for the route from Esk Hause to the Pike, in the view of expert climbers, was no more than a high road. And then Robin noticed that it was not a real mountaineer's rope. Though so professionally and lovingly coiled, it was only a stout clothes line that he had brought from his mother's kitchen. This sent Robin's eyes down to the boy's boots, because it is by their boots that you can tell the veterans. And it was as he had expected, the boy's boots were no mountain wear but the hobnailed boots in which he went to his work along some cobbled Yorkshire street. This was possibly his first visit to the mountains, but he had dressed the part well: he had coiled a rope around him like a veteran of the rock face. Robin's heart went out to them both, because it was so strange to see a lad turning back from a simple climb, with his rope so splendidly coiled. But Justin was less tender to that rope.

"The mist is probably only in patches," he said contemptuously. "Good God, it's nothing to be afraid of."

"The people wor' turnin' back." Humbled and crestfallen, the boy tried to justify himself. "They wor' all turnin' back."

"I've no doubt they were, old son. You can meet a lot of fools on a pass, and especially on Esk Hause, because it's a place where all roads meet. If they'd waited, the mist would have passed off. And even if it didn't, there's not the slightest danger on Scafell."

"Aw, isn't there?" The girl had sprung to the defence of her man. "That worn't what t'gentlemen said oop there. They said they wouldn't look at it in weather like this. They said it was a treacherous mountain, and you'd coom to harm if you lost yourself on Great End or Mickeldore, didn't they, Jim?"

"True enough, my dear," agreed Justin, "but you don't go anywhere near Great End or Mickeldore if you keep to the track."

"That's just it. They wor' afraid of losing t'ro'ad."

"Why? *Why?* It's cairned the whole way. There's a cairn about every twenty yards."

"Aye, but supposing the visibility wor' o'anly ten?" put in the boy, still sore.

"Well, then I'll tell you what: you leave one cairn, and she pays out that rope while you look for the next cairn twenty yards away. Then if you get lost, you can always work your way back to her along the rope."

"Aye, you could do that, I suppose," agreed the boy, imagining that this was a normal use of a climber's rope. "Are *you* goin' oop to the Pike?" There was admiration in his eyes.

"We certainly are."

"Mist or no'a mist?"

"Of course. It won't be the first time we've been on the Pike in a mist, will it, Robin?"

"No; but——" Robin was trying to save the faces of these children—"but I can quite understand anyone giving it a wide berth if they don't know the way."

"Aye," said the boy gratefully; and the girl nodded.

"Don't you listen to my brother," Robin counselled with a

smile. "He knows every cairn on Scafell, and he imagines everyone else does too."

And with that he said good-bye to them both in friendly fashion, and they smiled back and went on their way down the rocks; and he and Justin went on upwards. They climbed the sodden and clarty turf till they came to their private track by the ghyll-side which, after much scrambling, would bring them over the brim of the watershed and on to the tumbled ridge of Esk Hause. The mist was now spilling over the brim, and there was a new warmth in the daylight under this thick white blanket. They clambered up into the mist, leaving the clean light below their feet, and, after much heavy collar-work, the wind of a sudden saluted them for an achievement about to be completed. A little higher into the wind, and they were over the brim and on to the hause.

The hause was like a sea of grass-breakers running under the mist with rocks afloat on them, and Robin and Justin went switchbacking over these billowy tops till they came to the first shelter in the solitude of the pass. It was a shelter from wind, not from rain: four roofless walls at right angles to one another, and you sheltered in that one of the four bays which was screened from the current wind. To-day's wind was in the south-west, so they walked towards the northerly bay immediately before them. Three young men were already there, seated on stones against the wall and eating their lunches. They seemed a team of friends rather than of brothers, being quite unlike: one long and lean, another tall and heavy, and the third little and slight.

"Well, was it worth it, sir?" inquired the heavy one, as the two le Fabers came toiling towards them through the fog.

"Certainly it was," declared Justin. "Why, this is nothing. This isn't worth calling a mist."

"Isn't it?" scoffed the little man. "You try it a little higher up, sir."

"That's what we're going to do," said Justin.

And he unslung his rucksack and sat on a stone beside them.

"Have you been on the top?" asked Robin, also sloughing his harness.

"Have I been on the devil? Not likely. Listen, brother: he asked me if I'd been on the top."

"No. We're none of us heroes," explained the long thin one, who seemed to be a wit of the languid, unsmiling kind. "We went a little way, and the mist got thicker and thicker, and when it got thicker still, we turned about as one man and came back. It was rather like a flock of geese in the sky. We swung round as one bird and headed for home with our necks stretched out."

"But why?" demanded Justin, as one superior to such fears.

Languidly the young man picked an ancient and soiled red book from his pack. "Discretion overwhelmed us," he said. "Yes, sir. We'd just been reading this excellent book, and it says that crags and precipices abound on every side."

The little man snatched the book from him and turned its pages while munching a sandwich. "And that's not all it says. Listen to this, sir. Listen to what the gentleman says. 'By universal testimony the slopes above Esk Hause are specially designed for beguiling tourists into taking the wrong path, even without atmospheric accessories.'" He snapped the book shut. "That damned sentence was running in my head all the time, and I was never so happy as when these lads turned round, and I could do the same."

The lean and languid young man waved a hand at the surrounding fog. "This, I take it, is an atmospheric accessory. Well, there are heaps more of them higher up. Bigger and better ones."

"But that book's half a century old," objected Justin, now unpacking his own lunch.

"Granted, sir. It belonged to my governor. But I imagine Scafell is still much the same. I don't suppose it has shifted about much in fifty years."

"Don't know about that," suggested the heavy one. "It's rained a lot since then."

"Yes, and that would only deepen the crevices, brother."

"The mist is only local," said Justin. "I'm sure of it. It's a perfect summer day about two hundred feet lower down, and I believe that if you'd gone on, you'd have found it a perfect summer day about two hundred feet higher up."

And, as he made a show of eating his lunch, he was thinking, "Accessory? The mist is my accessory. It's keeping the people off the mountain. It will account for a climber's fall. These young men, and others coming down from Scafell, like the boy and girl we met just now, will exaggerate it, if only to justify their return, and those below will think it abnormal and the natural parent of calamity." It would not be the first time that a mist, brooding on Scafell, had hatched out a disaster.

And he fell to thinking how the young men, when they heard of the disaster, would speak to excited people in the valley of having met him and Robin at the shelter. How proud they would be of their exclusive story; how happy narrating it, while pretending to be shocked. Their faces would be grave, and their voices solemn, but their hearts would be lit up with their distinction. They would tell all how lively he and Robin had been, how free from any thought of death, how determined, both of them, upon continuing their climb. Yes, he must provide them with that part of the story; he must appear on merry terms with Robin, and Robin must appear as eager for the ascent as he. And he must contrive to identify Robin and himself to these witnesses.

"I don't think we're going to turn back, do you, Robin, old man? But I will, if you want to."

"*I* don't want to," Robin rapped out promptly, offended at the suggestion that *he* might be the one to hesitate. "Not for this. I never know why books try to frighten people about the Pike. This particular route is the easiest climb in Lakeland."

Good. He could not have spoken better.

"I quite agree with you. And I wouldn't mind betting the top's in the sunlight, would you, Robin, old man? We shall emerge out of the mist like Neptune rising from the sea." And he laughed with an ostentatious hilarity.

"Or Venus from the foam," suggested the wit.

"No, I don't claim to be Venus. But sometimes when I'm descending a mountain and come suddenly out of a cloud into the daylight, and see the habitations of men far below me, I feel, I must say, a little like the Archangel Gabriel descending with a message from on high."

"Gabriel? Is that all? Why not the Holy Spirit Himself?"

"Now, Bill, desist," rebuked the heavy man. "These gentlemen may be religious, or something. You never know whom you're meeting on Esk Hause. They may even be parsons."

"Well, then, let us say, like Lucifer falling from Heaven."

"Ah, that's much nearer the mark," laughed Justin.

"And as there'll be three of *us* descending in glory through the mist, I forbear to suggest Whom or What we might resemble."

"Blasphemous beast," his friend summed up.

"One of us *is* a parson," Justin disclosed, grinning. "My

brother. And what's more, he's no ordinary parson. He's a prebendary. He's a prebendary who's broken out for a bit. As for me, I'm merely a headmaster."

"There, I knew it. I felt it. Now look what you've done, Bill."

"Well now, isn't that just my luck?" The languid one turned to Robin. "I'm very sorry indeed, sir."

"Don't mind me," laughed Robin, anxious to put him at ease. And for the same reason he tried to be humorous too, though his heart was heavy. "After all, you don't often see a prebendary in shorts."

And Justin was glad that he had laughed and said that and seemed free from care. Everything was going well, and he added, as an example of the badinage that flies between good-humoured brothers, "Besides, he's High Church, and they never mind a little blasphemy."

Having forced down a second sandwich (it is not easy to eat in the last hour before action) he lit a cigarette and leaned back against the wall and looked at Robin quietly eating a cake. And he thought of him as a prisoner sitting down to eat a meal on the way to execution.

But Robin did not seem hungry either, and was soon finished with food, and lighting a cigarette. Justin drew a few more times at his own cigarette, while Robin gazed before him at the investing mist.

"Well, shall we go on, Robby? Shall we hoof up a bit higher? Just as you like."

"Of course we'll go on. There's no danger in this. Not yet, at any rate."

"Rightho, I'm ready." He rose and swung on his rucksack. "If we have to turn back, we will. Come along. Swing on your nosebag. Good-bye, gentlemen."

They lifted hands of farewell to the three young men and bent themselves to the slope. And they soon found it true, what the young men had said. The cloud thickened as they went higher. But its density was never so close as to shut out the next cairn. Ever the friendly and comforting cairns rose out of the mist and beckoned them upward. Though they could not see fifty yards they knew all the time where they were. They were climbing in the gap between Great End and Ill Crag, those two giant buttresses that shore up the north and east walls of Scafell. There was a silence in the mist, a white, close, cotton-wool silence that seemed to

quench all sounds at a few yards distance and muffle their
footfalls on the ground. Sometimes from far off they heard
the plaintive cry of a mountain sheep or the voices of men
—voices without visible bodies, which came falling through
the cloud and with a disturbing quickness assumed the
grey shapes of men; and these grey wraiths solidified into
laughing strangers who gave them a greeting and good news.
"It's all right higher up. Stick to the cairns and you'll come
out into sunlight."

They came to the parts where the green fell-slope lost the
last of its nap, and the massed rocks began. And climbing
from rock to rock, the cairns ever summoning them, they
guessed from the light now suffusing the cloud that they
were on the stairs that led to its roof. And they were right:
on the upper treads they issued into the sunlight. The sudden
clarity and brilliance, the sudden sight of infinite and floodlit
space, broke their breath with its beauty. Immediately befor
them, above a world-wide froth of mist, rose a chaos of boil
rocks, and there, behind a shattered and disordered pyrar
the Pike.

"This is like suddenly ascending into Heaven," Rob
moved to say, though there was little humour in his

"A damned barren Heaven," laughed Justin. "But
as I always thought. You parsons have fooled
heaven. There's no one here. A sterile promont
ever——" he climbed the rocks gaily—"General F
Heaven."

Up and down again—along a brief striding
last rugged crown, and they stood upon the Pi
there alone. The vast floor of viewless mist
rest of the world in the cellarage below. Th
here before them had sunk down throug
cloud.

Up here the silence was like the silenc
it had no link or truck with the roar o
below. Only after a little did they n
sunlight, as if they had isolated a cir
organ of the earth.

" 'The sun shone on all the statu
only the statue of Memnon gave

Robin did not answer. He
archipelago of mountain summ
cloud. He was identifying t

To the north-west the Gable and Kirkfell; behind these Red Pike and High Stile and, farther still, grey against the illumined sky and smoking with mist as if on fire, the shoulder of Grassmoor; to the south-west Bow Fell and Crinkle Crags and Grey Friar, with the Old Man of Coniston sulking behind. Beneath the rolling froth, like worlds at the bottom of the sea, one could imagine the long valleys with their pastures and their white roads and their farm-steads aloof in the fields.

They counted the summits on which they had stood together and then went down again into the deep sea of vapour. Down the shattered world of rocks, by short steps or long strides, from boulder to block, from block to fragmented shards; down what seemed a pile of the Creator's broken and discarded masonry; like Endymion when he went down towards the sandy bottom of the sea, and the visions of the earth were fled. Nothing but the steep of rocks as yet; no venturesome herbage in their seams and cracks; no sheep footing it from one stone bracket to the next; no human figure in a slowly lightening haze. Had it not been for the scratches on the treads of this rude stairway, which were the comfortable script left by the feet of earlier climbers, and for the kindly cairns which now beckoned them downward in the easiest path, they might have been clambering about the curve of some barren and lifeless planet.

Justin led. And all the while his eyes looked to the right. They peered through the mist on the right. Occasionally there was a clashing, melodramatic, break in the mist, unveiling headlands and green sunlit slopes and blue sky. Then closed and shut the world from him again. He was thinking that place, to the right of the cairns, where the first vegetation touched the rocks, and gradually the rocks gave place to a width of green fell which stopped abruptly at the brim of a rankled precipice. He remembered how that shawl of grass over the rocks slowly narrowed and steepened till at last it no more than about fourteen feet of dry grass and stones between the hanging rocks and the precipice. There were a few yards of this narrow tilt before it opened out again broad fell. But those few yards, that little canted between one safe place and another, had filled them to throats with a breathless but fascinating fear. A meet for Vertigo, that awful raked sill. No one would a man's frozen stance there, nor his head's sickening and his fall. Especially if his companion were heard

crying for aid, or found slightly injured after a distracted attempt at rescue.

He went with such speed down and up and over the rocks that he appeared to Robin, following behind, like a man possessed by a strange joy or a new purpose. His eyes had been curiously alight and his behaviour oddly excited all day.

"Where are you going, Justin?" For now he had left the cairns and was springing down the crags on the right.

"I've a fancy to find that place where we lost ourselves once before. The mist is clearing; it'll be all gone a little way further down, and we should have no difficulty in finding it. Come on."

"But who *wants* to find it? I remember it chiefly as a disgusting procession of precipices."

"*I* want to find it. And there was only one place where it was at all unpleasant. I'm always driven to find places that I knew long ago. I'm just lured to them."

"Oh well, we all suffer from that. If I'm near a place I knew when I was young, I have to go and look at it."

"Just so. And I can no more keep away from this place than I can from Pemberthy Road when I'm in the neighbourhood of Brook Green. Nor can Gerard. I met him mooning around there the other evening."

"You might quite likely have met me."

"Precisely, and if that's true about any place where one's been happy or suffered, how much truer is it of a place where one experienced both emotions at once. And to tell the truth, I shall never know which was the stronger in me, enjoyment or misery, when we catwalked along the narrow and abominable part last time. I'm going to try it again. Come on. I may not go on with it. I may turn back humbly like the lads on the Hause. After all, I'm nearly thirty years older now. And I shan't ask you to go along it if you don't want to."

"I'll go along it if you do."

"You remember what it was like, I suppose?"

"I should say I do! Who forgets a place that was something between a nightmare and an ecstasy? I remember that, if the slope had tilted one degree more, it'd have been nothing but a nightmare."

"And as it was, it was mainly a thrill. Observe that I say 'mainly' because I'm in the mood to be honest to-day. Let's go and see if we've still got the guts to negotiate those few sweet yards. After all, it's no worse than the Cumberland

Scar. We did the Cumberland Scar. There'll be no difficulty in finding the way back from there. We just keep the precipices on our right, if you remember, and they bring us to the corrie under Great End. There we strike the cairns again."

"Well, keep the precipices at a respectable distance on your right."

"I shall walk well this side of the nightmare's margin, you can be sure. The mist's getting brighter. Come on."

Soon the mist was above them, and the world was disclosed to them again, with the rocks beneath their feet glistening in the sun. They reached the base of the rocks and stepped on to the slope of vegetation which, though strewn with boulders and stones, was the first hint of a habitable world. The slope was broad and indulgent here, but its edge marched with the sky. Beneath that edge, as they knew, ran the chain of precipices, their seamed, primeval faces staring over Eskdale and knitting their brows at the brightness of the sky.

"Here we are. This is the way we came that time. I told you I could find my way blindfold on Scafell. Not bad after twenty-seven years." In an upswell of triumph at having found his way through the mist Justin forgot his mission on Scafell and became an adolescent boy again, vaunting himself before a brother. "Now there's nothing to do but steer due north. Actually it's a few points east of north. I remember that perfectly. But what need we of compass or map? The precipices guide us like a rope, and only a little way beyond them we sight the second shelter on the Hause——" he stopped, for as he said "we", he remembered.

Robin came easily behind on the long wide ribbon of fell. "It's much less awful than I thought," he said.

"There's nothing in it . . . nothing at all . . . except for one place."

Still, Robin looked towards the precipices somewhat anxiously. He had once seen those iron crags from below and far away, and he remembered their aspect now. They stood up in a dreadful frieze above the cataracted rocks and the outfalls of scree, their fronts not heeding the valleys but abiding the wind and the sun and gazing across the distances at eternity.

And they would have to walk within a few yards of them on that narrow and sloping stretch. His heart began to protest against the prospect; but no more to-day than at any other time of his life could he brook seeming a smaller and timider mountaineer than Justin; and he followed him.

Justin strode on. And all the time his brain, because it was the brain of a plotter, worked rapidly, shrewdly, and ingeniously. So ingeniously that now and then it paused to admire itself. At every second or third step it added a refinement to his plan. He saw exactly what to do. His heart beat fast and obstreperously, but more in excitement than in fear; though fear kept close to the excitement as both went along with him. Would he do it properly? Would he fumble and fail? God, he must not fail! If he failed, what then? How face Robin then? How walk home together? Supposing he failed to act at all? Supposing his arm did not move, *would* not move till they were past the only possible place? But he mustn't fail. Think of—think of what? Think of Robin becoming one of the great men of the world—just as Gerard had done—while he was thought of as a failure, and the one failure of the family. Think of Robin seeing him that night at the Orpheum when he was an object of pity to thousands—oh, thank heaven he had killed Bozzy for that—ah, yes, the memory of that humiliation, watched by Robin, remembered by Robin, probably spoken of often by Robin to Jessica, his wife, and to Gerard and Hector, put strength, an iron strength, into his will and his arm. And think—here was the final thought—Robin now knew the truth about Bozzy and the old Duke. Oh no, there was no hesitation in his arm. Robin should not reach the safety on the other side of that narrow sill.

And here it was. The slope was narrowing and tilting. It was now but a traverse on the steep mountain-side. A few paces more, and he must put his plan into action. Slowly, carefully, because of the increasing steepness, he side-stepped towards the precipice brink as if to look over it from a foot or two away. But suddenly he stopped; he sat down; he leaned his body uphill, and away from that brink; he grappled the grass with his fingers and forced his nails into the earth.

Robin came up with him. He reached his side. It was the side away from the precipice because he did not like to venture as near the edge as Justin had done.

"What are you doing?" he asked in astonishment.

Justin gave no answer. He stared before him and panted.

"Is anything the matter?"

"My God, Robin—my God—I—my head isn't what it used to be. I had to sit down. I felt that if I didn't sit down, I should fall over. I—I've never felt like this before. My head swam. Is it—is it affecting you like that?"

Instantly Robin made himself equal with Justin. "I've never liked this bit in the least. I didn't in the old days—I hated it—but I didn't want to admit it to you. I'm hating it now."

"But it's not—it's not paralysing you. You can stand upright."

"I've not been so near the edge as you. Every inch away from the edge makes a difference."

"I didn't mind it in the old days. Not like this. Hell, I'm stuck, Robin. I can't move, I can't do anything."

"You can work yourself backwards. I'll help you. Work yourself backwards. Every inch makes a difference. And when you can stand up, we'll go back the way we came."

Justin waited; he panted; then he replied. "No . . . No, I'm not going back. I've never turned back."

"Take my hand then."

Justin took the outstretched hand and gripped it tightly. "This is humiliating."

"Never mind. Damn humiliation. There's nobody here but me to see, and I'm not liking it any more than you. Now come on. A few steps and it'll be all over."

Carefully, leaning away from the precipice, Justin rose on one knee; he slid himself higher up and rose to his feet. "Never tell anybody that I failed like this."

"Of course I won't." Robin put an arm around his waist. "Come a little higher up still, and you'll feel perfectly all right. We can't fall."

Justin side-walked a few feet further up the slope, and then Robin, though his heart was a ferment, Justin's unexpected panic having added to his own fear, deliberately, after calling upon all his will, placed himself between Justin and the precipice. It was but two steps that he took, and yet it was one of the greatest efforts of his life. And, standing where he now stood, he summoned in terror the aid of God.

Justin, turning an eye, saw what he had done. It was what he had hoped he would do. "I don't think I can go on," he said, apparently transfixed and trembling. "I don't want to move."

"Come back," advised Robin.

"No. No, I won't go back. I've never turned back yet. But let me go my own way. *I'll* do it. I'm not going to be beaten." He leaned sideways towards the slope, so that his left hand could clutch at the herbage.

"Shall we try and clamber along the rocks above?"

"No, it'd be worse there. This isn't as steep as they are. I'd rather go this way. *I* shall be all right."

And so they went forward a few paces, Justin advancing like a crab on a hand and two legs, Robin walking erect at his side and watching his progress.

"Don't watch me," commanded Justin. "For Christ's sake don't watch."

Instantly Robin removed his eyes rather than hurt and shame him. He himself could have gone faster, and would have liked to, so as to be done with this dreadful shelf, but to help Justin he moved at his pace all the way, screening him with his body from any sight of the brink. Sighing, panting, pausing, Justin worked himself downwards a little way and thus edged Robin nearer to the brink.

And when Robin was near enough, not above seven feet away, Justin leapt up. "God, I'm all right," he cried. "Did you really believe I was afraid?" And, lunging forward on one knee, he gave Robin a sudden and violent push with both hands.

Robin cried out and fell; but he fell on his knee a foot or two from the precipice, and immediately in his terror flung himself on his breast, laying his weight upon the slope and clutching with his fingers at the herbage and the earth, as Justin had done. "Oh, God. . . ."

Justin had pushed violently, but not violently enough. Some suppressed recoil from what he was doing, some relic of the conscience that he had tried to destroy, some lingering trace, perhaps, of the old affection, some memory, too near the surface, of boyhood days—these had hung like weights on his hands. They had taken from his thrust just that minim of power which would have made it successful. Robin was not over the cliff. He was lying at his feet with a white terror on his face and in his grappling hands.

He looked up at Justin. Justin could not bear the look. Robin must go over. He must go over and out of sight. He must die quickly and know no more what had happened. There was no life beyond death, and Robin, dead, would neither remember nor reproach him any more. Robin was trying to crawl upwards so as to be further from the edge. He must not. This would mean failure, and Justin dared not fail now. What should he do? Stun him with a blow from a stone and then roll him over.

He stepped towards a large stone and picked it up. For a second, his eyes both wild and stupid, his hair awry, his forward knee bent, and his weapon in his tool-hand, he looked like one of the stone-age men. Robin was rising on a knee, and Justin struck him with the stone on the side of his head.

But again something—something below consciousness—the recoil, the old affection, the old memories—together with a fear of inflicting a wound that would sort ill with an accident, lopped from the blow that last and necessary ounce of power. Robin had cried to God for help, and so much of God as was left in Justin had impeded his hand. And the blow lost an ounce more of its force from the fact that Robin's body, insecurely poised on a knee, was compliant and unresisting. His head gave to the blow, and he fell to one side on a hand.

Robin was dazed by the blow. It shocked his whole body, but it did not stun him. Instead it, and its after-pain, filled him with a fury that was stronger than fear. It flung him on his feet and drove him at Justin.

Justin had tried to murder him. He had tried to murder him, even after he had placed his own body between him and death. Behind his precipitate and blinding fury he saw pictures of the old Duke and Bozzy and Primrose. To think that it had not been Primrose whose murder Justin was planning, but his own! Every emotion which Justin had raised within him these last few days seemed to have poured into the arms which were clasping Justin now: hate, vindictiveness, a passionate hunger to punish, love for the old Duke and Bozzy, pity for Primrose—and to these were added fear and the wild need to save himself and, strangest of all, a thought which had visited him more than once on this mountain to-day, but which he had always thrust from him when he returned out of reverie into sanity: the thought that, since he could not denounce Justin, and could not let him go free, the best solution for him and for all would be his death. Was a man ever justified in killing, not in hate, but in love? And always he had answered No. He had remembered who he was, and what he was; and that, even if the hand of an ordinary man might sometimes kill, it was not so with the hand of a priest. But now in his pain and fury the resistances to this idea were loosened. They were not enough. He did not remember who he was, or what he was. On this slanted sill there were neither Church nor priests.

The consciousness of his priesthood had dropped from him

like a vestment put on from without, and he was just a man naked. And the primitive wild stuff in him—the hate, the fury, and the fear—seized upon this thought for their justi-fication. "He is better dead. *Bozzy was what I call human trash, and best disposed of.* That was what he dared to say. And it is *he* that is the trash and best disposed of." The thought had boiled up into something like a lusting and gasping exultation at being the executioner. Besides, there was nothing else to do—and here was more justification. It was his life or Justin's. Justin was trying now to throw him over. Younger and more sinewy than Justin, whose strength had aged within him in the last wearing years, slighter and more active, he forced himself out of his grasp; he stepped back, eyes glowing, jaw projecting; and as Justin approached him again, he sprang at him and pushed his body with both hands towards the cliff. The fury, and the justifications it had seized upon, were enough. They put into his thrust that complete purpose and power which his brother had lacked. Justin staggered, cried out, looked at Robin, and went over the precipice.

"Oh Jesus, my Saviour!" Robin was alone on that shelve of turf, and realization was coming to him. "Oh Christ my God!"

§

After a moment of stillness like a catalepsy, he went to within two feet of the brink and looked over. His frenzied anguish saved him from fear but, even so, the fear laid a hand on his arm and held him as he looked over. He saw that the cliff was nearly vertical for some forty feet and then became a declivity of sundered rocks too steep to arrest a man's fall. Farther along the brink, however, the cliff was less precipitous: vertical for a few feet, it then became a concave flank whose rocks changed quickly to suspended scree, and the scree to boulder-strewn grass-slopes far below. It was as if here where the turf cap was so narrow a great mass had been reft from the mountain by a giant pick, leaving a gap like a quarry. Robin ran to this gentler brow and looked over. After looking down a vertical face, anything else seems easy, and there were no qualms in him but only anguish as he stood there sweeping the spoil of rocks and scree for a sight of Justin. And soon he saw him. He was lying among the boulders just above the first of the turf. One of the boulders, a large one, had caught him as he rolled, and he lay along it on his side like a man resting on a hard bed. His right arm was flung out on to a patch of turf above him, as a sleeper's arm is flung on to a pillow. Beyond the boulder's edge his long legs were flexed and hung limply downwards. His rucksack, still harnessed to his back, rested on the boulder.

And he did not move.

Below him, down by the mountain's hem, was a rocky and up-tilted defile, with a ghyll twisting down it; a deep and secret vale like a small sister of Langstrath. Robin remembered looking down upon that blue-green bottom, nearly thirty years ago, with Justin at his side.

A little to the left of where Robin was standing the cliff's gradient seemed easier still, and again he ran along the edge, and again looked over. And he saw that, yet farther along, a descent was possible—oh, surely it was—yes, down from rock to rock, then down that stable avalanche of scree, and so on to the billowing turf, and thence up again to the rocks where Justin lay. A third time he ran along the brink and, choosing the likeliest stair, began to descend. No fear went down with him; only the anguish. He picked a rash and headlong route down the angular debris, now jumping from a rock and falling, now hanging the full length of his arms and letting himself slip down a rock face to a foothold beneath. The rocks tore his hands and his shirt and at one point ripped the strap from his rucksack so that it fell loosely over one arm. He unslung it and flung it down the rocks before him.

Reaching the scree, he "shot" it, leaping into the stones with heels together and often carrying the surface stones down with him. How often had Justin and he shot the scree together! And so he came to the top of the grass where there was a starveling rowan tree, and some ferns awake under the rocks, and some bracken and fox-gloves that had climbed up from the green bottom. Here he could turn to the right and mount towards the place where Justin lay. He could not see him from here, but so deep had the picture of him lying there cut into his memory that he was certain he was mounting straight towards him.

"I'm coming, I'm coming," he shouted. "Justin, I'm coming."

And now, breathlessly climbing, he saw him again. He lay much higher and on a steeper incline than it had seemed from above. Could he get up to him? Oh, yes. He must. Wildly, wantonly, careless of himself, he scrambled upward. He put both feet on a large rock, and it loosed its hold and went down under his weight. He went down with it heavily, and his right foot caught in a rift. At once a sharp, sickening pain told him that his ankle was sprained, and a second later a stinging and a dampness at both elbows told him that they were torn.

Every movement of his foot was now a pain, but he dragged it after him and came at last to where Justin lay. And he sat on a rock just above him, as a friend sits on a chair by a sick bed.

"Justin . . . Justin. . . ."

He was not yet dead. He lay there, immobile, apathetic, somnolent; his face pale and bathed in sweat; his lips blue and parted; his breathing quick and shallow; his eyes open. They looked at Robin without anger.

"Oh, Justin. . . ."

Justin's left hand rested on his thigh, and Robin laid his fingers on it, afraid to do more than touch it. Slowly Justin lifted the hand a little way that Robin might grasp it, Passionately Robin grasped it and laid his other hand over it. There was a faint, answering pressure; and was there not something like a smile in Justin's eyes?

What did this last smile mean? *Vicisti*, perhaps. A last glimmer of the old raillery.

He did not speak. He was past speaking. And Robin, holding his hand and trying to comfort and support him by his prolonged pressure, wondered what to do. He dared not move Justin s body, for he knew there must be ruptures and fractures within it, and he did not want to leave him. He scanned the world for help. But they were quite alone on the slope. Above them was the mountain with only the mists wandering over it; below them this hidden re-entrant in the hills—an empty and sombre inlet that shunned inhabited vales.

But while he wondered what to do, Justin gave him his answer. His eyes were still open, and Robin could see that he had passed from somnolence into a coma. He was dying before him, quickly and with no troublesome tarrying.

"Justin," he said again, but in a whisper, as if he would not wake him from sleep; but there was no response; no movement of lips or eyes. His breathing—had it stopped?

Justin's sleeveless shirt was open, and Robin laid a hand upon his breast. He could feel nothing. He put his head against it and listened but could hear nothing. Justin's hand in his was limp, and his eyes were now glazed and dull and unreflecting. They seemed already to have sunk a little deeper into their hollows. His expression was no longer one of pain; it was the old wan look that had settled on his face of late years; the look of a man who knows that he has failed.

§

Yes, he was dead now. Robin, sitting on the rocks at his side, looked at the splendid frame lying there, cast off and broken, like a rotted branch that had fallen from a tree.

He raised his face as if to address the sky. "Oh, Justin, if you can hear me anywhere, forgive me. I didn't know what to do. All my life I will pray for you."

And again he scanned the world for help. Above him the skeins and ravels of mist drifted under the mountain top, aloof from human troubles and unrest. Below him the little ghyll, murmuring to itself, ran though the green bottom and turned from sight round the foot of a long green cape. It must be working its way southward towards the Esk, and it should be easy to walk along it into Eskdale and bring back help the same way. "If lost in the mountains, listen for water. Find it and follow it." How often Justin and he had said that, when bragging of what they would do if they lost their way. But the Esk ran for miles through the foothills before its valley widened and held the homes of men. And there were sharp throes and a racked pain in his ankle whenever he moved it. It would take him hours to drag himself into Eskdale.

If only there were someone else on this part of the mountain. The mist was diaphanous now, and melting into flakes and shreds, and the sun was in possession of most of Scafell. The people would certainly be climbing it again, and there might be some within sound of his voice. As boys he and Justin had often fancied that they had heard a distress signal, and secretly hoped they had, so that they could send back the right answer, displaying their mountain lore, and hurry towards the signal and bring off a rescue that would make them the heroes of the valley, if not of the whole country. And now, with Justin lying beside him, he put his hands to his mouth as a funnel and, pitching his voice high, sent six short clear notes up towards the breaking mists; then left an interval of silence, while his notes echoed among the hills; and again sounded his sixfold call.

Six times, perhaps, he sent that call up towards the summit, and then, in a pause, he heard, far above him, but not to be doubted, an answer. His own note, or one very near it, was coming back to him. Three times he heard it, and then a pause, and then the call three times again.

CHAPTER SIX

IN the Eskdale valley, hitherto unknown to him, Robin limped slowly along. Every step hurt him, but he felt driven to escape at any cost from the sight of men. It was seven o'clock the same evening, and he had left the kind and neighbourly house which had taken him in, and was now dragging his injured foot along a muddy and pebbly lane. He came to a farmyard and was greeted by the rich, warm smell of its midden. Entering the rough, cobbled yard, he passed a barn where some men were shearing the grey fleece from a large, patient, quivering ram. They were men very like the wind-worn shepherds, old and young, who had come to Justin's side, with stretchers and ropes and grumbling and kindness, and the ancient skills of the mountain in their heavy feet and large hard hands. They knew who he was, and no doubt they attributed his ash-grey countenance and baffled, helpless eyes to shock at what had happened to his brother. They did not know that it was shock at what he himself had done. They touched their caps to him.

Beyond the farm's last gate the hills began, and he dragged the aching foot through a fringe of bracken and fox-gloves till he came to the bare hillside, and here he laboriously sat himself down. . . .

When Justin's body fell, something else fell with it: Robin's trust in himself and, for a while at least, all his aspirations. After years, thirty years, forty years, of striving to be all that he wanted to be, after being beaten often to his knees but always getting up again and struggling on, he had done this thing. He had thrown his brother from a precipice in a wild surrender to accumulated rage: even with a ghastly exultation at being the executioner. No wonder that faith in himself, and all aspiring hopes, went down with Justin and lay at his side. He could have wept for this second death, if he were not discouraged beyond tears.

"I shall never know . . . I shall never know. . . ." Monotonously, rhythmically, he repeated this to himself. He meant that he would never know how far, in that storm of emotion which had driven him to kill his brother, there had been a few things which were not wholly wrong—few and small but there—and how far they weighed against the evil. There had been the need to save himself, of course, and to many this might seem justification enough, but he was not thinking of any motive so purely self-regarding. He was thinking that he had acted partly out of a blind love for Primrose, for the others of the family, for all the children, and even for Justin himself. Partly, but only partly. He was sure that this love had acted as well as the hate, but he would never be able to assess its share. His brain felt bruised, and the question was a strain and an ache behind his brows. All he knew was that he could never make enough of these better motives to balance the worse ones. There had been a preponderance of evil in it. The knowledge must always remain that carelessly, blindly, and while his thoughts were clouded with rage, he had sent Justin out of the world. There was no eluding this knowledge, no blunting it or lightening it. He must live with it always, and he must live with it alone.

"And what do I do now? What now?"

As he asked himself this, there came rushing in upon him, like a mill race when the dam is broken, just as it had rushed in upon him after the death of Bryn, and after the end of the war's slaughter, but never with such force as now—the knowledge that nothing mattered in the world but goodness and kindness and love, and that these were the things he loved.

"I shall go on. I shall just go on. There's no raising Justin, but *I* can get up and start again. I shall go on trying. I must do, because these are the only things I believe in."

And then he remembered something which had been so completely forgotten in these last few days that it might never have been. Yes, that question had answered itself violently. He must turn away from the great position that had been offered him. The hand which had killed a brother, largely in wrath, could not move among the unsuspicious people, clasping a bishop's staff, or giving them the episcopal blessing. Yes, that was certain; that was decided. And it was not wholly a disappointment, rather was it a relief, that the question had decided itself in this way. There had always been a part of him which had doubted his fitness for so great a charge, and it was not the weaker part of him but the better. The weaker had exulted in the offer. Yes, he was sure this decision was good; and he was glad this evening to do something that was good.

He was sure of another thing. Because the day's dark act
had not been utterly evil but had had something of love in it,
and because God could see this better than he could, God
would still accept his work as a priest. Of this he felt quite
sure. For the rest of his life he would go about loaded with a
secret, and God and he alone would know that secret—unless
one day—one day perhaps—he told Jessica and reduced the
dead lonely weight by sharing it with her. But let that be.
In the meantime God would accept his work, and perhaps the
memory of this day, ever with him, would put a new and
private poignance into the work and therefore a new power.
He would try for the rest of his life, by service to others, to
make amends for all that was wrong in his deed, and he would
offer his service on Justin's behalf too, and ask God to accept it
as some atonement for both.

"Perhaps He will. Who knows?"

A little while after this, seeing his way more clearly, he got
up and limped back.

§

But you will have observed that not once in this long
meditation, not for a moment, had Robin been troubled by
any fear that someone might suspect the truth.

And no one ever did. Justin, when he dreamed of damaging
Robin's career by contriving a scandal round his name, had
decided that this weapon would not cut: Robin was invulnerable; his reputation for goodness would put its armour
about him and make nonsense of any such assault. And Justin
was right. No one ever questioned Robin's story that they had
gone together to visit a scene of their childhood and that as
they crossed that hazardous ledge, Justin's head had failed
him, and he had lost control of himself and fallen. No one ever
doubted that Robin's lacerations and bruises, on elbows and
face, were got in his desperate and tumbling descent to his
brother's side. Why should they? The cataracted steeps of
Scafell had provided them with many such tales before. For
a day or two men spoke with interest of Justin's death because
of Gerard's wide fame and Robin's smaller distinction, and
then a night fell, and a new day began, and no one spoke of it
again, any more than they spoke of Bozzy's death one day
after the inquiry had been closed.

At least there was one person who spoke of it often; and
that was Hector. He was very proud of Justin's death and

much pleased with the notion that there was a curse upon the family. Sitting at his large table in his office at the bank, he would say sometimes to a customer, "Yes, it almost looks as though the story were true that there's a curse on our family." There was no such story, of course, till Hector invented it in his office, and the only curse behind these heavy events was the ancient curse of Self, which afflicts all our families. "We die violent deaths," he would expound. "First my youngest brother was drowned, and then my eldest brother fell from a cliff when he was climbing a mountain in Cumberland. He was a great climber. Probably my brother, Gerard—Gerard le Faber, you know, the actor—or my other brother, Robin, will go next. Funny fellow, Robin: he was offered a Bishopric and he turned it down, on the score that he wasn't good enough! Not a notion that ever worried any other le Faber. Yes, those two brothers have done very well in the world, I'm glad to say, but the mystery to me has always been that my eldest brother, Justin, didn't do better than he did. He was easily the most brilliant of us all and quite the handsomest man I ever saw. Sometimes I wonder if his fall was quite as accidental as it seemed. He was a disappointed man, I know—anyone could see that in his eyes just before he died—and he was the lordly type who would have elected to end his life in the grand manner and at an hour of his own choosing. Yes, and at a place that he loved, and the mountains were almost the only thing in the world that he did love. Ah, well, we shall never know. . . . Very good, sir, I'll put that matter through for you and let you know when the business is completed. . . . Of course, *I* may be the next to go. And I don't mean because of this old heart of mine, which may put me to sleep at any moment. What I mean is, I may meet a most untimely and disagreeable end in the course of a hold-up at the bank. You never know; and these are violent times."

And Hector would smile, and his customer too, for few people could look more substantial and safe than this portly, bald-headed, well-dressed man in his comfortable office at the bank.

The following titles have been reprinted at the request of the
London & Home Counties Branch of the Library Association and
can be obtained from Cedric Chivers Ltd., Portway, Bath.

Non-fiction

Braddock, Joseph	HAUNTED HOUSES
Cardus, Neville	DAYS IN THE SUN
Cobbett, William	COTTAGE ECONOMY
Day, J. Wentworth	GHOSTS AND WITCHES
Edmonds, Charles	A SUBALTERN'S WAR
Gibbons, Floyd	RED KNIGHT OF GERMANY
Gibbs, P.	FROM BAPAUME TO PASSCHENDAELE
Grant, I.F.	ECONOMIC HISTORY OF SCOTLAND
Harris, John	RECOLLECTIONS OF RIFLEMAN HARRIS
Hitchcock, F.C.	STAND TO: A DIARY OF THE TRENCHES
Jones, Jack	GIVE ME BACK MY HEART
Jones, Jack	UNFINISHED JOURNEY
Jones, Jack	ME AND MINE
Lowe George	BECAUSE IT IS THERE
Price, Harry	THE MOST HAUNTED HOUSE IN ENGLAND
Price, Harry	THE END OF BORLEY RECTORY
Stamper, Joseph	LESS THAN THE DUST
Tangye, Derek	TIME WAS MINE
Tangye, Derek	WENT THE DAY WELL
Thompson, P.A.	LIONS LED BY DONKEYS
Vigilant	RICHTHOFEN - RED KNIGHT OF THE AIR
Villiers, Alan	SONS OF SINDBAD
von Richthofen, Manfred F.	THE RED AIR FIGHTER

Fiction

Ainsworth, W. Harrison	GUY FAWKES
Anthony, Evelyn	CURSE NOT THE KING
Anthony, Evelyn	IMPERIAL HIGHNESS
Ashton, Helen	FOOTMAN IN POWDER
Barke, James	THE END OF THE HIGH BRIDGE
Barke, James	THE SONG IN THE GREEN THORN TREE
Barke, James	THE WELL OF THE SILENT HARP
Barke, James	THE WONDER OF ALL THE GAY WORLD
Barke, James	THE CREST OF THE BROKEN WAVE
Barke, James	THE WIND THAT SHAKES THE BARLEY
Besant, Walter	DOROTHY FORSTER
Blaker, Richard	MEDAL WITHOUT BAR
Brophy, John	GENTLEMAN OF STRATFORD
Broster, D.K.	SHIPS IN THE BAY
Broster, D.K.	SEA WITHOUT A HAVEN
Broster, D.K.	CHILD ROYAL

Broster, D.K. & Taylor, G.W.	CHANTEMERLE
Broster, D.K. & Taylor, G.W.	WORLD UNDER SNOW
Buck, Pearl	THE MOTHER
Buck, Pearl	THE PROUD HEART
Burney, Fanny	CAMILLA - in 5 vols.
Caldwell, Taylor	THE EAGLES GATHER
Caldwell, Taylor	TENDER VICTORY
Caldwell, Taylor	THE BEAUTIFUL IS VANISHED
Cloete, Stuart	THE CURVE AND THE TUSK
Collins, Wilkie	ARMADALE
Cookson, Catherine	COLOUR BLIND
Cookson, Catherine	FIFTEEN STREETS
Cookson, Catherine	KATE HANNIGAN
Cookson, Catherine	FANNY McBRIDE
Cookson, Catherine	MAGGIE ROWAN
Cookson, Catherine	ROONEY
Cordell, A.	RAPE OF THE FAIR COUNTRY
Corke, Helen	NEUTRAL GROUND
Crockett, S.R.	THE GREY MAN
Croker, B.M.	THE YOUNGEST MISS MOWBRAY
Cusack, Dymphna & James, Florence	COME IN SPINNER
Darlington, W.A.	ALF'S BUTTON
Davies, Rhys	THE TRIP TO LONDON
Davies, Rhys	THE BLACK VENUS
Dehan, Richard	THE DOP DOCTOR
Dumas, Alexandre	THE LADY OF THE CAMELLIAS
Dumas, Alexandre	THE CORSICAN BROTHERS
Eca de Queiroz, José	COUSIN BRASILIO
Ewart, Wilfrid	THE WAY OF REVELATION
Eyles, Margaret	MARGARET PROTESTS
Ferrier, Susan	THE INHERITANCE
Firbank, T.	BRIDE TO THE MOUNTAIN
Godden, R.	BLACK NARCISSUS
Golding, Louis	MAGNOLIA STREET
Golding, Louis	CAMBERWELL BEAUTY
Golding, Louis	THE LOVING BROTHERS
Greenwood, Walter	HIS WORSHIP THE MAYOR
Gunn, Neil	BUTCHER'S BROOM
Gunn, Neil	THE GREY COAST
Gunn, Neil	THE KEY OF THE CHEST
Household, Geoffrey	THE THIRD HOUR
James, Henry	WHAT MASIE KNEW
Jenkins, Robin	HAPPY FOR THE CHILD
Jones, Jack	RIVER OUT OF EDEN
Jones, Jack	BLACK PARADE
Jones, Jack	BIDDEN TO THE FEAST
Jones, Jack	RHONDDA ROUNDABOUT
Jones, Jack	LUCKY LEAR

Jones, Jack	SOME TRUST IN CHARIOTS
Jones, Jack	OFF TO PHILADELPHIA IN THE MORNING
Jones, Jack	LILY OF THE VALLEY
Jones, Jack	THE MAN DAVID
Jones, Jack	COME NIGHT: END DAY
Jones, Jack	TIME AND THE BUSINESS
Jones, Jack	CHORAL SYMPHONY
Kersh, Gerald	NINE LIVES OF BILL NELSON
Kersh, Gerald	THEY DIE WITH THEIR BOOTS CLEAN
Keyes, Frances Parkinson	VAIL D'ALVERY
Keyes, Frances Parkinson	IF EVER I CEASE TO LOVE
Keyes, Frances Parkinson	FIELDING'S FOLLY
Keyes, Frances Parkinson	LARRY VINCENT
Kirkham, Nellie	UNREST OF THEIR TIME
Knight, L.A.	CONQUEROR'S ROAD
Knight, L.A.	DEADMAN'S BAY
Knight, L.A.	JUDGEMENT ROCK
Kyle, Elizabeth	THE PLEASURE DOME
Lawrence, Margery	MADONNA OF THE SEVEN MOONS
Lewis, Hilda	PENNY LACE
Lewis, Hilda	THE DAY IS OURS
Lewis, Hilda	BECAUSE I MUST
Lewis, Hilda	STRANGE STORY
Lindsay, Philip	THE LITTLE WENCH
Lindsay, Philip	PUDDING LANE
Lindsay, Philip	THEY HAVE THEIR DREAMS
Lindsay, Philip	LOVE RIDES TO BUTTERMERE
Lofts, Norah	REQUIEM FOR IDOLS
Lofts, Norah	WHITE HELL OF PITY
MacDonell A.G.	HOW LIKE AN ANGEL
MacGill, Patrick	CHILDREN OF THE DEAD END
Mackenzie, Compton	POOR RELATIONS
Macpherson, I.	SHEPHERD'S CALENDAR
Macpherson, I.	LAND OF OUR FATHERS
Macpherson, I.	PRIDE IN THE VALLEY
Macpherson, I.	HAPPY HAWKERS
Macpherson, I.	WILD HARBOUR
Masefield, Muriel	SEVEN AGAINST EDINBURGH
Maturin, Charles Robert	MELMOTH THE WANDERER - in 3 vols.
Morrison, Arthur	A CHILD OF THE JAGO
Morrison, Arthur	TALES OF MEAN STREETS
Myers, Elizabeth	A WELL FULL OF LEAVES
Neill, Robert	MIST OVER PENDLE
D'Oyley, Elizabeth	LORD ROBERT'S WIFE
D'Oyley, Elizabeth	YOUNG JEMMY
D'Oyley, Elizabeth	THE ENGLISH MARCH
D'Oyley, Elizabeth	EVEN AS THE SUN
Oliver & Stafford	BUSINESS AS USUAL
Oliver, Jane	THE LION AND THE ROSE
Oliver, Jane	NOT PEACE BUT A SWORD
Oliver, Jane	IN NO STRANGE LAND